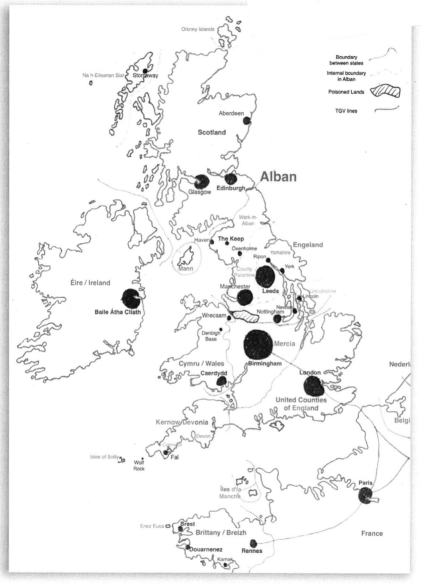

Orkney Islands

Na h-Eileanan Siar Stornoway

Aberdeen

Scotland

Alban

Glasgow Edinburgh

Wark-in-Alban

Engeland

Haven The Keep
Oxenholme
Yorkshire
Ripon
York
County
Palatine
Mann
Manchester Leeds
Lincolnshire
Lincoln
Newark
Wrecsam Nottingham
Denbigh
Base
Mercia
Cymru / Wales
Caerdydd Birmingham
London
Nederl

United Counties
of England
Belgi

Kernow/Devonia

Devon

Isles of Scilly
Wolf Fal
Rock

Paris

Îles d'la
Manche

Enez Eusa Brest
Brittany / Breizh
Douarnenez Rennes France
Karnak

Éire / Ireland

Baile Átha Cliath

Boundary
between states
Internal boundary
in Alban
Poisoned Lands
TGV lines

The Good Counsel of Alban

(Reimagined)

CE 2188

William Harding

First printed in Great Britain in 1989 by PUBeS l t d
First Published in Great Britain in 2020 by PUBeS l t d - Guillaume Arding

A catalogue record for this book is available from the British Library

1st Edition 2020
2nd Edition 2022 (Reimagined)

PB ISBN: 978-1-8380090-2-1

www.williamharding.co.uk
www.thegoodcounselofalban.co.uk

PUBeS l t d - Guillaume Arding

Rowan — for the zest you shared

C'est une bonne énigme, Iris, merci.

i

In oligarchal societies

power and control

by the apparatus of governance

shapes

the humanity

of that society

to serve its own ends.

We, the citizens, should be aware
of these dangers and act accordingly.

Contents

List of Main Characters

❖ from Confederation Helvetica (Switzerland)

Ardel Penaul	League Ambassador
Dahqin Stiwll	Ardel's consort (= Dah-kin)
Grandy Emembet	Ardel's patron, a Member of the League General Council
Matilde Bartouche	Grandy's patron, a Member of the League Inner Table

❖ from Fastness of Alban (see map)

Faerachar Strachan	The Reever of Alban (= Fay-ra-car)
Briged Jardine	The Good Sounding Counsel
	Mother of Faerachar, Kaet and Duncn
Kaet Jardine	Faerachar's half-sister
Duncn Axelsson	Faerachar's half-brother (= Dunc'n)
Regin Peterson	Under-Bursar of The Keep in Derwent

❖ from London, United Counties of England

SJ Letrap (Svenjon)	Trading House owner
Jarnie Paresh	SJ's Head of Security
Gabri Tabit	SJ's 'Go-for'

❖ from Cantref of Wrecsam, Fastness of Cymru/Wales

Owen ap Gaharet	Maer of the Cantref of Wrecsam
Gwyneth vch Dilys	Owen's mother

❖ from Fastness of Brittany/Breizh/Bertaèyn

Alun & Kirus Goffic	Twins, lifelong friends of Dahqin.
Peran Trelawn	Lover of Alun & Kirus.

The Letter

...from the dark of the stairwell...

**September, 21st, 2169 — Coteau de Valleyre, Villeneuve,
Vaud, Confederation Helvetica**

The letter arrived when she was alone in the house. It came from Éire; the stamp franked only a few days before. The address in the hand of her great-aunt Oona, the youngest of her father's aunts, the only one in her family with whom she maintained any contact. She saw Robert with his younger brother, up the hillside in the vineyard inspecting the grapes — the harvest due any day. Their son had left on his walk to junior school with his cousins. She put it aside and made herself a cup of strong tea. Out on the terrace in the warming morning light, she settled into a chair facing uphill across the vines and carefully opened the envelope.

A small photo dropped into her lap as she unfolded the single page. It looked to be of her, held by Oona, both looking happy; but the date of the photo was too early. And the letter had been written in 2158, a few days after she and Robert were married. Her fingers moved over the page, hesitating and quivering as the words grew into images.

The Sight of Kaet Jardine

He is already through the gate...

June, 12th, 2188 — Third House, Derwent, Wark-in-Alban — Kaet

It isn't always easy to work out what we really know. I remember with so-bright a certainty the day I told Faerachar, my older brother, we were to be joined by another brother. I was not yet four years old, and couldn't understand why our mother was crying so while rocking me, cradled in her arms. With hindsight I know it was few days since that sperm reached that egg.

"You will learn to live with this, Kaet, my sweet darling," Briged said through her tears. Then slowly smiled, kissing me.

And I have. It nudges. Suggests. Mixes the petty with the profound. Rarely, it is overwhelming. I make spare use of it.

I grew up here above Derwent. Our childhood was mostly a happy one. We had Briged almost to ourselves. I loved our playing and I loved going to school. Even though there was no avoiding history or philosophy. The tools of scepticism and discernment were drummed into us. I can still recite the mournful words we learned — *The Masters and The Slaving*[1]. The baleful events of the 20th and 21st centuries condensed into sixty-five lines; set into our minds as a caution against complacency. Human societies are fragile and need careful nurturing. We must each play our part.

All this I know and respect. After all, Faerachar is the Reever of Alban, the head of administrative government, and Briged is the Good Sounding Counsel of Alban. She is held in high esteem by those involved in governance and setting law. Lauded for her probity as the guardian of

1 *The Masters and The Slaving – page 468*

the ethical heart of our society. It is to her they first turn to sound the worth of their proposals and weigh their actions.

Me and Duncn, our younger brother, have our own lives. Well out of the politics and governing.

Then - this morning - just as nausea came, so did the fuzziness of sight. The name Ardel entered my mind. Little else came with it.

He is wheaten blond. His eyes the light lilac-blue of cornflowers. He is touched by darkening. He is already through the gate and does not follow the broad path. The sight has limits. It does not prepare me for how his arrival will affect our family.

Five days ago — I sat with Bridged in the cowled seat, amongst the camellias behind Second House. She was facing Nitting Haws and had finished meditating. The sun warmed that side of the valley, not this.

"Mum ..." She shot me a primed look.

"I have the proof, Briged. We can move on it now." The voice of Faerachar. The moment passed with his arrival.

"You said, Mum, Kaet. Carry on. I can wait a bit."

I shook my head. I love him, but not with that smile on his face.

"You two talk business. I have a painting to start. Briged – when you're free."

Walking to the beck I heard him say, "I shall send a Complaint to the League today."

After studying different trees hanging over the beck, I chose a group of three. I will see them clearly, with my easel at either of the living room windows; by the time Briged called in, the easel and paint table stood on a waterproof dust-sheet.

"Not the studio?" I had not heard her climb the stairs. "What matter do you wish to impart?"

"Mum, I ..." Still unsure of the words I need, my hands moved.

She beamed. "Pregnant." I nodded. "How long?"

"Five weeks."

"Tea?" She led the way downstairs. We sat at the big table in my kitchen. She stirred the pot for the third time, poured the tea, reached across and squeezed my hands as she looked away from me.

"I'm sending an Earth Mother to a Cymric woman who needs it."

"To Wales?" She nodded.

I faced my Earth Mother, on her little shelf, nestling on red silk in her yew-wood box. I sensed nothing of why she would do that, for our sights do not overlap.

Duncn was eight, I was eleven. Briged needed to work in peace.

"Please, Kaet, take him somewhere he can shout all he wants. Stay within sight of the house."

We wander into the woods. He charges off down a footpath leading to the river, paying no heed to my soft calling. His summer-light hair flicking in and out of the trees, he's chosen green clothes again. I look up the hill — I can see the house, so it can see me. I catch up with him leaning over the bridge rail at Cannon Dub, dangling his spit. We take the paths to Nitting Haws. The house is in plain view — tiny.

Duncn picks up stones for his collection and plays with ants. I am drawn towards the knub of rock on the edge of the little plateau. And there it is, no more than a duck's egg in size, and as smooth. Fondle it. Feel its power wheedling up my arms. Duncn stands on the edge of the drop, pushing stones over.

"Look what I've found! We need to go back!"

He runs over, peers at it, starts laughing. "It's a fat lady."

I put it in my forage bag.

Briged is still working. I chop purple beet and tomatoes. Mix them with the hedgerow salad we've plucked. Make cheese sandwiches and call her. She joins us on the terrace behind the camellias.

"Have you had a good morning's exploration?"

Duncn nods, mouth full of sandwich. I take a big bite.

Put the stone in front of her.

"Looks like an Earth Mother." She picks it up. "Mmm." Her face calms. "Does it call to you, Kaet?" I nod. "What did Duncn make of it?" Shrug my shoulders. Swallow.

"You know what he's like. He might have thrown it and I'd never see it again."

"Duncn, hold out your hand."

He sits up, watching it fall into his palm. His eyes go wide. Eyebrows rising, he pushes back into his chair; drops it onto the table.

"It's crawly. Weird stone. Don't want them things."

"What things?"

"Like Kaet gets. I make noises in my ears so I can't hear. Don't want to touch it anymore."

Briged ruffles his hair then puts some salad on his plate. She picks up the earth mother, still watching him.

"We'll make a box for her to live in."

"Kaet found that at Nitting Haws."

She lifts her head and looks out across the valley then swings round to face me. I see it cross her eyes and feel the rush in my blood. But it has gone, her tone is mild.

"How come you went so far?"

"I did check we were in sight of the house. He ran ahead as far as Cannon Dub. He wanted to play at Regin's, but I felt drawn to Nitting Haws. I felt we would be alright. This found me."

"You are sensible, Kaet. But we must agree some rules."

She puts the Earth Mother in front of her. Reaches over, squeezes my hands as she looks away from me, concern on her face.

She will always have concern for the three of us.

Sometimes she lets it show.

❖

Let me tell you ...

Three of us. Three fathers. Three houses.

Faerachar Strachan, Kaet Jardine, Duncn Axelsson.

Faerachar knows his father well. He knew mine well enough. He acted father to Duncn. Briged loved all three men in their times. Faerachar's she counts once more as friend. She holds my father's memory dearest. Duncn's father, when she remembers, with a little smile and sensuous words.

Unlike her own father. Bitterness churns inside, enveloped in anger.

We three know enough to leave it there.

Sometimes it comes to the surface.

First House, all but three centuries old. Back then, Briged was in consort with Alastair Strachan. Their politics — the commonweal — brought them together. Faerachar was born there. By seven he had witnessed for too long the anger that parted them. First House is Faerachar's now.

Second House, built for Briged. She met and loved my father, Iain Jardine. Took Faerachar to live with him in Edinburgh, where I was born. Two years later my father died. She was distraught beyond reason. Faerachar called his father. His arrival snapped her back to us.

A year later on a walk, me in my wheeler, she met Axel, coming up from the port. I saw his beauty — inherited by Duncn. He was in our lives for nine days. I said, "Gone!" when the door shut on the tenth morning. Later that day I told what I told, and she understood me.

Faerachar when twelve needed more time with his father. We left Edinburgh. Duncn was born in a tent set inside the unfinished Second House. It will be his.

Third House is mine. My design; my legacy thanks to my father.

Our child will be born here. I have yet to tell David.

Book One

The Fastness of Alban

All answers become clear in the light of time

June, 12th — Genève, Confederation Helvetica — Ardel

Ardel Penaul's phone buzzes with a message from Grandy Emembet, his Patron. He is to call on her as soon as possible. He shuts down the faxplex he is working on and heads for her office.

"Ardel. That was quicker than I expected. Are you bored?" She rises from her desk, indicates we sit in the armchairs.

"I am at a point in the report where the summaries are to be written. Your timing was good."

Our greetings out of the way, Grandy places her hands on a faxplex on the small table between us.

"When you leave here, write your summaries and hand over all your work to Patron Favre; she knows this is to happen. You are off your current assignment when that is done, Ardel. You have a Diplomatic Argument to sort out."

"Who am I going with?"

"This is your Solo. Succeed in this and you will no longer be a Noviate. Here are the details of the case." She pinches the thin rectangular document as she hands it over, making it glow.

I note the title of the diplarg — '*Complaint of Digression filed by The Reever of Alban citing as Respondent the United Counties of England*'. I scroll my finger down the sheet looking at the icons of sub-documents, then pinch to switch it off.

"You have three days to familiarise yourself with the issues. You must take a rest day before you go. You will be in London for two days and are to enter the Fastness of Alban on the nineteenth. Liaise with our

Section Bureau for travel and other needs. Incidentally, this is the first ever request from Alban for our services. The Review Committee suggests the main answers to this Complaint will be found there. They deem it suitable for a Solo. I'm sure you will succeed."

She indicates a decanter filled with a black liqueur. I nod. She pours some into small glasses and hands one to me. This is her mystery drink. I inhale the mix of blackcurrant and liquorice with herbal hints and sip, letting it coat my tongue.

"This is wonderful. Will I ever find out what it is?"

Grandy sits back, amusement in her eyes. "A toast. To success."

"Salut."

I drain the glass and place it back on the table, putting the faxplex in my security pocket.

"Go in peace, return in peace."

"I do. I shall." We touch palms.

"I am available at any time should you need."

I hand everything to Patron Favre with unseemly haste. She wishes me luck on my Solo.

Back in my office the churn of excitement is difficult to ignore. I read through the Complaint of Digression. It claims the threat of coercion on a local population in Alban due to uncertainty with borders. I know nothing of the place, and don't recall the name. I look up on the Registry files to see what is available — precious little comes back. I load that and some information about London onto the faxplex and head for home.

Thankfully I'm the only one waiting for a cab. Within a couple of minutes of pressing the call button a boxy eight-seater decorated with a hippo in a field of daisies comes onto the sidelink. I hold my persID to the control screen and tap in my home code. Once I'm strapped in the door locks and the cab picks up speed, joining the main flow of traffic on the highway heading north-east along the shore, taking power via the green line it follows in the centre of the lane.

I look out over the lake towards the mountains beyond the southern shore. Two huge jettes of water rise into the clear air, far out in the lake, dwarfing the original. When these three line up I am nearing home. The cab swings onto a sidelink. A few minutes later it stops outside the apartment blocks, under a broad canopy. I climb out, the door closes and the cab hums quietly away. I nod and smile to a couple of our neighbours heading out of the apartment tunnel.

"I'm home, Dahqin," I call out as the door shuts behind me. No reply. I slip my shoes off and under the bench.

Sunlight illuminates the pale grey colour range in the main room through ceiling panels. The local live-stream out across the lake shows on a large panel set on the far wall, next to the one small window. Heading to the workroom I draw my hand along the back of the big settee, stroking the leather. Scooping up Dahqin's workout vest I close my eyes, bury my nose into it. I carry it into the workroom and drape it over the gym equipment.

Switching on the multi-viewer I settle into one of the desk chairs. Usually I know quite a lot about the areas in diplarg. The Éireish issues on my last mission had been easier to solve for that very reason. I know where London is, but have never been there. Of Alban — nothing.

I write the name onto the touchpad with my scribbler. A hologram of Earth appears and spins, slowly zooming in on the Fastness of Alban, taking up the northern part of Great Britain.

At least I know the seat of government is The Keep in Derwent. And there it is sited on a headland on the west shore of a broad lake dotted with islands. Neither city nor town is shown close by. I put my hand into the hologram, into the valley with the lake, moving it into and out of the light.

Where is Dahqin?

Leaving the map in place I head for the kitchen, adjust the lights and get a glass of milk, taking a mouthful. As I let it trickle down my throat I reach across to the manga recipe book I'd left out. Clamp it into the holder at the back of the counter. I lay out the smoked lake fish, a large bulb of fennel, the ingredients for a peach salsa. Summer food. I love my knives, and choose a heavy one. As I slice, the damascene blade reflects the lights onto the splashback. The fennel must be sliced exactly as the recipe shows. The first sight of food on a plate is everything.

Dahqin emerges from Les Sept Nuits cabaret club, in the midst of goodbyes with his backing musicians and dancers. Switching his phone on, he sees Ardel's message from the morning, *Been summoned to see Grandy.* He rubs two fingers across his face, astride his lips. Phones the apartment.

"Dah-qin." The Swiss French accenting always makes him grin. He gets a smile back, the one with little dimples.

"I'll be about fifteen minutes. Just waiting for a cab. Everything's in place for my show. Glad to see you're in the kitchen. I'm so hungry."

❖

In the flush of excitement about going on my Solo, I'd forgotten his show. So I've let him talk about it non-stop since he got in, but finally he notices the unspoken *Finished?* on my face.

"Welcome home, Dahqin."

"Sorry, getting carried away."

He puts his arms around me, nuzzling against my left ear lobe until he feels me relax. Slowly he moves his lips in little hops across my cheek and onto my mouth. We kiss for some minutes. I know I'll let the meal go if he keeps at this.

"I love the taste of you." He kisses me again and I eat at him.

"We could ..."

I push at him, making him stand away. "You're hungry for food, remember. And so am I."

"What did Grandy have you in for?"

"I have to go on a simple diplarg mission. My trial Solo. I leave on the seventeenth." Dahqin's jaw clenches, then he lets it go.

"Promotion! Where?"

"Well, maybe. If I don't flunk it. Not far from Éire."

"Baile Átha Cliath. Your great triumph. How is the great woman?"

"She was being formal. She still won't tell me what that drink is. I've never seen it for sale."

"I like her sense of humour. Have done right from our first meeting."

"That still gives me sweats. I thought you'd taken some kind of kicker, you were so bouncy. Try the peach salsa, you might want a bit more seasoning."

"I bet there's an old monster in charge who'll rip you to shreds."

He tastes the salsa, nods, takes a second spoonful. Notices the disapproval on my face.

"That's just right for me. Well, I hope there's not. I want you back in full working order, and a full Ambassador. What've you got on Alban?" He holds up a wine glass.

"No, Genéva and cucumber soda, one cube of ice. Two faxplex is all they had. There's some short audio tracks, a few photos."

We eat at the raised counter in the kitchen, watching the live-feed screen on the far wall of the living room.

"So nice. You always get the flavours right. Drink was right too."

"I only followed the recipe." I run fingers up Dahqin's thigh. "You can pay me compliments later."

He rubs me on the shoulder, and gets up. "You won't get to see the show. It starts on the eighteenth for five nights. It's a trial run for a longer autumn season." I turn on the stool and reach for him. He shimmies away.

"Go. Get into your shorts. I'll clear up here and be in."

The hologram is still on; I'm reading from the faxplex. I see from the edge of my vision Dahqin pull on his workout vest, glancing in the tall mirror to check it hangs over his shorts just so. Slips past my following eyes and sits in the empty corner of the settee, his bare feet nudging against my thigh.

"Zoom out a bit, I want to see where you are going ... Oh, it's near Scotia ... Scotland, I think they call it."

"That's the name I couldn't recall. How come you know, when this faxplex doesn't tell me?"

Dahqin shrugs. "Breizh, Cymru, Éire, Kernow, Mann, Scotia are all Celtic lands. There's cultural links between us. Don't know anything about Alban."

"Do you miss Brittany much? You never say."

"My friends most. I miss the adventures I used to have with them. You still haven't met them. Or my parents. I want us to make an adventure of it. Every time we line it up, something causes you to be sent off somewhere else."

That's true, because twice I've volunteered into missions to avoid going. At least that's not the case this time.

"Adventures can cause issues. Anyway I get excitement in my job."

"Excitement? When the Protocols protect Ambassadors. I can always come and rescue you."

I dip my head and look under eyebrows — serious. Dahqin waggles his toes, he loves the seriousness of me. I stretch over and kiss him on the cheek.

"Well I think you won't need to."

"What does this Keep look like? Show me the photos. I can't imagine the adventure without seeing it."

I place the faxplex on the multi-viewer, and flick to the photos. There's only one of The Keep, taken from a boat it appears. He stares at it, clearly unimpressed.

"Weird looking thing. I'll study it later."

"Well in that case — Complaint of Digression." A female voice sounds, modulated to keep the listener awake and aware.

"Sometimes I wonder if you aren't still a boy, Dahqin."

"It's only years, Ardel. I don't want to grow up. Shifting round."

His head in my lap, I drape my left arm across his torso and he is asleep before the introduction is finished with. And I don't take it in. I look down at him, secure in his love for me — here in our own home.

June, 14th — Third House, Derwent — Kaet

Last night I told David of our child as we ate, and he stays over. He still maintains his suite in The Keep; shyly he spends more time here.

Briged left this morning on one of her regular seven day passes through Alban, being available to those she checks on. I return from my walk to the tarns and go to work on the painting while the light is right. The same two hour period each day when the weather fits. It's the light I want to capture.

I clean up for the day. I'm in the kitchen deciding what to do for the evening meal I shall share with Duncn; it's what we do on her first night away. Staring idly out of the window, touching the silvery irregular pearl that lives round my neck, I notice there's a truck from The Keep in our pull-in. Faerachar — it has to be — but it's very odd timing for him. First House is not visible from mine, but I recognise the dull slam of its front door over the sound of the beck. I put water ready for tea and turn back to the window. The truck is gone. I get a bottle of my ginger and nettle soda from the frige and go out to the seat by the bridge. Sipping, in the shade.

First House is mothballed; he's up to something. The last time he came and went in this mysterious manner was after Alastair had been elected to his third term as Reever. He worked a lot from First House. Faerachar called in there every day, for hours sometimes. No one realised it, but his father was not coping in the post — he's a thinker really. Faerachar was doing most of the organising required; he has a flair for that. Two years in, Alastair resigned. Faerachar stood before the Councils as candidate for Reever. Won the job; he was twenty-five. He fulfilled all the requirements — with his natural regard for the Ethical Code imbibed from a young age. Soon after Alastair moved back to the wilderness north of the Great Glen, handing the keys of First House to Faerachar.

I can't pin when Faerachar moved into First House completely. Whenever he fell out with Briged he'd go there. In the early days just for a few hours. Then, without any argument prodding him, he'd just go, sometimes for days. Well before his twelve weeks of Civic Service at the tail end of seventeen he was gone from Second House. He went straight to see his father on his return; never called in to see us for nearly a month. We are released from Civic Service two days before our eighteenth birthday. If Briged had qualms she never showed them.

I know almost nothing of what he did in the two year gap that followed. He says he just sailed away. He can spin a yarn — but maybe it was that simple. He has a friend, Charlie, who still has boats — never met him. Briged says they worked together in business before he was elected Reever. In that gap, he met Siobhagn. I remember his return.

Briged is showing me how to make drop scones. Duncn is doing something noisy outside. It suddenly goes quiet. She looks through the window, says. "Uh-huh."

He comes bounding in. "He's back! He's come back to see me."

He runs out again — yelling. I see Faerachar lift Duncn up and throw him higher. Brings him in under one arm, giggling and struggling — puts him down. Bobs down, gives him something. Out, Duncn runs.

"This is for you, Kaet. I have been neglectful. I promised once never to leave you."

He opens a small box, and hangs a silver necklace round my neck.

"You owe me nothing, Faerachar."

He holds me against him and I look up, but he is facing Briged. I am angry at him, though won't let the tears flow; pulling out of his arms I head for the garden. At the hall mirror, I look coldly at the oyster pearl hanging round my neck. Irregular, silvery, set in a silver clasp of two hands. Guilt brought this to me, I think. Then I hear the passion ringing in his voice. He does not call her Briged.

"She is Donegal in person, Mum. Her eyes the colour of shallow water rippling up a beach on a calm sunny day. Her skin the lightness of the softest sand onto which that water murmurs. She calls me, with her auburn hair, from the highest hills. I shall swim in her waters for the rest of my life."

She arrived a few weeks after he got back. The ideal foil for him. Stayed in First House a few weeks more, then disappeared and him with her — to a modern house down nearer the town.

Duncn arrives over an hour later than he agreed. There's a faint smell of fennel and beer as we embrace. Just as well I made no effort and went for pasta with an easy sauce and salad.

"Now I can cook the trofie. Nineteen minutes. Get a drink."

He opens the bottle of Alban Fastness Estates Dornfelder 2181 he's brought. Looks at me with his lost boy smile. Gets two glasses.

"Not for me now. Give me a sip of yours ..." Nice nose. Swill a little round my mouth. "Smooth. Fruity. Tannins balanced with a slight sweetness. Very impressed. How's Regin?"

He puffs a breath and throws up a hand; doesn't look at me.

"One look at that face. Plus his good fennel beer. How's Perdie?"

He slouches onto the smallest sofa. Shuffles his head about. Tuts once, puts his feet up.

"She's fine, but you know how she feels for Sam."

"This has been going on for seven years. Ever since you reconciled. In another week you'll head off. Probably go to Leeds this time. Get laid by strangers for three or four nights. Convince yourself you can be just friends with Regin. After a few weeks the wistful watching starts again. And he's just as bad as you, except he's not getting laid. Anywhere. When is Perdie going to be able to live with Sam?"

"That's what we all want to happen, but it'll upset the kids."

"It was your doing."

But — that's not quite true. He looks at me with sharp focus.

"You're pregnant. That's why I can smell blackberries. What else is in that infusion?"

"Horticulturist. You can have a sip and work it out. Here ... before you taste the wine you grew on those estates you manage. Yes, I am - five weeks I think. David knows, Briged too, and so will Siobhagn." He laughs at my obvious omission and shakes his head.

"That just came to me." With furrowed forehead, he continues, "If I could only see a way forward for us ..."

Duncn and Regin have loved since childhood. Lovers? Who knows when teenage fumblings slide into that status. I caught the changes in three line drawings — part-tints.

My first, the day Regin is allowed to live full time at Second House. My gift to them. Briged had a sound-proofed door fitted towards her end of the bedroom corridor before she agreed. Both still fifteen years old — joy on their faces — in shorts and tees. A tangle of legs and arms on their bed; anticipation making them glow. Regin is the older by ten days and twelve weeks. Two and a bit years of riotous life follow, till Civic Service separates them for half a year, other than those ten days in the middle.

My second, at Regin's request. I am in their bedroom within minutes of his return, them holding their poses. He, thumb by dick, pushing down his pants. His focus is on Duncn's part-seen face, who I see naked from behind, returning the look across his left shoulder. Clothes strewn at their feet. Regin gets it as his eighteenth birthday gift. Eight days later when Duncn is called up for his Civic Service, he is alone with it for twelve weeks. Half the time Regin is elsewhere, often staying at his parent's, I guess, but maybe with Sam or Perdie, their friends from school.

My third rendition on Duncn's return, is much larger. I take some persuading to be there. They are on their bed, naked, kissing, on the point of copulating, the pose gone in seconds. The fastest outline sketch

I ever made. Two people longing too much. Too hungry.

The drawings survive the night of Harvest Moon, one period later.

It starts after Briged has gone to bed behind her sound-proofed door. I am still awake and catch the rare tension in their voices, so open my door and stand in the shadows out of the moonlight on the stairway. I can hear the cold logic of Duncn disowning his love – deaf to Regin's pleas. He angrily manhandles an equally angered Regin down the stairs, each bitter step resisted. His anger ramped up with jealousy because of the unborn child nestling in Perdie's womb.

Certain he will destroy all reminders of their love, I flit to their room. Take the three drawings to my attic studio and lock them away.

When I come back to the landing Regin is already out of Second House, the front door being locked for the first time in my memory. Duncn stamps back up the stairs, slams their bedroom door without a glance at me. A window opens and bangs shut. Sounds of rampage. I run from the house, scooping up the bundle of clothes. Regin is crouched naked by the beck, sobbing, shivering. I am distraught myself – wanting this not to be real. I enfold him, feel his heaving heart. I see bruises as I dress his unresponsive body. Fetch his shoes from the hallway. Sit hugging him, until the moon crosses over the south; until his pain allows him to talk – in snatches.

He always wanted to be a father. Wanted them to be fathers. Now he would be. Three months is too long. Without Duncn.

Who is still wrecking his world. We walk from the noises, down through the woods to his parents' house in Grange.

"Why does he need to be so cataclysmic? This pain inside. Like I'm ripped." He starts crying again.

"You'll find the strength, Regin." I hug him hard. "Using the word cataclysmic – in this state of emotion – you'll find a way to get through this." He laughs bitterly; wipes his cheeks.

"You will always have me to talk with. You are brother to me. You are part of my family." He nods, holds my hands.

"He loves you too much. His green brown-rimmed eyed jealousy

17

drives this. It is not good for either of you. Build your family with Perdie, concentrate on that. His love for you will not wither. Leave him to stew; time will bring him back. I'll bring your belongings down later."

I kiss him, watch him enter, and turn homeward into the dawn.

Briged sits in the kitchen. "Something here is awry, Kaet."

I burst into tears, arms outstretched. "Mum ..."

"Where did you go? A calling? Did you hear me?"

He is holding out my mug of blackberry concoction. His face relaxing. I take it from him.

"Sorry, Duncn. It's nothing. What did you ask?"

"I said — that just came to me — about you being pregnant. By the time I got to musing on why I can't see what the future shall be for him and me, you were gone."

"How long?"

"Couple of minutes. That's got a nip of ginger, some blackberry fruit, but mainly young leaves and a few fermented older ones. I think there's spearmint rather than peppermint. A modicum of very young nettle shoots. It's based on a weak version of your nettle beer, which you've rid of alcohol."

"Good nose, Horti."

Happy, he goes to the hob. Forks out a piece of trofie and bites it. Satisfied, he slops cold water into the pan and drains it. We eat and reminisce, as we always end up doing. At the end of the meal I try another sip of the wine.

"Will this lay for a couple of years?" He nods vigorously. "Can you get me a bottle so I can celebrate the end of weaning."

"I can get it now. There's a couple of cases at home."

"Next time."

"No, now. Your Mother can care for it. There's room on her shelf." He is up and gone.

I go to my studio behind the kitchen, bringing the two drawings in their canvas slips back to the table. Clear the plates. Top up his glass — reseal the bottle — and sit down.

He bounds in, sets the bottle on her shelf with a flourish. Sits down, beaming at me. Turns to the canvas slips, and the beam goes. He's never asked about them. Slides his left hand cautiously onto them. Looks at me — akin to fear in his eyes.

"It's time you revisited them."

"Where's the third one?"

"Hanging above the foot of his narrow bed in celibate Regin's tidy room."

June, 16th — Genève, Confederation Helvetica — Ardel

Everything is in place, I called in on Grandy who voices approval of my plan of action. I am primed for my Solo. This is the start of my rest day. Leaving Dahqin asleep, I'd cycled down through the woods to the lake promenade. The sun is high in the sky, a few wispy clouds over the mountains to the south. Choosing a seat in the shade of the walnut trees giving a clear view of the lake, I order rosti and a milky coffee. I settle this scene in my memory — my ritual before going away. There's just my packing to finish.

"I'm home." I go straight to the bedroom, see my vest and shorts laid on the neat bed. Sounds of weights clunking down carry from the workroom. I emerge from the bedroom to see Dahqin standing under one of the sun tubes, over by his piano, mopping his face with a towel. Damp patches on his vest and loose shorts; eyes in down-slope mischievousness, no telling where iris and pupil meet. His slightly open smile, tips of his teeth parted, voice huffy.

"Hi. Earlier than I thought." He heads into the kitchen and gets some water. "You changed quicker too."

I follow him in. "I took your hint. Much more to do?"

"About thirty minutes. And your formal clothes are?"

"Thrown on the couch, like I never do. I cycled down to see Grandy — my clothes are in the wash-basket. I'll cross-train." I hold Dahqin in a bear hug. Look down at him looking up.

"You mean watch me."

Backing him into a corner, I claim kisses from him. He licks light sweat from by my armpits.

"You've been edging me the last three nights. You'd better mean it tonight. I'm away for days."

"You've played along with it."

The muscle along the top of Dahqin's left shoulder feels the nip of my teeth. Dahqin pushing into them, sighing out little breaths. I push a finger into those breaths, his lips closing round it, his tongue slipping along it. Nibble up his neck to his ear, love that his eyes are barely open. I breath in his scent. Feel his hands snake up under my vest giving me little twitches as his fingers skitter over my skin. Thumb and finger tweak at my nipples, getting them hard. Dahqin hard against me. He releases my finger, slides his mouth onto mine. We slow down; tasting. The swooping sound of nasal breaths as we slake with our tongues back and forth. A buzzer sounds and Dahqin pulls away.

"Thirty minutes. I want you sweating on the cross-trainer." Leads me by my hand into the workroom. "Twenty minutes on that. Then you help me do the final bench presses."

Dahqin sets weights, strips off his vest, throws it to me, and pulls on the bar. I drape it round my neck, watching abdominal and chest muscles tense.

It has gone midnight. We ate late, a light picking meal, lounging on the big settee, while watching an old romantic film. Me just in shorts, Dahqin in a beach-wrap.

I watch his lightly snoring figure. My packing otherwise finished, I pick Dahqin's vest from the wash-basket and slip it into my small backpack.

June, 17th & 18th — London — Ardel

The journey from Genève to London will take six hours. I can forget work for now — little smiles play with my face — and still feeling the pleasures of last evening I recline the seat and close my eyes.

Two officials receive me in London with the respect due an Ambassador — this is how I want things to be. I am so happy. Everything follows the Protocols with an easy delivery. I am lodged in the Government Guest House, well above the river dykes. My top-floor room faces the river. Upstream a huge bay can be seen in which sit a couple of islands settled with tower blocks. The far shore is covered in buildings as far as the hills I can see in the distance. I am taken on a tour of the district, regaled in a good restaurant, and am careful to respond in a correct manner to everything that is done for me.

Next day the meetings with various bureaucrats flow efficiently one into the other. I inspect the records of the sessions held during the period in question. There are no references to Lincolnshire. The area vaguely identified in the Complaint consists of marshes with isolated islands. It crosses from Alban through Mercia and into the United Counties of England. From the map the Complaint seems unfounded. The final agenda item is reached well ahead of schedule, every document loaded onto my faxplex. I thank my polite escorts for their time and effort.

They leave me alone in the Public Gallery watching a session in the Parliament. After half an hour, wondering why procedures are so arcane, I wander out onto the streets. I find a place to eat in the sun, on the edge of a square with dolphin fountains, amongst grand old buildings. Bronze lions guard a tall column with some martial figure on top. Beyond that the road leads down to the high dyke and a clear view of an upstream reach of the river. Two barges are heading through the bridge at the far end.

There is an appearance of being relaxed in my comfortable well-fitted suit and classic sunglasses. As I move to look about me the slate blue material, shot with silver and black, shimmers; there's a flash of dark crimson at the breast pocket lip and the slits along the cuff buttons, which matches the lining. I toy with my phone, but there is no one I can, with purpose, call. So I put it in its secure inner pocket. I pick up the menu, but don't really look at it. The waiter arrives, holds her touchpad towards me. I see her name, take off my sunglasses, smile.

"A small white beer, please, Janey. What is today's best vegetable special?"

"Definitely the aubergine parmigiano with sticky roasted sesame oil. It's got walnuts in it. Comes with a green salad." I order that.

Sitting forward, elbows on table, thumb under chin, fingers under nose, the other fist against my jaw bone, I try to look the part I want to be. I watch pigeons. Solo. She comes back with a glass of water and the beer, sets the table. I acknowledge her, put the sunglasses back on, sit back, drink some beer and really begin to relax. I watch people. The meal is delicious. When she clears the table I compliment her on the recommendation.

"Thanks. I love the colours in your suit. They suit your colours."

Walking through little back streets and alleys, I dawdle, looking in shop windows, and noting oddities. Just filling time. The wind builds up, blowing in from the east; dust swirls in the air. Turning my back to the wind I return to the Guest House. I call Dahqin soon after. It's become my role to soothe him as best I can as each first night approaches, but he's more confident than I expected.

"Going into Alban on this Solo is your first night. It's unsettling you, I can hear it in your voice. You'll be fine. I'll be fine. It'd be great if you were here for me to sing to, Ardel. Like the very first time I saw you. But other people pay us to do what we want to do. We both have to get used to this."

Our conversation lightens into intimacy.

June, 19th — London to Alban — Ardel

The Consular Agent of Alban arrives at the Guest House exactly on time. I put out my hand palm up, the Agent his palm facing in. In attempting to align, our fingers interlock.

I am embarrassed, but the Agent laughs out loud, clapping me on the upper arm.

"One way or another, hey! That caught me out. Got everything with you? My name's Frederick Wright. What do I call you?"

"How do you think I should be addressed?"

"Well, my choice, as we're travelling together for the best part of the day, is you call me Fred. That's my diminutive, as I like to say. Is Ardel okay?"

"Not as I was expecting."

"Marvellous. Let me take that bag with wheels, Ardel."

We take a taxi. He chats me onto the train, and when we are seated, hands over a faxplex.

"Details of your travel from here."

I go through the information. It proclaims — rather vaguely — I shall be meeting different officials along the route to The Keep, giving me time to acquaint myself with the country.

"This mentions various places, which seems clear enough. But there are no times."

Fred says that allows flexibility when seeing the country. The train journey is over after five stops and eighty minutes filled with snippets of dubious information and casual asides.

"Grantham. Time for a quick bite to eat. We'll go to the Angel and Royal. From here on it's slower going, I'm afraid. We have to show you the marshes east of here. You need to get a feel for the problem. A driver will be here in about forty-five minutes."

"What do you know of the Protocols, Fred?"

"Protocols? For what? Everything I can tell you is on that faxplex. Is there a problem?"

"I will note that. Let's get something to eat."

The restaurant in the hotel is a warren of small rooms. Fred chooses one with only two tables. He orders some kind of pie and a local beer. I settle on soup, Chilled Pea Green Summer, dark rye bread and water. A plaque on the wall claims nine hundred and eighty-five years of serving travellers. When the driver turns up, Fred rises to greet him; turns to me, holding out his hand palm up.

"Well, Ardel. It's been a very pleasant day so far. I'm off back to London now, I'll get the bill. Jimmy here, will be taking you on to Newark. He'll show you the watery landscape. Good Luck."

Amazed, I automatically drop my palm onto Fred's.

"Thank you for your ... help, Fred. It's been ... illuminating."

We leave Grantham into hilly country. Half an hour later having driven through green countryside and a couple of small villages, we are standing on a high platform above the steepest part of an escarpment. It drops away to a broad bight of water, dotted with islands and swathes of marshland.

"We're in Mercia here." Jimmy hands me binoculars. "Go three-thirty degrees on the compass. On that peninsular is Newark. It's in Alban. You'll just make out the spire of the church."

"Ok."

"Now go five degrees. Beyond the first island. You'll see Lincoln. The cathedral up on the summit of its island. The sun's shining on it. Looks golden. That's in Alban too. All this water out here to the east is salt. The water the other side of Newark is fresh. The Trent valley's flooded as a reservoir and to minimise salt water incursion."

I hand the binoculars back.

"Got any questions? I'll answer them if I can. If I don't know, I'll say."

"Where do I begin, Jimmy." I shake my head then look him in the eye. "Do you know anything about the Protocols?"

"Only the little I remember from school. I know what they're for." He narrows his eyes. "Are you an Ambassador?"

"Yes. Do you know why I'm here?"

"I was told to bring you here and explain the flooded landscape of Lincolnshire. And show you where the border runs. Is that wrong?"

"Not entirely. Then you take me to Newark, where ... What?"

"One of the Fastness river cruisers is waiting to take you up to Ripon overnight. Someone'll take you on from there to The Keep."

"That sort of ties in. What do you do for a living, Jimmy?"

"I work for the Fastness Estates, in Lincolnshire. Specialising in hydrology and flood defences. As you can see, there's not much to do." He creases a big smile and laughs.

"You picked me up in Grantham. That's in Mercia. Completely open borders?"

"Sort of. It's a bit complicated. The Mercian Border Force'll be tracking me. Our Boundary Patrol does the same with them. This is the best viewpoint for this part of the coast. Storm surges don't care about political borders. We work together up here."

"I need to check a name." I pull out of its security pocket the all-important faxplex with the Complaint.

"Where's Holbeach Drove?"

"That was abandoned years ago at three metres. It's behind us." He turns round and checks through the binoculars. Hands them over. "Go one-six-five. There's two little lighthouses. One green. One red."

"Got them. Is reclamation planned down there?"

"Lower a bit. It was in those marshes this side of them. They've been talking about reclaim for decades. That's well inside UCE. It's London land. See the little settlements on the few islands? Reclamation might keep people out there. But it's really to protect Peterborough."

"So Alban isn't involved?"

Jimmy laughs, takes off his wide-brimmed hat. Shakes his head, scratches at his hair.

"No. It's a waste of effort, that style of land management."

He starts towards the truck.

"Forty-odd years ago this was Alban. After the inundations slowed the Council of Lincolnshire received a petition for a sounding of the electors. Grantham lost a lot of its hinterland to the sea. It made economic sense for them to be part of Mercia. Old links die hard, though. The Five Boroughs might be split, but it's still Danelaw for some people. Newark clings to Nottinghamshire. You'll be looking that up, I can tell."

He begins to climb into the vehicle — stops half in. Grins at the puzzlement on my face.

"It's amphibious, Ardel. Bird-bone structure and inflation collars are what floats it. There's some marshes and a river we can cross on the way. You're a good excuse."

June, 19th — Newark to Ripon

The boat heads downstream soon after he boards. It has one long deckhouse. A young man leads Ardel through the saloon into a small cabin with a tiny shower and toilet cubicle. He squeezes past Ardel to get out and stands in the doorway.

"I'm Jesp. I'll tell you when supper's ready. It'll be here in the saloon. Do you want anything now?"

"Just water, please. Are there binoculars I can use? I'm Ardel."

He puts out his hand — Jesp steps back, laughs nervously, then extends his for the shake. Glances quickly at Ardel's eyes. Gestures with his thumb over his shoulder.

"The binos are by the book rack. Bird books, and the like. There's a water fountain by the frige. Glasses and mugs by it."

Ardel sits on deck in the sunshine, watching the watery world slide by. They pass through the first lock, the crew working the ropes. Occasionally there are ruins. Some in clusters might be from the Upheavals. In one place the remains of a soaring bridge, pointing south-east, sticks out from a high embankment. He turns to the woman sitting near him, reading a book made of paper with a soft cover.

"What happened here?"

"Used to be a big road. Ended up going nowhere."

"Can you get them on faxplex?"

She flips the book. "Expect so. Don't use 'em. I like these."

Lines of wind-driven generators, marking out the embankments, turn slowly in the warm breeze. Through the binoculars he can see hedged fields on the rising land behind the reservoirs. She gets up to deal with the mooring ropes as they approach another lock. He picks up the book, gently touches the pages. The title — *I Told Him, Get On With It* — printed over a cartoon of a frowning woman in bright colours. He carefully lays it back where it had been.

They sail into a salt-water estuary, which grows ever wider as they progress. She's back reading, giggles quietly and lays the book down.

"Are you wanting a drink? I'm Sal." She's still amused.

"Please. Ardel."

He eyes the book, but feels her footsteps coming down the deck.

"It's a slice of life, that." She hands him a mug. "Sweet-beet."

He thanks her, sips at it — pleasant, slightly earthy taste.

She picks up the book, giggles again. Turns a page, takes a mouthful of the drink. Occasionally clouds block the sun.

He drifts to the summer of his fifteenth year. The joyful energy of sexual attraction. The thrill of being covert with the younger of the two crew, on a cruiser his parents hired in France.

"Won't be long. We're changing the battery pack." She's passing the boat ropes through mooring rings on a jetty. He opens his eyes, stretches, arms above his head.

The hills are higher and closer. They are alongside a small crane. She goes ashore and slews the jib out over the hatch in the deck where they have been lounging. Eventually two people come down the jetty on a trolley carrying the large battery pack. Their talk with Sal is in a dialect he has problems understanding. He goes to the cabin, showers and changes into shorts and tee.

Soon after Jesp calls him to supper. He sits opposite Sal and one of the two helmsmen, who nods at him. The table is screwed to the deck between banquettes. Nothing is said, and they are both soon gone. Jesp brings his food. He takes his time with it. It's tasty and wholesome, though nothing special. Jesp is working behind the galley counter. Lithe. Easy to watch.

He catches Jesp looking at him reflected in the shiny splashback, a little smile crosses his face when he's clocked. When he turns with his plate of food in hand and comes to the table, the smile is still there. Their knees brush as he sits down. He mumbles sorry; the smile holds.

"If you want anything special, like. Just say." Their eyes meet.

"I will, Jesp." Placing his cutlery on the empty plate, Ardel drops his left hand onto his thigh — feels a nudge as their knees touch — brings it back into view.

"Er ... Have you worked on this boat for long?" Jesp bursts into laughter, nearly chokes. They slide into flirty banter.

... It is dark when he slowly wakes. Jesp is by the bunk in briefs.

"Is this the something special?"

"You know fine it's yet to cuum." Jesp emphasises the word. He lays a hand on Ardel's chest, slowly slides it down past his abdomen.

"Are you in this for lust — or something else?"

"Lust, of course." Jesp takes his hand away. "I'm so horny, and you're an Ambassador. Never had one of those."

"Now's the time." He puts Jesp's hand back.

"I think it's time we made it special." Pulling Jesp's head towards him, he moves in for the kiss. ...

Ardel lurches awake from the dream. It's his hand. He can hear Jesp and one of the helmsmen talking. He gropes in his bag and pulls out Dahqin's vest.

June, 20th — Ripon — Ardel

Jesp greets me cheerily when I enter the saloon.

"It's Ripon. Where you're bid farewell. What d'you want for breakfast?"

The muesli, salted buttermilk and honey eaten, the mug of coffee drunk, I sit out in the early morning sun, chatting with Jesp. The boat is moored to a stone wharf. This is only a small town — ten kay population at most, I reckon — and dominated by a large church. There's a few animals in the fields across the river. A warm front is bringing a bank of dark clouds through from the west.

A dirty work truck drives onto the wharf. Jesp elbows me.

"That'll be for you. I recognise him. Safe journey, Ardel. Maybe another time." And he's gone before I can respond.

A scruffy man gets out, walks towards the gangway.

"You'll be the vip, then. Give me that." He takes my wheeled case.

"I am the Ambassador. And you are?"

"Me name's Graff. I'm to take you towards Keep."

"In this? How long is the journey ahead?"

"Aye. In this. Two comfortable treks, Ambassador. Not too hard. Up over fells and down the other side — I'm driving — other side."

I deposit my bag behind the passenger seat and climb in.

"As you please." Graff secures the bags into a safety net and we set off at a slow pace through the town.

I notice a neatly painted sign as we cross the river — For Every Right, There Are Obligations

And by the church — Everyone Counts For Something

In the Market Square — Probity Is The Essence

They aren't overly large, but distinctive enough to notice.

"What are those signs for?"

"The Ethical Code, Ambassador."

The cultivated land soon turns to shrubs and spinneys of trees. Soon we are driving through thicker woods, along a broad metalled road; grass growing in the middle. I try to strike up a conversation.

"That front looks angry. Do you think it is going to rain soon."

"Aye."

"Do you think it will last long?"

"Shouldn't."

We cover a few kimetres.

"Are we using this truck all the way to The Keep?"

"No." Through the leafy canopy the first drops of rain spatter onto the windshield.

"How are we getting to The Keep then?"

"Horse." I go to respond but compress my lips. Horses were not mentioned in the itinerary Fred handed over.

We drive on for a few more kimetres. With the rain falling too heavily, Graff stops the truck in a clearing. Hunches forward over the wheel. Thunder rolls nearby.

"Where do you live, Graff?" He faces me — considers me.

"Where *you* take to horses."

"You will not be coming with me?"

"Ambassador, I've a farm to look after. Fell Riders'll take you."

"Fell Riders?"

"You'll be safe with 'em. They're superstitious folk, but they'll look out for you." The rain eases and the sky lightens.

"You own a farm?"

"The Fastness Estates own the farm. I look after it." The last few drops patter on the roof. "That's it for today."

The road surface is rougher and the motion of the truck tiring. I doze fitfully. I awake sluggishly when we leave the road and climb steeply on a rock-chip track between high banks. Stunted trees and thick copses of thorn bushes stand to either side, casting deep shadow. We swoop down across a wooden bridge spanning a fast flowing river, round a sharp corner, turn between two massive doors in a high wall and come to a halt. Stables, two houses, a large barn and various smaller buildings all of grey stone, make an enclosure hiding in a scoop in the hills.

"You'll eat?"

"I will, thank you."

"The Riders." It's muttered. He does not point or turn to look at them, but I see his eyes flick in their direction.

Two men short of stature, with weathered faces, bandy and black haired, stand watchfully in the weak sunlight. They have four cobs with them, the largest with cargo panniers; colourful bridles and reins prinking against their dark hair. I clamber from the truck and nod to them. The younger one nods back. Lugging my tote bag I follow Graff into the farmhouse.

"Toilet's in there."

Dressed in my rough-travel clothes I return to the kitchen. A bowl of hot broth and some bread sits on the table. As I'm finishing, Graff comes in from the yard.

"'You'd best go with the Riders now." He pauses. "You do ride?"

"Of course."

He hands over a riding hat, over-breeches, and a rolled up rider's cape. "Hand them back at The Keep."

June, 20th — Over the Fells

By mid-afternoon they are above the trees, the older man leading, climbing all the while up an ever steeper pass. The land on each side is sodden. Little rivulets coursing together join the torrent in the narrow watercourse they are following. High up a large raptor drifts. The sky is clearing of clouds. When the sun shines on the hillsides it lifts the colours. The warm wind tugging at his hair and fluting across his ears is not yet tiresome. Cattle, sheep and horses, in small numbers, feed on the open rough pasture. He surmises from the Riders' clothing that the cattle and sheep provide their livelihood. Occasionally he sees isolated buildings and narrow roads in the valleys below their route.

The young man calls out. He looks back, they are the first words either has uttered to him. Ardel searches in the direction he is pointing and sees a stag with his hinds. Their silence gathers round him again. They pass a sheep carcass being picked at by ravens and crows. The older man turns round.

"Dogs."

During a break they offer him dried meat, which he graciously declines. He's shown how to relieve himself without befouling the surface, scattering bacterial powder into the hole before putting the sod back. Once they are moving he discretely eats a protein bar. Late in the afternoon the young man attempts a conversation with Ardel in the common tongue. It takes both of them some time to break through the accents and limited vocabulary.

"We are called Roamers. Riders. We ..." He speaks to the older man. "Horses." He pats the neck of his mount.

"Them we love like our women." He looks pleased, eases. Tells him they live in small family groups scattered all over the high fells in this part of Alban; they do work, like this, for The Keep.

As they reach the summit of the pass the leader turns to him again. "We stay with my family this night. At sundown we reach them."

It is another hour, the sun not quite touching the horizon, when the leader speaks for a third time.

"Here is my family."

He waves towards a gully that cuts into the hills south of their path. They file away from the track and descend along a ridge. As they pass, he points to a curve of wall in a dip to the west.

"When you need. What I show you before. Men. Down at camp, he shows you in the stream where men wash. Do not enter the water above this place."

It is gloaming when they reach a fire burning outside some caves set in a cliff-face. A couple of men, lurchers in tow, amble over to the leader. They unhitch the pack horse, chattering as they take the panniers off, laughing at something.

Or someone. Ardel checks his phone — no signal. Tuts, then quietly says, "I shall hear a voice I comprehend, or be nothing."

June, 20th & 21st — Over the Fells — Ardel

I should have realised earlier, the language is their own. No links to any of the languages I speak so fluently. I might as well be in the panniers. I am cut out. Solo. The young man jumps from his horse. I am envious of his poise. He disappears back up the ridge. I see now the well-worn path.

The saddle is not like those I am used to. It is softer, more comfortable, but the aches will be the same. My dismount is not elegant. The cob has treated me well, not pushing to test my control. I feel an affection for her, standing to the side of her head, eye to eye, rubbing my hands across her neck and cheeks. Holding the reins, I let her nudge at me. The bridles have no bits champing across their mouths. I like that — their deep love for these horses. One of the men taps me on the arm, gives me two carrots and grins. I thank him and snap them in two, leaving one bit on my open palm, hiding the others in a closed fist. She pushes at the fist.

"You have been a good horse to me." I let her take the lot, the one on my palm she takes last. Rechecks my hands when she finishes.

The man laughs. "She loves you ... While you have carrots." He takes the reins and leads her downstream, following the others.

I stretch and flex, slowly turning to view the camp. I can see the tops of a couple of tents beyond a hummock. The leader talks quietly with a woman he had acknowledged when we arrived. He points at me. She turns, looking straight at me. Black hair falling down her back pulled tight with a ribbon. Her dark blue skirt, over trousers, printed with peonies the colour of my suit lining. Gold bangles at wrists and ankles, necklaces and earrings. He comes over.

A pot hangs over the fire. There's meat in it, and no choice. People are gathering.

"You will eat with us. A stew of sheep."

"Thank you. It smells good."

The leader turns, says something that makes them laugh.

"I joke about your cornflower eyes, wheaten hair, your tallness."

"I don't mind." I smile. "I am Ardel. What is your name?"

His smile goes.

"Ask not the names of those you meet on the moorland. Their souls must pass you by." I hear annoyance; I fix a mild expression. He makes a strange gesture with his hand. Looks into the shadows.

"You are a Taran on a quest." He joins the others and gets them laughing again. I can't stop my frown, and she is still watching me.

"Come. I show where is men's water."

He's back from the latrine, hair wet. We head downstream, beyond the cobs and some bigger horses. In what once had been a quarry I see two covered wagons and some carts. A track goes down the valley to the south. Another stream joins from the left.

"Not up there. For the women." We round a spur. A third stream. An easy climb to a pool, spilling over smooth rocks.

"This is for us." He lifts a flat stone off the top of a small pile, pulls out a jar filled with leaves.

"Always put lid back and fit this stone the right way." I wash my hands as he does, rubbing a leaf between them.

"What is this?"

"From a bush. I don't know in the voice you speak. It cleans and is ... smooth." He moves thumb and fingers together.

"Smooth to touch. No harm to this water."

"Yes I can feel. The skin is nice."

"Only this here. You wash by the latrine. You'll see."

"Why come here, then?"

"Calm. This pool, the women's pool are for ..." He spreads his hands apart, palms up, his eyes closed.

"The other man said not to go in the water up from here."

"My father. He means above camp. Our food water we take from there."

"This camp is a simple way of life."

He laughs at my naivety. "Not really. Life does not need so much. We are here Spring to Autumn. Summer camp. When the winter comes we go down to our houses. Your phone", he mimics me looking at it and shaking my head, "does not work up here. You tell him your name is Ardel. You do not me, so I tell. I am Michal. But you not to use near my father or mother. She is the one looks at you and sees."

He looks shy.

"I don't use this tongue much. You are the first time since winter. Come."

A group of younger children wait by the horses. They run silently ahead of us mingling into the adults around the fire. His mother beckons me over, pointing to a folded blanket. I sit cross-legged. She hands me a dish of stew and a bowl of black tea. I eat listening to the cadence of their language. Invisible, it feels. Except to Michal and his mother sitting together.

I can feel my eye-lids drooping; she prods my arm, mimes sleeping. I follow her to one of the caves, to the glow of a tea-light. Just inside the entrance a bed, with towel and bottle of water on it. When I look round she has gone. My bags are on a trestle. I pocket my torch, and throw the towel across my shoulder. The light of the quarter moon is enough to follow the path. And the latrine is not as I feared. It is an ecological type, spotless, with lighting, and a shower.

I walk cleansed, on the edge of the fire light, to the men's pool, followed at a distance by two of their lurchers. Strip off. The pool feels cool after the heat of the day. The dogs lay on the bank opposite me. Wild animals, cough-bark in the distance.

I climb into bed surprised by it's softness, and thankful. The flickering tea-light picks out the markings of an old mine. I blow it out. The murmur of their voices carries to me.

They wake me early. I am enlivened by a plunge in the pool, my mood better. We set off over a higher pass, then descend over a series of lower ones, stopping once. I think I see a railway line away to the north, but cannot make them understand when I ask about it. Soon after we enter a dense wood, the first since I have been with them; when we emerge I catch no other sight of it.

"These few buildings we see. Are they ruins or in use?"

"If there are dogs", Michal says, "they are lived in."

His father snarls. "Farm dogs I don't like."

"Some of those we've seen are huge."

His face is grim. "Killing dogs."

"What!"

"People sometimes." He faces front. "In the next valley we stop for food."

The land is changing. The buildings lived in, dogs or not. I can't make out what is growing under the canopies between the walled fields. When I ask they shrug.

We stop at a low building backed by a stand of stunted oaks, on the outskirts of a small urb. Big windows face a field of grass bounded by thickets of gorse and hazel pollards. A few horses are already tethered by the well-spaced water troughs; trucks and tractors with trailers are parked on a gravelled standing. I watch them picket the horses at a water trough right at the front. His father brings two shiny brass padlocks from his saddle bag. They look ancient. Michal sees my look as he secures the panniers.

"Don't worry, these are for the eye. It's market day for the farms. Our horses, people don't touch. They bite if we are not with them. We watch from in there."

It's busy, outside and in. People at square-topped stands conversing in the local accent. They talk too fast for me to understand much of it. The long bare tables are quieter. Michal leads us to the window end of the closest one. A young lad follows us over, sets down three mugs of some frothy cold liquid.

"What d'you want?" He looks at Michal's father.

"What the cook says is good." I don't see a menu and nod agreement. They both drink. His father avoids eye contact.

"My friend, what about me troubles you?"

He rises from the bench. "Cannot say. What is to come, will be."

"I do not understand."

"Shadows fall on you, Taran. On the long day, darkness."

He makes that funny gesture again and walks away. Michal does not move, though a crooked grin comes and goes.

"Why does he call me Taran?"

"You sound words like they do." He takes a swig, licks his lips. "What are you, if not Taran?"

"Swiss."

Raises his eyebrows, turns down his lips.

"What he says. As my mother says it, it's not so bad." I go to ask him, but he closes his eyes. Moves his head three times side to side.

I sniff at my mug. Wrinkle my nose. "What is this?"

Michal grins. "Honey beer. Strong. Here, if you don't want it."

I go for water and when I return the cook's good meal is on the table. It's another stew, this time with dumplings, and a dish of boiled potatoes. I make do with some of them, two dumplings and the bigger bits of mushy vegetables, pushing my bowl away long before they finish. Michal spoons the remains into his own dish.

"How much longer?"

"Near four hours." His father is almost looking at me.

We ride away from the settlement over yet another pass. Cross a broad river coursing through boulders and up a narrow lane under concrete and brick bridges. I catch a glimpse of railway tracks, but lose sight of them as the lane carries up through a gully and peters out onto yellowing rough grass. The wind catches at me. Lifts the mane of my horse. I fasten my jacket – pull the strap of my hat tighter. Away in the distance on each side are part-views of large lakes. I recognise the remains of a Roman road we ride beside. In the valley to the east, two small lakes in shadow. We zig-zag down to the west. Passing the end of another lake and climbing more bare fells we stop on the crest.

"At last." I can't hide my relief. The valley opens out, seeming filled by the broad lake with a few islands. Silvered by the sun, the river draining the lake runs north amongst water meadows. Below us in a side valley I see a small town astride another river.

"The Keep is there."

His arm outstretched towards the western side, Michal's father is watching me. As I turn my face towards him, he looks away. Nothing resembles the photo Dahqin and I had studied. But then the sun shines on the dome.

"I see it."

Michal's father nods, grunts; sets his horse moving.

We cross the river on a suspension bridge that sways with our weight. Trot the cobs across the water meadows onto a curve of road going through aspens and Scots pines to The Keep. The lower parts of the building are covered by creepers of various kinds, a multitude of greens. The upper stories of grey stone are clear of them.

Michal's father remains mounted outside the narrow entrance tunnel pointing to a cabinet on the wall. I stand facing the mare, she nudges at the pocket where I have a carrot waiting. I rub the dull chestnut nap on her neck when she's finished and do a rider's stroll to the screen — touch it.

A face appears. "Yes?"

"I am Ambassador Penaul; here at the behest of the Reever."

"The Reever is due back soon. In his absence you are welcome. We're sending down a cannion." The screen goes blank.

"Cannion?"

"Cage. It goes up." Michal yawns, lifting my luggage from the pack horse. The cannion arrives. Grille doors slide open. Inside are benches fitted with grab handles. Attached to the side a wheeled cage. Michal opens it, puts my bags in, latches it.

"Thank you for your company ..." I almost say his name and it shows on his face, but a smile takes over. As he ties the reins of my mount to a trace on the pack horse, I take a final look in her eyes, rub her nose, and get a nudge from her. The leader looks directly at me, makes his sign as he turns his horse. Michal waves a hand without looking back, and they are gone into the trees.

June, 21st, The Keep in Derwent, Wark-in-Alban — Ardel

I stand in the sun, removing the over-breeches and riding hat. A voice comes from inside the cannion.

"Get in, Sir, please. Sit down on the left, and hold on."

"Okay. I'm seated."

"Thank you, Sir."

I drop the hat and breeches onto the floor and clean my hands in my sanitiser bag. The doors slide shut. The cannion rises up the shaft. A few seconds later, with a slight jiggle, it moves sideways, speeding along straights and curves alike, in and out of dark tunnels. There is a little jolt, the cannion goes down, for quite a time. A bump. The light goes out. Moving sideways, slowly. Something slides. A thud. A humming sound. The cannion descends. Not far. A clunk, which gives an echo. Complete darkness. Silence.

I feel my pulse, it's too fast. I need to hear a voice.

"This is Ambassador Penaul. What has happened?" No reply.

There's a plink. The ringing sound of a drip of water falling from a tap into a bowl. Dampness in the air.

"I'm hanging over water." I sniff a few times. "Seaside?" Cattle had been drinking from the river, and The Keep is well inland.

"This is Ambassador Penaul." Silence.

Training takes over. I remember *When in Tight Situations* in the flat voice of the shaven-headed trainer.

"Talk calmly. Act in concert." A gallows humour snort escapes. "Me and myself. In Solo concert." Needing to rub my legs and buttocks, I stand up slowly. The cannion sways in a jiggeredly fashion. Finding a handhold I do a few squats.

"Take stock. Assess. Focus. Do not fear. Resist panic. Centre." It has to be a malfunction.

"Do not crave for what is missing." My torch and phone are in my work-case.

"Peering into darkness brings fear, not knowledge." My eyes already closed for just that reason.

"Fear is worth fearing." They will get it fixed soon.

"Fixating on the passage of time is a danger." I take off my time band. Put it in the security pocket of my jacket with my persID and Warrant badge. Zipped away. In the other pockets, two half-litre soft packs of water, one each side in their special pouches. Protein bars, oral chews, skin freshener, nasal wipes, sanitiser bag. Touchpad. My fingers close round my army knife, wrapped in a kerchief. Dahqin's.

"Emotion and attachment must be resisted."

I must not — but surely, just one little sniff — I can't resist. My sigh blots out the quietness. I push my hands into the sanitiser bag, rubbing the cloth with unnecessary vigour. Sniff them; neutrality.

There is a loud 'Plop!' Momentarily the pin-pricks of fear move up the nape of my neck. Then another one sounds.

"Deal only with what is before you."

The cannion is gyrating gently.

"I must reject anger. Centre and Calm." I sit cross-legged on the floor, imaging the smells of butter-lights, frankincense and sandalwood.

The meditation gains me some calmness. More attuned to the sounds of the space I know there must be marine fish of some kind in the water. But what could live in this darkness? As I push myself up, I feel a small pebble.

"Assess." Pick it up. Setting my touchpad to stopwatch I wait with my eye lids cracked open. When they are accustomed to its dim light, I drop the pebble. The touchpad is crammed with useful presets. I am twenty-one point two three metres above the surface. "Maybe useful."

I lay down. Try to cat-nap — but for that one must feel secure.

A horrifying slithering sound overhead has me jumping up. Something smelling rancid passes the grille door. The loud spl-lu-shh! is followed by an explosion of slurping, plopping and unseen motion. My jacket and trousers feel clean. Out comes my sanitiser bag. Catches on Dahqin's kerchief.

"Adventures! Definitely raise issues."

I loudly force out breath. The frenzy lessens. "It's just fish."

I feel for a grab handle, sit in the darkness, head pressing against the panelling.

"All answers become clear in the light of time." The voice and its tone surprises me, but it is mine. That thought came out of nowhere. A door higher up in the space opens. Light, though dim, makes me squint.

"I am very, very sorry for your treatment," a gentle voice says from beyond the door. "A moment more and we shall haul you out. The pause is to give your eyes a chance to adjust."

The light in the cannion comes on. I shield my eyes.

"You are the Reever." I feel absolute certainty. I become the calm voiced Ambassador. The Protocols can start.

"I am the Reever, Ardel. We have violated your neutrality, and I am the slighted Complainant you have come to help."

The voice is pleasantly accented, but alluring. I put on my time band. So, the sun will soon be gone to night.

"How have you used this unexpected confinement, Ardel?"

"I have had time to meditate, Reever. I have a list of questions of the why? variety." I peer down. The noises seem not so loud.

"Do not worry what is down there. All answers become clear in the light of time." A cold frisson passes through me.

"It is not so far, nor so fearsome as my imagination made it."

"Perhaps the real function of imagination is to let relief wash away fear, Ardel." I say nothing.

The cannion rises, trundles out and deposits itself on the floor of a corridor dimly lit along the base of the walls. The doors open.

Five people stand there. Two of the women are in uniform; badges proclaim them Boundary Patrol members — the first I have seen. They remove my luggage from the cage, unclip it and wheel it away.

"Do you need a hand, Ambassador?" the younger man asks.

"No, thank you. I do wish to freshen up though, and change out of these clothes. Before anything else."

"Of course, Ardel." The other man steps forward. His hair is the colour of the mare's, there's a streak of white each side. It's wavy, in a similar style to Dahqin's when newly cut.

"I am Faerachar Strachan. Reever of Alban. I offer my sincere apologies for what has befallen you in these last few hours. I hope you will accept them."

There's familiarity in his eyes. I feel mine giving way to his; darker blue than mine, with sandy flecks. I steel myself, look back up. He has authority pulsing out of him. But that won't shield him from what I shall say during our tête-à-tête. That phrasing of his features — that's a clever one. Smiling without the eyes or mouth denoting it. Lulling one into liking him. Together with his voice, dangerous.

He was definitely not on the photos Dahqin and I looked at. Nor is it his voice in the audio of the Complaint. He holds out his right palm. I place mine onto it.

"This is not how I expected to meet you, Reever."

"I understand entirely. I am truly sorry, Ambassador." I lift my hand away. "It will take a couple of minutes to get to your chamber. If you need to..." He indicates a nearby door.

"I can wait." The younger man puts my luggage in the cannion. I feel the nip of anxiety.

"You need to know these important people. They will be looking after your domestic needs. Martha ..."

She puts out her hand. I realise in time, and shake it. She's slim, upright, her handshake firm. A bit shorter than Dahqin. Not afraid to hold my gaze, but then, she's probably older than my mother. Wears her greying hair short. I want to say how much I like her fitted suit. Short upstand collar. Sage green and cream wool mix with twisted lime green trim on the jacket edge and down the trouser seams — at the cuffs too. Flat shoes the same tone as the satin buttons. Very stylish. Complemented by her eyes. But this is not a permissible path to tread.

"I am Martha Jenkin, Ambassador. The Bursar of The Keep. Anything that is awry you tell me or Regin and it will be solved. I have assigned him the task of ensuring you get what you need."

He smiles at me — a welcome vision. Nothing special about his clothes, but he's neat. Short-sleeved, open-necked white shirt and dark-grey shorts, carefully creased. Light grey socks reaching just below his knees and soft black shoes. Hints of tattoos at the left arm and open shirt.

"Regin Peterson." We shake. "I'm Under-Bursar." My height. Black haired and very pale skin, about my age. I don't dwell on his eyes, not with the Reever watching. He registers my tension as the Reever places a hand on my left shoulder.

"We're all going up in this cannion, Ardel. You and Regin will get off by your chamber. I will see you when you are ready for food. I really cannot apologise enough."

"The Protocols, Reever."

"Of course."

The Bursars seat themselves opposite one another, my luggage between them. The Under-Bursar produces a bag, turns it inside out, picks up the over-breeches and hat, and ties it. She takes it from him. The Reever moves his hand behind my left elbow and steers me the two steps back into the cannion. It lifts off the floor, moving along high up in the corridor. After a few metres it stops, moves backwards. There's a slight jiggle and it is rising through a shaft. It passes, too fast to count, many floors. When it stops the Under-Bursar lifts my luggage.

"I'll take my work-case."

"I will see you soon, Ardel. Regin, do your stuff."

"This way, Ambassador. Have a good night, Martha," he calls as the doors close.

I notice a small mirror high up against the ceiling, showing the doors and around the adjacent corner in the corridor. We head the other way, passing a few doors, each with a tag letter and number. The door he stops at is larger, with a name plate — Coleridge.

He pushes it open and I enter, following the sweep of his hand. Hanging my jacket on the hooks by the door, I notice one pair of room slippers. They fit snugly.

"You are the first ever Ambassador to use these rooms." His English has a mild accent; easy to understand. I meet his steady gaze.

"How do you wish me to address you?"

"Regin is my given name and will get my attention. It is our custom to address each other so. Martha and Faerachar might be further up the pecking order than me, Ambassador, but all of us count for something.

Each of us with a name that grants no precedency. How should I address you?"

The Protocols mark my position, gird me with titles and demand deference. Quietly a clock ticks away seconds. He is a person, the same as me; tasked with looking after my needs. I have a desire for his respect.

"Ardel is my name, Regin."

"Ardel." He tilts his head. "Thank you."

I have passed his test. He begins his stuff, pointing to a low set of drawers set against a large desk.

"Your work-case will be handy on that. Power points are under the lid on that side of the desk. I'll show you the rest."

There's a pleasant feeling in the room. Fabrics in shades of silvers and greens, strokes of black dashed across them. Each section of wall with one contemplative painting. Pushing aside a heavy curtain, he takes my wheeled case into the bedroom. Hefts it onto a similar set of drawers next to a wardrobe. Smooths out a wrinkle on the bed cover.

Points to an ottoman. "Extra bedding."

Opens the washroom door. I can see clear over to the far side of the lake. I look from the window to him.

"The blind's concealed up there if you want it, but you're twelve floors up. Why waste the views." He checks everything is just so.

"Plenty of towels in this cupboard." He pulls out a bathrobe, almost the colour of my eyes.

"You're a nice bit broader than I guessed." He holds it for me to try. "Too tight on the shoulders. Next size up, then."

He leads back into the main room, puts the bathrobe on my work case. I pass the settees and armchair, a glass-topped table between them, to the tall windows set within an oriel. Kneeling on the cushioned bench I take in the vista. A place to relax — someone in your arms. He looks up from his inspection of the frige.

"You're facing south-east, that's Lady's Rake above the trees over that side. You'll want some drinks in here. I'll bring a list of what's to hand. Anything else we'll try to get." He opens the glazed double doors that lead onto a broad terrace, letting in a breeze; comes over to me.

"Got your phone?" We palm them on top of each other.

We both say "How do I spell ..." at the same time, laughing together.

"Just seen the tag on your case. Mine ends g-i-n. Faerachar won't be dressed formally. Call me when you're ready. I'll come to these doors."

I follow his gaze, when I turn back he is gone. The bathrobe too.

The sun is shining only on the higher peaks that face west, though I can still pick out details on the far shore. Clear water in the shallows on this side shows a gravelly bottom. Lawn reaches the water's edge. Amongst trees a large boathouse with jetties is sited. A passenger launch is crossing to the other side.

From the shower I watch the rapidly changing light on the fells. Wander round the main room, drying — inspecting the paintings, checking in drawers and cabinets. The desk drawers are stocked with graphite–fed pensticks, little notebooks of paper made from wood. There's bottles of coloured ink and dipping pens with various nibs. One cabinet near the frige holds bottles of various drinks. There are some liqueurs — none of them black. I won't drink any of this on my own. The glasses I find are varied and old, histories to be told. There are three matching ones, small. Very thin glass, narrow stemmed, acid-etched patterning from a slightly wonky transfer. Papa would love these. He told me about this type of marking, it's three-sixty to three-thirty years old. Exquisite.

A knocking at the terrace doors — it's Regin. I'm surprised to see it's almost dark out there. Hadn't noticed the room lights creeping up. I wrap the towel and call him in. He puts the bigger bathrobe on the settee nearest the bedroom, it's initialled with a tiny AP on the lapel.

"I tried calling you, but your phone's not responding. Faerachar is wondering if you need sleep more than food."

"Food." I check my phone. "I've got no signal. Haven't had since I left Newark. Wait here, Regin. Give me a few minutes."

I've laid out clothes I want to impress with. I reach for Dahqin's vest, just a little sniff.

"Informal, you said." There is no answer so I look up. He is leaning on the near side of the armchair with a clear view of me. He nods — I stare at him — no hint of abashment, he stares right back. I drop my towel and begin to dress.

"It's a nice night, Ardel. I've laid the table outside. It's vegetarian. Do you drink alcohol? Only I've got a good local white to serve with it."

"Vegetarian's good. And yes, wine. Did you know?"

"Know what?" A tiny sneak of insinuation in his voice.

"I'm vegetarian."

"Of course. Martha's very organised. She got information from your office. How do you think I guessed at the bathrobe and slippers. I'll tell comms about your phone. Use the internal one for now."

He goes rummaging in the desk and plugs in an old-fashioned handset. "Just press the button, someone will answer."

I follow him along the terrace. The table is large enough for four and nicely set for two. Damask for the cover and napkins. Glasses for the wine not over-large. The lighting well-judged. Bread on a board in the centre, water in a clear shapely bottle with two heavy tumblers. Just as the Protocols require.

The Reever is talking to someone further down the terrace. Regin pings a glass on the butler trolley. They look up. His companion is taller than the Reever, so taller than me; dressed in black and I can't make out his face. As he moves away he disappears into the darkness. Regin too has gone.

The Reever comes over with a smile on his face. I wait for him to stand by his chair.

"Bread and water." I say as we sit.

"You are the first Ambassador here in a hundred and thirty-eight years." He pours the water. We both sip. Put the glasses down.

"The Protocols are important. But I'll not read from a script."

"What happened with the cannion?" My teeth bind.

"Poorly worded instructions on my part. Compounded by your escort intimating you were not to be trusted, it seems. If apologies could wipe

46

the mistreatment away I would say them forever. But you either accept them now, or not."

There is sensuousness in his passion. My anger feels petty.

"I will accept your apologies as sincere. To do otherwise would not be diplomatic."

"I believe you jest with that last phrase, Ambassador."

"I'll try my best to be light." Our eyes hold, his appear contrite.

"I can give more details."

I wave my hand. "In time for my report, Reever, before I leave."

He gives a little huff, moves the bread board closer to me.

"Let it please you to break the first bread, Ambassador."

"If that is your wish, it is mine."

"Let there be trust between us."

"I would be honoured to receive that indulgence."

I break the loaf. Hand the board towards him.

"And I with yours, Ardel."

"You play with me."

"While the Rules are thick with Protocol and how to deal with the Ambassador — and I would be the last to breach such august pageantry — allow me at least to be human." He rings a little bell.

"This is our territory. The people in this Fastness have put their faith in me, and I will strive to protect them by all the means at my disposal."

He stops as Regin comes out with the wine in a cooler.

"Thank you, Regin."

The Reever takes the bottle and unseals it. Pours some into a small glass Regin holds — who does the nose, swooshes it round — takes the lot. I watch his Adam's apple move as he swallows.

"Better than 2186's. The finish is just smooth enough to leave the apple sharpness nicely on the tongue. It will go well with both courses."

The Reever is focused on Regin, nodding.

"Regin's got a better palate than me, Ardel. This is the very first bottle of last year's pressing."

He takes the bottle from the Reever and serves us — places it by me.

I study the label.

"This grape — Fendant — we call it Chasselas. Are the vineyards near here?" I address the Reever, but Regin owns it.

"A few kimetres north of here. The Estate Manager knows his viti- and his viniculture." There's an edge to his voice, matching a look of wistfulness.

The bouquet takes me home — the smell of childhood — the taste of grapes right off the vine.

"It is very good. I like it a lot."

"Food, Regin. Please." We both watch him go.

"The League should be the one straightforward entity on this entire globe. Nothing else is quite what it seems. In the Cantons above all you should know the truth in this. Yes, I play with you. I play with all who enter our Fastness. It is through play the truth may out, so good can rise." He takes a sip of water. I am about to respond, but his hand comes up, palm facing me.

"I know you, as Ambassador, must be strictly neutral. Such neutrality will be left inviolate by my playful proddings. They are aimed at you, Ardel, not the Ambassador you mask behind."

He holds his left hand out, palm up, angled, the fingers loose and curled, ceding me the space to talk. I take my time, sipping water.

"It is thought to be impossible to separate one from the other. It is only in the Cantons an Ambassador can truly relax and safely forget the Rules."

Regin reappears. Places the plates. Old Japanese ones, a milky base swirling with sea colours. Sitting on them, five small bright yellow pancakes, plump with sweet pickled cabbage and scallions. Toasted nori squares, mirin mayo and thickened teriyaki sauce in little cups of cabbage leaf. Raw crispy kohlrabi sticks. Better looking than I can make.

"*Okonomiyaki*. This looks beautiful, Regin."

The Reever finishes chewing the small morsel he has tasted.

"He says the name properly, like you, Regin. And they taste fantastic, as always." The praise brings a flush to his face.

"Your cooking?" He beams at me, nods, swings away. I eat slowly, avoiding the Reever's eyes. Easy with food this good.

"Regin's an exceptional chef. Bit younger than you."

"How old are you?" My Ambassador's voice cuts in.

"I am nigh eleven years your senior."

"Then you are forty."

"In a few weeks time. He's all but eleven months older than your consort."

I squash my reaction. "We must set an agenda and timeline for resolving the Complaint to everyone's satisfaction."

"Everyone counts for something. Is tomorrow acceptable?"

"Given the late hour, yes. I have seen the site mentioned in the Complaint — through binoculars from inside Mercia."

"Do not doubt my motives. They are pure. There is a long way to go to prove this to you, but it is the task I have set myself. You will not always believe what you see and hear."

He rings the little bell. A woman comes and gathers the plates, checks the water.

"Regin says five minutes, Reever. Is the bread finished with?"

"Yes. Thank you, Bess."

"Did good man Jimmy take you to the viewpoint?"

"Of course. The border there seems hardly to exist."

"Yet it does. What do you think of the Complaint?"

"I will wait until I have seen your evidence before reaching a conclusion. But I warn you, so far your Complaint is about as solid as the marshes around Holbeach Drove. Why have you given me the information to demolish your case?"

He sits back comfortably. His face amused somehow.

The main course arrives in a shallow cast iron oven dish. The aroma is complex. Savoury and sweet, a hint of sour. Vegetable and fruit. It is coloured by turmeric, tangy with lime, smelling of ginger and the fresh chopped coriander wilting on the surface. Regin is more relaxed.

"I call this Gamboge Garcinia[2]. The other pot has smashed floury potatoes to soak up the juices."

He serves it into wide white bowls. A large dollop of the potatoes to one side. "Do you wish for more wine?"

"I have enough for this meal, thank you, Regin. Another beautiful looking dish."

"Then I too have enough. Are we the last of your diners?"

"Yes, Faerachar. What time do you want breakfast set here?"

"Tomorrow is the long day. Ardel, sunrise over the eastern fells a little before seven. Is that reasonable for you?"

The more we get done, the sooner I can go home.

"Yes, Reever." I sip a spoonful. "This is amazing, Regin."

My mood is mixed. I never got an answer to my question. He slid round every attempt I made. He talked about the political structures in Alban. How power comes up from the people. How they argue into a commonality on every issue. How they don't have political parties, as such. I'll add it all to the registry file. Still no signal for my phone. I'd love to talk with Dahqin, though right now he's in the middle of his show. I compose a message that tells Grandy I am safe, goes into the barest details of my greeting, and gives apologies for missing the prescribed time of transmission on this and the previous night. It's sent on the HiSec satcom. It's not late, but sleep comes quickly.

I wake from a dream, the pillow is damp, hair stuck to my forehead and neck. I heave out of bed, unsure where and in which room I am. The moon was a slim crescent over the eastern fells when we were eating. It should be low and further west — but I can see by its light. When I get to the outer room the hue is a flickering yellow. A huge fire burning on the eastern shore. Still naked, I go out onto the terrace. Lean on the parapet in the cool air. From the direction of the fire comes the sound of voices.

2 *Gamboge Garcinia* – page 478

Mid-summer night revels. Higher up, further north I see a small fire, but it's gone in minutes. Somewhere in the shrubs below an upset baby shrieks. I know it's a small deer, but it always jolts me. I turn and look up to the top of The Keep. It rises in three more banks of pale stone. On the top is the shiny black dome, wearing an animated reflection of the fire, flickering and breaking into pieces disappearing into nothing. It's of a piece with the oddities of the last three days.

As for the dream, there was no mistaking the eyes that lured me into the pool. They hadn't woken me; encountering the unseen things in the water had scared me witless, in the way dreams can. That and the mocking laughter he threw at me. The smell of the lake reminds me, I want to know why there is salt water in the cistern. An owl flies silently down over my head. Makes me jump. I'm chilly now, and yawning. Time to get back in bed — there'll be fireworks later. I smell Dahqin's vest by the pillow, and put it under my head.

June, 22nd — The Keep in Derwent, Wark-in-Alban — Ardel

I wake up slowly, getting my bearings and feel like tucking down again. Disconcertingly, a drink has been placed on the bedside shelf. I sit up and bring the glass to my mouth. Something green, fizzy and herbal smelling, mildly alcoholic too.

"Mmm. Nice."

I leave some and go to the washroom, still half asleep. What are the questions I need to ask the Reever? Salt water first. I wag my index finger. No. Why had he sent me off with Jimmy? With the Roamers? By the time I get through the shower, watching the colours of early dawn changing, my questions of the Why? variety are little clearer. Then I remember the chill that made me flinch when he told me Dahqin's age. I check my phone — still no signal. To help order my mind I play a morning raga on the multi-viewer. To the sounds of tabla and sitar, I finish the drink while checking my clothing. It's the bubbles popping on the tongue that make it so enjoyable.

It sounds daft, but I'm sure the Reever's been flirting with me to gain an advantage. He's subtle, but the little clues are peppered all over. Well, that can work for both of us. My knee length bodysuit with the hood — nice soft cloth. I like the feel on my skin. Don't have to carry a hat then. And one of the loose fitting over-shirts will help counter the heat. Ruffle my hair — a light gelling, a bit of gloss to the lips. Check in the mirror.

The table is set, the Reever sitting, watching me advance. If my attire has any effect it does not show on his face.

"I bid you good morning, Ambassador. I see you are dressed for the weather we expect. The skies should be clear all day."

I respond and sit down, waiting for him to make his moves. He's wearing loose-legged trousers and a plain short-sleeved top. Those eyes unreadable this morning and nothing to tell from his face except an easy hint of humour. After some moments of silence he rings the small handbell.

"Breakfast arrives with the sun."

Regin comes out, bearing a large trencher covered with a high-domed lid. At the same moment the tip of the sun rises over the eastern hills, lighting the pale stonework and Regin in a rosy glow. The Reever stands, and as the trencher is set on the table recites from the Protocols.

"I hope you have no forbidden foods, no tastes you cannot stand. We have old-fashioned foods here. I know you are used to your own foods. Are you prepared to try what we set before you?"

"I will try each thing you set before me. As for my taste, it may not please. It is accepted by all that local fare is local taste."

"Then shall we be pleased you have but tried to satisfy our cooking's honour." He lifts the lid from the trencher. It looks and smells delicious. I can see nothing odd.

"I shall do my best."

"So much for Protocol in the early morning."

"We must address the Complaint before the morning is out."

"We shall start now, over this repast, if you so wish. But I beg you not too much Protocol between the two of us."

"I admit no objection to your request, Reever. Unless necessary for dealing with the digression."

"Very formally put. We shall eat now, Regin."

He splits each dish between us. Takes the trencher. Comes back with a jug of the green drink and a pot of tea.

"That will be all, Regin, I shall let you know when we are finished." He goes inside shutting the door behind him. The sounds of crows and gulls calling are a background to our silence.

He's looking at me with smiling eyes. "Are you going to eat, or am I to starve as well?"

"You have a strange way of putting things. I think you'll not starve on my account."

"There's an exercise gymnasium near your chamber. If you require to use it, ask."

"Is there ever going to be a lineal conversation with you?"

"I remember the trivial things betwixt other, weightier, matters, and mention them as they come to me. Putting off the saying of them would lead to their being forgotten, like fallen leaves in an autumn wind."

He pours me a drink of the green liquid. "It's nettle beer. You like it, I believe. You left nothing this morning."

"I see you will do things your way, irrespective of the Protocols. How shall I solve the digression facing you when it makes no sense."

"*The digression facing you*. Very quaintly put. It says so much about your frame of mind. This digression will grow if it is not tackled now — head-on — by the League."

"If it is so urgent, why was I left in the dark, literally, for hours yesterday? Half a period has passed since you first sent the Complaint. And your Complaint does not cite a recognisable digression."

"That is almost true. I mean that without some solution the digression I need to bring to your attention will grow of its own accord and face the whole Confederation and the League with a transgression."

About to take a mouthful, I hesitate, putting my loaded fork back on my plate. "Is what I must sort out so serious?"

"Yes." He carries on eating.

"It said nothing in the Complaint about something this serious."

"It does not have to. The Rules are not that binding. I have used something trivial, well, made up as you have realised, to bring you here. Mentioning the real reason may alert those who are causing the problem."

"I do not know if this is real or a dream." The feelings, first stirred in me in the cannion in the dark, spill into my speech.

"You had better explain your treatment of me first. Your poorly worded instructions and my seeming lack of trustworthiness, based on a weird superstitious nonsense. And while we're at it, why is there salt water in the cistern all these kimetres from the sea. What carrion eating beasts live in that blackness with all their plopping?"

"I warned you would not believe what I tell you. You will get the answers you require; though they may not be the ones you want to hear. Finish your breakfast. The Digression can wait a few more hours."

He starts eating again, and neither says another word, nor looks at me. When his plate is empty, he drains his glass and stands up, almost knocking over his chair. Anger flashes across his eyes.

"Well, Ambassador, are you prepared to ride a horse in those clothes selected so carefully for my delectation?"

I stand up; I am not going to be looked down on. "Yes! I am!"

"Good! I shall come to your chamber soon. We have something to witness." The tone is one of authority. I would complain about the lack of Protocol, but to what end.

"I shall wait for you."

I sit, glaring at his receding figure; poke at the remaining food on my plate, take a mouthful from my cup of tea. It is lukewarm. I am annoyed and bested. I, not Faerachar, should be in charge of the agenda.

And there — he is not a title.

I go back to the chamber in a fury, angry at myself, as much as with him. He must abide by the Protocols, and stick to the direct matter of the Complaint. Someone knocks heavily on the door. Steeling myself for a confrontation with him, I focus on being the Ambassador.

"Come in!"

A woman enters — who I've not met before. I've seen the face though, hers being the only woman in the photos. She's short, but I can feel her stature, and see it in her eyes. She's another stylish woman. Fuller head of hair than Martha's; pale, but lively with flashes of colour. Her claret suit does not outshine her. Her shoes — for utility.

"I come at the Reever's orders. I am the Steward of Alban, Ambassador Penaul. Margot Salkeld. I am to conduct you to him."

"And where might that be, Steward?" I've set my voice too cold. I hold out my hand, palm up; there is a noticeable pause before she responds to my gesture and my question.

"Below, Ambassador. By the lake." Her voice is accommodating. "You do not know The Keep. Please — follow me."

I match her tone. "Very well, take me there."

She faces the cannion shaft doors.

"Steward here. By Coleridge. Going to stable tunnel."

A couple of minutes later we are heading down to ground level. We land by stables, at the inner end of a short tunnel out towards the lake. I follow her across the lawns and through the trees to the half-hidden boathouse. Beyond boats stored ashore, and a half-dozen in the water, a sleek boat with a cuddy is moored at the entrance of the covered dock, Faerachar sitting on the stern seat. He stands, makes a slight bow.

"I, the Reever of Alban, do welcome you to our land and trust that together, as Ambassador and Reever, we can sort through the Complaint of the Diplarg with the United Counties of England. We should decide the method to bring this matter to an orderly and speedy conclusion as we cross Derwentwater." A faint smile at his lips.

"I am sure we shall."

"Ambassador, meet The Steward," he says, mocking formality. I learn, later than I should have, that keeping to the Protocols requires absolute complicity.

"The Steward will keep a record. Boatman!" A figure moves out of the shadows — hands me a lifejacket. We settle, one on each side seat close to the Reever. The boatman casts off the ropes, pushes the boat from the quay with one foot, jumping in as it moves away. We proceed slowly.

"Reever, I must find out — today — exactly what was said in the Public Hearings in London to cause the digression in your Complaint. You already know my thinking on this. There is no mention of Lincolnshire in the records I have seen in London. When I am convinced that exact references validate your Complaint, I will act to ensure dealings between Alban and the United Counties of England are honourable. Until then I will do nothing which might be considered partial."

She is facing me, watching both of us, without animation. She took the seat that puts the sun behind her. I resist putting on my sunglasses.

"Well said, Ambassador. When we leave the boat the Steward will return to The Keep and have the papers organised ready for your perusal. Do not think we shall try to cheat you. We adhere to the Conventions of Confederation as we adhere to life." He smiles that dazzling smile. "Until then, I wish to show you something."

"Before we go further I would have answers to my earlier questions you so casually brushed aside. Why was I incarcerated in the cannion in that cistern? I would like to weigh your explanation."

He deflates with a sigh. Her look is that of a mother faced by a teacher questioning her errant child.

"I like to be the one to make guests welcome, to surprise them in some way. Make their arrival memorable. As I had been held up by an unforeseen incident, I told the Castellan to keep you in the dark until I arrived. He took that literally, as a coded instruction, because of the frequent gesturing against evil-eye by your escort."

"Evil eye! What do you mean? I was conveyed in a most strange manner at your behest into this Fastness and with escorts you provided!"

I look up into the sky, my hands out, wanting to shake him.

"Your Consular Agent might as well have been a hired comedy actor. I can only assume he is good at the routine work. I was an excuse for him to have lunch in an ancient pilgrim hostel, on a day away from the desk. He claimed to know nothing of how our interaction is supposed to work. At least Jimmy is a thoughtful and straightforward man."

"You are angry, and I do not blame you. It is my own fault."

"Angry! That is something of an understatement. Effort went into giving me the skills of calmness. Torn to shreds. An Ambassador handed across the fells like a parcel. Preposterous! And you expect me to accept all this with equanimity."

I shove my sunglasses onto my nose. She looks directly at me – a little glimmer of respect.

"Anger in an Ambassador. Well. You dealt with Baile Átha Cliath on your own, though with a guiding hand, I might add. Well done. You have had a long training at your job, going to places I have not seen. I know your exploits, Ambassador. You do not know mine. Some things get learned in the Fastnesses better than they do in the Cantons. What do you or your Patrons know of this Fastness of which I am Reever? What was there on the faxplex you studied in your apartment, your lover in your arms? Nothing. That is the answer. Nothing! The knowledge was never sent, nor asked for. Fault on both sides. You know where some of the boundary is. It is a river. Oh bravo! The League is not sure of the rest. Well, never mind; join the dots. You have your hologram maps, and you can see the shape of the land. You see how it folds and bends and how each vista changes. The beauty of this small thing in your apartment fascinates you. When you are tired, you switch it off."

I turn my sunglasses towards him. Faerachar looks around, away from me, ticking off the views. I look in the same directions and wonder if I see the same things. But know I am seeing them as a tourist. To Faerachar the land and what makes it is a precious thing – a known and favoured one. He turns back to face me, his voice soft, as I first heard it.

"A poet will choose a word to complete the setting in the making. Each word is looked at, and turned, this way and that, inspected as it takes on other meanings. The poet tries it in place, but alas it does not suit. The word is set aside and another tried in its place." He reaches over — surprised, I let him take hold of my hands.

"It is like that, being Reever, Ardel. But I don't work with words, whatever you think of my use of them. I have to work with the people I have around me. They are more complicated than words. It is not so easy, always, to set them aside when they do not quite fit in every way."

"That is an excuse for the Castellan. Not you." He drops my hands back in my lap. Sits back.

"The reason for the false Complaint was to get an Ambassador here. Something is afoot that threatens the Confederation's established order. And I needed to see someone before I could trust how to tell this to the League. I believe you may be that conduit."

I feel my lips form an O. Take off my sunglasses. Look from one to the other. They both bear my scrutiny. I can't think where to go with this. Solo. I am Solo. This is no longer a simple diplarg.

"Is this something amongst the Rulers?"

"It is not the Rulers we are afraid of. It is the rulers of the Rulers who worry us."

"The populations? You are worried by them?"

"I do not mean the visible rulers, I mean the invisible ones." He leans towards me. "What do you know of this land's history? Of society here. Before the Upheavals, I mean."

"Enough, I think. We covered it at college in some detail. Why?"

"Your League." Faerachar shakes his head. "You have much to learn about this place and our ethics, Ardel. And, I fear, the journey I thought to take you on is going to be longer even than I suspected. Do you believe in the Earth Force?"

"I might. Amongst other things."

"Can you feel it here?"

I look around, try to imagine. "What does it feel like?"

"You will know when you do feel it. It is not something that can control us, any more than we can control it. It is there, and some feel it, others don't. We need to be cognisant."

"What has this to do with these invisible Rulers?"

"Boatman, to the eastern shore." I can hear the wake now, feel the wind. He smiles sadly at me.

"You don't understand yet. You are thinking I am psychic. I'm not." He turns to the Steward.

"Please see the papers are ready in my office, Steward. Tell David to bring everything he has regarding the faxplex. We shall be back just before sundown. Dinner for all of us before Ardel sees the evidence. Martha has that arranged already. You have the guest list?"

"Yes, Reever. To all of that. Is Kaet omitted by forethought?"

"No! Margot, tell her. Thank you." For the first time a smile settles on her heart-shaped face, her hair blown back by the wind of the boat's passage.

"Are you suggesting I am psychic."

"Not here."

"What is in the salt water in the cistern?" He laughs at me. "The water in the cistern is salt. I could smell it."

"There are many things you will find hard to believe. Yes, it is salt water. You know all water has life. You will be shown."

"I will hold you to that, Reever."

"We are at Landing."

The boat is nearing some wooden jetties built out from a shelving beach. He stands up, motions me to follow along the narrow side deck and onto the bows.

We jump ashore. I cast my lifejacket into the cuddy, watching as the boatman manoeuvres away from the jetty. The Steward now sitting on the stern seat, facing forward, bolt upright, plumb centre.

"Come, Ardel, we get ponies here. It is not a long ride. I do not want your buttocks to get too tender."

"They will recover in time." I turn to see him going into the trees. I jog over the road and into the tunnel they make. There's a rookery across three big limes, though the birds are quiet. He's heading towards a cliff amongst steep slopes. A thicket hedge breaks the view through the trees. I catch up with him beyond it, facing a terrace of tall stone-built houses.

"We crossed the fells up there. Never saw this."

"These were built towards the end of the Upheavals."

"I cannot see this from my room."

"From the very top of The Keep you would, but only the roofs. This is where some who run The Keep live. It's where our children are."

"Children are sweet, no doubt, but they usually annoy me."

"You sound like my sibling. At least admit the only reason for the League is to preserve the human race, against its baser leanings. Which means children do matter to you, whatever else you think."

"I meant ... I shall never be a parent."

"I am aware of that, Ardel. Who could think otherwise of you?" Faerachar is soft-voiced as he speaks. I catch a glimpse of his appraising eyes. But he chuckles and heads for an archway through the terrace. They are built as an harmonious square. Each side with an arch in the middle. We reach stables in a yard hard against the cliff. He takes a hat and over-breeches from the groom; takes the reins of a pony, fusses it and mounts.

"Mandy, please get the Ambassador some over-breeches and safely mounted."

There seem to be no paths, and the trees obscure the true position of the sun. My only sense of direction is upward.

"I hadn't expected so many horses in use."

"All energy sources are ultimately fallible. What better than a self-feeding vehicle to take to the fells."

"Where are we heading?"

"You will still see The Keep when we get there."

"I have been told about wild dogs. But I haven't seen any."

"There are wild dogs, wild boar and wild cats. Lynx the biggest. Deer too. They do not worry us. Not usually."

"The Riders said there are killing dogs. Used against people."

"They probably were in the Upheavals. Certainly not ethical. And illegal, then as now, of course. Survival makes many things possible. It is best not to dwell on it. Nightmares are not easy to stop once they start."

"Like things going Plop! in the dark."

"What else did the Roamers tell you?"

"Forecast darkness ahead of me. So I can tick that off."

"I'd not reckon so lightly as you. Though you may be right."

"He said I was Taran a couple of times."

"Ultimately you are a Taran, on one side at least."

"How do you know that?"

"I merely point out we are both commingled with Éireish stock. I can hear it in your voice. Nothing more."

We are stopped just out of the trees, on the edge of open moorland. There's a clearly defined bridleway leading towards and through a maze of walled fields.

"That's what Michal said. I thought my English had the tiniest French accent." He's amused by that.

"It's with certain words. You have pronounced them like that a long time. More impressively, I have never heard anyone call a Rider by their name. How did you get that? They have a taboo around it."

"My diplomatic skills are not wasted on everyone."

His laugh is deep, throaty, it breaks ice, making me join in.

"It was by accident. He could tell me his name because I didn't ask him. I did ask his father, that's when the ... evil-eye ... signs started. I got told off, called a Taran on a quest. Michal heard me say my name. He told me his when we were alone, showing where I could and couldn't go in their camp site."

"Let's work the ponies." Faerachar pushes his mount into a trot. We chase after them, my pony making me work for it. Faerachar reins-in beyond the enclosures. In the centre of the plateau, within a ripple in the turf, we reach a circle of standing stones. All very different in shapes and sizes, a small cluster sits inside on the eastern edge. None of them are huge, but they make me feel insignificant.

"We went north of here." I take off my sunglasses. "The light here seems polarised." He's nodding.

"We don't know their true purpose, there is some dubious alignment with the motions of the Sun and Moon. Theories come along now and then. There are sites like this all over these islands." He dismounts, takes binos from his saddle bag; leaves his horse to forage.

"From your window you would just make out this spot with these."

I dismount. He hands the binos to me.

"Let it join mine."

The top three floors of The Keep are clearly visible; the distinctive oriel window of my rooms as if set on the ground of the hillside. This has to be where that fire had burned, but there is no scorching anywhere nearby.

"I want you to witness something." We cross into the circle through a wide gap between the largest two stones; head to the inner stones. He faces a thin slab of rock stuck into the ground like a broken-off giant spade blade, strokes it a couple of times.

"Today this stone was directly between my bedroom in The Keep and the point of sunrise on the fells to the north-east. Touch it."

"Why?" I feel bullied and prepare to refuse.

"Just touch it." He's softened his tone. "Go on."

Suspecting a trick of some kind I slowly extend my hand towards the stone. He's watching intently.

"What do you expect to happen?"

"Perhaps nothing will. It all depends on you."

"On me?"

"Just touch it. Nothing bad will happen to you. I won't let it."

"For what that's worth."

I put the middle fingers of my left hand against the stone. There's a feeling I've felt once before. When being vaccinated for tetanus, and the nurse hadn't buffered the solution. It's a swirling creepiness within my arm, surging in little bursts up and down. I take my fingers away. It stops. I feel a deep-seated happiness. I put that hand, palm-flat, back on the stone. Feel it happening again; look, puzzled-faced at the palm when I remove it. Touch it with the fingers of my right hand. "It's hot."

"I knew it!" He's triumphant. I want to try other stones and head towards the lowest one in this group.

"We need to move." The command in his voice pulls me out of the compulsion. I follow him out of the circle. He whistles and the horses amble across to us.

"We are going back by a different route. There is one more thing I want you to see. We should keep to time."

As we ride onto the bridleway I look back at the stones. I feel compelled by forces not in unity. Them and Faerachar.

We ride alongside each other, little faster than walking pace.

"What was that sensation? Is it only that stone?" His face is serious. "I suppose I must wait, give it time."

"Yes, Ardel, give it time." The bridleway crosses the fell above the square of houses.

"That's Lady's Rake ahead, isn't it?"

"Yes. You will get to know this place well. Much of what you think of me is based on my underhand ploy. I made you touch a stone, and you felt something, searching your soul, perhaps. I do not know, though I know of the feelings. You are not the first to feel the stone and so be reached."

"Reached?"

"How else to describe it?"

"I don't even know what it has done, if anything. You may have set the whole thing up to confuse me. How would I know?"

"You never will, not totally. In life it is best to remember this. Listen to what is told you. If it is told as the truth, believe it as the truth — for the sake of the teller. If your intuition says it is not the truth then accept that too — but hold it to you. Still believe — for the teller. He lies for himself — not for you. Why bother to face him with his frailty when you know the answer anyway. I have tampered with nothing in the circle and never will."

He looks out over the lake. "At times I see fires burning there. Yet in the morning there is no trace upon the grass."

A coldness shoots through me. "You ... you see fires there?"

"Yes." He flicks a look at me. "You've seen one, haven't you."

"Last night. I am used to sleeping easily in the dark at home, but now ..." Faerachar turns his face to me.

"There is this graver matter I wish to bring before you, the real reason I brought you to Alban. I have told you I am not psychic, so I am well informed. Your swallowing is dry, there is a water bottle in your saddle bag." I take it out and quench.

"Some things come to me from looking at you, or taking your hand, for example. You wondered how I knew the age of your lover. From you I can guess your lover is male, maybe boisterous, and that while he loves you, sometimes you're not sure of the depth of it. But from you I cannot tell his age or his name. It is Dahqin Franz Stiwll."

"Dahqin! And his full family name? How do you know his names? How do you know our ages?"

"What would Grandy Miriam Makda Emembet say to you under these circumstances? How would she mentor you?"

"Are you trying to undermine me?"

"No. I am glad you were sent. I'm trying to make you see that I have knowledge I should not have. My methods seem to be working, though the Good Sounding Counsel will likely not approve of my ethics."

He coughs to clear his throat, and drinks half his bottle of water.

"I could give any Ambassador such intimate information. You may understand what I have found. And we may act in unity to confound the perpetrators. But we may not succeed. Which is my biggest fear."

"You seem to know what we talk about in our apartment."

"No. I get that from you, with a little intuitive guesswork. You follow Regin with your eyes, and lower your tone with him, too much for me to miss. Does Dahqin have dark hair?"

"Not so dark. And he's a bit shorter. Have I encroached into his space?"

"He will tell you if you do. The first question is easiest because it is the most simple, but the simple answers are often the hardest to believe. A case full of faxplex was found in the south of this Fastness, on the seventh of this month. I felt entitled to check its contents."

"Whose case of faxplex was it?"

"When I read one of the faxplex I was shocked. The first part is about you Ambassadors, Grandy's name is on it, so is yours. All your personal data including lineage, consorts, for example. It is up to date according to the faxplex."

"Why not just hand over the box to the Ambassadors' League and let the Council sort it out?"

"I would have, if they had been sealed. But it had no League Seals or codes to protect from my eyes. Someone has gleaned the information from a study of secure League files. That someone is surely within the League. It is well known that no one can slip through an electronic trapdoor into the vaults of the League."

What he says is true. Our data systems are not linked to the outside world. It is the only secure resistance to hacking.

"How do you know Grandy and I are linked?"

"Everything is cross-referenced in the lists. Anyway I want to find out what is behind this illegal set of faxplex. Whatever it is, there is a conspiracy to do something. Whatever it is, the currency will be power. Gaining this sort of power means the ability to gain immense wealth. And you must have immense wealth to gain such power."

"But in the Confederation power is carefully balanced and controlled. It can't be bought and sold like common trade goods. The Confederation and League are not likely to crumble because of this information alone, surely."

"There are many ways to control populations. Many of the Confederation's Civitas and Fastnesses are actually oligarchal in nature. Power and control by the apparatus of governance shapes the humanity of that society to serve its own ends. The citizens should be aware of this and act accordingly if they want to maintain an equitable congress."

"Why trust me? What makes you so certain I am not part of this conspiracy."

"Maybe I am part of the conspiracy." He says it glibly, holding my gaze. He stops his pony and resettles himself in the saddle.

"I know – I know because the stone told me."

Mine is fidgeting. I let him trot a few paces, then make a show of controlling him.

"Where are we going now? You said you had something else to show me." He starts his pony walking, I get mine alongside.

"I do, it is a pleasant view, and I want you to see it as I do. Or as close to that as you can. It will take us to the southern end of Derwent. There is time for this, before sundown. Take some pleasure before the torments ahead. It's barely one and a half kimetres."

"How did you find the faxplex case?"

"It came from an airship."

"I thought airships didn't come over Alban?"

"They would not, ordinarily. We knew it had come from Hamburg heading to a place in the north of Cymru. It crossed over the wrong river. Who knows why? They shouldn't, but these things happen. Like its cargo bay coming open spilling goods from one side of the border to the other. What landed here we will send back to the Cymric side. Some went in the river and presumably some has gone missing into grateful hands."

He concentrates as he slips ahead, onto a narrow part of the path.

"I hatched a scheme to alert the League. With the information on these files I could not have wished for a better choice had I asked for you personally."

"On what grounds?"

"You are young and alert. You are not complacent. Not yet."

"Do you still have these faxplex?"

"Of course. They are the most important part of our evidence. But we have to send them on in one form or another."

"What! Why?"

"To lull our adversaries into thinking they are still hidden from view. Still safe to act."

"When will you decide on that?"

"It's already done." We are descending a track cut across a scarp, and I am about to ask him for more information when he holds up a hand.

"This is one of my favourite views." Faerachar stops his horse again.

"Ardel, I will do anything to stop a return to the stupidities which unfolded all those years ago. To keep the freedoms we now enjoy here we must fight by any means we can against those who would impose their will on us."

"Isn't that a morally unsound argument?"

"Intellectually — yes ... Pragmatically — no. I have known for some time that certain unethical trading houses want to set up bases in this Fastness. The Fastnesses are the soft underbelly of the Confederation. You must know this?

"Compare the Civitas to beehives where the entity is both provider and taker, each part being necessary for the well being of the whole. But it is not like that in most Fastnesses. We thrive like solitary bees. By spreading far enough apart we fill a whole area and live in harmony with it. The trading houses play the role of bee fly, apparently interested only in flowers. But their eggs turn into maggots that consume the bee larvae. The real masters are the insect-eating birds, snapping up bees and bee flies alike. Don't look so puzzled. You will have to check on these insects later.

"We know the trading house with the base in Cymru is interested in opening one here. If they were ethical, they could have years ago. I know what they have done in Cymru. Like a cancer the credits they hand out are spreading. Only they convert them. The end result will be the same for trading house and citizens. Slavery to a system of greed in the pursuit of the enrichment of the few.

"That is why I read the faxplex. And why I can say any means can be used to counter them. They ruled for hundreds of years by letting nothing stand in their way. We must not let them resume their position. And I hope you will come to understand why I say these things. The Upheavals were hard-fought battles to find a more equitable way. We cannot afford to slide back."

"Am I to see these faxplex?"

"The originals, of course. Though some information is very wrong. My father is listed as the Reever. That ceased years ago."

"I didn't suspect this Fastness was governed by dynasties. Did your father die?"

"It isn't. And he hasn't. He is well and very hearty. He lives in the far north, beyond the Great Glen. My mother lives also."

We trot onto a lane that rises towards a group of three large houses amongst trees.

"We'll stop here for refreshments."

June, 22nd — Third House, above Derwent — Kaet

Standing back, surveying the painting on my easel, I'm satisfied thus far. The trees shading the small stone bridge over the beck in front of Third House are faithfully replicated. The angle of the sun at this time in the afternoon is perfect for the one job I have left. The sleight of hand. The sun-dappled patches of yellows and whites to be added to the individual leaves closest to the viewer.

Every window in the house is open encouraging a little draught through the rooms. I hear the horse-gate on the lower cattle-grid clang shut. Then the sound of walking horses. I feel the jittering across my shoulders. The thought comes — *He is through the gate.* My brush hovers above the watercolour paste. I put it into the dirty water jar, cover the pastes and go out to our little bridge that leads from The Three Houses across the beck to the lane. From the shadows I see them coming into view, in conversation.

"Faerachar!" Both men look up.

"Kaet! Hello my darling. How are you?" I walk over to the small paddock in front of Second House as he leads Ardel across the bridge.

"Same as when you last saw me. I keep smiling as you know. What about you? You look elated. Haven't seen that in a while. Who's this?"

Faerachar swings down. We hug, kiss lightly each other's cheek. He keeps an arm round my shoulders. Says nothing.

"It's been quiet up here. Now, who is this blond young man?"

Ardel dismounts rather stiffly and I glimpse a faint silvery aura. They've been to the stones. He doesn't realise his ability. And he's trying to hide his curiosity about us, but it's on his face. He judges the full-length over-dress made of thin linen which hangs loosely from my shoulders.

"This is Kaet."

He puts out his hand, palm facing up. I go as if to shake, he's easy to play. Place my palm on his: feel his energy. He's unsettled.

"Hello, Ardel." So is Faerachar now; I ignore his questioning face.

"You're a bonny lad." Very bonny. I mimic David's accent. "It does na' tak' much t'see where your interest is."

Faerachar thinks this highly amusing and claps.

"Don't be cruel. Ardel doesn't understand, and you know it. He is the Ambassador sent by the League to help us."

"I know what you are. I'm sorry, Ardel. I have a mischievous spirit. You dress as you have, so you shouldn't be hurt if I read it the way it's meant to be read. Even if it isn't for the likes of me."

A flush of colour crosses his face. "Now what have I said?"

"I am just wondering how you know why I dressed like this?"

He speaks good English, French lilt, but with a hint of brogue.

"Oh, come on! By the way you look around you."

"I'm going into the house," Faerachar says. "Show Ardel the sights and then we can have something to eat and drink, maybe?"

"Make yourself comfortable. You know where everything is. Get started." He strides off towards Third House leaving us in the sound of splashing water. There is an awkward silence from Ardel.

"It's lovely here," I spread my arms vaguely towards the beck. "I'm sorry if I seem rude to you, it's not meant as that. You won't find much diffidence up here, leastways not from the likes of me."

I hold out a hand and he almost takes it.

"I'll show you the view."

"I thought I was being careful, but time and again Faerachar has ..." He pauses, looks me in the eyes. His are exactly as foretold.

"Now I feel you know even more about me. It is most disconcerting. Who do I dress for? Usually it is only for myself."

"You still are, even if you're out to gain some advantage. You're responding to something Faerachar has given off and trying to get him to react. Aren't you?" He clicks his tongue.

From the centre of the bridge the whole valley northwards comes into view. I can make out Bassenthwaite Lake. I barely notice The Keep most of the time. He sighs.

"It gets me like that. It's why I like living here. What's it like where you come from?"

"You mean you don't know. Sorry ... Similar in some ways. Though the lake near us is much larger and the mountains much higher."

"I have been to the Cantons. Once — a quick tour." Astonishment on his face. "We do, some of us, travel you know. We aren't as insular and simple as you think, Ardel."

"Why are you so defensive?"

I laugh. "Defensive? That wasn't being defensive. It was me taking the mickey." He frowns. "Making fun of your assumptions in a gentle way."

"Oh."

"Come on. Faerachar might have made a drink by now."

We amble towards Third House.

He's got his hands in his over-shirt pockets. It feels natural to push my arm through his, he flinches slightly but doesn't resist.

"Go on, ask me."

"It might be impolite."

"In which case I shall probably tell you that, but still give you the answer anyway."

"You seem very sure of yourself."

"Of course, I'm in my home."

"Are you related to Faerachar?"

"I care deeply for him. I think him one of the most gentle men and trustworthiest I have ever known in my life so far. But he has a temper and can be very stubborn."

"His temper I've met. Unfortunately it raised mine. You have the same way of giving information that is not to the point. You don't look alike but I think you are brother and sister."

"We have the same Mother, but different Fathers. I'm nine years younger than Faerachar."

Outside my door he stops and turns to face me.

"Where does your mother live then? Faerachar told me his father lives in the far north. Where does your father live?"

"Our mother lives in Second House." I point to the middle one. "You'll get to meet her, I'm sure. My father died when I was two."

He is about to commiserate.

"There's no sorrow about it. Such things are."

"I think I will see you at dinner tonight. Am I the only one living down there, do you know? It's huge."

"There's a few who do. Bet you're in Coleridge. It's a bit like a hotel up there. Work goes on round the clock in The Keep. Let's go in."

He drops his over-breeches and hard hat onto the bench in the porch, next to Faerachar's.

I adore my home. Inside its thick walls the hall is lined with wooden panels. I take off my shoes putting on my felt slippers. He reaches for some that look his size. I lead him upstairs to the living room. He takes it all in. The bookcases covering the southern wall right up to the narrow windows showing the hills beyond the trees. The large window looking out to the north. To the left side of it is my old-fashioned telescope. My easel by the windows looking over the beck.

He goes to the telescope. I know from its angle that Faerachar has moved it. He bends down, looks through it, flicks his head away then looks back. I can guess it's focussed on the doors in Coleridge that lead onto the terrace. He turns to face me — thinks it might be me.

"Faerachar."

He understands; grins. Next it's the easel — studies the painting.

71

Leaning back slightly, his legs nicely tensed. One hand under chin, the other arm across his stomach, hand supporting that elbow. Doesn't like to show emotion, but can't stop himself. I want to sketch him. Looks out at the trees and back to study the art. Glances at the paint table. Then faces me.

"I like the fluidity of your work. The light too."

"Thanks, it's how I make a living."

He moves on to the old oil paintings, then to the book shelves. That'll keep him occupied.

"You can take any of them out to look through. Or borrow."

"Thank you. I probably shall." One book's caught his eye.

"Nicolo Machiavelli. The Prince." A warm voice to listen to.

"I'm going to speed him up. I'll leave you with your thoughts."

June, 22nd — Third House, above Derwent — Ardel

I watch her go, the fragility implied by her linen overdress, denied by her forthright nature. I feel I've known her for a long time. I can hear her talking to him. Not the words, just their murmurs; high and low, soft and hard. I pull the book from its place.

"Il Principe, autore, Niccoló Machiavelli." It sounds better.

This is printed in the language Maman instilled in me from my first memories. I know this book, have studied it so well. But never in English. And never before felt the fragility of paper carrying such weighty ideas. I open it carefully, and turn the pages slowly because the paper is delicate and yellowed. The printing date is 1969. I put it back on the shelf. About to shut the door, I see *Insects of the British Isles* on the shelf below.

I sit with it on the arm of the big settee — looking north at the view. These books are rare, worth a fortune elsewhere, and yet here they are just everyday.

"Do you like books, Ardel?" Faerachar has silently crept up behind me, but I'd sensed him.

"These fascinate me. How are they preserved?"

"An anti-oxidant of some kind and neutraliser. I'm not sure of the process. Aren't they lovely."

"Yes. Where is Kaet?"

"She'll be here in a moment. We've been talking to Briged. What are you looking at?" I show him. "Ahh ...The bee fly."

"Is it in here?"

"Of course it is. Maybe you'll meet Briged if she has the time. You'll like her."

"Who is Briged?"

"You look up the bee fly. I shall be back."

This book is twenty years younger than the other. I find the entry. The photo shows a brown furry fly, wings defined by black veins, its long proboscis almost inserted in a small flower. It feeds on nectar, but its larvae on bee larvae. So ... If let into the Fastnesses the unethical trading houses would fleece the community, weakening it. Weakened, they could more easily control them. And once that happened ...

Hearing them coming up the stairs, I go to the window and use the telescope to view the landscape.

"I hope this will be to your liking?" Kaet says. She carries a large tray covered with dishes and jars; behind her Faerachar with another. They set them down on the table amidst the settees.

Faerachar flops down on one of the smaller ones, his feet up.

Kaet gestures to the larger settee, "Sit on this one. That end. You'll get the best view then."

"So, you are the famous Ambassador. I had imagined someone more regally dressed, but I suppose you'll do." The woman who stands in the doorway, if younger, could be Maman.

She smiles at my obvious amazement. "Cat got your tongue?"

"I am sorry. I ... How are you? No, I mean ... How do you do?"

I hold out my palm, she grasps it, turns it and shakes my hand.

"Proper connection. I am fine, young man, however you ask. Now, I cannot have you going round referring to me as the Reever's Mother, so you had better address me as Briged. It is my name."

"I am Ardel, but I suppose you know that already."

"It has been mentioned. And it is how I shall address you in any case. Ambassador is far too grand a title to fit into any of these rooms. You'd best leave that for The Keep."

Finally she lets go of my hand, moving to the settee and sitting where Kaet had indicated I should.

"Sit by me," she pats the cushion between them. The refreshment is nut bread with butter and conserves, and lime flower tea, sweetened with honey.

"What causes you to stare so?"

"You look remarkably like my own mother."

"Ha! Either your mother has aged somewhat in appearance, or ours is much younger in looks than we have been led to believe."

"Don't be cheeky about my looks, Faerachar. You're walking the same road."

"I meant ... you resemble her."

"I know what you meant, Ardel. You'll get used to our fencing. You'll have to learn to bite back or we'll talk all over you. Now behave yourself, Faerachar."

"My mother has an accent different from yours."

"At least you and I can converse using our own idioms. People do cling to their own forms of speech. I dare say they will be careful in front of you, for they've never before had an Ambassador to deal with. When our children learn common tongue at school they are taught it is bad manners to speak anything else in front of outsiders."

"At least the common tongue allows easier understanding between peoples. It certainly helps us with our diplomacy."

"Do you think everything is understood? I find that quaintly naive of you ... Ambassador."

"Faerachar" Briged's tone is scolding, "Ardel is still finding his feet here. And you had better make sure you help him stand on them firmly."

"I think you underestimate your abilities, Ardel. You're at a disadvantage with my dear brother because you're uncertain what information he has about you. And you can't cloak yourself against us. Can he, Briged."

"No. Trust your own skills. No one can teach you how to use them. With discretion, is the key. You will be alright. Above all, at core, remain yourself." She stands.

"I am going home now. Duncn will be here soon. I shall see you tonight, Ardel, at dinner."

I stand and proffer my hand. With a low chuckle, she shakes.

"You learn our ways quickly enough." She pats Faerachar and Kaet, who do not rise, on the tops of their heads.

After the sound of her footsteps recede, Faerachar sits up and stretches.

"So much for Briged. We must head back to The Keep. Thanks for the afternoon tea, sweet sister."

"Try to find time to come back here before you return to the Cantons, Ardel."

"I shall try to make that happen. It has been a pleasure meeting you and Briged. I'm hoping your brother will answer all my questions."

"In shall. We can say our goodbyes outside, readying the ponies."

We head around the southern end of Derwentwater. Some distance from the houses we meet another rider. His face and hands are dirty – I assume from his work, his body suggests that. Faerachar stops and greets him amiably, but pointedly does not introduce me.

"You're well, I trust."

"Aye, well enough. I've been checking the marked timber stands for felling. Some areas still need a lot of undergrowth cleared away if we're to get the best trees out. I'll be in The Keep tomorrow. Got a meeting."

"I'll see you later."

"Aye." Without looking at me he rides away. He noticed me though, for the glance rate was high, but none long enough for me to grasp.

"Who was that?"

"That? Oh, that was Duncn."

"The same Duncn your mother mentioned?"

"Yes, the very same."

"Well, he's good-looking. The best looking man I've seen since I came to Derwent."

"Really? Fanciable would you say?"

"Very." I smirk at him. "Who is he?"

"The love of Briged's life."

"Really? You're joking." He's no older than me.

"Why should I be? He is the image of our mother's paramour, if I may use that term."

"I don't know what to say."

"Say nothing then."

"It is not that I am shocked, you realise."

"Of course."

"It just wasn't the answer I expected."

"You suddenly seem very open for an Ambassador. Easily jerked into showing your reactions to what faces you. Shocked into betraying your moral boundaries. And anticipating answers. Not at all how I imagined Ambassadors to act."

"Since leaving London, as arranged by you, things have happened to me that were not dealt with in my training. Four years I have been going on diplargs and watched the laid down procedures followed to the letter. In none of those places has an Ambassador been treated in the way I have been. And you expect me to accept the information assailing me without a ruffle of reaction."

"Finished?" He's got a look of indifference on his face.

"No! I have not. You keep treating me like a young boy, as if you have something to teach me. Maybe you do. I am at a disadvantage, because you, as Kaet said, have certain information which allows you to confuse and bewilder me. And I wonder if I really shall know what it is. Sure, you have confirmed the original Complaint is fiction. Briged told me that all I have to do is trust in myself, yet through your actions I feel confused and bewildered."

"Now have you finished?"

"Almost. I am totally in your hands in this, and you know it. Do not belittle me. I must regain faith in myself, and I need to regain it. There, I have finished."

"At last, plain speaking. What did you tell your patron last night?"

"I had a most unusual greeting. I will not conclude my judgement until I find out more."

"And what do you intend telling her tonight?"

"That will depend on what you do next."

"Let us ride in the last of the day's light for The Keep. Stay with me if you can, Ardel."

Faerachar gets his pony off at a fast pace. I trot mine into the dark glades of trees above the lakeshore — sure of it finding the path.

June, 22nd — The Keep — Ardel

I am left by my escort at the entrance of the Audience Chambers to wander through a pleasant area with plenty of plants between the groups of armchairs and low tables. Large folding windows open onto a terrace facing south along Derwentwater. A thickly carpeted corridor passes a dining room windowed on both sides. Muslin curtains waft gently on the terrace side. I count twenty place settings on the dressed oval table.

"They're out on the terrace through those curtains."

Regin is alongside me: it is a very thick carpet.

"Are you cooking?"

"Not for this number. I'll be keeping an eye on things. Ardel, allow me to apologise for creeping in and putting that drink on your bedside shelf this morning. That'll not happen again. A fresh jug of the Nettle Fizz will be in your frige every day."

"It was a little disconcerting. Thank you, in any case."

Realising my arrival is unnoticed I wait a moment just outside the opening. There is a discussion about a dispute in the Peak District, wherever that is. Something to do with commoner rights on Fastness Estate lands.

"The Procurator Fiscal hoped it could be settled without you getting involved."

"It will be, Margot. That's the Procufisk's arena, and I'm leaving it alone. That's not my point."

"But what if it it breaks commonality?"

"It won't. It's simply a matter of timing. But I should always know about these affairs." Faerachar turns to alter the position by which he rests against the parapet.

"Ardel! How long have you been there? Let me do some introductions of those you don't yet know."

I can't recall one name by the end of the fast round we made. He says it won't matter. Kaet takes my arm – hands me a drink.

"Porto tonico. Hope you like it. I'll take you into dinner when it's called – get you seated. Sorry, Faerachar, carry on."

"Ardel, there'll be six different people sitting with you over the course of this meal. I've chosen people who can tell you things about this Fastness in the quickest way without boring the arse off you. I want you to understand how our society operates. They don't need to ask you about the League, and there won't be small talk from them. You can make it go where you want. Kaet and Bridget will be the brackets for you – they know what to do if things bog down. Only one of these people works here, and he'll come along with the pudding. I'll introduce you now. David!" Kaet wanders away.

"David, stop gossiping, and come over here."

He levers himself away from the parapet, where he's been talking to Duncn. His skin is shiny, his jawline is accentuated by the low lighting reflecting off it. He's taller than everyone else here. Tops me by half a head. I realise it is who I saw talking with Faerachar last night. His hair is pulled back in rows, into a small plait. He is so well defined, dressed in the type of clothes I like to show off in. Can't match him. I manage to keep my face strictly neutral.

"Hello, Ambassador."

Firm shake, he says nothing else, inclines his head, the faintest smile. A woman touches his arm and he faces her, focusing on what she is saying. Glances at me, gives a little wave, and follows her.

"There is just one more person for you to be introduced to."

He is facing Duncn — the paramour. Kaet is leaning against him, both laughing. Faerachar takes me over, Kaet winks at me.

"Duncn. When you and Ardel met earlier, I was remiss. I think both of you are upset with me."

He puts out his hand, grips mine hard as if to shake, but just holds it. The eyes looking up at me from under long lashes are glistening.

"I'm glad to be properly introduced to you, Ardel."

His tongue brushes across his lips. He relaxes his grip as the little finger slowly strokes the edge of my palm. My heart is thumping so heavily the others must be able to see the pulse at my temple. I can't control what my face is showing and I hold my breath, until Duncn releases my hand when Faerachar coughs theatrically.

A gong sounds. Kaet leads me away to the table.

The meal over, we head through the Audience Chambers to a suite of offices. Faerachar signals Margot Salkeld to join us.

"I am going to be very candid, Reever. Would you rather hear what I have to say alone?"

"I need the Steward as my witness. Come into my office."

It is huge. We have entered through glass doors sitting across the angle where two long walls meet, each fitted with working surfaces of varying heights. There are free standing work tables to each side of a wide central aisle. On some, stacks of papers and faxplex. The third side, curved, almost completely glass. In daylight there must be spectacular views across Derwentwater. A few lights from the small town of Keswick and those from the Township twinkle through the trees on the far side. There are four sofas and two tables by the windows to the right hand side.

Directly facing us along the central aisle, separated from the general office by glass walls and doors, a beautifully crafted desk curves in opposition to the outer wall. It is set on a dais, backed by a narrow screen — the only break in the glass wall. Burr walnut in the main. Three panels of stone sit centre and mid-wings in the top. The colour of that stone in the circle; all highly polished. On one wing stands a sleek multi-viewer, of Danish manufacture. On the other, communication devices from the same source. On the centre stone panel, a large piece of pale leather, tooled round the edges in Celtic swirls, sits to soften the surface for writing; on top a pad of light green paper, embossed with *Reever of Alban* and bordered with the colours of the female holly. A glass jar dull and crooked, holding some pens and graphite sticks, is clearly ancient.

The chair behind it is the most stylish and best ergonomic design available. In front, not blocking the view of the centre, sit two upright padded arm chairs, upholstered in the same fabric as used in my rooms; each has a scribe's drop-leaf of ash. The style of the desk is redolent of the nineteen-thirties, though the overlapping front edge of the top is sealed by the knobbly bark of the tree. Only in The Praedicatum, the League Elders' sanctum, in Sion, in Valais, have I seen such careful portrayal of thoughtful power.

The Reever sits behind his desk, motions me to the right-hand of the two armchairs. The Steward sits in the other. I fix the scribe's drop-leaf in front of me and place my touchpad on it. Breathe deeply, while recalling the appropriate words of the Rules.

He has the authority built into him enhanced by this setting. But I am to judge him. And eleven years his junior. I have never witnessed censure administered to a Ruler. Yet now on my Solo, I must do that very thing. Before a witness older than he, I shall issue a Notification of Censure. He gambled a ploy to get an Ambassador here, and whilst he must take responsibility for the method he chose — he has got his way.

In the silence of this inner office I press the record button.

The Steward has left. Sent homeward by him with thanks for her support, and hearty farewells, in what I take to be his usual manner.

My judgement of the Complaint must be reviewed by the Jurisprudence Court. If it holds, I shall no longer be a Noviate but a full Ambassador. If it holds, he must ask the League for absolution of his misdemeanour. He will then issue a fulsome apology, which the League will deliver to the slighted Civitas of the United Counties of England. He will be rapped over the knuckles. And he will be forgiven.

"Show me what the stolen faxplex hold."

He takes me to one of the bigger stand-at tables. Next to the multi-viewer sit two scuffed equipment travel cases; he lays a hand on one.

"They are safe in here. I've ordered coffee. It's an excellent roast of our local crop. Very low in caffeine."

"It grows here?"

"We have some remarkable controlled environment growing houses. You must ask Duncn to show you. He is rightly proud of them. David's bringing the coffee now. We can start when he gets here."

"What is David's role in this matter?"

"He is the Communicator of the Fastness, did I not say?"

"No, you didn't. Neither did he." I don't hear the doors.

"What didn't I, Ardel?" His accent is distinctive. Thanks to the pudding course, I'm used to it now.

"You don't mind me calling you Ardel, do you?"

"I've given up on deference for the moment. I'm trying to find out why you are here now."

"Skill." He puts the tray down. "How do you want this?"

"Plain, please David."

"I know my way through the information."

"I need a faxplex from my room." Faerachar reaches for a phone.

"I'll go with him, Faerachar, it'll save time."

He takes me through to a stairway and down four flights of stairs.

"How did you get on with all the information thrown at you?"

"Touchpad has it all. Including your Scotian tones. I'll transpose it into a report later."

"Briged and Kaet must have been a welcome duo. She's got you sussed, has Briged."

"Sussed?" We come out in a corridor through sets of fire doors.

"Worked out."

"Oh. She knows my character already."

"That's right. She's a complex woman — quite ruthless in her way. But I respect her a lot." David indicates a change of direction.

"Talking of her — Duncn has what relationship with Briged?"

"He's her youngest son. Why?"

"Curiosity. What does paramour signify to you?"

"Paramour? Lover, doesn't it? Without checking I couldn't give a better definition. Why ask that?"

Through another fire door, and we are by my rooms. He stands in the doorway as I take the faxplex from my work-case.

"I was puzzled by the word earlier in the day. This is all I wanted, we can go back now."

"What context was it used in?"

"It does not matter."

Seeing David's shrug of resignation, I touch his shoulder.

"I think I am being ... wound up."

"Faerachar then. Duncn's another halfling."

"Halfling?

"Yes. Briged had him when Kaet was four. They're always pretending they don't know one another with strangers."

"Who else knows what is on those faxplex?"

"Three know the significance of them. Margot, Faerachar, me."

"Can you be sure of that?"

"Yes. There's a dozen people work with him in that office. All of them have worked with him for years. But they haven't been working on these."

"I hope you are right."

The doors to the office silently open as David holds his hand vertically towards them. Faerachar is not there.

"We can start without him, Ardel. Check your information."

I put my faxplex onto the multi-viewer.

"What's that for?"

"I need to load a verification app into the cache for the duration of what we are about to do, David. I will know which files are originals from the League. At the end of the session it will wipe."

"I'll trust you."

Two cups of coffee, and a lot of stretching later, I have seen enough of how I progressed through the ranks of the Noviates.

"This is fascinating. I must keep my feet on the ground. But frightening that such information is here outside the League vaults. What did you make of all this?"

"It's not for me to imagine, Ardel."

"Have you got a consort?"

"Not as such, but we're heading that way. I think you like her."

It takes me a moment.

"Kaet? But you barely said two words to each other all night. I thought ... Well it doesn't matter."

"You couldn't but look me up and down. Inappropriate or not, it's honest ... and a bit flattering. But you are smitten with Duncn. Obvious even to me before Kaet mentioned it. That was the longest string between us tonight — seven words."

"Seven words?"

"Those two are lusting for each other. That's a bit of a red colour, Ardel." His laugh is infectious. "Is the information on you accurate?"

"Scarily so. When is Faerachar coming back? I've some questions about this."

"Ask me, Ardel."

"All right. What does he intend to do with these faxplex?"

"I've made copies which don't have all the cross-references in them. They look the same at a glance. They can't be replicated either. Faerachar says they won't know the difference."

"He said a set has been sent back. What if they have another set?"

"He says the people who traded in these only have the one copy. I don't know why he thinks that. These are the originals that fell. You'll be getting these as evidence."

"What knowledge does he have to reason with, David?"

"Survival in a rough world, I guess. This has been his crusade from before I came here."

"He said something about survival before. He might say needing to survive gives an edge to one's ability to imagine. Show me Dahqin's file. Faerachar got his name and age from it, and he has some level of security clearance."

As information scrolls over the flatscreen my mood dips.

"What's the matter?" I look up to see concern on David's face.

"There are things Dahqin has not told me."

"Do you think Dahqin has been keeping secrets from you?"

David swears; I jump.

"I didn't mean to frighten you."

"Then why that smile?" David says.

"It's a hell of a coincidence, is it not? His vouchsafe and my Mâitre being the same person?"

"Trust in his innocence, Ardel. He may know nothing about her work. David, get the sheets with the cross-references on them. It's easier to see the connections then. Ardel, you have no objection? You can easily check on Dahqin once you have seen how it fits together."

"Can we put it on a low table over there? I need to sit down."

I slouch back on one of the sofas by the windows, watching David put the sheets in order.

"Start here, Ardel."

June, 23rd — The Keep — Ardel

Two hours later, in the early hours of the morning, bleary-eyed and tired, I compose a message for Grandy and send it on HiSec. Though my phone has a signal it doesn't feel safe to use; every message and phone call is logged in Genève. I hope my use of only one part of a coded security warning will draw Grandy's mind into thinking I am being devious rather than remiss. On my way to bed I look out across the lake. A few lights to show human existence. No fire. No clue to where the circle stands, its ancient roots gathering the earth force.

... Dahqin holds a lance, watching me sink into the soft mud floor.
"Dahqin!"
He ignores me, looking away. I struggle up, left hand over heart. Dahqin's face changes into Faerachar, into Regin, into Duncn and back to him.
"You don't love me any more."
"Of course I do." ...

Hardly awake, I pull his vest onto the pillow, roll my head onto it. Let the rapture of his aroma soothe me, and go into blank sleep.

Book Two — Part 1

Missing Trade Goods

Reckon it's a case of finders keepers

June, 10th — London, Trafalgar Square

In a room in a building in London a man sits at his desk, tapping its surface with a platinum toothpick. Two powerfully built men watch him. He turns from staring at a picture on the wall to looking out of the window. Below the window's elevated position is a broad concourse with real fountains and a column, depicting some one-time hero of the people who once populated London. People scurry by the monumental column and its guardian lions in the heedless pursuit of being busy.

"Ants!" The two men remain silent. "Ants," he repeats more softly. He slowly faces the two men.

"It's been a week. Still nothing, hey?"

"No, SJ, nothing."

"Well I hope they are in the river rather than in the wrong hands. Still, if one of the ants has found the boxes they won't know what to make of them anyway. But if they're in Alban, it's the wrong hands."

He starts to tap the desk again. He bunches the fingers of his right hand, looks at his fingernails, and flicks the fingers outwards, at the same time he blows quietly through his lips. He taps the desk for a few more minutes.

"Gabri, get back up there and tell that Maer to keep looking and listening. And make sure he gets the message about keeping his mouth shut. If they find the box you know what check. Arrange for everything they find to be sent on to the base, including the faxplex."

The younger of the two men rises, makes a slight bow, and leaves. SJ leans forward focused on the other man.

"Has anything else come out of Birmingham yet?"

"Nothing, SJ. But I'm not 'finished. I still think it was deliberate. Nothing was dropped over Mercia."

"Jarnie, I'm satisfied with your efforts there so far. A pity about losing the co-pilot, but ..." He leans back again.

"We don't know where that guy ended up. You should have let me finish it."

SJ shrugs.

"You're going to have to cross into Alban at some point soon, Jarnie. The people we have been in contact with are very interested in dealing. If we can get in like we did in Denbigh, get a base for the airships; I'll be able to grow even faster. "

He turns back to look out across the square.

"You have the names and addresses of the main people. The one you need to talk to lives near a place called Sedgeworth. I'm not sure if he's telling it right about his ability to lead a group in the council in Leeds to push for the changes we need. He says they monitor the phones, and as you know, the last two guys I sent up there were chucked out in less than a day. I still want an entry into Alban, so avoid the Boundary Patrol. I'll leave the details to you. Keep me updated."

"Sure, SJ. I'll keep out of their way." He asks for the use of SJ's personal cab and driver to get to the border in the right place.

"Okay Jarnie, you've got it." He rises, performs the same deferential bow as Gabri, and leaves.

"Ants and spiders," SJ says, staring at the closed door. "Ants and spiders."

He considers himself a spinning spider. Jarnie and Gabri are definitely ants — even if soldier ants — they are still part of the crawling masses. All of them can be controlled. He needs more patience than ever now all the strands are coming together and the web is nearly complete. The only worry he has concerns the relative size of his spider compared to the others. He has not come this far, and put in this amount of capital, to be eaten by another marauder at the moment of triumph.

He wonders briefly if the Rulers would ever know what had happened.

He doubts it — because they are too busy listening to the other ants out there to realise their impotent power is being usurped and bypassed. The Great Enterprise, as the conspirators refer to it, has already come a long way. The information in the League files is just more fuel he has been told. He becomes aware of his fixed and vacuous smile only because his jaw starts to ache.

"Ants!" he says and turns back to stare out of the window.

June, 12th — Cantref of Wrecsam, Cymru

For once, in his position as Maer of the Cantref of Wrecsam, Owen had asked no proper questions. Seven days back his friend Rhys Parry, who works for a trading house based in Denbigh, the Cantref to the southwest, had promised him some credits. All he had to do was organise some people to search for trade goods that had dropped from an airship. The population in this part of Cymru is not big, but when the news spread that people would be paid to search for some lost freight he had plenty of volunteers; choosing the right people was the difficulty.

Owen has persuaded some inhabitants in the area to return things they just happened to find, but a significant amount remains missing. In particular, the cases that have been given such importance by the pushy man from London, have not turned up. Now he's back in the area and doesn't care that Owen's biggest problem is crossing over what Gabri calls the River Dee and he knows as Afon Dyfrdwy. It forms the boundary between Cymru and Alban in this area, and the greater part of the goods seem to have dropped over the river.

Two nights ago that man — Gabri — had made sure Owen was in no doubt that all efforts must be exhausted. He hopes the man will believe his contention that the cases have gone into the river and swept towards the sea. He is in difficulty because no one will agree to cross the river and search the far side.

"Try just that bit harder," Gabri had said. "I'll be back in two days, at the same time." Then he had disappeared back into the night.

Owen sits under some trees on a little hill at the end of a low spine of land reaching back towards his home and the mountains beyond. From this vantage point above the river he stares across the valley into Alban. There is something about the place that leaves people on this side of the river feeling uneasy. It is not just those bare hills in the distance. Cymru has bigger hills and mountains of its own — mountains with legends of fanciful creatures and mystical doings in the dawn of the world. No, the feeling comes from the emptiness of the land on the Alban side of the river. And the warning notices placed haphazardly on the Alban bank are stark.

'Poisoned Lands. These are dangerous to all animal life including humans!'

It looks like good land in places, but there are no humans or animals for most of the time. Especially noticeable is the lack of small birds. Some local traders had been to Alban in the last few years, but not bothered to go back. Too weird and empty, one of them had told him. Then this airship had gone astray. Rhys Parry has told him with all the navigation devices, those things don't lose their way. Yet it did. And as for its cargo bay coming open and raining goods around the place, that too is queer. He does not fancy crossing the river into the strange Fastness, so how can he expect others to do it for him.

Biting into his cold pie he chews at it thoughtfully; he doesn't have the authority to order people across. Taking a swig from his flask he swills the liquid round his mouth and swallows it with the morsels of pie. Cider is his one weakness, but he is careful not to overindulge. A brief thought of his wife and their sons canters through — four of the little rascals. I do okay by them, he decides. The population of the Cantref of Wrecsam lives peaceably enough amongst themselves, content to leave political dealings that inevitably come up inside the Fastness to the Maer, in most circumstances. I do alright by them too, he thinks, and if it leads to me being disliked some of the time, so be it.

There is something going on in Denbigh that Owen now knows more about from the last Maer's Meeting. Somehow outsiders there are becoming involved in Cantref affairs. Rhys Parry had introduced that toughy, Gabri from London, on his last visit, after persuading Owen to take the credits. Then two nights ago Gabri hinted about ways of getting people to do things in a tone that left him uneasy; making him feel obliged to do what he was told.

Owen picks up his binos and scans the water meadows. He spots two teams of his searchers close to the riverbank. Lifting his head slightly he looks into Alban, moving his field of view slowly along the track set way back beyond the far bank. He'd seen the occasional wagon moving along it from time to time, but not today. As he swings further round a group of people flashes into focus. That makes him jump.

The area is supposed to be uninhabited. They are really close to the river. One of them is standing on the front seat of a wagon with horses hitched, looking through binos at the closest of Owen's search parties. The rest are sitting in the shade under the trees – five of them altogether. The likelihood of trouble is remote. Everyone knows that the only way to deal with disputes across the external borders is through the Confederation and the League.

In the Fastness of Cymru any disputes with outsiders are dealt with at the Senedd level in Caerdydd – though the Maers are the ones reporting upwards. There are always plenty of squabbles and problems between the different Cantrefs and Maers. Some settlement meetings are very lively indeed. Though Wrecsam faced Alban across the poisoned lands he had never had any human interaction across the border, and heard of none on the grapevine.

His search party nearest the river is completely unaware of their presence. He begins to wish he'd never taken the credits. He makes another sweep of the valley. Just the one group over there. He sees one of them put something to his mouth. Owen stands up, reaches for his phone, and can't remember which group is closest. Seconds pass before the sound reaches him – a long mournful wail. His nearest teams stop what they are doing and look in the direction from where the sound comes.

Swinging his binos to check on the Albans he finds them out in the open, waving and shouting, moving slowly along the far bank closer to his team. He runs to his horse and makes for the river. Part way there he hears a gunshot. The wagon is on the Cymru side of the river being emptied by the time Owen reaches the riverbank. He nods to his men, and stares at the people from Alban, for now he can see they are all women, two of them right here in the wagon. He raises his hand in a friendly gesture, but doesn't know what to say to them, it is so long since he'd used the common tongue.

"How're we going to get all this back to the compound, Owen?" one of his search party asks.

"Was that a gunshot?"

"They shot a heaving line over for the towing ropes, Owen."

"You two, go and bring one of the trucks and a trailer. You," he points to another with a horse. "Ride round the other teams and tell them we'll meet back in the compound. You three stay here with me."

He watches the women haul their wagon back across the river, hitching up their horses to pull it up a ramp he'd not noticed. They move off towards the track beyond the trees.

"Right let's sort through this lot."

Most of the stuff is clearly trade goods. Some packages badly damaged, others pristine. Amongst them are three smaller boxes — two strongly made.

"The girl in charge said to be careful of this little box. But it's just a weird lump of stone." The man is pointing into the smallest box, which is glass-topped.

"Blowed if I know. Give it me. Is it a woman? Pass me those two cases." He puts the small box in his saddle bag. The bigger cases contain carefully padded faxplex. He hopes they are the ones Gabri is looking for. "Never again."

It is dark by the time Owen gets home and he is looking forward to a good meal and a some cider. Bronwen makes a good cider and he will enjoy it all the more if they have found what Gabri wants. Then he can get back to being Maer. No more doing things for credits.

He has a glass of cider before eating. The kids are in bed and Bronwen has eaten. She chatters away about the problems the kids have brought home during these days he has been so busy.

"They were causing havoc at the pond again. Chasing the ducks with sticks."

"Well, the ducks are Runners, Bronwen."

"It's not funny, Owen. You'll have to tell them, mind. It's not good if it's only me telling them. We should share that chore a lot more than we do. First thing in the morning."

"I will, love."

There is banging on the door. Owen looks at her and yawns noisily as he get up. Bronwen can hear male voices speaking in low tones. She hears the door shut and covers his plate with a lid, then picks up his glass and takes a sip of cider.

There is something funny going on that Owen won't talk about to her. She suspects it is something more than the airship cargo, and hopes it will not be like the affair of the summer before over sheep in the forestlands. That had taken days of Cantref Meetings to reach agreement. Life is too short and precious to spend it fighting over some sheep. Why is it always this way with these men?

"I think we've found the boxes you want. They were the other side of the river."

"I need to check 'em," Gabri says. "Got a multi-viewer here?"

"At my office."

"I need to check they're what we want, then I can get out of here."

"It's not a long walk." Owen leads the way towards the Cantref office.

"I don't want no one seeing these, not even you. D'you follow me?"

"I follow you," Owen says flatly. "Don't worry, I just want to go back home and have my tea."

"Sensible man," Gabri says as he slaps Owen on the back.

"Ach!" Owen says. "I nearly forgot — there's a small figure you need to see."

"Don't forget too much, mate."

"I won't. It's with the other goods up in our compound. I meant to show it you. In a fancy box. Doesn't look like anything else."

"Show it to Rhys."

"I'll only be a few minutes, I need to bring the viewer in here." Owen says once Gabri is sitting in a small back office.

Gabri looks around him. There are some coat hooks by the door — waterproof suits hanging off them. The furniture has seen better days and the office equipment is obsolete. He expects the multi-viewer will be old and slow. Stuck on the wall in front of the workstation is a planning chart covering sixteen lunars, and a map of the Cantref, dotted with freehand annotations. It clearly shows the river. To the south east of Wrecsam it is within the Cantref; to the south for a stretch it is the boundary with Mercia. To the east it forms the boundary with Alban before opening out into an estuary. On the opposite wall is a printed map of the Fastness of Cymru and a calendar.

"So, he got 'em to cross the river."

He idly tries a drawer. It is unlocked, holding some notebooks. He flicks through one; columns of meaningless figures. Boring. He doesn't care what SJ is up to, but he hopes these faxplex are the right ones, because he is impatient to get back to London. Sod all this pissing about in the wilderness.

Owen puts the newish multi-viewer on the desk and powers it up.

"I'll be at home finishing my tea. I'll lock up here when you've finished."

Owen hears a grunt and closes the door behind him. He leaves the building quickly, feeling very angry at himself, and walks home slowly. By the time he reaches their door he has calmed down. If he hadn't listened to Rhys, when he'd brought Gabri along that first time, he could have left them to sort out their own solution.

Bronwen is dozing in one of the large chairs. He sits at the table, uncovers his plate and quietly eats the remains of the meal and empties the glass of cider. As he puts the dirty plate and utensils into the sink she sits up with a start, peering around blinking. Seeing only Owen, she smiles.

"Is that the end to the day's business?"

"Don't ask. I have to wait for that *gentleman* to come back. And, please, don't ask me any questions about it."

"I wasn't going to, Owen, but you are worried by something. You can't deny me that."

"Yes, by what's happening around the Cantrefs. At the moment I can't tell you because I don't really know."

She looks up at him standing by her chair and puts her hand up to his arm. "Don't bottle up too much."

"I won't. I'll have another glass of cider. I don't know how long he's going to be. If you want to go to bed, just go."

"Owen, if you're having another glass, I'll join you. We'll see out the night together."

"Bronwen, what would you want most if we ever got a bit of extra cash?" She looks at him dubiously for a moment, but sees the dreamy look in his eyes.

"I don't rightly know. How much is a bit — exactly?"

"Ahh ... Five hundred." He doesn't dare tell her it is ten times that.

"Well, I can get the kids something from Mercia. Good quality clothes, like, something different."

"No, Bronwen, not the kids, not something that's practical and everyday, even if it is good quality. I meant, what do you want most. You know, what do you dream of having that isn't everyday."

She is a bit overwhelmed by this. This is a departure from the Owen she's got used to. He is kind and dependable, and he looks out for the kids and her well enough, but he has never before shown a flight of fancy like this.

"I don't know Owen. I'll have to really think about this. I haven't had a dream–anything to think of for years. I used to dream of finding a good husband. Well, I got you. And I used to think about having well-behaved children ... Still, getting one of them right was a miracle if you ask me, particularly four with four sons."

Her tone is serious and she sees him frown before he realises it's their usual banter. She picks up one of his large hands in her small ones and smiles at him.

"I couldn't wish for a better partner, love. You know that."

There is knocking on the door. Bronwen starts to rise.

"I'll get it," Owen snaps. Then strokes his hand across her hair as he stands. "Sorry, Love. This won't take long."

Gabri is happy — he has completed his mission. He hands over the credit notes to Owen.

"As promised."

"What about that small figure?" Owen asks.

"Make sure Rhys gets it tomorrow and hand those faxplex only to him. There's a large open field up by the warehouse compound."

"Yes?"

"Well, you'll need eight strong men up there around mid-morning to take the lines from the airship. Rhys will be here first thing. Just do as he tells you. I'm heading off now. And remember — keep your mouth shut about our business. I'd hate to have to come back."

"There's no need for your threats. I'm a man of my word."

"Remember that when you've had a bit too much cider."

Gabri steps back into the darkness and a small shaft of light is all that can be seen moving silently along the road.

He stands in the doorway watching the light bob along. He clenches and unclenches his fists. After a few minutes he hears voices and a door open and shut — a metallic sound, followed by a stab of bright light and the burring hum of an electric motor. Rhys must already be in the area, but that doesn't sound like his truck. He is instantly listing suspicious incidents and characters in his mind. He is about to return to the kitchen, when he remembers the faxplex boxes in his office.

June, 13th — Wrecsam

It is barely dawn when Rhys knocks at the door, waking Owen.

"Flaming hell, Rhys, could you not sleep last night, then?"

"I slept fine, but I've been up these two hours getting here."

"So ..." Owen began, but decides against asking questions about what and who concerning Gabri. "Was the journey easy?"

"Easier than it used to be. I've got a new truck."

"Ahh. Come in and I'll get you something to drink. Are you hungry?"

Owen has always got on easily with Rhys, which is why he had been drawn into this enterprise. Perhaps Rhys's ability to get on with everyone he meets is what the outlanders want most from him, Owen thinks. Then recalls previous conversations and feels the knitting in his guts. From now on he'll have to think twice before speaking.

"Yes, I'll have a drink, and I'll take some food, Owen. Whatever you're having will suit me fine." Rhys smiles.

"What time do you expect the airship to show up? I've got to get some men in to hold the ropes. Have you ever done it before, because you know fine well I have not. What are the ropes for?"

"We've plenty of time yet. Just to hold the airship still. Don't worry, I'll tell your men what to do, there's no problem, I've got anchoring points." He picks up the mug Owen places in front of him. "Bronwen's brew?"

"Not this one, this is Mam's, it's like pop. Best thing for the morning. Bronwen hasn't dared to make it yet on two counts. The first, it might not come up to scratch and that will upset her. The second, it might turn out better and upset Mam. She keeps telling Mam she hasn't got the time to do it."

Owen is rummaging through the cupboards getting out pans and crockery, when Bronwen comes in and shoos him to the table.

"I'll get you breakfast more quickly and quietly than you two can manage."

The two men sip their weak beer and talk of everyday matters.

"What brings you back to Wrecsam so quickly, Rhys? You're spending as much time here as at home these days. How's Megh and the kids?"

Her friendship with Megh stretches back to childhood.

"Megh's fine, the kids too. When are you coming for a visit? You know there's room to stay."

"I'll come over with the kids when there's a break in their schooling."

She had lain awake for a long time during the night thinking of the credits Owen mentioned. Things are not bad in her life. Owen has always worked hard and provided. But the fact is he can't prepare breakfast, and it brings into focus the separation of their roles in life. It has been nagging at her for sometime now. Ever since seeing a program from Mercia on how the Upheavals had really started because people had demanded real equality of opportunity and treatment in society — and not been given it.

Events in the last few days — Owen's overbearing protectiveness and the mysterious and unexplained night-time activities about which he says nothing — had finally lumped together this morning with the men's dismissal of her from their conversation and into a mute domestic serving role, and she aiding them. Sure, there are conversations between women of which men know next to nothing, and she supposes it's the same with men. But now she wants some change in her role.

She cooks eggs, bacon and spiced sausages with some tomatoes. Listening to the mundane, even inane things they say to one another she wonders if she really wants to bother. She can't think of one woman of her acquaintance but is left out somehow by the way the men organise themselves. She knows it's not the same across Cymru. There are some women she knows about who have no men in their lives at all, even with the kids, but with these she has almost no contact. Perhaps she should actually seek out the company of some of them. Her desire of husband and kids has been realised. But she has not been fulfilled as she had wanted.

Rhys makes some comment about the sheep dispute and the likelihood of its recurrence. Those mangy sheep, she thinks, brought right into the kitchen. Rattling two plates down onto the table she flips food onto them, pushing them in front of the two uncomprehending males.

"Thank you, Bronwen," she says in a thin voice. They mumble back an approximation of thanks and set to eating the food. Instead of joining them and having some food of her own she leaves and goes upstairs.

Through the door she hears a muttered, "Wrong time in the period?" from Rhys.

The pilot manoeuvres the airship right to the piles of cargo where the temporary mooring arrangements have been set up. It takes the best part of four hours to load all the cargo by hand. Knowing of SJ's angry reaction, and the removal of one of the pilots concerned, Rhys has twice made sure the bay doors are locked shut before allowing it to lift away. With the airship gone the spectators melt away leaving the compound to those loading the remaining cargo into Rhys's truck. Owen invites Rhys home for a snack before he heads back to Denbigh.

"Bronwen?" Owen shouts from the door. "Any chance of a bite to eat, love?" Owen removes his boots and goes towards the kitchen. This time noises can be heard in the house. Rhys waits by the boots.

"Is she there?"

"Bronwen?" Owen calls up the stairs. "Are you there, love?"

"I'll be down in a moment. Put the kettle on. I've managed to get some coffee to drink. Get the cups out."

Bronwen makes a jug of coffee, ignoring them. Leaving it to brew, she places slices of bara-bridd and a dish of butter on a cutting board between them, then sits down and looks at them both.

"Sorry about this morning, Bronwen," Owen says. She nods slightly in acknowledgement and softens her expression.

It is only after Rhys has left that Owen notices the box with the stone figure, dropped on the road near the house. To keep it safe he hands it to Bronwen, saying they need to look after it until he hears from Rhys what's to be done with it.

Looking through the glass lid she can see it is a rotund sculpted stone. The box had been made with care and lined with a scarlet material. The latch on the lid stiff, but made to be opened. She takes it out, turning it to view it from every angle. The figure of a mature woman with a benign face. it is much smoother to touch than its appearance suggests and it feels warm as she handles it.

After some minutes she places it on top of the box, on the end of the narrow shelf that holds the fir cones, stones and snail shells the kids have given her over the years. Standing back and looking at it from a greater distance she absorbs the sensuousness of the curves forming the female shape, so takes it off the shelf again, gently rubbing its smooth surface.

Silently she tells herself — Yes, I will sort this out with Owen. I know I have the strength to do it, and I know he'll listen. Their smallest son runs into the kitchen, sobbing. She puts the figure into the box and turns her attention to him.

Two days pass before Owen gets an answer from Rhys. The stone figure is not part of the cargo from the airship.

"Reckon it's a case of finders keepers," Owen says to himself. Bronwen's always touching it so she shall keep it. Then he promptly forgets about it as other Cantref problems take his mind off such little things.

June, 15th — London

In SJ's office in London, Gabri is recounting his findings to SJ, the delicate tinging of the platinum toothpick punctuating his oration.

"So," SJ says, interrupting Gabri's flow. "The faxplex are in the base."

"Course, SJ. No problems. Rhys Parry should have confirmed."

"He has." He turns to gaze out at the square.

"Do you think that Maer will keep quiet?"

"Yeah. I don't think we'll have any problems with him. He was glad to see the back of me."

"There was a query about a small stone figure."

Gabri starts feeling clammy — glad SJ isn't looking at him.

"The Maer told me it was a little stone in a box, nothing fancy."

"Was it part of the cargo we lost?"

It sounded cordial, but SJ had swung back watching him.

"I didn't check, but it didn't sound like the sort of thing you trade in. I took a guess it was something picked up with the real payload. Besides I told the Maer to give it to Rhys Parry to send on. I'll go back in my own time, if it's necessary."

"It wasn't part of the payload. Rhys has confirmed it's not on the manifest. But you didn't know that. Next time let nothing slip. Our operations demand attention to detail. That's why we're successful. And I want to stay that way."

SJ settles back in his chair.

"It's taken ten years to build that base to where it is. I'll have that Fastness in the palm of my hand soon. After all, there are a lot of credits burning holes in people's pockets right now. We'll get all of it back. We always do. And a lot of favours owed afterwards. Once started, they can't resist the lure of lucre."

SJ turns back to face the window and puts his feet on a small table. He rocks slowly back and fore.

"Gabri, I want you to check out the operation at the Birmingham warehouse. We're still losing goods."

"Okay, SJ. I'll get onto it right away."

As soon as he is alone he turns back to his desk and types a code into the phone terminal. It is a few minutes before the screen lights up and a face comes into focus. It is a death mask — meaning nothing to SJ — of Cosimo Medici.

"How is our enterprise flourishing?" The voice is synthesised.

"The faxplex are secured."

"Good. Now we can move forward again. Do you know where they were found?"

"Not exactly, but near the River Dee by Wrecsam."

"Any signs of tampering?"

"As far as we are able to ascertain the code tags are intact."

"SJ, I know you're a busy man, and I can see why you had others make the necessary checks. If we are to unseat Sion from its — what might be termed holy — position we shall need every scrap of information in the world we can use to manipulate them. If capital is to be used in the way it should be used, to the advantage of those who have it and understand it, we have to break the spiritual hold of Sion. Those faxplex are the key. You will get a set of codes to ascertain the authenticity of the faxplex. Only you are to use them. And SJ, remember you are one rather vital cog, but a replaceable one."

The screen goes blank. Looking at the white screen he wonders who is behind the mask.

SJ wants to maximise his profits. He could screech into the fabulously rich bracket within a very short time were it not for the limits put on profit making by the strictures of the Confederation, aided and abetted by the League. The equitability demanded in society is not at all helpful to the business entrepreneur. He does not hide his views about the need to liven up the capital markets. They are why he was approached in the first place. Even after joining this conspiracy he had been told to maintain the same high profile. He is happy to do so. What he wants to do is win and be seen to win.

He knows the information has come from someone in the League itself; for what motive he does not greatly care. They have been bought is all that matters. Everyone will accept a price.

Whoever is behind the mask is watching him. Which niggles SJ, as he is in the scheme wholeheartedly. But now he has to check the faxplex personally.

June, 16th — The border lands of Alban and Mercia

Jarnie's camouflaged figure slides across the southern boundary river of Alban where it is still narrow. A flit of dark-greens and black in the failing moonlight, in the region just to the east of the poisoned lands. The inflatable bodyboard pulled back to the Mercian side by SJ's driver. The role Jarnie plays is something he considers natural – he wants to be martial; the Confederation is too sedate. Sure, it has its defence forces and they are well trained, but with no recent experience of real warfare. The years of peace have seen to that.

In those forces Jarnie had risen as far as he could and stayed with them for as long as was allowed in any one stretch. When the ten years was up he had wandered into the wildernesses of the east acting as security for a trade mission. The mission had returned, but he had stayed on and spent ten years as a mercenary soldier, in the chaos of the jungles of Asia. SJ had met him while concluding a commercial venture with Jarnie's then employer. Soon afterwards he returned to London and took up employment as head of security for SJ's trading house. He found Gabri and trained him. There is still more to do – Gabri is not so ready for calculated violence as Jarnie would like.

Climbing the northern bank of the river he lays low in the shrubs. He waits and watches through the next couple of hours, until the light of dawn becomes discernible. Then he surveys the land once more through his binos. The previous afternoon he saw a group of people in a horse-drawn wagon pass along a track about one kimetre beyond the river. They had not seemed to be going anywhere or doing anything in particular. Jarnie's objective is a line of hills that runs north, rising steeply from the river valley.

He checks through his binos for the compass bearing of a particular clump of trees on an isolated hilltop. Then scans through three-hundred-and-sixty degrees. Satisfied he is not under observation, he sets his radio to seek. Rising stealthily from his hiding place he weaves across the open ground towards the trackway, heading for the shelter of an overgrown heap of ruins on the other side. As he crosses the trackway his radiophone emits a piercing howl. Jarnie knows there is an electronic system alerting the Boundary Patrol.

He checks the clump of trees again and selects his next refuge. Dashing towards it he veers and ducks. In this fashion his progress into Alban continues throughout the day. He eats condensed rations little and often, drinking his bottled water in little sips. By staying under cover as much as possible he keeps out of sight and out of the sun.

During the afternoon he reaches the clump of trees near the summit of their lonely hill. Beyond that hill is another barren valley to cross before reaching the escarpment cutting the southern edge of the range of higher hills. In a hollow amongst the trees he sets proximity sensors and sleeps for a few hours.

He wakes as the last of the daylight turns into night. Away to the south he can see the lume of light from Birmingham. He's travelled nearly twenty kimetres during the day; now he aims to cover double that distance in the quiet of the night. He eats, sips some water, pees and sets off. Scanning through a complete circle picks up no human images, so he descends into the dead lands and marches west. Jarnie travels for six hours before napping again — the proximity sensors set, his pack beneath his head, a knife by his hand.

With the first light of dawn he wakes, listens carefully and gets up. Staying hidden he relieves himself. He chews on a protein bar and pulls at the pack to get his radiophone. It is not in its pocket — he quickly searches round the area. His knife remains where he left it, and it is impossible to tell if anyone has been into the shelter of the ruins in which he made his camp. It is his instinct to have stowed the radiophone back into the pocket. Carefully pulling his pack apart he checks through the contents. His binos are still there, and his gun but it is missing its magazine, and the spare clips are gone.

He sits rigid, momentarily unsure of himself. They must have gassed him. He had done that before, but never left the quarry behind. He reasons they are playing with him, and his pride makes him accept the challenge. Knowing he is under observation, but sure of his craft, he decides to be bold. Striking camp he sets off westwards, out in the open, away from all cover.

Jarnie had urged SJ to get someone to act as a go-between with those prepared to push for change in the financial governance rules in Alban. And that job is now his. He knows that communications between SJ and these people are constantly interrupted by signal failures. He suspects there is a more sophisticated government system in Alban than SJ is prepared to admit. SJ has a fixed idea that the Fastnesses are all easy to manipulate, because the populations are used to a loose form of governance. That might be the case in most of them, but Alban is different. Rumours are rumours, though sometimes they are based on a fact or two. The rumours about the way the Fastness is run — where outsiders are not shunned, but somehow vetted on arrival and watched — are too many and from different sources for there not to be truth in there somewhere.

Getting changes to the right rules is not going to be easy. They are framed in constitutional terms, and set as if in stone. There seems to be fewer divisions in the populace, like they had exploited in other places. There are some strange notions about society that make little sense to him. He isn't sure SJ understands them either. He's been told that the government consists of an administration held to account by a complex system of councils and public voting. Most importantly there seem to be no formal political groupings in these councils, which makes identifying the most useful influencers difficult. The contact he is hoping to meet in Sedgeworth is a member of the Governing Council, the central council for Engeland. He speaks well of his influence amongst other councillors, but has warned SJ that he is under scrutiny for so-called unsound practices. One of Jarnie's objectives is to assess this man to see if he lives up to his self-proclaimed potential.

June, 18th — Alban

During the day Jarnie travels through open woodland skirting the north side of the trackway that follows the boundary. In late afternoon he sees another group of people in uniform on a horse-drawn wagon. They are travelling east, in no hurry. The group stops a good distance from him and after unhitching the horses and giving them nose bags, settles down to rest. He decides to test their reaction and saunters past them — keeping his distance.

To his amazement they display no discernible interest in his presence. After a while a truck and double-trailer come into view. The group becomes animated as the truck rolls to a stop. The horses and wagon are loaded into the trailers. The people climb into the large cab behind the driver, joining others. He hears their banter and laughter clearly. No one has given him more than a cursory glance. The vehicle heads west a short distance before turning north into the hills. Jarnie watches through his binos until the truck is out of sight.

Crows land where the group has waited and pick at the small remains of food they have left behind. He waits a bit longer before moving back into the cover along the base of the hills which curve to the north with the track climbing into them. As darkness spreads across the land, Jarnie sets off, keeping between the track and the summits. He begins to hear sheep, and knows he might encounter dog packs. He also knows the dogs will likely leave him alone as the sheep are an easier catch. He is confident enough that anyone meeting him out in this open land cannot jeopardise his mission. The removal of his gear worries him, but he focuses on succeeding, refusing to accept the worry.

Somewhere in the distance he hears dogs yowling. The moon will soon rise so he'll see better what lays ahead. He looks west and sees strange greenish lights, down on the plain. He drops to the ground, and cautiously looks again, but the lights are gone. He hears laughter above him on the hillside, and voices talking in a language he can't understand. Down on the plain the green lights are flickering again, twirling and moving like figures in a ghostly dance. Somewhere nearby he hears a creature moving through the coarse grass. He stays quite still — the lights on the plain keep moving, breaking up and reforming to start the dance all over again. Soon the voices above him are silent.

The moon has risen and its blue light flooding the landscape has diminished the intensity of the green ones in the valley. Then he hears a rustling noise in the air above him and sees a huge bird shape sweeping back and fore across the sky to the east. There is sudden silence and the bird has gone. When he looks to the west again, the green lights have disappeared. Having seen some inexplicable things when in the east — things beyond his rational mind — Jarnie cannot stop the hairs on the nape of his neck stiffening. He remembers scoffing at the tales of the poisoned land inhabited by spirits, but now he can't block them. The green lights on the plain start dancing again.

June, 19th — Alban

Because of his unease, Jarnie travels less distance during the night than he wanted. He hopes he has eluded his observers in the open spaces of the hills. To make himself more secure when he rests, he places trip-cords outside the shallow cave that is well hidden at the base of a low cliff, amongst undergrowth in a copse of birch trees. In the rapidly cooling air heralding the onset of day he is dozing fitfully and becomes aware of sounds around him. Before he can react he feels himself slipping into darkness while struggling to defend himself.

From the Castellan's Security Force base in the foothills he is sent to The Keep in Derwent. Within a couple of hours the still drugged Jarnie is inside The Keep, his presence known only to the Castellan's Security Force and the Reever.

The Communicator's specialists have amassed a huge amount of data from his phone.

June, 19th — The Keep, Derwent, Wark-in-Alban

When Jarnie comes round he is in complete darkness, half-squatting in a metal cage less than a metre diameter, which is slowly gyrating in an unknown void. His knees and back are pressing against some sort of padding. He has limited movement of his shackled hands but can feel in front of his face and chest there is a square of steel mesh — a dozen squares each way, each as wide as his two middle fingers; the rest of the steel is perforated with holes into which he can fit his little finger. He is wearing soft shoes but is otherwise naked. He is surprised he is not cold, and slowly stands up.

Smelling salt and seaweed he believes he is on the coast. Something smelling rancid shoots past the cage and sloshes into water and something down there causes a lot of noise. A clear voice comes out of the darkness.

"Jarnie Paresh. What is your business in Alban?"

"I am on a walking holiday."

"We require your acquiescence."

The cage lurches down. He knows he is being softened up, but in a way he has never used. The tortures he applied relied on the prisoner seeing exactly what was in store if co-operation was not forthcoming, and either way the outcome was usually fatal. Here, close to the Civitas of Europa, it is difficult to believe death will result from any interrogation he undergoes. The worse thing Jarnie faces is the prodding and goading of his own memory; what he had done to others might yet be done to him. In the darkness, with only sounds to fix his mind on, he cannot stem that rising tide. Another question is asked.

"I was doing what I was told." Again the cage lurches down.

"What are your orders concerning the individuals you are supposed to meet?"

"My name is Jarnie Paresh."

This time the cage does not drop. Sounds of doors opening and of machinery moving. Something passes the cage and some minutes later enters the water. Then something overflowing rises alongside the cage, and something sploshes into the tank. He is wetted and smells and tastes the salt. Time passes.

Still no light penetrates his dungeon. If he spills the truth he might be let out and can always go back east. Restart his interrupted career as a mercenary. As long as you do what they want, they don't care what you've done, just how you've done it. If he can survive, he might get away — somehow.

"Who is your boss?"

"My name is Jarnie Paresh."

"SvenJan Letrap employs you to handle security in his trading house, Paresh." When he remained silent the cage dropped again.

"You're wasting your time trying to force me to talk." His tone is mocking.

A light flashes on, flooding a glass-sided tank of water with its gleam. It is level with his face and only a metre away. In the water pink, eel-like creatures flick and writhe. He grimaces at the sight, mesmerised. These must be in the water to which his captors are dropping him with each non-answer he utters. A large fish, damaged — but still twitching — is in the tank.

Nothing happens immediately, then one of the creatures hooks onto the fish and curls itself into a knot pulling away chunks from the dying body, and the others do the same. Blood spills into the water, but even so he can clearly see the creatures slowly entering into the cavity of soft inner parts. Soon none of the creatures are outside the carcass, which twitches and jumps with the movements of the internal feeders. Jarnie feels sick. A far worse death than any he had ever devised waits in the waters below. The tank is emptied and rises out of his sight. The light goes out leaving him in darkness.

"You think that'll make me crack!" he yells. It bounces back at him in the damp air. He is left to swing.

It is a long time before they ask more of him. A narrow beam of light illuminates his face, acting as a beacon, about which the cage swings. The motion, though gentle, leaves Jarnie with motion sickness.

"What is the real motive your boss has for sending you into this Fastness?" It is a different voice.

"Getting all those trade goods back."

"Come on, Jarnie. Nothing remains this side of the boundary — except you. We know his long-term interest is in setting up a base here. He sent you to meet with contacts in Alban."

"As you know so much, what more can I tell you?"

"We think you can fill in some gaps."

The cage moves slowly downwards.

"The fish was dead, at least," another voice says.

"I was sent to find the missing goods," Jarnie hears the rise in his voice. The cage slows down, barely descending at all.

"You, his head of security were sent for that?"

"We are just underlings." The cage stops, begins to ascend.

"You say the faxplex are the only thing that matters. Yet we see from your phone you are to meet and assess a list of contacts. Don't say you aren't paid to think. It's obvious you are."

Before Jarnie can respond, the cage drops the remaining distance to the water surface, stopping with water lapping into its base, covering his feet. Jarnie spits out the mouthful of spew.

"What contacts are you talking about?"

"You haven't knowledge of what is on your phone?"

"I don't know what list of contacts you mean."

"We have more questions for you, Jarnie."

The light goes out and the cage rises rapidly. A door swings open and the cage trundles out, coming to rest in a small room. The lighting is very bright; he sees two men in boiler suits wearing mirrored glasses. One of them approaches.

"What is so important about the two boxes of faxplex?"

"I don't know what their importance is. It was supposed to be a simple transhipment. It would have been if the bay doors hadn't come open on that airship."

Suddenly the cage is lifting away from him and the bottom drops open. He lands awkwardly in a narrow pit in which he barely fits, grazing himself. His eyes are almost level with the floor of the room, and he notices it dips gently towards the pit as if it is a central drain. The man is looking down at him, while the other moves a small transparent tub with a little water in it close to Jarnie's face and sets three of the pink creatures into it from a bucket. As the creatures writhe they release slime into the tub.

"See how quickly the tub fills up," the man says. "What was the purpose of sending the faxplex to the base in Cymru?"

"Security. It's safer there. We have our own armed guards. We aren't allowed that luxury in the Civitas."

The tub is brimming with slime and it begins to overflow.

"Where did your employer get the faxplex?"

"Somewhere in Deutschen, I don't know where, but all our trade goods usually come through from Hamburg. I don't know any more than that. He isn't the kind of boss who tells more than is needed. And he wouldn't keep anyone for long if they asked questions like that, either."

The slime rolls in a glutinous dribble over the edge of the pit in front of his nose.

"What is on the faxplex?"

"Something to do with the League. SJ was always going on about the League being too bossy for the good of business."

"See. You do know something. What would you propose to do if we let you go?"

"Go east — back to my old employment. I don't think you'd let me return straight to London."

"There might be the means of making it worth your while."

"You want me to spy on him? He's a very careful man who pays me well to work for him. You'd need to top that." Jarnie laughs derisively.

A lever is pulled, the edge of a large tank drops. A swarm of hagfish shoots in a slither of slime across the floor and into the pit. Jarnie yells in horror as the pink creatures slide over him and fall about his naked body. The slime rises quickly to halfway up his abdomen and he shouts and promises and curses, while he waits for the teeth to bite into his flesh. For the pink worms to invade his innards. Waits for the pain to begin. Prays for the slime to drown him first. He can feel the sinuous bodies knotting and unknotting, curling round his legs, pushing against his prick, slipping round his balls, pulling at his arse. The slime is just below his shoulders, the teeth tugging at his skin.

"Finish it," he whines. "Let me out or finish me." In his mind pass faces of those who had pleaded with him to shoot them. And he sees himself standing there laughing at their pleas, revelling in his power. But his tormentors are looking at him with neither humour nor pleasure on their faces, and he cannot see their eyes. The slime is edging over his shoulders. As best he can he scrabbles at the creatures where he feels teeth tugging at his skin.

"Okay! I'll spy for you." He is gulping now, the slime almost at his mouth. Suddenly the hagfish are sluiced away – back to the cistern. Cold water washes over Jarnie and he sinks as low as the pit dimensions allow. He looks down and seeing blood running on his skin; he spews and shits. Two more men appear. He feels a sling passing around him and is pulled from the pit.

"Take him to the medical room."

He spends the night in a cell. Comfortable though the bed is he does not sleep. Every time he dozes off a wave of nausea sweeps over him and leaves him sweating. Jarnie has never been captive before, nor interrogated.

June, 20th – The Keep, Derwent, Wark-in-Alban

He is told he will be transported to the border and expelled from the Fastness. He will not be allowed back. He does not believe they will let him out alive, as they cannot believe his promise of spying on SJ. He is astonished when they show him everything they have gleaned from his phone; leave him with a printed copy to look at. They say it's his to take back to Mercia and beyond. All the coded security of the trading house had not stopped them from reaching the data. He is given a medical report, and shown that the wounds are clean, superficial and not from the hagfish, but his own nails.

In the afternoon they take Jarnie to an area of moorland, well to the south-east of The Keep. None saw him come – none see him go.

"Exercise yourself," he is told when they stop. They sit by the truck chatting. He is unrestrained, and dressed in his own clothing. He has his pack, filled with the evidence they had gathered. He suspects a trick and does his exercises, remaining within reach of his captors. They ignore him. Eventually a larger truck arrives from the south. His new guardians usher him into it and head back the way they have come, following lanes and ancient trackways. With the sun setting they let him out. They pack food and water into his backpack, adding his knife and binos.

"Exercise yourself. Follow this track south. It leads to where you crossed into Alban. You should be out of Alban by this time tomorrow. You will be under observation. We will know where you are."

For hours he runs, before stopping in a small copse of trees on the lee-side of the hills. He looks back over the way he has travelled, but there is no sign of pursuit. One thought goes round and round — they captured me before, so can again. Exhausted, he lays down to rest.

When he wakes the sun has gone down. He starts south again, keeping high in the hills. Just before complete darkness envelops the land, he hears horses and voices. The same strange language he had heard before his capture. When they are almost upon him he lunges up and makes a grab for the nearest horse, unseating the rider. Before the man or his two companions can recover, the horse is galloping away with Jarnie. The fallen rider in tandem on another mount, the three set off in pursuit — ululating. Soon another group of riders appears heading off the stolen horse. One of these riders whistles shrilly. The stolen mount stops dead, pitching Jarnie to the ground.

With them is a large dog which gets to his prone body first. The riders pull the dog off, but there are teeth marks on his shoulders and neck where it has bitten him. There is no life in the prone body; Jarnie's neck is broken.

June, 21st — The Staffordshire Peak District, Alban

Early in the morning the fell-riders report to the nearest Boundary Patrol base that a horse was stolen late the previous night and the thief took a fall and died. The Boundary Patrol report it to the local Procufisk and head for the scene, but are puzzled not to find a body.

Unknown to them in the early hours a Security Force team had already removed Jarnie and his backpack. With implanted trackers they had no trouble finding the spot.

The Castellan does as required by the Reever, under strong protest. He issues orders to the Security Force team to dispose of the body by placing it carefully in the Betch, a small river flowing out of the poisoned lands in Alban into the Afon Dyfrdwy.

June, 21st — Cantref of Wrecsam, Cymru

Jarnie's body, fully clothed, has been found trapped in the millrace weir, just upstream of the tide-head in the estuary.

In the few years he has been Maer, Owen has never had to deal with a suspicious death of an unknown person; the actions to be taken are clear in the Laws of the Cantrefs. It involves the police — the Heddlu, the Cantref law officer — the Canghellor, and the nearest Registrar, as well as the local doctors' committee, for a post-mortem.

To the Maer falls the duty to appoint special constables from the Enlistment Roll, to aid the Heddlu in the collection of reports from the population in the vicinity of the incident — or as wide into the Cantref and adjacent ones as deemed necessary — which isn't exactly a helpful phrase. The Maer is also responsible for notification of the death to all administrative districts bordering on that in which the body is found; within and without the Cantrefs. Therefore he has to inform three other Maers, the authorities in Mercia, and last and most troublesome, the authorities in Alban. Getting in touch with the Mercian authorities is easy, but Owen has no idea how to inform the relevant people in Alban. The advice from Caerdydd is not really helpful — report it to the nearest administrative centre in Alban. But they can provide no up to date information. The only person he can think of who might have contacts is Rhys Parry.

June, 21st — London

SJ is checking through financial reports when he receives an urgent coded message from Rhys Parry. There is a photo of Jarnie's body with brief text. He sits back in his chair and turns to stare out of the windows.

Jarnie is dead. The fact and manner of death do not really concern him. Jarnie, like Gabri and anyone else he employs, is eminently expendable. No, what matters to SJ is the loss of an important piece of his plan. At least the Maer in Wrecsam has no information about the body. There must be no link between him and the body in that river. He ponders a moment more. Jarnie had definitely crossed into Alban from the south. His driver had taken him to the crossing point and waited until mid-morning before reporting back directly to SJ.

Deny any knowledge of the dead person, he sends back. He swears loudly. Now he has to find someone to replace Jarnie.

June, 21st — Wrecsam

Owen's Mam cannot recall a murder in Wrecsam in her lifetime. She looks at Owen, a sharp expression on her face.

"I mind it was what had gone before. Too much killing. Too much blood. And what for, huh?"

She chops vigorously at salad stuff and adds it to a plate with boiled eggs and ham. He cuts and butters some slices of bread, sighing.

"There's no mystery it was all for keeping power. Well, those that had it, lost it with their deaths, and there's a truth."

She puts the meal in front of him, goes and gets a glass of beer.

"Don't go getting ideas into your head about power, my boy."

She wafts the glass towards him before putting it down. She sits in the chair Bronwen favours and watches him over her small spectacles, her hands together in her lap. Her white hair is held back in a large bun — when brushed out it falls to her thighs. Her weather-tanned face has seen a lot of wind and sun.

"They'll bring back bad times if they're let to. The less you have to do with them the better."

He wants to confide in her about the credits and his worries, but her certainty on almost any issue always makes him feel weak.

"What are you thinking about, Owen?"

"I'm wondering how to get in touch with the authorities in Alban."

"Cross the Dyfrdwy and ride north-east."

"Send someone into Alban? In person?"

"It's only the other side of the river, Owen. What's wrong with my suggestion?"

"Well, nothing, exactly. It's just that people don't go over there. Not normally. Do you know anyone who's been?"

"There's a fact, and I do ... Me!"

He twists his head round to look squarely at her.

"You! — You, Mam? When did you go? You never told me."

"And what's to tell. I often go to Alban. Where do you think I get the peace and tranquillity I want? Not here. Mind you, it is an eerie place for the first few hours ride. But it is peaceful."

"Is it true that no one lives there?"

"Yes, there is poison in the ground and lots of ruins. I was told, but I don't know if it's true, that it'll take another four hundred years before the poison has washed away completely. Anyway, I always take my own water, same as the locals."

"You know people from Alban?"

"Of course I do. Strangely enough, they're people like you and me. They don't speak our language, and the common tongue's odd. But ..."

Noticing the little stone figure and its box are missing from the shelf by the stove, she frowns at him.

"You'll get a crick in your neck, twisting like that. Turn and face me. That's better. Now, when are Bronwen and the boys coming back?"

"I don't know yet, Mam. I thought you said you liked peace?"

"I like both in their place. I want to be able to choose. Tell me again why she and the boys went off to her parents? It's not like her to be so spontaneous. But I'm glad they weren't here when that body was found. Have you had a falling out?"

"No! I don't know for sure why she decided to go. Drop it, Mam. Now, do you know anyone I could talk to in Alban?"

"You're just like your Dad was. But who am I to talk. I don't know anyone you can report this death to, but I know people who will be able to help me. I can wear the Dragon badge for you. I am on the Enlistment Roll."

"How do you get over the river?"

"I have a boat tucked away. I'm amazed your teams didn't find it."

"How do you know they didn't?"

"Because the shed has my name on it, and you'd not've been able to keep your tongue still once you got home." A smile forms.

"Owen, my lovely boy, you're not bad, but you are a typical man. If a woman gets ahead of you, you'll want to trip her up. Well, your Mam's so far ahead now you can't stick your long shanks out far enough. Shall I be your messenger to Alban, or will you try to get one of the men of this Cantref to cross the demon's river?"

"You go for me, please, Mam."

He never asks her how she copes, or what she does. Since his Dad died there is so much they have not discussed. True, they had clung to one another for a while in the aftermath, but he had left home to live with Bronwen as soon as he was able. He does not see her but once a week. She usually calls in to see them — she likes Bronwen. He'd always known she was strong-willed — even his Dad had not argued with her once her mind was set. But crossing to Alban on a regular basis? He shakes his head and laughs.

"Now what are you laughing at?"

"Me. Me and you, Mam." She starts laughing with him.

"I'll go whenever you want me to. Can you manage not to starve without a woman pandering to you?"

"Of course I can," he says indignantly. "I'm quite able to feed myself. Is tomorrow too early?"

"No, I'll be glad of the excuse. I'll use my own horse as always."

"I'll have everything ready for you. Shall I see you for breakfast?"

"Oh aye. Tell you what, love, you can have that ready for me too. I'll be round by nine."

For once he follows her out and watches her go towards her own home. She looks back and gives a little wave. He waves back, but too late for her to see. Not fancying going back into the empty house, he wanders down through the water meadows and heads downstream. He follows a vague path through the grass to the bank. It is years since he has wandered aimlessly like this. The river isn't very wide really, but the mental barrier it erects — and those few notices — prevents nearly everyone from venturing across. And superstition has taken over from logic. He knows his Mam is right. Industrial poison made the land on the other side uninhabitable. There's nothing otherworldly at the beck and call of the Reever of Alban; even so he feels uneasy.

He wonders where his Mam's boat is hidden, and pictures something neat and tidy, with carefully embroidered cushions on the seats. He sits down cross-legged where the stone revetment finishes, and tosses wild barley heads into the current — idly watching them float away. When the midges start to irritate he gets up and heads back across the fields to Wrecsam.

At home he finds a message from Rhys; no contacts in Alban, but if Owen establishes contact, can he pass the information on, it might come in handy.

June, 22nd — Wrecsam

Owen is up in good time to get breakfast ready. It'll be a long day for her, and she'll need a good meal.

He makes porridge, taking great care to follow exactly how Bronwen and his Mam add the ingredients. He is careful not to add too much salt into it as it cooks. He always grumbles it isn't salty enough for his taste, and Bronwen always counters by telling him it is possible to add salt, but not take it away. He puts the pot on the stove where he knows Bronwen always puts it.

He dices potatoes into a pan of water and adds some salt — enough, or too much? He can only guess. Now, what does he like the taste of? He goes to the herbs hanging by the back door and picks off some thyme, throws that in and covers the pot. He needs to slice some bacon and — Damn! He hasn't collected the eggs for the last two days. He goes out to the chicken roost. Rummaging around he grabs half-a-dozen eggs. The rest can wait till later. He returns to find the porridge glooping and bubbling. There is a smell of something charred. He puts the eggs on the table, picks the porridge pot from the hob and empties the contents into another pot that he places to the side of the hot plate. He fiddles with the thermal fluid controls of the hob, then dumps the burned pot into the sink and runs water into it.

He goes to the cold-room and pulls down the bacon piece. Slicing four rashers, he places them on a plate by the eggs. He hasn't been up to the dairy lately for any milk and has used the last of it in the porridge. He is still thinking about the milk when the potato water boils over leaving the air tainted with another smell of burning. He grabs the pot from the range, scolding himself in the process, and thumps it down on the table. An egg rolls slowly over the edge. Owen curses. He is wiping the remains of it from the floor when his Mam comes through the back door.

"Very domesticated," she says, taking off her jerkin. "If I can be of any help, just say."

"I am trying to get you breakfast. So far I've burned the porridge, half-cooked some potatoes, overheated the stove, and smashed an egg on the floor. On top of that there's no bread and milk left. Are you brave enough to test my cooking as it is? Or should I start again."

"I've brought you some milk and bread — I was informed you hadn't been to get any."

Then, laughing gently she says, "I'll try your porridge, but honestly, son, I'll finish the rest of the cooking."

She resets the thermal fluid controls.

"You'll have plenty of time to cook in the next few days. You can experiment then, if you don't rope somebody else in to cook for you."

She sits at the table. "My neighbour Rachel would be happy to oblige, so she can tell everyone how I abandoned my son in his hour of need. You've got enough to do besides. At least people round here are glad they don't have one of those Maers who strut around full of their own importance."

"Well, if you don't mind doing it, I won't say otherwise. You might be right about getting someone in, though I don't think I could put up with Rachel. I haven't fed the chickens, I've just thought."

He pours the porridge into two bowls and hands one to his Mam. She sips at the first spoonful, nods sagely, takes a knob of butter and stirs it into her porridge, then tastes again. Owen reaches for her bag and stands the bottle and loaf on the table. She pours a little milk into her bowl and again stirs, then eats at a steady pace, a slight smile on her lips. Owen eats quickly, facing her across the table. That smile could turn sweet or acid.

"Well?"

She signals him to wait. When she finishes, she licks her lips.

"Not bad for a first attempt. You might have used a bit less salt, there's always extra in the butter. But it was nice, especially the slight caramel flavour."

"Caramel flavour?"

"Burnt sugar, love — I'm teasing. Don't worry, you'll get it right by the time Bronwen gets back."

"She still hasn't let me know how long she'll be away."

"Oh, she hasn't?" She nods a few times.

"Owen, when she gets back be more thoughtful. Don't take her for granted ... And don't tell me you haven't been. You have been."

She moves to the stove. Taking the potatoes he had started cooking she puts them back to boil, and gets out a skillet to cook the bacon and eggs.

"She isn't going to be impressed by those credits you got for finding those lost goods, you know. It isn't material things Bronwen wants. She wants you to realise she has a mind of her own. If you can help her blossom as much as she wants, you'll do all right. Don't sit there like a ninny with your mouth open. I know exactly how much you got too. I know a lot about what goes on round here you thought was secret. I'm your Mam, and I care about you. Watch out for yourself with that Rhys Parry. You know I've never taken to him, charmer that he is. Too full of himself by half, and too nice with it. He'd sell the heart from a statue."

"How did you find out?"

She strains the potatoes and mashes them with an egg, butter and milk, puts the bacon on top and covers the pot while she cooks the remaining eggs.

"How do you think? I was out on a walk in the dark night. I overheard that Gabri fellow and someone else. They were talking about you and the amount of credits you were to be paid. They said some other things too, and if they are right I might just move into Alban."

"What things? What on earth would you want to do that for?"

"Rhys Parry is mixing with a rough lot. They aren't going to stop because they've paid you for the work. They'll soon be asking for favours, like they ask for favours in Denbigh. That base of theirs — never seen it, have you."

"No, I haven't, Mam. I've not been that far up the valley since it was built. And to be honest I'm not much interested."

"Yes, well. Maybe you should be. Those credits of yours — I'd give them away to the people who helped you. They'll only bring you trouble if you spend them. I've a feeling about this. It wouldn't surprise me to find out the dead man was mixed up with that Gabri somehow. Now, I've said my piece. Eat this food, and I can be off. You will be coming to see me over, won't you?"

"Of course, Mam. You don't think I'd send you out to that strange land without seeing you on your way, do you?"

They eat while talking of past times. Of Owen's childhood. Of the trips they had taken into the mountains. Of the tales his Dad told about the land over the Severn. Owen can feel the stirring of the deep swell of emotion that has lain damped all the years since his Dad's death.

He had seen the tree fall wrong and knock his Dad to the ground. He had been a kid, barely twelve years old. He had run screaming to help him, but it had been too late. There was no helping, only the sadness and unfinished tears. He had taken on the responsibilities of adulthood so seriously that his childhood had been lived as if an adult; an adult who did not understand. He had moved from mother to marriage, fathered kids, become Maer.

As Maer his ability to accept responsibility was an asset, and the responsibility for others allowed him to hide his hurt even deeper. He looks up at the sound of her voice.

"Come on love, don't go dewy-eyed on me. Be strong for me."

Exactly those words she had spoken as they watched his father buried. He has not seen his Mam cry since she knelt by his body out there in the woods. He had been strong for her then, he must be strong for her now. But he can't trust himself to speak, so he only nods.

It is mid-morning, and they let the horses walk slowly down to the Dyfrdwy, meeting no one. They turn onto the track Owen had taken the previous evening. He remains silent, though now feeling stronger. She allows him his silence, quietly singing to herself.

"Mam, what arrangements have you made for looking after the animals and garden?" he finally ventures.

"Whatever you need get from Ifar — the rest is his. He'll be doing the looking, so it's only right he gets something for it. You know I might be a few days?" She stops her cob.

"Listen now, I've told everyone who normally gets told, I'm going away for a few days towards Gwynedd. Don't forget, I don't want anyone knowing I'm in Alban."

"What if someone's seen us coming this way?"

"Tell them we were talking and went for a ride along this way, say I went round by the coast route. It's miles away, they'll never know. You know what they're like."

"You've got it all thought out, haven't you."

"Someone has to. Don't mind about me — no harm will come my way. I'm an old woman, and despite what you've been told to the contrary the lands and people of Alban are friendly enough. Ah, but there's another thing, don't tell Rhys Parry anything about me. Promise me now, not one word. Promise me."

"I've got my own doubts about those arrangements with Rhys, Mam. I promise." They ride on in silence. She points ahead.

"My boat's in a shed hidden amongst those trees." Owen lets himself laugh, the more to counterpoise the other emotions.

"What's so funny then?"

"I came for a walk down here last night. I couldn't settle. I walked exactly where we've come this morning, but stopped right here before going back. It's years since I came down this way."

At the shed they let their horses forage. She turns to Owen and gives his arm a hug, then smiles sadly at him.

"You missed too much of your childhood, Owen. I know how it is, love. I never told you how much I missed your Dad. I was feared you'd get too upset. I started coming down this way at night ... when you were asleep. I came to be by myself. I wanted to be with him. How I loved him. But you were there, needing me, and I couldn't show you how I felt. Couldn't let you let go, because I thought if you grew up quick enough you'd get over it. I'm sorry now, but it's too late."

"I understand Mam. I knew you loved him and wanted me to be brave, and I didn't want to let you down." He pulls her into a hug, adding, "You be careful. I don't want you doing any heroics."

"Don't be silly, man. It's not another world over there, it's as safe as here." The words are out, and they just look at one another.

She pats his arm.

"You know what I mean. If there is anything causes problems I'll be leaving enough good people in my wake that you'll get to know. You be careful now. I want someone smiling on me when I get back, and you are all I've got. Now, enough of this foolish talk. Let's get my boat out.

You're no oarsman, but it shouldn't be too difficult for you to bring the boat back."

"I'll try rowing you over if you want."

"No, I think I'll show you how it's done." She pushes the boat out on its trailer.

"Where did you get this from?" He is disappointed by its lack of adornment.

"Years ago I found it. Drifted down from who knows where. No one came asking after it, so I kept it."

She walks the boat down the sloping bank into the river, tying the painter to a tree. He hobbles his horse as she pushes the trailer back into the shed, and is about to lock the door. She tuts and hands him the key.

"Make sure you lock it up and take this key home with you. If you decide to use it while I'm away just be careful."

She calls her cob, gathers the reins and ties them loosely to a stern rope. Putting her panniers and saddle into the boat, she climbs in.

"Get in Owen. Get in. And sit there." He makes the boat wobble until he settles. The horse walks into the water as soon as the oar blades touch the surface, and starts swimming. Rowing steadily she guides the boat smoothly, heading for a slope amongst the trees.

"Come on, son, before we're through the best part of the day," she chides as she ties the painter to a small tree. Owen clambers along the boat, hanging onto each side to steady himself. Then he too scrambles onto the soil of Alban.

Leading the horse up the bank he waits for her. "Now you're sure you want to do this Mam?"

"As sure as I will ever be. Will you be alright with the boat? I usually pull it up this slope and between these bushes."

"Of course I will. As right as I was with the breakfast."

"I love you, son. You know that."

"I know Mam."

He hugs her to him in an uncharacteristic action.

"Take care."

"I will, Owen, I will." She feels the lurch of his emotion. "There, my Luvvie, don't go dewy-eyed on me."

He breaths deeply and shudders, then stands away from her. "Hahh! Silly."

She leaves him be and mounts her horse.

"Look after yourself Owen ap Gaharet. And after Bronwen and the kids. They'll be back soon, and when they are give them my love. You mind what I've said."

He walks across to her and pats her on the arm; she turns her horse, and trots off. He watches her go. She is a tiny figure when he suddenly yells after her.

"Maa-am! Maa-am!"

She doesn't look back.

"You haven't got a badge of authority," he says, sighing. "I didn't bring one with me."

Then, in the first moments he has been truly alone since his Dad died, he sinks to the ground; letting his sadness emerge before sobbing it back into its hiding place.

Book Two – Part 2

The Good Sounding Counsel

You are no ordinary person

June, 22nd – Riding into Alban

After leaving Owen, Gwyneth rides north for two hours then stops to ease her body. She had not turned round to see him attempting to stop her, and would be unconcerned about the lack of a badge of authority. She is quite capable of creating her own authority.

The day is dry and sunny, though to the north clouds top the distant hills. The troopers in the local Boundary Patrol observation post watch her head northwards and promptly turn to other things, for they are used to her travelling through. It is late when she enters Tarporley. She gets a welcoming reception from people she counts as friends, who give her good company, food and drink, and a bed for the night. They cannot otherwise help her quest, but make enquiries of the nearest Procufisk, in Northwich, who agrees to see her the next morning.

June, 23rd – Northwich, Alban

Having listened to Gwyneth's story the Procufisk seeks advice as to how she should deal with this matter, there being nothing in the rules about such reports being necessary. It is late in the day when she gets a response; telling her it is best that Gwyneth be sent to The Keep in Derwent, because the matter is of interest there. Gwyneth and her cob are lodged overnight on a nearby farm.

The Procufisk makes sure she is adequately prepared for the journey north, with a route map clearly marked. She is prevailed upon to take the morning horse train, which stops at most stations, but will allow her to reach The Keep within the day.

June, 24th — Getting to The Keep

Travelling on such a train is a novel experience, and her horse takes some persuading to enter the horse carriage, but she is glad she listened to the advice. Gwyneth leaves the train at Oxenholme and rides to a livery-hotel in the valley to the northwest where she seeks confirmation of the route.

"There's only one way to follow," the man who takes her order assures her. "But so long as you don't mind company, you're in luck. Our lad has a job in the township at Derwent, and he's going back there shortly. If you're quick with your meal he'll not mind waiting for you. I'll hurry your food up and slow him down."

He disappears into the back of the building. A few minutes later he introduces her to a man in his mid-twenties. Brown hair frames a narrow face with brown eyes and an embarrassed smile.

"This is our James. You don't mind, do you lad?"

"If you'd rather not wait, just say so. I prefer plain speaking to false politeness."

"I'll wait for you, no worries. But I usually keep a good pace."

"My horse has come a long way, but had a rest on that train. I think she'll last the pace out. My name's Gwyneth." He continues to smile at her for a few moments, then turns away.

"He's a bit shy, is our James, but he knows the fells."

When her food arrives she eats it quickly. Getting her horse back fed and watered, she waves to the waiting James and swings up into the saddle. Together they clatter out of the yard.

"Mind you don't go daft," his father shouts from the front door.

They leave the small settlement riding in silence, on a wide bridleway alongside the metalled road, until a huge stretch of water comes into view.

"Mind if we put on a bit more speed? We've still four and a bit hours to go and I like to make good time down here along the mere."

Gwyneth shakes her head, and he pulls in front.

"We'll start climbing over the pass soon, we won't keep this up for long," James shouts back to her.

126

Soon enough they slow down as the track swings first south then round a huge stump of rock hard up against a small lake, to head north once more through fertile flatlands dotted with a few houses. They pass through a village and enter a steep-sided narrow valley.

"I don't like this bit much," James says, the horses now walking. "It's better once we reach the top of the pass."

As they crest the pass the valley before them seems almost filled by another lake.

"There's a dam at the other end. They use the water for drinking and to make electricity."

"There seems to be no shortage of it up here, James. Everything seems to be electric. D'you know how often those trains run?"

"I haven't ever used one. Other than Oxenholme the nearest stations are away to the east or west of here. We don't have much use for them. And ... um ... I prefer to be called Jamie."

"Glad you said. Jamie it is."

They follow a road along the eastern edge of the lake. The sun is behind the mountains, though the air is still warm and the gathering clouds still patchy. At the northern end of the valley the road snakes higher up before splitting. They take the western branch which swoops down across the river formed by the outfall from the dam, crossing a slender bridge before climbing up the hillside west, where they leave the road for a bridleway. They ride out of the shadows into the glorious colours of sunset, crossing a small plateau near a stone circle.

"I don't like this place at noon," he says gloomily. "Let alone at this time of the day."

Gwyneth is not affected by whatever causes his unease. Instead she feels a tranquillity she would like to dwell in.

"The Keep is down there, on the other side of Derwentwater. I'll deliver you to the door. It'll be easier."

"I hope I get time to recover before they throw me out again."

"They won't throw you out."

"It was meant lightly, Jamie."

"Oh, sorry."

Jamie leads her down through the edge of Keswick, across the valley floor and over the suspension bridge. He takes her along the lakeside wall of The Keep and leaves her with a groom at the stable entrance.

"Thank you very much for your company, Jamie."

"You're welcome, Gwyneth."

With her horse settled, and her letter from the Procufisk presented, the groom heads to the cannion shaft and calls control. Sounds come down to them from above.

"It'll only be a moment. The cannion will take you to the guest levels. You'll need to sit down, it moves fast."

Gwyneth does not know what the young woman is on about, but knows the answers will come. She is glad to leave the saddle, feeling the rigours of her journey. Next day will be hell.

"Do you know who expects me?"

"No, Ma'am. Someone will meet you up there."

"Thank you, Luvvie."

The trip in the cannion is fast and when it stops Gwyneth is feeling less than brave. She steps into the corridor, where a young woman greets her.

"Hello, Gwyneth. My name is Sarah. This room, B6, has been assigned to you. You must be tired and in need of freshening. The washroom is through that door. Place your riding clothes in the laundry bag and leave it in the corridor — I'll get it cleaned for you. There are some refreshments on the table. Black tea is fresh made in the flask and milk is in the frige. Do you want anything else?"

"My dear, this is fine. I've been travelling for three days, more than my old frame is used to. Can you tell me why I am here? Well, I know why I am here. Can you tell me who wants me here?"

"The Reever is interested in hearing your story himself. I'll come back in two hours to take you up to dinner."

Refreshed, she opens the window wide, takes in the complete vista and sits with her feet up on the window seat. Behind her the view is across tree-tops to bare fells. She faces Derwentwater and the eastern fells and can see the outlying houses of Keswick. She drinks some tea, and has a couple of biscuits. The peace of the room beckons her to snooze. She is soon snuffling, her body letting go of the jogging motion of her riding.

Gwyneth is escorted to the Butlery tables by Sarah, and introduced on first name terms to Briged and Faerachar. When offered a drink she asks to taste the same white wine that Briged is drinking, but screws her face, then notices a jug of green slightly cloudy liquid on the trolley.

"Is that nettle beer?"

"Yes, Gwyneth. Would you like to try it?"

"Please, Faerachar. This wine is a bit too sharp for me."

"Do you drink wine at home?"

"Never had it, Briged. Fizzy low alcohol drinks I make from the hedgerows, that's my lot."

"Well, your good health, Gwyneth."

"Iechyd da, Briged."

"I hope you have been well looked after on your journey north."

"Indeed, by welcoming natives — my friends, and young Jamie."

"Yes, cheers, Gwyneth. I have been told you had good company on the way here. Thank you for agreeing to come here at my request. I am the Reever of Alban, and the cause of you being this far north. I hope you are not incommoded by this."

"My accent should tell you our languages are not the same, Faerachar. So some other word than incommoded, please."

"Ah! Yes, Gwyneth, sorry. I had never thought about your language until I saw the declaration and questions you brought. Written first in Cymraeg — if I have that right — then the common tongue. What I meant is — I hope it is not too troubling for you."

"No, it is not. And you have a close enough sound to the word for our language. Well, as I told the first official I met, I have time to spare.

129

I am of an age when I can do things for my own pleasure. My son, Owen is Maer of the Cantref of Wrecsam in Cymru, and I have travelled on a legal purpose for him."

"The purpose is understood. But you intrigue me. Why did he have you come into Alban across the Poison Lands on a horse."

"My choice. I've been coming into Alban that way for years. I need to call him, to let him know what is happening, but can't."

"Ah! again. I will get someone to sort that out." He goes inside.

"When did you start coming into Alban, Gwyneth?"

"Well, Briged, let me see ..."

Faerachar reappears. "Gwyneth, this young man will get your phone working."

After telling Owen she is okay and will call him next day with her plans, the conversation turns to the reason for her being there.

"I am sorry we cannot help identify the man found in the river near Wrecsam. We are also not aware of any reciprocal agreement with the Fastness of Cymru in such cases, but it has been flagged up to our legal authorities to suggest something similar be put in place here."

"Moving away from what Faerachar has said, Gwyneth, what we would like to do, is use this opportunity to gain an up to date idea of how things roll along in Cymru. Knowing our neighbours is not a bad thing, and we need to improve the situation. There is already local cross-border activity, along the north coast, but the Poison Lands have necessarily impeded it in the area round Wrecsam. We have tended to adopt the word Cymric to denote anything coming from there — person or other — I hope that is not an offensive thing to you."

"No, Briged. We use various words other than Alban when referring to here, and some of them would, I hope anyway, make you laugh."

"I do know, Gwyneth, from speaking to the Border Patrol base northeast of Wrecsam that you cross over at least three times a year, and spend two or three days in a couple of small towns north of the empty lands. You've made friends amongst us. That's good."

"So, Faerachar, I'm watched. Briged, I started coming over soon after my son left home to get married. I needed space of my own. I was questioned by the armed guards for about ten minutes that first time in 2167. They were casual enough, and decided I was an adventurer they could trust. Now I just wave and say '*Bore da*' — time has mellowed things."

"So your son is similar to this one in age. Sons can be a boon and sometimes a nightmare. I hope yours is not so trying as are mine."

Briged flicks a dismissive glance at Faerachar.

"I hope I am more boon than bother, Briged."

A gong sounds. Faerachar leads them through the Butlery, down a spiral stair, into a small dining room. The fabrics are the same as those of the Reever's office, and accommodation suites. A large oil painting of Derwentwater, with picnickers on the lawns alongside a boathouse dominates the room. The women's clothes suggest it was painted in the Edwardian era of the early twentieth century.

In front of the large window with views across the water, the table is set with white damask and plates with yellow borders trimmed with gold. The lighting is mellow to suit sunset.

"The menu takes a bit of a liberty, Gwyneth; some of our local fare, that are our versions of yours. I hope you enjoy it nonetheless."

"My taste is broad, Faerachar, and my appetite yearning."

Gwyneth has a weak beer, while the others have the white wine. They are served a dome of Laver mousse on a maize cake alongside a round toasted slice of spelt bread topped with *Caws Pobi*.

"It's unusual to have them served on the same plate. But they look beautiful. I'll go for the Laver first, it's the more delicate of the two."

They follow her lead. Faerachar tells her they were often fed Rarebit as a meal when they were younger.

"And Porphyra seaweed has always been harvested from certain parts of the coast, by those in the know."

"Ahh. This is how I would cook the laver. Strong bacon flavour — I like it." She is equally pleased with the *Caws Pobi*.

"Every one makes that slightly different. There's no single recipe."

The conversation flows easily between her and Briged. Faerachar becomes a witness to their exchanges, with no part to play except as a foil when Briged expands on her earlier comment on sons.

The main course is slow-cooked mutton with seasonal root vegetables, creamy mash, podded peas and pea shoots. Gwyneth is persuaded to try a red wine to accompany it.

"Alban Fastness Estates Dornfelder 2181. It is a very smooth wine, Gwyneth, not a bit like the white. Just smell it before you taste it. The production of this came about through a collaboration between my other son and the person who has cooked this food for us."

"I'll bring Regin out when we finish this dish. But only if the wine greets your palate well." Faerachar pours a small amount into her glass.

She tries the wine, nods, holds out her glass for more, and they set about the food. There is no conversation, just little noises of appreciation.

"That mutton was superbly tender. And that wine went very nicely with it. So satisfying. Introduce the genius, Faerachar."

Regin bows to the praise from Gwyneth, and when asked for a suitable dessert he recommends a sticky rice halwa with flame raisins, saffron, and coconut water, saying it isn't overly sweet.

Faerachar excuses himself, leaving the two women talking about family life. Soon after, Briged proposes a nightcap of Spanish chocolate.

"It's rich and creamy, with rum — Regin makes it so nicely. It'll be fine to last us for the rest of the evening. The night is warm enough, so we can drink it out on the terrace under the stars."

"You can now be on a holiday, Gwyneth. When was the last time you spent a deal of time away from Cymru?"

"I've only been out of Cymru into Alban to the area around Tarporley and Cuddington — never anywhere else. Gaharet worked in Telford in Mercia for many years, when Owen was small. But I never visited him there. There was a special bus from Wrecsam. He went on a Monday morning very early, and back late every Friday evening."

"You have not mentioned him in all you have told me of your son."

"Maybe tomorrow, in daylight. But not as I am about to go to bed."

Regin arrives, setting out a small jug of warmed rum, four amaretti, and two glass mugs filled with hot creamy dark chocolate.

"As you are staying here tonight, Briged, what time do you want breakfast?"

"Regin, serve it in my apartment, at six-thirty, please. If you bring me the menu I shall order what I want now."

As he walks away, Briged smiles at Gwyneth.

"A sudden thought occurs; I am due to go on a short tour of four cities in Scotia. I would like to have you come with me, Gwyneth. It will make a change to have a companion, and it will allow me to show you how this Fastness lives. Would you like to join me? At our cost, of course. I plan to leave tomorrow on the half-seven shuttle."

"I would love to come on such a trip. I trust my horse will be in good hands here. But I only have the everyday clothes I wear at the moment. I would not like to feel too much out of sorts."

"I shall be wearing my usual trouser suits for my work hours. In Glasgow, we shall see you well-kitted out, I use a hire place that will dress us to be noticed, Grandmothers though we be."

"A dressing-up party. I'll go with that, Briged."

June, 25th — The Keep

Eating breakfast in Briged's apartment on the upper level of The Keep, Gwyneth notices an earth mother on a shelf by the doors to the small south-facing terrace.

"Where do those little women come from, Briged? I have seen only two others in my life, they look the same."

"They are made here in Keswick, using the same material as the mother-stone at Rigg. The glass–topped boxes are just a neat way of keeping them pristine. I made sure one went with the trade goods being returned to Wrecsam in the days before you set out on your errand."

133

"Why did you do that?"

"I had a strong feeling there was someone who would benefit from getting one. When you appeared I thought it was you, but you haven't mentioned it in that way. I wonder where it went?"

"It ended up with my joined-daughter, Bronwen. Owen's wife, the mother of my four grandsons."

"Joined-daughter — that is a lovely phrase. Where did you see the other one?"

"At the official's house in Northwich."

"The Procufisk's house. The significance of the earth mothers must not be downplayed, Gwyneth. They are an ancient symbol of the potency of women. Whatever the secret of the stone itself, I only know it can help channel a force for good. Women are often more in tune with the feelings engendered than are men."

"Bronwen had it on a shelf in her kitchen with things the boys gave her — big snail shells, bird feathers and the like. I didn't get to ask her where it came from, for when we got news of the dead body, she took the four boys and went off to her parents. I noticed it was missing and asked Owen why she'd gone. He was evasive. I told him when she comes back to treat her with more respect for who she wants to be. Not just a provider of household comforts."

Briged gets an earth-mother from her bedroom. Sliding it out of its box, she passes it into Gwyneth's cupped hands.

"Cosset it. It is the essence of all we women are. It is the adamantine hardness woman needs, to endure and triumph in the face of the vagaries of man. It emphasises — without any allurement — those parts man concentrates on as objects of his desire to take to himself and own. And by its nature it gives us the strengths we need to overcome the wiles used as they seek to bind us."

Gwyneth feels the lightest of tingles through her arms.

"Bronwen is sifting her thoughts on her place in the world. I hope — I think Owen is capable of absorbing the changes."

"This is the force of the earth telling us women to awake, Gwyneth.

To bear our role not just with fortitude; to look within our own kind for the depth of love and strength we need to live well alongside, but without submission to, the other half of the human species. This force does not require our submission to itself, our devotion, or our adoration. It simply is there in the earth itself, in the magnetism flowing through the stones. It murmurs '*Be who you are*' and if you take that call to heart you will be allowing yourself to flower. To face man eye to eye, and show him — I am mine, no one can own me but myself."

They are driven to the mono-link station near the Keep and take the scheduled service to Haven.

"We shall take a train from Haven to Carlisle and from there to Glasgow. The route is scenic, and we can talk easily as we watch the countryside pass by. I want to know about Cymru."

June, 25th — Conversations on the journey into Scotia

Between Haven and Carlisle their conversation carries on from breakfast.

"Men have to realise for themselves their very strength is their greatest weakness, and their entitlement is their downfall. It is a continual struggle to get them to see for themselves. No condescension, no entitlement, no coercion, no fear. In this Fastness, if we are lucky, we might be on the third step of the stairway and this has been on the go here for over sixty years. And I don't know how many steps in the stair. I am following the lead of others. Only by being true to our own spirit can women give up the part we play in our own enslavement to man's ego. And we have to start with our sons, Gwyneth."

They are alone in the buffet carriage as they cross into Scotia, so Briged again asks about Gwyneth's husband.

"Owen was twelve years old at the time Gaharet died. They were thinning stands of timber. The tree smashed his body all but in two. He watched helpless as the life went out of his Dad. And that was his last picture of him. He couldn't drive the truck, so ran home over seven kimetres. Sobbing into my arms, blathering out this tale of death. To try and calm him, I told him to be strong and not be dewy-eyed. Dewy-eyed! It was a torrent. And though in shock, I couldn't let my inner scream join his convulsing body as he shuddered out his grief.

"I rode him back to those woods with a picture in my head of what I would find. With him hanging onto me, still sobbing. We had to wait for the men coming from town to lift the bloody tree off him. And look ... I had to look at what my son had seen and would never lose from his mind. His beautiful strong face contorted in his dying. I knelt down and caressed his chilled face, all gone to death. And the keening inside I wouldn't let out in front of Owen.

"I used to go out into the night once he was asleep. Wet, especially wet, snowy, sweltering or fogbound. Go down near the river, to cry my heart to fatigue and scream at the moon."

She stops talking, the tears coursing. Briged hands her a big linen handkerchief, which Gwyneth holds to her face, and in the sobbing, flashes of a smile break the grimaces; the mixture of grief and better memories that rips through one's soul. She stands up, and Briged with her. The embrace is long, Gwyneth letting herself out of Briged's arms.

"Thank, you Briged I needed that very much."

She faces the scenery, and Briged leaves her be. The train enters the winding valley through the hills, as Gwyneth carries on her tale.

"I had loved him so and I still miss him. He was a gentle man. He treated me with respect. He was a man as you describe, who let go his entitlement. But in our son I fear I locked that in by my oft repeated, 'Come on love don't go dewy-eyed on me. Be strong for me'. How many times I said it that awful day, I don't know. I said it at the funeral. And I said it — oh, how stupid — only the other day before I crossed into Alban. He was emotional when we were talking about his Dad, something we had never really done. I could see in his eyes he was building up to let go. And I said it. That damned phrase."

She shakes her head. "*Iesu Mawr!* Aahch!"

"When I rode away I didn't dare look back in case he was gone to pieces. I made him bury his grief, not let it go. It's not too late — d'you think — for him to let it go. Oh, Briged. What messes we make of them, by letting them cleave to men's view of how they should be, gleaned from the men they see around them ... And now I'm bawling again."

Briged reaches across, but she holds up her hands, the tears stopping.

"Let me be for a while, Briged. I'll be fine. I haven't told anyone that in thirty-odd years."

"I'll get us some tea, Gwyneth."

With a pot of tea to consume, Briged tells her story of striving for an equitable society, and of her children.

"My first consort was Faerachar's father, Alastair. For some years I had been telling my friends and anyone else who would listen, man must voluntarily give up the entitlement taken for granted, which sets woman into a diminished status in society.

"At the time he was pushing a new concept into the discussions about reforming politics. He said what the body politic of the people must focus on is the broad commonality existing in humans. Then the differences instead of becoming barriers to reaching a consensus, are whittled away. The idea of giving up an entitlement — the outright win — so that a compromise could be reached, entered the politics of this Fastness. The change in attitude towards social justice within the Fastness that this made was quite dramatic. When first I put to him the parallels with my ideas he would not see my point. He thought man was done.

"Faerachar was born in First House. He was seven when his father and I decided to separate. Our discussions had descended into battles. I was emotionally drained and had all but stopped talking to him by then. After I left, he came fully to endorse the notion that man must give up the arrogance of entitlement so that woman could be truly freed into an equality which brings the differing halves together in mutual respect.

"Had we been still together he might not have become so fired up in espousing the necessary changes. His pain from our separation made him go over every argument I had put to him. He listened to his own voice, when he had stubbornly not listened to mine.

"Over his twenty year span as Reever he consolidated the concept. Commonality is now our political creed — but like all things human — there are dissensions within some parts of the populace to this notion. So it needs nurturing still, probably forever. Because lessons have to be taught anew to each new baby who comes along. Applied to young minds that are finding their ways in this fragile world through learned behaviours, the ideas have generally become accepted as normal.

"Kaet's father, Iain, was my second consort. He was much older than me. He had come to The Keep on some errand of which I knew nothing. We met over a meal, where he expostulated ideas on how to reach a deeper equality between woman and man to Alastair. I fell in love with him for his ethos, his humanity, and his ideas of how this Fastness could grow in a different and balanced way, to a better future for all humans."

"I moved to Edinburgh with him and Faerachar, and Kaet was born there. I never did find out what in Iain's past brought him to urge the adoption of these simple yet powerful, and ultimately, difficult to enact, ideas I was trying to promote. But difficulties or not, these fathers acted in concert with me and my band of determined women and drove these ideas forward."

"More tea?" Briged orders another pot.

"Faerachar showed, right from the start his sister was important to him and her equality too. He had absorbed my ideas while his father and I argued so vehemently about man's disregard of woman. As he grew towards a teenager, he would pull me up when he thought I was not equal enough in my treatment of Kaet compared to him.

"Iain died from a brain bleed when Kaet was almost three. Suddenly I was left alone with the two of them. My grieving was in plain sight. I just let go, no thought in my head to hide it or expose it. Let go my proper care for the two of them. Oh, not completely. But after a few weeks Faerachar got in touch with his father who came and would have bundled us back here to First House. Although he needed the help, Faerachar didn't want to leave Edinburgh and was very forceful about it. It was the shock I needed to concentrate on the children and move on.

"When she was nearly four I was out with Kaet going down Cable Wynd towards the port. It was a bright sunny day, which at that time of year was rare. She started repeating 'This blond, this blond'. I was fully blonde at the time, but she wasn't looking at me. There was a beautiful blond man, younger than me, coming towards us. He could clearly hear her, for he looked around. Nobody else was in sight.

"We spoke to each other across the road. He said 'I must be this Blond' and asked my name. As I tell you this, I can still feel the thrill that went through me. Axel was in my life for ten days. I never saw him again. We gave each other nothing more than the time we had together. It was sexual attraction and diversion in all the best glory of it.

"My power of sight has never been strong. As the door closed behind him — Kaet said 'Gone!' with all the finality the word can be given. When Faerachar came home I told him Axel had left. He said 'Kaet told me this morning I'll have a brother'. At that moment I knew she was gifted and burdened. I cried far more for her than I did for me at Axel's going. I remember looking at him horrified. He has told me that at the time, he feared from the shock visible on my face, I had been hurt beyond repair by his saying it.

"Faerachar asked to be with his father more, so we moved back. All his spare time outside his education Faerachar spent with his father. Imbibing the role of Reever without consciously being aware of it. He got used to helping out, as Alastair worked a lot from First House — taking over those tasks Alastair was least good at discharging. Faerachar got elected because he showed such understanding of the role of Reever. Some will always believe it came about through being our son. It did not. He has been re-elected once already. He made strong bonds with the officials aiding his father. The Steward and the Castellan are still with him from that time."

The train has reached the southern outskirts of Glasgow.

"Our journey is nearly over, Gwyneth. And so is my story. Duncn was born in a tent inside the shell of Second House. It was apparent at an early age that he would seek his happiness with other men — and my task was helped by his love for Kaet, and for Faerachar, who acted like a father to him. Between them they made sure that his trait, looking inward to the epitome of maleness with his kind as it does, did not isolate him from understanding that all men, whatever their interactions with women, have to take the same steps as those who are drawn only to women by their sexual chemistry."

"I have no personal experience like you, Briged, to know how it is exactly with the men of Duncn's nature. I am acquainted with joined-women, having no men in their lives. For some the fathers of their children are like him in their own loves.

"Gwyneth, I know that my son is isolated at times. I have tried to get him to open up to me about it, but he doesn't really. I know platitudes when they are fed to me, Duncn is a dutiful son and good with them."

June, 25th to 29th — Stirling, Perth, Dundee and Inverness

Gwyneth being suitably kitted out for the next four days they set off by train for Stirling. Briged explains she has no formal structure to her visits. Sometimes it is simply meeting with the workers in the different organisations and having conversations during their breaks, giving them access to the very top of the administration. Very occasionally something momentous comes to light which means she has to spend longer sorting through the ramifications.

"My intention is to show you the places I visit for my work, only as a passing moment, Gwyneth; for you to sense the way we work. In each of the four cities we are visiting I have good friends — who I'm sure you will find easy company — and one or more of them will be taking you away to see the various sights each place has to offer. We'll meet up in the evenings, when you can tell us about your life in Cymru. This cannot be a one-way street."

"That sounds a good plan to me, Briged. I'm inquisitive and amiable by nature. As you realise I can tell a tale or two. The beauties of my land will shine in the telling."

And so, as they go from Stirling, to Perth, to Dundee and Inverness Gwyneth meets the good friends. She tells of the historic towns and castles along the north coast and amongst the mountains; recounts the myths of the land of her birth. And in between talks of present day life in Cymru. It is at heart a good place in which to live, she emphasises, but women and men do not interact as here in Alban. It feels to her more traditional.

"And seeing how things are here, I am determined, when I return home, to chivvy the women I know into calling the changes. I'll need more earth mothers, Briged."

❖

June, 30th — The Keep — The Plum Orchard

They arrive back from Inverness by powered glider, a flight that both thrills and terrifies Gwyneth.

They are heading for a seat looking out over the water, in the shade of the acacia trees surrounding the Plum Orchard. Briged stops under a small tree.

"Victoria plums. Let me find you one to eat, Gwyneth."

Facing the water they enjoy the juicy sweetness, in a comfortable silence. Licking her lips, Gwyneth throws the stone into the long grass between the acacia trees.

"It will grow or not. I have one more question, Briged. Your role in this Fastness? You were treated with deference everywhere you took me. You seem not to have a position of power, yet you have this apartment in The Keep. You are no ordinary person."

Briged laughs. "My official title is The Good Sounding Counsel. It is pompous, and not of my choosing, but it is descriptive of my role here. I am considered the fount of ethical knowledge, which is foolish. So I do not allude to it very often. I do not want any officials to be too formal with me. I want my feet firmly on the ground. I want to trust in the earth force to guide me, not the accolades of other humans. It is considered a high office. Does that answer your question?"

"Yes, it does. You are such an inspiration. I feel emboldened by your example, enough to start ruffling feathers when I get home. I am so happy to have met you, Briged, and would like our friendship to thrive."

Book Three

Grandy Emembet and the Bagad
He might well have hidden talents

June, 23rd — Genève, Confederation Helvetica

Ardel's untimely communications are worrying Grandy. After the communiqué he sent from London, only the daily message as he passed through Newark had been at a scheduled hour. And where is yesterday's message? She knows his HiSec satcom is working, for it auto-pings, though she has been unable to get a response from his phone. She has a planned itinerary for him, sent from the Alban Consular Agent in London. He should have been in The Keep by midday on the twenty-first, yet the message for that afternoon had been sent late in the evening. It informed her that his reception had been unusual for an Ambassador, but gave no further details. She falls asleep considering sending a Runner to check up on him — an automatic fail of his Solo. The message from him in the early hours does not wake her.

She listens twice to his message — then a third time. She can hear the tiredness in his voice and he chooses the words with great care. But he has jumped in heavily with his judgement, and the tail-end point is very unsettling.

"Play."

"This is Noviate Ambassador Penaul, I append my code." There is a momentary silence as the machine verifies Ardel's code.

"Authenticated," the machine says and Ardel starts talking.

"I send you my felic ..."

"Skip!" Grandy feels one set of felicitations from Ardel is enough for the day — three unthinkable.

"I have weighed the evidence placed before me and listed later in this report, and find no breaches of the Rules have taken place in Public Hearing in the Parliament of the United Counties of England in London. In essence there are no grounds for the Complaint of Digression to have been sent ..." And so it goes on for eight minutes. Grandy finds herself wandering from the words to the tone of his voice, until it draws her back with his conclusion of the diplarg.

"... Thus I have issued a Notification of Censure on the Reever of Alban. But my investigations have brought to light evidence that requires careful consideration of other actions. With this in mind I request your ... *disinterested guidance* ... through these matters. It seems to me from the evidence to hand the original case can be answered fully only when all information is correctly analysed. I end, your Noviate Ambassador Penaul, and append my code." The machine verifies it.

Grandy stares across her office. A Notification of Censure is heavy diplomacy – he must be sure – and his message should therefore have warranted a more urgent classification. Yet he chooses not to do so. The last paragraph is not standard format, and mentions extra evidence. The most worrying phrase is '*disinterested guidance*'. The phrase is part of a dialogue for use in situations where the League itself might be in danger. It signals a need for stealth, and should mean the issue going straight to the Security Branch for action; in such circumstances the phrase would be part of an elaborate grammatical exercise in question and answer. Ardel has deliberately used it separately and has emphasised the words.

She will scan his voice for stress patterns. This was supposed to have been a standard and simple diplarg on which any young Ambassador could be tested to prove suitability for promotion. What on earth could this new evidence be? A Runner cannot solve this quandary. There are two possibilities. One is to summon Ardel back to explain to her in person. The other is to go to Alban herself. What is Ardel doing up there? Possibly he is distracted by some man, she thinks irreverently. If so, there's one person who will know.

June, 23rd — Genève — Dahqin

After the stupendous reception for our final show, I don't stay long celebrating with my troupe. I head home, wanting Ardel there, or coming in later — a hopeless desire. I've not heard from him in five days. Dowsing my hope when I notice the message on the phone, it's still disappointing to hear Grandy's voice. It's too late to call her now.

I wake very late in need of carbs. I take a tub of pasta salad — my go-to intake — from the frige and leave it to warm up while I phone.

"Grandy. Got your message."

"How is your show doing?"

"Fine, Grandy. Last night was the best reaction I've had for this run. I should have told you and Kazzia, but it was a trial run, and it was the last night."

"She would've liked that. Never mind."

"It's on again in the autumn. I'll get you gratixs for that."

"Thank you, Dahqin. I'm sorry I haven't called you since Ardel's been away. How are you doing without him?"

"You know how I rattle on whenever I start talking, well now it's just to myself. Thankfully the show has kept me going up till now. I did have a long talk with him on his last night in London. I hope phones are secure; Ardel seems to think they aren't that perfect. And he spoke to me from somewhere in Mercia when he passed through there. Since then — nothing. That's why you've phoned me, isn't it? Something has happened to Ardel, hasn't it?"

"Nothing nasty has happened to Ardel. But I'm wondering how things are between you. I know how you two are generally — you're a pair of flirts who tease each other."

"Oh, sure we mess around, but it's nothing serious. He was alright when last he spoke to me. Why?"

"I am hoping you can enlighten me about Ardel's frame of mind when you did speak. All part of my role as his Patron."

"He sounded a bit concerned, but he always worries about me before the first show in a run. I recorded some of the call from London. Maybe you'll pick up on something I've missed. Why don't you come round? It'll be great to see you."

"I shall. I'll be about forty minutes, Dahqin."

That was not our usual light chatter. I start rubbing my chin — won't shave until tomorrow. I know she cares for both of us beyond her role as his Patron, but even so. I eat, trying not to think of whatever situation Ardel is in. My imagination is too volatile. I'll have to get used to this sort of thing if Ardel becomes the full Ambassador he craves.

My wistful sigh empties my lungs — blowing out all my aspirations to travel to the wild places Ardel will get used to visiting. We've been consorts for over four years now, and while we've been to other places in the core of Europa, he's not joined me on a trip to Brittany.

I take the food into the living room and turn on the multi-viewer, watching the topog of Derwentwater glow into focus. Only a few minutes of it and I'm getting maudlin, so switch to a travolog about one of the Southern Zone desert regions. A line of camels with indigo clad riders descends across the slope of a large dune; the wind the only sound. I zoom in until a close up of one face hangs in the air, level with my face. Only the eyes are visible in the flash of face left uncovered by the deep blue cloth. Dark and unreadable, they stare at me, then Grandy announces her arrival.

"Glad to see you, Grandy. Do you want something to drink?"

"I'll have sherbet water — please." I take her cloak, indicate the hologram. She stands by it, studying the face.

"Aren't the eyes gorgeous, Grandy. I sometimes feel I can climb in and be with them."

"Dahqin, you're too romantic for the Cantons. No wonder Ardel chose you to live with him. There's never any chance of him getting bored with you around." I hand Grandy her drink and we sip in silence for a while, then Grandy looks directly at me.

"You know that what we are to talk of must remain between just the two of us."

I nod vigorously.

"I was taken aback by the last report Ardel sent from Alban. It should have told me how the diplarg was progressing, and what date he expected to be back in Genève."

I stop the travolog, switching back to the topog of The Keep.

"How can you get things through to him when they don't seem to have phones?"

"The League doesn't rely on them. We have our own more secure system of communicating."

"That's left me feeling depressed. His Patron can get in touch with him when I can't. Can Ambassadors send personal messages that way?"

"Not possible. Except in very dire circumstances. Great thought has gone into choosing patrons and Ambassadors who are correctly matched. It is no accident I am Ardel's patron. The accident is I like you — importantly, I trust your discretion. Hence this conversation."

She sips at her sherbet water, watching me. I hold my tongue.

"What did you discuss about this diplarg?"

"Nothing. He told me he was glad he could do the briefing at home. To be honest, I only wanted to see the topog and what The Keep looks like — though I did sneak a peek at the photos of four people. I'm not interested by the diplomatic information. I fell asleep when he went through that. But there's very little detail about how the place runs, or what its society is like, is there."

"It goes back to the beginning of the Confederation. Not all of the Fastnesses sent back data, and no one followed up on Alban. Let's see that faxplex."

"Grandy, you'll probably only get useful ideas out of the first few minutes. Um ... there's not much conversation towards the end."

"Dear child ... I do believe you're blushing. Don't think any of your depravities can shock me, I'm quite capable of listening to the raw sexual indulgences of men without the least embarrassment, especially such young ones."

She is enjoying this moment — and she's not finished. She would never try to embarrass me in a public space, but she's making the most of this private one.

"You men are such juveniles where sex is concerned. In the last two hundred years you've learned no more than in the previous three thousand. That is why there are so many woman at the top in the League, and in many of the Civitas, I might add. You should do a bit of research. It'll knock out your complacent idea of the world revolving around the stage from which you happen to be thrusting your loins at the audience. You little minx."

"Grandy, is that how I come across?"

"Of course, my darling. Maybe I overstate it slightly, but it's why you're such a big hit. Women and men adore you, but then — your form is made to be adored — especially with a backside like yours."

I escape to get the faxplex, cursing myself for making this offer.

"I thought you'd glory in such praise from an older woman."

"I'm trying to."

Thankfully the multi-viewer projects a flat-screen view of Ardel, fully clothed, relaxing on a big bed. We talk briefly about his Solo giving him the equivalent of my first night tensions, and supporting each other. For a couple of minutes Ardel talks about his day and his thoughts about the next leg of his journey into Alban. Then the call takes a turn as we become amorous. I stop the multi-viewer. Grandy is smiling wickedly.

"I really am astonished, Dahqin. You are marvellously inventive, but a little over-eager. Still, that last bit is very entertaining. Are you sure there is no useful conversation after this?"

She makes a move towards the multi-viewer — I pluck the faxplex off the top.

"Honestly, Grandy, there isn't anything."

"Goodness, you are an embarrassed young man."

The blush is making me sweat. I plead with her to keep this between just the two of us. She assures me she will, but tells me how stupid I am for keeping such recordings. I feel decidedly silly.

"What remains to be seen on that faxplex could be dangerous to you and especially Ardel. I advise very strongly that you destroy any such recordings and learn to rely on your own memory."

"I know you're right. I want some wine, Grandy. How about you?"

"Yes, it would be rather a pleasant change. You are an eye-opener Dahqin. And still hot under your tan — such a delicious shade."

"Grandy! Please! Can we talk about something else over the wine? Like, what are you going to do about Ardel?"

"Surely. I promise with all my heart." There's a smile twitching at the corners of her lips. Sighing, I take the faxplex back to its hiding place, and get the wine.

Grandy's eyes are closed when I return with the Chasselas. As I pour it into the glasses she opens them, watching my movements.

"I may have to travel to The Keep myself..." she murmurs.

"No chance of me tagging along, I suppose?"

"No!" She says it sharply, then pauses.

"My plans depend very much on a meeting tomorrow morning. Not such a simple assignment after all."

Looking at me directly now, she lifts the glass to her lips.

"Hope for a successful conclusion."

I nod, sniff at my drink and quietly say, "I hope he's alright."

"Of that I'm certain. No use being melodramatic with what we know. It is unthinkable that an Ambassador could be in physical danger."

Slowly she swirls the wine round the glass.

"Ardel is being so careful in his report..."

She sips the wine in silence — stops me refilling her glass.

"What's the problem, Grandy?"

"I must go home now, Dahqin. Thank you for your indulgence. It has been very helpful. Pay heed to what I said about those recordings. His report may not mean anything sinister."

She pats my arm, making me frown.

"Ardel didn't like it when I joked about the Reever snatching him into his horrible clutches. Do you think Alban is dangerous?"

"I have no reason to think that. I shall contact you tomorrow."

"When tomorrow."

"As soon as my meeting finishes. Walk me to the cab link."

Out in the cool night air waiting for a cab to arrive, she looks around to make sure we are alone.

"Dahqin, if you wanted to leave Genève without drawing attention to yourself, how would you do it?"

"I take the standard tgv services. Dress down, light luggage. Why?"

"I may need to travel incognito." She suddenly leans forward and kisses me on both cheeks.

"Sleep in peace."

"I'll try. But you have worried me."

"It is seven years since I last ventured into a Fastness. It is not a step I take lightly, Dahqin."

We touch palms as the cab comes to rest. She taps her persID on the driver panel, the door slides shut and the vehicle moves away into the darkness. Shivering from the chill of the early evening, I walk back to the apartment.

June, 23rd — Genève — Grandy at home

"I might have to go on a journey," Grandy tells Kazzia, as they relax after their supper.

"For long?"

"Maybe a week, maybe a whole period."

"No! When?"

"As soon as I can arrange things, two days at the latest."

"Not much notice. Is it anywhere exciting?"

"It's not what you would call exciting, I think. Into a Fastness."

"Oh. Not me at all. Ardel?"

"Something like that. I won't know for certain until tomorrow."

She sighs at Kazzia, who pouts back in sympathy. They have not spent much time apart in the last eight years; a period sounds very long. Grandy brushes her hand over Kazzia's arm.

June, 24th — Sion, Valais, Confederation Helvetica

Grandy starts early the next day for Sion, arriving in plenty of time to enter the refectory for breakfast. It is nearly a year since she was in the Praedicatum. Settling herself at a table against the wall farthest from the door Grandy can see all who enter. Some merely nod, others greet, and a few come over and ask how she is and, politely of course, why she is visiting. In Sion diplomacy is the essence these people breathe, eat, and bathe in. She gently turns aside all questions other than those regarding her wellbeing. Her smile is welcoming when Bartouche comes over — her breakfast on a tray.

"Let us eat together, Grandy."

"That pleases me."

"I am in sore need of counsel."

"Is this a matter beyond your writ?"

"It may well turn out to be so."

"Either it is or it is not beyond your writ."

"I wish to talk this over with a wiser head than mine."

"That is why I am here. What is the subject you left out of your message yesterday?"

"I dare not say — not here. I ask for private audience. You know me well enough to realise I do not lightly step outside the bounds of our regimentation."

"When we withdraw to my chamber, then. How is Kazzia?"

"She is fine."

"I truly believe you will always be together."

"I know you think that possible. Always and ever are concepts too big for me to contemplate in the affairs of my heart. We shall survive through moments in time."

They leave the refectory into tall hallways, peaceful and echoing. In the centre of a crossing a fountain trickles sounds into the air as its waters fall on tiny bells set amidst ferns. Her chamber is at the end of the southern hallway. They sit in armchairs facing the window with views across the river towards Dent Blanche.

"You have my undivided attention for as long as you need. Grandy, I have never known you so beset with uncertainty and guarded in our correspondence."

"You know Ardel Penaul, and are aware of his capabilities; his readiness for promotion. It is his Solo we must discuss."

"What is the problem your protégé faces?"

"The first leads to the second."

Bartouche slightly reclines her chair, and closes her eyes – giving Grandy the space in which to be candid.

"Regarding the diplarg – he has sent me his interim report of closure. The evidence sounds conclusive. But on the strength of it he has issued the head of government in Alban – the Reever – with a Notification of Censure. He is still a Noviate; it might be a precocious action, though he is capable, and the Reever has accepted it at face value. When I am satisfied he has it right, I will advise him to send it for confirmation by the Jurisprudence Court."

"And the second."

"He craves disinterested guidance on something he has seen."

"From the Formula of Defence. That is clearly a security matter. Why come to me with this?"

"Because of who you are what you represent."

"And other members of the Council?"

"I do not know the others as I know you."

"So you do not know who to trust. Does my position on the Inner Table sway your reason for trusting me, Grandy?"

"No, it is because of your years as my Patron I trust you – wrongly or rightly. The greater power of good help me if I misjudge this."

"Why not assume he has mangled the process. He's on his Solo. Why should you not forward this to the Security Office?"

"He singled out the phrase without its checks and balances, and stressed it in his reading. He is open about the Censure, but not this other thing."

"Tell me something of his work history and his home life."

Grandy quickly covers his recent work, and his domestic situation. She mentions Dahqin's career. It is the only time she hears anything from Bartouche.

"Ahhh ... Yes. That young man."

Grandy cites the comments about Ardel's suitability made by the Appointing Council.

"Would you say you like him?"

"Yes, Bartouche. Yes, I like him a lot."

Bartouche rises and crosses to the window — the mountains are still snow-capped.

"When I die I want my ashes out there on the grass." She comes back to her seat. "And his consort — Dahqin. How long have they been together now?"

"Almost five years. Both were quite young when they met."

"That's true."

"You know him?"

"Merely coincidental. Let us concentrate on this diplarg grown wild. Have you had the usual voice checks done?"

"Yes, all of those prescribed."

"You are very worried then. Have you been to see Dahqin?"

"Yes. I wanted to make sure there were no emotional tensions between them."

"I take it there were none or you would have ordered a recall. How much does Dahqin know?"

"Of the dilemma; nothing. Of the diplarg; no details. But he's been studying a topog of Alban. He likes to dream of adventures. I would say he knows more than Ardel about the lie of the land."

"You want him to go with you."

"I ... haven't asked either to go, or for that. It is not politic. It was something he mentioned."

"Grandy, Grandy. This is so unlike you. You are thinking of chasing after one young man and dragging his consort with you on supposition; maybe gut reaction."

"But it's ..."

Bartouche holds up both hands.

"We shall have some rose tea and almond biscuits and then we shall chase over this dilemma once more." She places an order for the refreshments.

"I know already what the cautious, sensible, course of action is, and so do you. It is a recall for consultations. Let us listen to his report."

Bartouche hears it through twice. They sit with tea and biscuits to hand. When Bartouche snaps a biscuit in half, Grandy is surprised by the noise.

"I understand your dilemma much better now, Grandy. He does sound confident of his position with the diplarg. But that disappears when he tries to make you aware of a danger he wishes not to draw attention to. I know enough of young Penaul — he has a good head at his disposal."

Bartouche orders lunch to be served in her chamber. As they eat she questions Grandy about lighter things; holidays taken with Kazzia, shows in which Dahqin has featured and is planning.

"I have very humorous memories of a younger Dahqin, the little devil. He called his band of friends The Bagad. Sometimes it is necessary to revisit old acquaintances. Let me know when that show is on in the autumn."

She chuckles quietly to herself. But when Grandy tries to elicit more information about their connection, Bartouche returns to the issue of getting to Alban.

"What exactly did he say, Grandy, that made you think of taking him along in the first place? Which most certainly is unorthodox."

"He asked if he could tag along. It is typical of his throw-away comments and I dismissed the notion. But when I asked him how one could leave the Cantons without drawing attention to oneself he didn't hesitate. Take the standard tgv, was his answer. Travelling up here I've thought more about it. He comes from Brittany so he's lived in a Fastness. And he knows how to make sure one is noticed, and how to keep a low profile."

"There may be something in what you say."

Grandy leaves the Praedicatum soon after lunch is finished. She calls Dahqin and asks to come directly to see him. On the journey back to Genève she mulls over what they have agreed. Ostensibly she is on a vacation, and can take with her whomever she wants. Her work in the League offices will be channelled through Bartouche's secretariat, as will her communications and expenses. The lodging of Ardel's Notification of Censure will be delayed. Because HiSec transmissions are logged by the Communication Section in Genève it is only to be used for messages concerning the original diplarg. Ardel will get a message to let him know Bartouche is his point of contact while Grandy is away, and that his request for support will be given the fullest attention.

"He will wonder where and why I have gone."

"Grandy, if he is as smart as we think, it will do him no harm. Let him have some doubt in his experience. You say Dahqin has been studying a topog of the area in their apartment, so go there and make your plans. Pick his brain. He'll already have a plan in mind."

As they part Bartouche holds Grandy's hands in hers.

"There is always the chance young Penaul is totally wrong, in which case we must deal with this another way, when he gets back. Travel in the spirit, Grandy. May you succeed."

June, 24th — Genève — Dahqin

Grandy said she'd be here mid-afternoon, I was deep asleep when she called and I went right back into it. So when she arrives I have to leap out of bed to let her in. I'm still drained, and she's lucky I grabbed my briefs.

"Is that all you're going to wear?"

"Afternoon, Grandy. You got me out of bed. Five nights with adrenalin rushing round takes it out of me. You're lucky I found these. And I was dreaming that I found Ardel but couldn't wake him."

"Oh ... I don't know what to say to that, Dahqin."

"It could have been worse, it was only a dream, and you stopped it. What do you want to drink? I'll put something less revealing on."

"I'll find the coffee. Want some? Too late on the revelation Dahqin —
but do."

"Yes to the coffee, please."

I return freshened up, wearing shorts and a vest. She's made the
coffee. And I'm still yawning.

"I have patronage to go to Alban."

"Right. How are *you* going? Will you need me to do anything?"

"Help with my plans, please." She puts a faxplex on the counter.

"Okay." Now I'm really disappointed. She lets the silence gather, her
face trying to convey empathy for my feelings.

"You see, I thought ..." Then she grins. "I did wonder if you'd come."

"Yess!" I drum on the counter. "You had me fooled there."

"From that, I take it you want to go on this mad escapade."

"Absolutely. I'll always chase adventure."

"The first thing — I am leaving tomorrow."

"Wow! That is urgent. It's not a problem for me."

As we stand drinking coffee, she tells me that she hopes he is right in
his assessments. If he is wrong, though, it means he will be re-assessed
and have to do another Solo; not good for his self-esteem. She fiddles
with the mugs and rearranges the utensils on the work-surface.

"Ardel might find it very, very hard. He takes his work very seriously
and he's focused on it. I've known people leave the League over such
incidents."

"If he got into that sort of mind it would matter a lot to me, Grandy.
It could make him withdraw from me. Of course, I'll always get by —
something, somewhere, will always crop up. But Ardel? I suppose we
don't know what each other wants in the final analysis, do we?"

"No. We always hope our partners want to include us."

Another coffee in hand I lead the way into the living area. She activates
her faxplex, takes out a scribbler and goes down the list of what she wants
to achieve today. I set the topog to show the area of Europa between
Genève and the part of Alban with The Keep.

"We should not draw any attention to ourselves when leaving the

Cantons, and by the quickest, yet least likely route imaginable. This is where you come in, Dahqin. You've been studying Ardel's way through the land as well as the topog will allow you. Do you have any ideas?"

"I do. The Keep is near the west coast. If we go to Brittany we can get a wind-boat up that way. No one will know where we are at sea. Plus I know people we can trust absolutely to help us with that."

Grandy leans back and shuts her eyes.

"I should be able to organise this myself, but I feel out of my depth."

"Leave the journey to me. I'll tell my parents I'm taking a last minute break and bringing a friend with me. We take the tgv to Paris and go on from there to Brittany. When we get there we plan again — face to face with my contacts. What do you think?"

"It's fine. Won't your parents mind?"

"Not at all. Well, not too much. They don't see a lot of me, so they put up with what I throw their way."

"We must pack light, you said. I shall take the normal comms kit an Ambassador has, it's very compact."

I let her carry on listing the things she thinks we need.

"Have you been on an expedition like this before?"

"Of course not Dahqin."

"You've seen too many old flix, Grandy — in monochrome. You sound like a heroine on an expedition."

"That's exactly how I feel. Don't you?"

"Definitely not a heroine. I'm just going home. I shall probably feel more excited once we are sailing."

"Are you capable of limiting the amount of clothes you take?"

"Of course, Grandy. My friends' father's rule was: *Only take half of what you get out to pack.* I shall follow it as always. My Bagad, used to go on expeditions all the time. Have you heard of Karnak?"

"No. What does Bagad mean?"

"Gang. I'll tell you about Karnak at sea — plenty of time then."

"Show me your planned route. I want to see what your mind has hatched."

I go through the routes. She's got a quick brain, and asks a lot of questions to which mostly I have no answers. I coin a new catchphrase.

"We'll have to see when we get there."

I want to know why she seems so jumpy about what Ardel has found. She looks at me for a few moments, rises and starts to pace about the room — one arm clasped about her waist — sipping from the mug in the other hand, at what we have agreed must be the last coffee of the day.

"It's nothing tangible."

She moves her hands apart as if trying to define the limits of her uncertainty. She's over by the raised counter — where we often take our meals — between the kitchen and living area. She drains the coffee and puts the mug down.

"I feel Ardel has stumbled into something momentous. Something big enough to make him uncertain."

For a moment I think she's decided to say no more, but then goes on in a bit of a rush.

"You see, Ardel is a studious and careful person. You said you don't discuss your careers much, so you might not know this. Ardel is the top of his peer group, he is a star in his way. He's got an edge, and should make an ideal Ambassador. He understands perfectly the protocols and regulations ruling the work of the League. He is in touch with the nuances which make diplomacy diplomatic. So when someone with his capabilities sends a message, which includes important phrases that are truncated and hacked, it means he has done so deliberately. Our job has been accomplished easily these last hundred years, and maybe we have grown complacent." She resumes pacing.

"I'm not telling you anything out of the ordinary. You could hear this in many a bar in Genève. People here believe the world is getting used to our way of sorting things out. I know for a fact, chaos still thrives in the Middle Zones. But in the Eastern and Western Zones we can sort things out. There have been reports in Council saying certain interests — and it is never stated which — are getting restive. I would hazard these interests are those which were supposed to have realised the errors of their ways when the League first came into being."

She sits next to me and briefly touches my arm.

"If it is the same interests I fear there may be turbulence ahead."

"As they say in the airships." It's glib, and I wish I hadn't said it.

"I am going to spend some time with Kazzia. She's at home this afternoon. What time do you think we should leave tomorrow?"

"Um ... I know a tgv arrives in Rennes, about now, and another later in the early evening. There is one in the morning, but we can forget that. Wait a minute while I check." I go to the multi-viewer.

"If we take the 0830 for Paris we can catch the tgv to Rennes for the afternoon. Leave it with me, I'll book the seats."

I've booked the trains — packed one bag and a chest pack. It's all done quickly and I am relaxed. An early night is calling. We are to meet at 0800 in the station. I'll be there at seven.

June, 24th — Genève — Grandy at home

Kazzia takes the confirmation of Grandy's departure in her stride. Short-notice arrangements happen all the time in her job. She's relaxing after their supper, watching a costume drama.

"It is supposed to be a last minute decision of mine to take a holiday. It's the flimsiest excuse, and anyone who knows me won't believe it."

"You are the exact opposite of Lady Spontaneity."

"I can't make up such stories just like that. What shall the reason be do you think?"

"Leave it to me, darling. That's my line of business — I'll think of something plausible. You will be safe, won't you?"

Grandy snorts. "I'm pretty sure I'll be fine. I'm taking Dahqin with me. I'm trying to convince myself it's for cover. But the more I say that the more I think he'll be just the reverse."

"He'll be okay. He's single-minded and focused when organising his shows. You've never seen him outside the little circle we know here, or on the stage. He might well have hidden talents."

"I hope being inconspicuous is one of them."

Kazzia holds out her arms, and Grandy settles alongside her, nestling her head against Kazzia's breast. Looking up at her lightly freckled face she says, "I want you to pander me."

Grandy's brown eyes appear almost black, her skin lustrous. Kazzia runs her pale fingers across the frizzed black hair and leaning down presses her parted lips to Grandy's dark temple.

June, 25th — Journey to Douarnenez, Brittany — Dahqin

The tgv to Paris is not fully booked, even so we find ourselves with immediate neighbours. We talk of my show as if it featured someone else, and Kazzia's career as a commissioning producer for an unnamed media company.

"You do seem to know how to get around without attracting attention, Dahqin. I thought you courted it?"

"True on both counts, Grandy. For my work, I only travel first class on the tgv, and my agency makes sure I am seen."

Grandy is very tense. Although she is good at appearing casual when making sure we are not under observation, I can see it, because I'm pretty good at it myself.

"Do you see anyone in this carriage?"

She shakes her head, then asks me to tell her something about my life before moving from Paris to Genève.

"I don't see anyone either. I used to be very good at hiding myself out of sight. When I was younger, and wilder — don't look at me like that, I've calmed down a lot — I used to go on expeditions with friends in our school holidays. There were six of us. We would draw lots and the chosen one of us had to disappear by that evening, leaving just one clue behind. The others had to find him within the space of three days. At every change of location another clue was left."

160

"Did you always find your quarry?"

"Not always. But the clues had to be good ones, otherwise the quarry had to pay a forfeit. We hardly ever got a bad clue, because the forfeits were awful."

Grandy yawns. "You'll have to tell me more about it another time. Unusually I feel so sleepy. I know this probably is paranoia, but I would prefer it if you stayed awake. I don't want to lose anything."

"I've never lost anything on a tgv yet."

"Dahqin, I wish there was absolute certainty for why we are doing this. Things might be less dangerous than I imagine. For once, I wish all messages were sent by Runners, as they used to be."

"How long would a Runner take to get to The Keep, for instance?"

"About twenty-four hours, I guess. They always use the quickest routes. You know in some ways ... Why are we whispering? We've got to stop acting like this." She continues in a normal voice.

"In some ways technology has not advanced as much as we would like to think. Particularly in personal transport. What do you do in Brittany ... No ..." She yawns again.

"I really need the sleep. Tell me when I wake up, Dahqin." She adjusts the seat to 'Slumber' and closes her eyes.

Left to my own devices, I take out a comiplex purchased at Genève terminus. It's the latest adventure in a pulpy comic series I love. The muscled hero rushing across the galaxy to save the planet of humankind's birth from destruction at the hands of various villains. As a youngster I dreamt of being such a hero. It isn't as alluring a story as I had hoped.

How shall I explain Grandy to Mam and Papa? For a start — she is a she — and so much older than me. Ardel's parents are easy. I find mine cloying in their inquisitiveness; all but impenetrable in their thinking.

Mam mostly treats me as a semi-exotic animal. She cuddles me with a grip of desperation and constantly reaches out to touch me, as if to convince herself I am actually there. Papa's not so bad. He hugs me at arrival and again at departure, the rest of the time staying behind Mam, watching her rituals.

About them and their life together I know practically nothing. As a kid I never heard an argument. As a teen I had been aware of the times when tensions ruffled the air in the house. They appear to be devoted to each other. It's my assumption they are, but I never saw any affection between them like that showered on me. Maybe there had been none left after my portion was allotted.

It is so different with the twins' parents. And the twins — how I have neglected them; presuming now on the capital of our love. As an only child I spent most of my waking hours with them. I now know I have an ability to lead; popularity was easy. At school I was always the mastermind behind the pranks. I made the plans; others executed them. They got caught; I went free. That is another thing I have had to accept about me. I am able to inspire loyalty from those I get to know. But my use of them; their silence to protect me. Their devotion. It all adds to the rancid taste of my betrayal of them; a sense that I am unworthy of the attention my parents, and the twins in particular, put my way.

I only addressed the matter of my loyalty to another, mostly subconsciously, after I met Ardel. The thing about Ardel that drew me in was his ability to stand away from his surroundings, including people. It was a combination of self-confidence and — I only realised later — a fear of being rejected.

A mutual friend introduced us at a party. We spent only moments talking before someone butted in and I let them drag me away. The amused and resigned look covering Ardel's face stayed with me, and I kept searching the rooms for a sight of his blonde features. He found me attractive — it was there on his face. Knowing I was desirable, and could usually get anyone I wanted, made me blasé.

He had not been haughty in his manner, but he had remained aloof beyond the effect of my charms. Every time I caught Ardel's gaze, I shot him my best smile. He had responded each time with a rather shy smile, and stared with those blue eyes, at something deep inside me, it felt.

"If you are interested in that one, you'd better make a grab before he moves out of your life for ever."

I took the mutual friend's advice and we exchanged phone numbers. She had not been wrong. Ardel would simply have added my form to an extensive gallery of unfulfilled encounters — faces to dream of during lonely evenings — and wandered off into the night.

I waited for Ardel to call. But the shaky hand punching the numbers into the phone, and the suddenly dry throat swallowing rapidly, hoping the desired face would appear, was mine.

Ardel has refused to promise faithfulness, and it is that very lack in him which brought out my loyalty. I had forever played the self-regarding Adonis they all desired, and all forgave. Back then the real Dahqin remained as unknown to me as to those I dealt with so badly, so lightly. Until I was refused such adoration and loyalty by someone who obviously wanted me. I paid attention to what Ardel did, to where he went; found myself going to bars because Ardel might be there. I saw other men who attracted me, that ordinarily I would have drawn to me. I turned away from them before the moves began, bored with the game. Ardel was always pleased to see me and I always had a brilliant time when they were together, but me it was who did all the running.

Only when Ardel was about to return to the Cantons, to his parents, and his posting in the League, did he make an advance to me. He had not previously mentioned he would be leaving Paris, but dropped it into the conversation while casually asking if I wanted another drink. We had not even consummated our relationship. Ardel had been as careful of giving too much too soon, as he was of starting an affair with me in the first place. It was the most chastening experience of my life, and the thought of him slipping out of it forever left me crestfallen, and uncharacteristically silent.

"Don't be so sad about it. You can come and stay with me in Genève. Maybe you could get a billing at one of the places there?"

That night, nearly five years ago, was the first we spent together. Whilst I still flirt with all and sundry I am Ardel's, heart and soul. And here I am still doing the running.

June, 25th — Journey to Douarnenez — Paris to Brest

When the tgv reaches Paris the sky has wisps of white in its brilliant blue. They have an hour to spare; Dahqin takes Grandy to a cafe he knows well. It is where he had most often met Ardel, and where he sometimes performed in the evenings. The terrace overlooks the river. Many of the buildings are less than a hundred years old, and only a few relics of the past had been rebuilt when the urb rose from the chaos of unpredictable weather patterns and the rubble the upheavals had scattered in its passing. Like most urbs it is smaller than its predecessor.

Dahqin had enjoyed the time he spent in Paris. His career had blossomed and consolidated by the time he met Ardel. He regales Grandy with episodic tales, but the reminiscence is weighed down by the reason for their visit. Now, rather poignantly, he points out sights to Grandy, who does not know Paris as he and Ardel had known it.

They arrive at Gare Montparanne with little time in hand to board the tgv. Grandy watches new territory passing as a flash of smudged greens and browns. This journey across northern France does not excite her enthusiasm.

She looks at Dahqin, asleep now, the alternating sunlight and shadows of trackside trees flashing across his face. She has never before seen him asleep; his face displays an innocence and serenity, making her feel content. It does not last long, for following on that idea's heels marches the vision of what his face and body portray when his eyes are open and the muscles controlled. She laughs silently to herself. For all his boyishness Dahqin can never be an innocent in her mind. The carriage is almost empty, and though trying not to, she dozes off. She awakes to see a smiling Dahqin. The tgv is crawling.

"I thought you were going to keep watch while I slept?"

She shrugs, but looks at the baggage locker over their seats.

"I've checked, Grandy. They're still there. We're coming into the terminus at Rennes." She nods at him and stretches.

On the way to the local platforms they freshen up, and go outside to a small kiosk selling coffees. He asks for them in a language she has never heard him use.

"It's Brezhoneg, Grandy — the language in my heart, from my part of Brittany. Their coffee is the best in Rennes."

"What do we do at the end of this train journey?"

"Go by boat. The ferry runs except for the winter, it's too often rough out there then. Today the wind should be moderate."

"How long does it take?"

"Just over an hour. It's a quicker route than by train or road."

She listens carefully to the chatter around them. There are snatches of French, and two other distinct languages she can separate, but not understand. He continually looks about him. Travellers always make cursory glances at each other; no one seems interested enough to keep checking on them. As they wait for the announcement of their train's departure, Dahqin fiddles with the straps on his pack, then with his timeband, and finally he twiddles his thumbs. A state of frozen expectation descends on the assembly. The train is delayed somewhat. A ripple of silent shifting plays through the crowd. A couple of coughs from one corner, and a few exchanged glances between those who know this is not extraordinary. Eventually the three carriages hum into the terminus, and they board.

"Don't expect it to start out on time, Grandy, the driver will have gone for his break."

"I'd forgotten all this hanging around when travelling outside the Cantons. How does anything get done on time?"

"You're forgetting the rule of pace. It doesn't matter if it gets done the day after tomorrow instead of today."

"I am. But when one has been travelling all day, it is nice to get the journey over and done with."

Despite Dahqin's pessimism they start on time. The train stops at stations in the middle of what seems nowhere, passing through large tracts of woodland, crossing small rivers, until they trundle into a terminus near a wide estuary. They take a bus to the ferry terminus on the Kae Armand Considère. Tickets in hand Dahqin leads Grandy down a ramp onto a pontoon where a large catamaran is berthed. On the top deck he picks two seats in the shelter of a windbreak, away from the quayside.

"So this is Brest."

"Yes, Grandy." He points across the water.

"Those big ruins are the remains of a base for subs which used to operate from here. There are some even older ruins down the coast. Too strong to wipe away, too weak to stay completely in one piece. Every so often some Member of Assembly suggests blowing them up. They never will. There are remains buried in concrete all over Brittany — atomics mostly — what an inheritance."

"When does this leave?"

"On the half-hour, Grandy. It might get a bit chilly up here when we get outside the estuary, but we can move downstairs then."

"Dahqin!" A man's voice calls out. They look around to see a young man of similar age to Dahqin standing outside the wheelhouse.

"You're coming home. Why didn't you let me know?"

June, 25th — Journey to Douarnenez — Dahqin

"Alun ... How are you?"

I smile as I stand, climbing over the seat as Alun comes to me. We embrace — he's laughing in joy as much as me.

"Alun is an old friend. One of the wild ones I mentioned."

It's so good to see the sea-green of his eyes and their sparkle. I introduce Grandy as a friend, which at this moment is truer than I ever thought. Alun takes her hand and bowing low, kisses the back of it. I'd not remembered rightly how wonderfully their skins tan with the weather and sun. His dark brown hair is cut short — it really suits him.

"Enchanted." Grandy approves of his act.

"I haven't seen you for a long time, Dahqin, and you are a worse correspondent than me."

166

His face radiant he chants our courting rhyme so sensuously in Brezhoneg. There's a flutter in my breast.

"Aye, Alun, but a lot of things have changed in my life. Remember me telling you about Ardel?"

"Ardel? Oh, the last guy you wanted to bring home. About three years ago. Yes, I remember you talking about him."

His mouth straightens and I feel terrible.

"Don't tell me you are still with the same blonde lawman."

He sounds okay, but the radiance has gone.

"That wasn't how I described him. Grandy, I wouldn't describe Ardel like that, would I?"

"How about horny hunk?"

Ignoring their jibes I slip an arm across Alun's shoulders, wanting him to know I still have ... my emotions are unsteady. I change tack.

"Going back home, Alun? I take it that's why you're on the boat."

"Yes, sort of. You know I was running the local boat across the bay, well now I run this one. When we dock in Douarnenez, then I go home, at the end of my shift. Are you staying long?"

"No, Alun. This is very last minute. Can we talk with you during the trip?"

"Of course. Come into the wheelhouse now — you know the etiquette. Bring the bags with you. Dahqin, your eyes keep sweeping the quay. You're not hunting, are you?"

"With you to hand! Of course not. Just making sure we're not being watched." I see Grandy's look of warning.

"Alun and I are the closest of the bunch. We still love one another."

It was worth saying; his brightness is back.

"You are my ideal, my brother, my lover. Grandy, whatever I can do for Dahqin I will attempt. Whatever the problem facing you both, I will try to help you overcome it."

My Bagad is still in being with this man at least.

"What do you think, Alun?" The shading windows are set dark by the sun, hiding us from those outside.

"One person — but probably he's after your body."

Grandy's laugh is so ribald, bringing tears from her eyes.

"Most of the passengers are locals. If you are being followed — it's him."

"He's been with us since Paris. It may be coincidental."

Grandy taps my arm, she looks from me to Alun and back.

"He looks familiar. He was at the station in Genève. I need to decide who sent him. And how he knew we were getting that train."

"Then, Grandy, you must decide against him for now. That's how we played it in the Bagad — Huh? Dahqin. If he's come with you all the way with such a small backpack, he can't be staying for long."

"Alun, look what we've got. We may be away for a period."

"Dahqin, what on earth are you involved in? You always make the most mundane matters so exciting."

"Alun, as Dahqin trusts you, I trust you, but the fewer we meet the better. What did you tell your parents?"

"Practically nothing. Mam moaned about the lack of notice, but even when I tell her well in advance it's never enough notice. I told her I was bringing a friend, and would only be seeing them and the twins. And they weren't to tell all and sundry ..."

"The famous Franz is coming home," Alun interrupts.

"Franz?"

"My real name, Grandy. Dahqin's a nickname."

Alun reaches out and flicks my mop of fine dark hair.

"I told them we were passing through on a trip to Kernow. I said nothing of our business. Is he still there? I can't see him."

Alun goes to the docking window. "He's boarding."

As Alun helms the vessel away from the berth, we settle ourselves into spare conning seats, watching the urb slip by on the right, the walls of the old fortresses still standing over the estuary.

"They rebuilt those in the Upheavals, Grandy. It was after Brittany declared itself a Celtic land."

"What did he say to you in the rhyme, Dahqin. His cadency had such passion in it, and you responded to that, but shut him down."

"It's an old Breton verse from centuries ago. The closest it gets in French is 'If my lover promises we can be together tonight.' But there's no rhyme or rhythm then. We were lovers."

My voice catches. She lays her hand on my arm.

"You started to tell me about Karnak? Is that the right name?"

"Yes. It's a series of standing stones. They're found all over this area, but Karnak is special. There are stories trying to explain the lines and lines of stones standing on that heath. Armies turned to stone who will one day awaken to save us from deadly peril. Pretty naff really. But difficult to dismiss when you are a youngster hiding amongst them with mist swirling about you, and five screeching hunters hard on your heels. On a bright day the atmosphere is one of wonder, you know. Why are they there? What are they for? Who took the trouble to put them there? It's only when you blunder into them in the mists, especially on a moonlit night, that the awesomeness of the stones settles on you. I don't think I've ever experienced anything so frightening as my first night amongst them."

"Are they far from where your parents live? I mean, is there any likelihood I'll get to see them for myself?"

"No, there isn't time. It takes a whole day to travel there, and not back until the morning. Maybe some other time, when we aren't chasing after missing Ambassadors."

"Try not to let that word out to anyone. Friend or not. I don't want any loose ends. I still haven't thought of a plausible story for hiring a boat to get to Alban. Have you?"

"I think going to Kernow is enough for a start."

"I don't know anything about the history of this area. How old are those walls originally?"

"Don't know, they must be a few hundred years old. I only remember certain bits of history — usually ancient stuff."

"The myths, you mean." She laughs.

"Yes, but are myths and history so different. You know, if we say we're heading for Kernow, and say we want to go for six days — then we can change our mind and head for Alban after we sail. The crew will tell their base where they are heading in any case. That's mandatory."

Alun closes the docking window and sets the auto-helm.

"Home soon. Are you glad to be back?"

"In better circumstances, Alun, I'd be glad. We need to hire a boat as soon as we can. It really is a rush-through."

"Kirus has nothing to do, if you can handle sailing with Kirus."

"Kirus. Yes, yes, of course I can. They're twins, Grandy. When you say nothing to do, are you telling me he'd be prepared to crew a boat for me, I mean us?"

"Not any boat. Our boat. The Blondyn. We're in the charter business, and unless he's taken work today, he has a boat to hire with himself at the helm for at least a couple of weeks. You could get him to go alone, you know that, don't you."

"Would he really, Alun."

She's seeing right into my core. I have nowhere to hide the joyful hope that's pushing round me, and she's heard it in my voice. She puts her hand back on my arm – which helps ground me.

The sea is calm, with the usual long swell from the south-west giving a slow rolling motion to the catamaran. Grandy closes her eyes as we chatter away at the 'Do you remember when ...' memories. She falls asleep – occasional snuffles sounding – so we switch to Brezhoneg. She'll understand not a word, but I can hear the passion from the rhyme in both our voices.

June, 25th – Douarnenez – Dahqin

It is an easy passage home. The man, we've taken to calling The Shadow, leaves the boat without looking back when it docks at Kraozon in the north-western corner of the bight – despite having a ticket for Douarnenez. Which neither proves nor disproves our suspicions. After a short passage the boat enters the main harbour of Douarnenez in the south-eastern corner of the bay. It looks the same as ever. Gulls sit on the roofs of the buildings along the harbour, occasionally letting out small cries and stretching their wings. A few people are fishing near the bigger boats. We wait for Alun as he hands over to his relief. He wants to meet up later, but I'm not so sure.

"Come round and arrange things with Kirus. It'll save you doing it tomorrow." Grandy thinks this a good idea, so I have no choice.

Mam and Papa are very happy to see me; their greeting exactly as I had imagined on the train. They are clearly at a loss as to the relationship between us. When Mam asks if I can help her with the meal in the kitchen, I swiftly tell her it's separate rooms. Sitting at table the conversation is slow and about the entertainment business.

"And what sort of roles do you play, Grandy?" Papa says.

"As diplomatic as possible," she replies and no other explanation is needed in the laughter that follows. They concentrate their attention on me, the son they seldom see, as they both frequently tell Grandy. She finds it amusing when I don't always respond to Mam calling me Franz. At nine o'clock I make excuses, and we go to Alun's. I promise Mam we will not be too late, and that I will spend most of the next day with her. Making sure we are a good distance from the narrow lane where they live, I throw my arms out and twirl along the pavement, shouting.

"Aaigh! Aaigh!" Feeling released, I see Grandy some way behind me.

"It's like this every time I come home. It's so stifling."

"Maybe if you came home more often it wouldn't be so bad. They wouldn't be so starved of you. How often do you talk to them?"

"Every couple of periods or so. I've never been very chatty with them."

"Is that why you left for France, back in your youth?"

"It's not so long ago, you know. It's one of the reasons."

"Nearly five years with Ardel. And what age when you left here?"

"Twenty. Seven years. It's never felt so long. I wonder what I would have been doing if I hadn't left?"

"Still running with the wild pack, structuring their lives instead of your own."

"You think that would be so?"

"Not until the trip from Brest. Your conversation with Alun, until you switched to Brezhoneg, gave me an insight into a Dahqin I don't know. A bit like that faxplex the other night."

"You were sleeping — snoring."

"Trying to meditate, at first. Your stories were intrusive in an interesting way, and I cannot deny overhearing. It's a habit from years as a diplomat. Yes, I did drift in and out."

Reaching the door where Alun lives, I use the heavy knocker. When the door opens, it reveals an unknown youth who nods to Grandy, and responds to me with a very surprised look. He silently bows as we enter, motioning us to walk ahead of him. He's bound to be the lover of one of them; a reminder of me when I was eighteen. We climb two flights of stairs and go into a dark hallway. In the main room large cushions are placed on low bases to form seating. The walls are hung with muslin — the place resembles the interior of an elaborate tent.

The youth is using a radio.

"Alun, Grandy's here."

"I'll be right back."

"I'm Peran. Do you want a drink?" I can't place his accent. We settle onto cushions while he goes for the drinks.

"Weird taste in decoration," Grandy says. "I could not live with it."

"Alun always wanted to be a prince and ride about on a white horse. We used to devour the documentaries. Like that one the other day with the camels. We were going to ride the world's wastes looking for adventure."

"What happened?"

"I ran away to Paris to escape everyone, Alun included."

"What drew you to Paris?" The question remains unanswered, as Peran comes back with the drinks.

I ask him how long he's known them. Peran seems surprised by the pointed interest. He is from Kernow. He had come over on a sailing trip two summers back, met Alun and Kirus, and not gone home. He sometimes goes with Kirus as crew on the longer trips of the Blondyn, and sometimes works on the local fishing boats, or in their father's boatyard.

"How often does Kirus go on long trips, Peran?" Grandy asks.

"He's had four trips this year. I've been on three of those. The other trip was to Q'imper, and he didn't need crew for that because the charterers wanted to sail."

"I know that trip well. I've done it many times." I hear the note of condescension in my voice; it makes Grandy frown.

She changes the subject back to her needs.

"What is Kernow like? That's where we're thinking of going. Where would you head for if you were on a trip?"

"Tamar, Fowey or Fal. It's all good for boating. From here Fal is the easiest to reach, and probably the best. What are you looking for mostly? A few days of gentle sailing? Sandy beaches? Getting up to moorland? It's got all that." He looks puzzled for a moment.

"Same as here really. Just the people are a bit different. Not so friendly at first. We aren't so open as these Breitones."

He's garbled that word and now he's looking at me closely.

"Where are you from?"

"From here." It's so curt. I'm annoyed that I'm needled by Peran being here. A frown develops — realisation spreads across his face.

"Oh... Are you Dahqin? They talk about you all the time. You know Alun and Kirus really well then."

"Yes. I've known them since we were small."

Grandy is looking at me with disapproval.

"I thought it a bit strange you coming round to the Tents. And asking about me, an' all. Alun only said about Grandy. Normally people who hire the boat go to the yard."

Sounds of the outer door shutting, then footsteps coming up the stairs and through the folds of cloth.

Alun comes in with Kirus right behind him, standing there open-mouthed, a stunned look on his face. Probably on mine too. It is impossible for her to tell Alun and Kirus apart, but not me.

"Dahqin!" He closes his eyes and shakes his head. "Dahqin. Hey!" Kirus opens his eyes and arms. I almost skip to him. We embrace and kiss. Such laughter. We gather Alun into the hug. As we swing round I catch sight of Peran's face. Alun sees it too for he pulls away, goes to where Peran sits, kissing him. I hear his reassuring tones. Kirus has me in a hug from which I can't escape. I'm just that bit shorter than them.

"I can't breath, Kirus." He lets me go. Brushes a hand across my cheek, mouth and chin. It lands on my chest.

"So! Dahqin. It's you who want to use our boat. Ahh, man! How long for, my Lord?"

"At least six days, maybe longer, Kirus." He wrestles me to the ground, I resist but he is so strong. Finally I push him away and sit up.

"Don't worry Grandy, this was quite normal between us two."

"It still looks to be, Dahqin. I do wonder what set of man-boys I've landed myself with. I need you to take our business very seriously."

"Yes. Sorry, Grandy. Kirus, we need to hire your boat to get across to Kernow as a start. If we wanted, are you prepared to take us further north, up past Cymru."

"I'll take you anywhere you want to go, Dahqin. And I'll bring you back. You know that. The Bagad together. Right?"

"Of course, but ... Well I haven't exactly been paying attention to the Bagad of late, and you might have other priorities."

"No way. If one of the Bagad asks for help then we should give it freely — it's just us three now. Wouldn't you help us if we turned up in Genève?"

"Of course, but this is", I pause, struggling because I hurt Kirus so much by leaving, "more than I've ever asked before. That's why you have the choice."

"There is no choice for us with you, Dahqin." Alun hugs Peran more tightly as he says it. "Peran, go get a couple of bottles of cidre from the café, please."

As the door shuts, the three of us are wandering in the space — I knew they'd moved in, but never seen it.

"Grandy, we have to tell them more."

I can see that Grandy is still not sure which is which. They are dressed in white tee-shirts and orange shorts, their hair cuts are too close to call — their tans and smiles identical. She's looking at Kirus.

"You three trust one another implicitly, Alun. What about Peran?"

"I trust him like I trust these two. Alun, you?"

"Kirus, sit here next to me — now!" And when he does, she flicks his thigh with her fingers.

"Ow! That stung."

"Seriousness for the rest of this discussion. We are to be back at your parents at a reasonable time, Dahqin. And you Kirus, you behave."

Peran returns and hands out glasses of cidre.

"This is what I need from all of you who are coming with me. Absolute seriousness when it is needed, with enough light humour between to keep us sane. Now, go ahead, Dahqin. You explain what we have to achieve."

I describe our voyage as simply as I can without mixing in why she has to go on it. Alun is unhappy because Peran is needed as crew. He feels he misses out doubly, and makes no secret of it. Kirus and Peran start to tease him about this, and it ends in another bundle on the floor, from which I keep well clear.

"I take it the saga is concluded, Dahqin."

"Yes, Grandy. Anything you want to tell them?"

"Only to remind them ... Are they alright?"

They slowly untangle and sit up.

"It is vital our trip be kept secret. We don't know what we shall find at the other end. What Dahqin has not told you is that we are on League business. Do you understand the importance of what I say?"

"Yes, Grandy. Kirus, speaking. When do you want to leave?"

She shoots him a narrowed-eyes look — while keeping her smile under control.

"How soon can you be ready, Kirus?"

"By tomorrow afternoon, Grandy."

"Dahqin. How will your parents take it if we leave tomorrow?"

"Mam, won't like it one bit, but I'll spend as much of tomorrow with them as possible."

"Alright, Kirus, tomorrow evening. We'll wait until after Alun is back in port." She empties her glass, tilts her head towards the door, and we return to my parents' home.

June, 26th — Douarnenez — Dahqin

Breakfast next morning is interrupted when Papa ushers Peran into the dining room. I take him back into the hallway.

"Always something happens," I hear Papa say as I close the door.

The news Peran brings is that the Shadow is in town.

"He tried to follow me, but I lost him in the alleys."

"He might think you are me, Peran. I know you are a lot younger than me, but there is a resemblance, don't you think?"

"I am in my twenties, so not that much age difference."

I let it go, I'd swear he was younger than that. I make Peran's visit the excuse for broaching the subject of our departure.

"Kirus reckons it'll be westerlies tomorrow, the best moment to leave will be this evening, getting the south-wester to help us round Ushant."

My parents look at each other, and Mam's eyes become moist, but Papa takes her hand. She makes her smile of sadness.

"I didn't think we'd be leaving so soon." I look at my plate, but see her looking at Grandy.

"This is so normal for one of Franz's visits. We see so little of him. I wonder afterwards whether he has been here at all."

"Please, Mam, don't."

We get into a bit of a tussle over my slipperiness as a visitor. I'd arranged two visits and Ardel couldn't come on either at the last moment, but I can't tell them that was why I didn't come. I can feel it heading towards tears from her, and Papa is getting flustered.

"Blame me for the last two years," Grandy interrupts.

"I am Ardel's patron, and his last two holidays with Dahqin have been ruined at my behest. I am guilty of not considering the other obligations Ardel may have had to fulfil. I must admit it was the same with my patron when I was younger. Ardel has asked for leave at the end of his present assignment, Dahqin. You must not let me or him forget this time."

"I won't. I was asking Ardel about that before he went to Alban." Grandy, ignores my slip.

"Do your parents know what Ardel does?"

I shake my head — too surprised to speak.

"We work in conciliation services. We have to be discrete, and sometimes act at short notice. I wonder — I saw you have a fixed line phone. Could I use it please? I would like to speak to Bartouche, a confidante of mine."

"Bartouche?" Mam is suddenly all brightness. "That is my family name, an aunt of mine with that name lives in the Cantons."

Mam and Papa are both animated: the family connections are scrolled through.

"Matilde's name is also Bartouche?" I know her by our surname.

Mam goes to the sideboard and brings an address book over to Grandy, I see the old photo of Matilde stuck by her address. Grandy looks carefully and says her friend doesn't live in Lausanne.

"She might be the same woman." Papa doesn't want to let it go.

"I think I'd best try the number I know," Grandy says, excusing herself.

"What do they do, dear?"

"Like Grandy said, Mam, it is work requiring caution and diplomacy. Ardel and me never talk about it. I don't think Grandy would like us to talk about it either."

They say they understand and will not breath a word to anyone. I wonder about Mam, she always knows the latest gossip in this town. Papa is silent at the best of times. Even when he imbibes too much alcohol he seems to remain silent. I just have to hope Mam can resist the opportunity of boasting about Franz and his connections.

Within a few minutes Grandy returns and puts money on the table, insisting they accept.

"She's definitely not the woman you know of."

We leave the house soon after, Grandy making the excuses. As soon as we are out of the lane, I have questions bursting out.

"Who is the Shadow? Is it who you think it is? And what's all this stuff about Matilde? Isn't Bartouche Ardel's ultimate boss beyond you?"

"I don't know about the Shadow, Dahqin. Bartouche is your Matilde by the way, but she doesn't want your parents to know that at this point. And she is not happy about us having a shadow. I told her he was up against you and your horde. She laughed and said you were acting true to form. Getting her private number from your mother has given us a way to reach her outside the direct League links. It should be safer, but she urges caution."

Feeling uneasy I look back and glimpse the Shadow ducking from sight. We hurry on, scarcely talking at all. At the harbour she wants to see the boat she's chartering. I casually indicate a catamaran with two aerofoil masts set on strong pivots. It is hi-vis yellow with black patterns on it, and painted on the larger mast the Gwenn-ha-du denoting the Fastness of Brittany. On the outside of each hull in large black letters is the name 'Blondyn'.

"It doesn't look very big from here."

"They never do. Wait till we get on it, it'll feel big enough." I do not add — until we get to sea.

"And it isn't what I would call discrete colouring."

"None of them is, Grandy, although this is the brightest." We walk around the harbour, occasionally glimpsing our Shadow.

"Let's sit awhile and watch things. See what he does while we have a drink." We walk away from the harbour and go to a cafe on the Kae ar Porzh Vihan.

"It means Quay of the Little Port, Grandy." I order spritzers and a dish of unsalted anchovies. I'm glad to be out of their home, glad to be away from their scrutiny. Not glad to be shadowed though.

I know, if ever I manage to get Ardel to come to Brittany with me, we could spend no more than a couple of day's with my parents. If only

Ardel would agree to a sailing holiday, we could live on the boat and visit Mam and Papa for a few hours dotted over the vacation. The Shadow sidles by, and we both face him off, for he immediately looks away and goes to another cafe.

"Your parents watch you all the time, don't they?" Grandy says, staring at our follower.

"Yes, exactly as I dread. Did you get that with your parents?"

"No, I was sent to a school away from home. The time we spent together at holidays was never enough for me. I didn't want to go away. Now, when I see my parents, they talk to me as if I am an acquaintance they meet every so often. I have never been their child in that sense."

"We'd better head back, Grandy. Kirus said he'd come by this afternoon to rescue us about four o'clock. We'll go to the Tents and from there by a different route to the boat. Maybe the Shadow will have faded by then."

Stopping at the cafe where the Shadow sits, Grandy goes right to his table and stares down at him. She's got nerve. And she's loud.

"We are going to sit on the cliffs for a while. Don't worry we'll be coming back this way."

He looks around to see if anyone is listening; some youngsters on the next table look across.

"He's been following us, but we don't know why."

The man clenches his jaw and crumples his napkin. The youngsters lose interest — probably think she's weird. We quickly walk on, looking back every few metres, but he remains at his table.

"Can we get back to your parents' another way?"

"Of course, it'll be easy to lose him if he stays down here."

We climb the cliffs by a well marked path and approach the woods. She stops and sits on the grass, I lay full length beside her.

"There's an air of otherworldliness about this town," she says. I watch her arms waft to each side encompassing the view.

"Most of this place hasn't altered since before the Upheavals, has it? That church. Still there as it must have been for the past six or seven hundred years. Is it still used for worship?".

"By a few, I think. I don't know what their religion was like before then, but it must have been radically different to what they have now. The thought that somewhere out there", I sweep my arms apart, "is a power greater than me, is enough. I don't need to prostrate myself to it. Being out there makes you realise how small we are."

I sit up, clasp my arms round my knees, and rest my chin on top.

"This part of the bay hasn't altered much from the old maps I've seen. This town sits high enough for most of it not to have been affected by the rise of sea level. But some of the land on the coast south of here has altered drastically. That's what belief in an earth force is about for me. A force I can't fight, one totally oblivious to me and my dreams."

"You may be right, Dahqin, I can't say either. I wonder what those who go to the church believe. Really believe, I mean. It must have been an awful shock to find what you have sincerely believed in all your life, about the road to salvation and redemption and all that, started out as a political movement to overthrow a puppet king in the so-called Holy Land. Other beliefs have had it easy, some of them still make sense. I'm glad I wasn't around to have to adjust my beliefs to a new reality."

She stands up, ruffles my hair and looks around the vista again.

"It's nearly noon now. I don't think we should be late."

She raises one hand and waves vigorously at the small figure watching us from the base of the cliffs. He sprints towards the cliff path; we run into the woods.

June, 26th — On the Blondyn

The good-byes have been short. Dahqin's Mam clings to him as always, tears in her eyes, while his father hugs him briefly. Only a judicious comment from Grandy dissuades his parents from coming to the harbour. They leave with Kirus and go to the Tents via the little alleys which loop about the town. There are still a couple of hours before they sail, and Kirus suggests if they are at all sleepy now is a good time to have a rest, then he goes to check over the Blondyn.

Dahqin takes up the suggestion and is soon snoring, but Grandy cannot catnap, so she helps Peran prepare stores for the voyage. She mooches around the flat while he takes the stores down to the vessel. It is decided sunset will be the best time to leave, when most people will be getting their evening meal or watching the glory of nature — rather than a boat leaving.

The sun is low in the sky, large, red and oblate when they reach the pontoons. Scattered rain clouds hang about the horizon, high above, thin wisps of cloud herald a change in the weather. Of the Shadow there is no sign and on boarding Grandy and Dahqin immediately go into the cabin out of sight.

"It'll probably blow tomorrow. We should be well north by then." Kirus says to Grandy, as he backs the boat out of its mooring. The aerofoil controller motors hum as they pivot first one way, and then the other. Peran stands at the bows aiding them back with a long sweep. Alun walks along the jetty, smiling at him, his heart aching. The Blondyn turns into the channel between the boats and gathers speed towards the entrance. Peran pulls in fenders and tidies the ropes away.

Kirus gives a final wave to Alun, who turns away and walks slowly along the pontoons towards the ferry boat, hands pushed hard into his pockets.

"How long have you been sailing, Kirus?"

He laughs.

"You mean, am I experienced. Practically all my life, Grandy. Same as Alun. Our father has a boat repair business, so we sort of drifted into it when we were small, similar to Peran in Kernow. Dahqin came along with us when we were kids and took over. He's a good natural sailor." He checks around the harbour.

"When did you last go out?" He addresses Dahqin — who is lying with his eyes shut — but gets no answer.

"Well, he'll get enough of a refresher on this trip. We'll split the work between us. Do you want to help with the watches?"

"Of course. I have not sailed before, but I'm a quick learner."

"Just remember to shout loudly if you aren't sure and we'll come running. It's easy. This boat will practically sail itself." He turns the boat through the entrance, and it momentarily stalls as the sails adjust to the new heading and relative wind direction.

"Peran, can you check the charging rotors? You two can creep out now, but keep low."

Grandy comes into the cockpit. The windscreen gradually darkens until they can see more clearly along the strand of orange light reaching the boat. Behind them red pigment seems to ooze from every atom of the town's fabric. Please, Grandy thinks, let this problem of Ardel's be other than a prelude for a blood-bath.

"I think the town looks better from out here. Glad it's not really that colour all the time though." Kirus says, as he concentrates on conning the boat while it picks up speed.

"It will be one day — somewhere in the future," she tells him.

"I wonder what life on earth will be like then. At one time it was thought we would have colonised the stars." She shakes her head with some sadness at the human race's attempts to control fate, and turns to face the darkening shore.

"We can't even sort this planet out, let alone another. Its taken us two hundred years to get back to where we were with space exploration."

"It'll get choppy further out as we lose the lee, Grandy. The swell has had a few days to build up. You'd better make sure your gear is well stowed. Peran will be making a snack later."

Grandy goes below to her small cabin. There is a hammock-cot, furnished with a thermic sleeping bag, she rolls her own on top, and puts her equipment safely away into the netting pouches. Feeling the increased movements of the vessel, she tries to tune her own movements to it. Almost regular — but not quite — the pitching and rolling make her uncomfortable, and she grabs at the catch-holds a couple of times as she returns to the main cabin. Peran is working in the galley area, chopping for a salad. She offers her help, but he grins at her and declines. Stepping into the cockpit she pitches onto the seat beside Dahqin. Already they are leaving the enclosing arms of the bay.

"Feeling okay?" Dahqin looks at ease, and is just far enough along the seat to have the wind riffling his hair.

"Don't fight the movement, Grandy. You have to learn to move with the boat, not against it. Just relax enough to flow with it."

"It's a bit much to cope with. You know I can relax better than most, but this motion leaves me decidedly unrelaxed. How can you flow with something this irregular?"

"You just have to — there isn't really any other way. Watch how Kirus and Peran move around the boat, you'll soon get used to it." She sighs and nods.

"And you might need help against motion-sickness. They'll have tablets or patches on board — just ask."

Grandy shakes her head. "It's not yet necessary."

"I'd forgotten how much I love being out on the water. You know I said I missed the sea — well I really have. It's in my blood, in here," he thumps his chest.

"Look to the sun. In a moment, just as the last little bit goes below the horizon there'll be a green flash."

"Oh Dahqin, it's not true. It's simply a trick of the light."

"Is it? Does that make it any less special? Just because we are tricked by an interplay of colours doesn't mean we should dismiss it. If we applied that to everything, romance would be dead. For you Ambassadors, dealing with facts all the time, maybe it is dead — but for us adventurists, dealing in possibilities and dreams, romance is alive and well. Kirus, you believe in romance, don't you?"

"Of course I do. If I didn't I wouldn't be out here trusting my life to chance. I thought life itself was romance, especially when amongst those we love." He turns to look directly at Dahqin, and slowly smiling flicks up his eyebrows.

"You, men. I think there is a place for solid facts, but I see I'm outnumbered by romance. In any case it will have to await another sunset for me to witness the phenomenon, seeing as the sun thoughtlessly disappeared while we argued. You should realise diplomacy is not so much about facts, Dahqin, it's about reconciling differing beliefs in events. Now, Kirus, where do you plan to head for on the other side?"

"Fal, as Peran suggested. If the weather goes round to the west and blows we can shelter there until it goes over. If we're lucky, and it doesn't we can head right up past the Wolf and straight for Cymru. It all depends what the weather brings. The forecasts are good, except for this blow."

Peran appears, goes to a locker and pulls out a folding table, fixing it in place in front of Grandy. He closes the outer panels at the aft end of the cockpit.

"It'll get a bit chilly, but before we close up completely we might as well eat out here in the last of the light. I'll pass the food out, okay?"

Grandy grabs at the tray he passes through the companionway, nearly dislodging the contents as the boat lurches.

"Relax, Grandy."

She glares at Dahqin as she hands the tray over, for the way he says it. When the plates and utensils are handed out, she braces herself more carefully before taking them. Finally Peran comes out with a pot of tea. She notes he doesn't bother to hold on. Damn these men! She determines to master this trick before the trip is out. Over the cold meal they sort out the routines of watch-keeping. Kirus will have Grandy on watch with him to teach her the use of the instruments, so if necessary she can keep short watches on her own.

Having missed the earlier chance to sleep, Grandy is tired. She also feels queasy, and decides to go to her cabin. Without saying anything, but with a kind smile, Peran holds out a hand as she rises from the seat. She lets him drop the small white tablet into her free hand.

"Just chew it."

She nods, putting it in her mouth, and leaves them talking about the most suitable landfall dependent on the wind.

❖

June, 26th — Douarnenez

Alun watches the Blondyn moving away along the sun's reflection path, and, hands still in pockets, reaches the end of the eastern pier. He leans against its beacon tower seeing all the lovers he has ever known sailing away from him. He also feels the jag of jealousy, which he gets every time Kirus and Peran go to sea. But it is worse this time; seeing Peran and Dahqin together starkly emphasises the physical similarities between the two. He cannot ignore that the only one he loves more than his brother is Dahqin; he has never stopped loving him. And now the three of them are away together and he is left with tumbling memories.

After half an hour he can no longer distinguish the shape of the Blondyn against the rapidly darkening sky. The few lights which illuminate the roads of the town have come on, and he starts toward home, deciding to go to his local cafe rather than retreat into the empty womb of their tented abode. He turns off the harbour front into the deserted main street and catches a glimpse of the Shadow moving along behind him. He turns into a side alley and starts to run, and quickly loses the man. He is almost home when he is grabbed at from another alley. An instinct borne of the years of playing with the Bagad makes him jump and sprint away. Just in time, for a heavy blow strikes him in the middle of his upper back. His assailant loses balance and tumbles to the ground. Thoroughly alarmed Alun disappears back into the maze of lanes and races for his parents' home.

"What's the matter?" his father asks. "Where's Kirus and Peran?"

It is a week since they have seen any of the three, and a concerned expression settles on his mother's face.

"They've taken a charter to Kernow, Pap. With Dahqin and a friend of his. I was attacked in the main street, down the harbour end. Some bloke tried to knock me out. He got me in the middle of the back. It's sore."

"What on earth made someone try that?" His father raises Alun's shirt to have a look, and tuts.

"Let me have a look, Bedow."

There is a burn where the cloth grazed across his left shoulder blade, and the beginnings of a large bruise just below the nape of his neck on that side. His mother rolls his shirt over his shoulders and gently prods around the area.

"Do you know who it is?"

"No, I don't, Pap — he's not local."

"Nothing is broken or out of place, Alun. I'll put some witch-hazel on the bruise, and salve on the graze. It'll be fine in a few days."

"Thanks, Mam. It's the shock of it happening at all."

"Do you fancy coming for a drink after your Mam's fixed you up?" He winks at her. "We can have a chat over a beer."

With a drink in hand, and friendly neighbours around him, Alun feels safe. He gives his father a brief recap of the events of the last two days without breaking the secrecy he promised. His father listens without interrupting. Alun has two things clear in his mind — the man is after information about Dahqin and Grandy, and he's dangerous.

"Spend the night at ours, son. Tomorrow I'll come down to the ferry with you. I think we should find out who this character is. Let the Guard get hold of him and see why he wants to go thumping a Breton on the head."

"I should tell Dahqin what's happened."

"You think this man knows where the Tents is?"

"Yes. And he has an idea where Dahqin's parents live, because Peran lost him close to there, and Dahqin said he was waiting for them in the main street. He'll find this place eventually and I don't want him sniffing round here."

He looks round the bar and back to his father.

"I'll call Dahqin and let them know about it. I can maybe lead him off into the wilds and try to lose him."

"And you think that will get rid of him?"

"I have to try and draw him off."

"Alun, you have a job. Remember. And you know nothing of him. He might be alone — but what if he can call on unlimited resources? I admit trying to knock you out in one of the main streets seems a bit stupid. He obviously wants something badly enough to attack you. How far is he prepared to go? He could get everything you know out of you and leave you to recover. But he might just be nasty, and go further."

"Well I thought of leading him down to the standing stones and freaking him out there."

"This isn't one of your boyhood adventures. You're facing someone who may be ruthless, certainly desperate enough to cosh you in a Fastness where he doesn't speak the language. But he must have had somewhere to take you after hitting you. Probably to the Tents as you were close by. Why not stay at ours for a few days and we'll keep an eye out for him. Get the Guard looking for him. I'll have a word with Dahqin's father. Make sure they're careful."

"I still have to get the radio and call Dahqin while they might be able to help."

"Come on, finish your drink." Bedow pays the bill and they leave, looking about them carefully.

They enter the Tents via the fire escape at the rear of the building. Kirus had altered the half-height door so they could enter and leave the place unobserved by the man they call the Crow, who lives across the road from the front entrance to the Tents. He habitually notes all the comings and goings of people from the homes around him, and makes sure everyone else knows about them too. Especially about the twins.

Alun ducks in. "If the Crow talks to him he'll know who's who, and where to find everyone. I bet he's watching the main door."

His father creeps in, quietly pushing the door shut behind him. Alun hands the pencil torch he always carries to Bedow.

"Watch where you tread."

"You and your damned fabrics." Bedow is flailing through the folds of cloth in Alun's silent wake. He catches up with him at the big window of the main room. Through the diaphanous hangings Alun can see the Shadow skulking within the entrance to the Crow's building.

"What are you watching him for?"

"Just realising how fragile everything can be, I suppose."

"Philosophy!"

Alun shrugs and goes for the radio. Gathering bits and pieces of personal apparel, he shoves everything into a backpack and returns to the main room. His father is watching the watcher, Alun pats him on the shoulder.

"Philosophy? I'm ready to go."

They leave the way they had entered. Alun carefully placing the false-wood cover over the tell-tale lock. From the ground the door looks no different from any other on the ladder.

Despite trying frequently over the next few hours, Alun cannot raise the Blondyn on the radio. At first he does not accept it, but as frustration turns to panic, and tiredness exhausts panic into troubled drowsiness, he gives in and goes to bed. He does not have a restful slumber, and is up before dawn trying to raise the Blondyn again.

June, 27th — Douarnenez

He punches the identifying numbers of the Blondyn into the radio and waits nervously as the tones pip out.

"Blondyn! This is Alun!" the Brezhoneg language harsh in Alun's urgency. He feels time slip away — he will be safe for now, escorted to and from the ferry — but will have to come to a decision on his own. It is his neck; only he can save it.

"Blondyn! Blondyn! This is Alun!"

"Alun? It's Kirus."

At the sound of his brother's voice Alun lets his breath out in sobs and squeaks of laughter.

"What's the problem? You sound weird."

"The Shadow tried to clobber me. Why didn't anyone answer me last night?"

"Somehow the volume got muted and I only discovered it about an hour ago. What do you mean, clobber you?"

"He attacked me, tried to knock me out. He's watching the Tents. I'm at the Nest. Where are you? I need help."

"Shite! Between Wolf and Tater Du. What do you need from us?"

"I don't know. Who the hell is that guy? Find out from Dahqin or Grandy. I thought of chasing out to Karnak."

"Why?"

"To mess the trail a bit."

"Don't do that. What does Pap say?"

"The same as you. I wish I was with you lot. I'm frightened — this is very scary."

"I'll talk to the others. Stay tight. I hope the Crow keeps his mouth shut about the Nest."

"So do I."

"I'll get back to you, or Dahqin will phone you. Alun, I love you."

The radio beeps and goes silent.

Alun lays back on the bed in which he had spent their teenage years sleeping and playing with Kirus and Dahqin, and drifts into a doze, waiting for the breeping call of his phone.

June, 27th — On the Blondyn — Western Approaches

Kirus rouses Grandy and Dahqin.

"He must be working for someone who saw me with Bartouche. Someone in the Praedicatum. I can't believe he is acting officially."

"But, Grandy, what do we tell Alun to do? Shouldn't we go back and get him? We can be back by tomorrow evening."

"I must go back, Kirus."

"Why?" Grandy challenges Dahqin.

"There will still be three of you on this boat. Kirus, you must get Grandy up to Alban — and that does not need me here. Ardel is at the other end already."

He looks to Grandy; she nods her head.

"So there's no point in all of us going back. Much as I miss Ardel, I want to see Alun safe and well, too. I know he's with a tough bunch with Bedow and his friends, but it would only take an unguarded moment and he could be injured or ... If anything happens to him and I haven't tried to help him — Ardel in my life will not compensate."

"And I've no substitute for Alun except ..."

"Don't, go there, Kirus."

"Nothing. Everything. You know my feelings. Why you?"

"I don't know this boat. I'm not dissing Peran's abilities, Kirus. But he needs you here. I'm going to help Alun and get him safe."

"Have you got a plan?"

"No, Grandy ... But I will. Kirus, how do I get back quickly?"

"We go into Fal and you hire one of the hifoils based there to take you back to Douarnenez. They go twice as fast as us."

Kirus turns the Blondyn towards Fal.

June, 27th — Fal

As they sail into the inner harbour at Falmouth, Peran points out a weird looking multihull in one of the marinas.

"That's the one you need to hire, the HiTail-it. Fastest one in this port. It's owned by my Uncle Charlie. It could be available. I'll try calling him."

There is no immediate response to Peran's call; they land Dahqin at a public quay. Grandy and Kirus intend waiting in Fal until he has hired something, but with uncertainty about the weather holding in their favour he overrides their arguments. As the Blondyn turns south, rounding Pendennis Point for the sea, Dahqin goes in search of the fastest wind-boat in Fal.

June, 27th — On the Blondyn — Sailing north

The Blondyn fares better than Kirus hoped; the wind remaining strong and favourable without going to storm strength. Passing between Kernow and the Wolf, they are well up the coast of Cymru when the wind veers unexpectedly more to the west and begins to increase in strength. Kirus sets the Blondyn to head into the building seas as closely as possible, crawling away from Cymru to gain a lee under the coast of Éire.

"It'll be a long slog tonight," he tells them.

Grandy has got to grips with some basics of navigation and watch-keeping duties under normal circumstances, but the motion of the vessel in this stretch of sea throws her off balance completely. She takes another tablet and follows Kirus's advice to sleep through it.

June, 28th — On the Blondyn — Sailing north

She gets up when dawn is breaking and the motion much easier and promptly finds herself on watch — issued with very strict instructions from Kirus — giving him and Peran a necessary break.

They are fully under the lee of the coast by the end of Grandy's watch, and between showers she is able to see white houses nestled in small groups on the hillsides behind the coastal dunes. As the Blondyn heads northwards dunes turn to cliffs and they pass two harbours backed by small urbs. She sleeps during the afternoon. When she returns to the deckhouse, Kirus keeps her company and asks about her life.

"I was born in Genève, though not of the western bloodline as you can see. There are all the right genes in me somewhere, but I cannot be bothered to recount them. Suffice to say my parents are wealthy and from the family patrimony near Gondor, though they never go there. We can claim a lineage directly to the House of David and beyond. The eastern branch has a more complete record of its line than the rather shadowy path by which the western branch tells its story, whatever Sion says. Despite the Derg and the other Subjections the Amharic Copts managed to save most of the old records, and there is no fuzzy five-hundred year gap in our family history."

"I think my family tree can only be traced back to the resurgence of the Celtic Lands, Grandy. Dahqin has something a bit more historic and *noble* in his mother's family. Something his mother has always gone on about. She still is actually. It's why he's called Franz, we think. It's a very strange name for Bretons to give their children. He hates it and only they use it. Dahqin's more meaningful — to me anyway."

"I can sympathise. Grandy is not my given name, I accepted it from my peers at school. I will not even attempt the lengthy process of repeating my given name, but it goes halfway to covering the genealogy of my family." They are watching the sun disappear behind the mountains set back from the coast.

"When we first met Alun, he said a rhyme to Dahqin with such emotion. It was beautiful. Can you say it in Breton for me. I loved the sound of it."

"*Mar ham guorant va karantit, da vont in nos o he kostit.*" His cadence is exactly as Alun had sounded it. He puts a hand across his mouth, and looks away from her, swallowing a few times. He laughs a little, then faces her.

"What did Dahqin say about it? It's really a male talking to a female, but that's not how he and I mean it."

"Lovers promising to sleep together — then he changed the subject. How do you mean it? In Common Tongue?"

"If my lover promises me, I shall couple with him tonight."

She probes Kirus for stories from the childhood the twins had shared with Dahqin. When she calls Peran out, the rain has stopped and the sky is already lightening. They are sailing fast on a broad reach, so Grandy sits on with Peran, drawing out his life story.

His family owns a boatyard and have traded across to Brittany, so far as he can tell, for a couple of hundred years, certainly from before the Upheavals. He has a couple of sisters and a brother, who are enough to help run the business in Fal, so his moving to Douarnenez was no problem, and he fitted right in. His Uncle Charlie on his father's side has a trading business and operates cargo wind-boats and some others like the hifoil. His father had suggested he worked for his uncle, and though they get on well Peran didn't want to work with him. Anyway, it is much more pleasurable to work with Alun and Kirus, and now and then for their father. He tells her meeting Dahqin had been weird, because the twins have mentioned him lots in all their storytelling, but he'd never seen a photo of him. There aren't any around and he's never thought to ask to see one. Alun had described only her, as if she'd be on her own, and Kirus thought she would be too. He thinks Dahqin doesn't like him.

Grandy gets up late in the day. With night approaching Kirus decides it is better to shelter on the east side of Mann. Setting out at sunrise next day will give plenty of daylight in which to make landfall, for the topog and their charts give insufficient information on where best to land to reach The Keep. He anchors the boat under the lee of low cliffs backed by hills, sheltering a semi circular bay. At the northern end of the bay two piers stick out a short way from the shore, with a small harbour nestling beyond them. Ashore, faint lights shine out from a cluster of houses around the harbour.

June, 29th — On the Blondyn — Reaching Haven

Anchor on board, Kirus sets the boat about and it quickly clears the bay. The wind has shifted and the waves are smaller, though a short swell remains making the boat's motion choppy.

By the time they reach the eastern shore the wind has decreased, knocking down the waves, so they can reconnoitre safely. High, scrub covered hills rise from the narrow coastal plain. The shore is a warren of dunes covered with coarse grass. The sun is hidden beyond the hills, and they lose its warmth as they move inshore. Dahqin had identified a southern inlet that showed good shelter. Using the notes from him and the topog they find the entrance amongst sand dunes. There is a bar of some kind, and the waves are breaking over it.

"That'll only be safe at high tide and in certain winds." Kirus checks over the charts again. "We'll try this harbour further north."

The sand dunes give way to low banks leading onto grassland. Further north massive concrete structures are sighted, some part way in the sea. Large skulls have been painted on them in the faded colours of the rainbow. On one of the largest mounds 'Here Stalks DEATH' has been painted in enormous letters. Peran translates it for Kirus.

"It's atomics, isn't it?" Kirus says, equating the structures with those in Brittany.

They are closing up to a headland where the strata of stone are slanted and jointed like a lop-sided brick wall. The ruins of a lighthouse perch precariously on the cliff edge.

"There's someone in that building." Kirus is looking through his binos at a small hut near the ruins. Then the radio squawks into life.

"Vessel Blondyn, south-west of Bees, tune radio to 77 and call."

"This is the Blondyn, from Brittany."

"What is your business in Alban?"

"What do we tell them?" Kirus asks Grandy.

"Um ..."

A long list of questions follows and Grandy builds her reasons for being in Alban into the answers she gives Kirus to pass on.

"This is the first time I've been questioned like this, Grandy. Éire, Cymru, Kernow, France, Viscaya, Galicia. There's never any trouble landing. Usually I just sail in and fill out any forms after tying up."

After a very long wait the radio crackles back into life.

"You have permission to enter. Sail north about four kimetres to the fairway buoy for Haven and the pilot will meet you."

"Thank you, Madame."

Kirus turns the Blondyn onto a heading of twenty-five degrees and adjusts the sails to suit the course.

Book Four — Part 1

Waiting in The Keep

Safely in the arms of another

June, 24th — The Keep in Derwent — Ardel

There is a streak of sunlight on the wall I face. I stretch lazily, wondering how to spend my time. Waiting to get a response from Grandy will be frustrating, so I need to be doing something physical. Nothing is scheduled with the Reever or any other arms of government. The idea forms that I should gather information about Alban. But that can wait for a day.

There's the glass of water I put on the bed shelf, but no Nettle Fizz. My memory jogs — I have to get it from the frige. In a minute. I close my eyes again, turn over and smell Dahqin's faint aroma. The dream comes back to mind. I shake it off.

I can't help wondering what Dahqin will do with his time now his latest contract has ended. Grandy will check in on him. I hope he's got some work in the offing, otherwise by the time I return home he'll be morose and grumpy; feeling unsure of my affections. Which is silly. I love Dahqin so much and can't imagine anymore what life would be without him. But I'll never admit as much to him. Rather, and I know it's a little selfish, it is really important to me that we are as independent from one another as we need. I know he has deep-seated loyalty to me that feels vaguely obsessive, which can be dangerous. And I have sometimes pushed the envelope out to the edge of what Dahqin will accept, but the alternative won't work for either of us.

We do get off on telling one another about the little outside incidents. I can feel one in the offing — vaguely obsessive I could be about Duncn. But I have a serious purpose to fulfil here. My Solo. Time to get out of this bed before that pre-dinner scene from last night expands. The sun is well up in the sky and I need a good work-out.

A woman answers when I use the internal phone.

"Good morning. This is the Ambassador. I have been told there is a gym near my room. Where do I find it. A plan of The Keep would be helpful to me. Please."

"I will get someone to come to your chamber, Ambassador."

"Thank you. Oh, can you tell me if an hour in the gym will make me too late for breakfast?"

"No, Ambassador. This is Martha, the Bursar. You can request food whenever you need it. Come along the terrace from your room. There is a Butlery just inside the recessed door, by the tables."

"Thank you, Martha."

Now I check the time, it's not so late as I thought, I have not yet got used to the difference in time from Genève. With an hour of training, breakfast can be finished by ten o'clock. Whatever is said about the abuse of power and privilege by Faerachar, it seems those living and working in The Keep have a lifestyle better in many ways than mine in the Cantons. Dressed for the work-out, I store that thought away. When ready, I open the chamber door to the corridor and lean against the door frame.

A man dressed in Boundary Patrol uniform soon arrives from the direction of the cannion shaft.

"Ambassador. Here is the plan you requested. The Castellan sent this also. The gym is just a few doors along."

He hands me an envelope and a multi-coloured 'Guide to The Keep' — I put them on the desk and follow him back the way he had come.

An hour and a half later feeling primed and satisfied, I sit in the sun, outside the table canopy's shadow and out of reach of the south-westerly breeze, eating a light breakfast while studying the plan of The Keep. It is carefully drawn so the casual visitor may reach the places to which they are permitted. I assume that status for today. Nothing is shown about large sections of the building; no means of entry, and no designation of purpose. The level my chamber is on, and the one above with the Audience Chambers, where we had the meal last night, permit the greatest access. The Reever's Office is not marked. Immediately below where I now sit there is a large Rest Area. Relevant cannion points are clearly marked. At ground level the Main Reception, the Stables, the paddocks, lawns and Boathouse have access. Somewhere, low down at the core, is the cistern with its strange inhabitants.

I want to get out of The Keep and spend some time on my own. By the Butlery entrance there is a service phone.

"This is the Ambassador. I wish to speak to The Communicator."

"I'll patch you, Sir." There is a pause, then the sound of David talking, with other voices in the background.

"... don't leave it like that. Tidy it up. And get it okayed before sending. Hello, Ardel. What can I do for you?"

"David, can I come and see you?" I could ask for what I want over the phone, but I would like to strengthen our rapport.

"Um ... Well ... Sure. Look, can you find the canteen?"

"Is it the Rest Area? That's all I've got on this plan. One floor below mine and to the south?"

"Y-eah," he says hesitantly. Then, "Yes, that's it. I'll be about ten minutes, maybe a bit longer."

"Okay, I'll be there."

I go back through Coleridge to the nearby cannion shaft. I am still checking for a call button when the shaft doors open. It looks just like the one I was first in — I sit down. There are no controls and before I can say anything it is going down. When the cannion stops I'm right by an entrance to the Rest Area.

It is busy with groups of people chattering whilst having food and drink, and constant movement in and out. I was not expecting this. The Secretariat of the Council House in Genève could manage to fill such a room, but this is Derwent, in a Fastness, and no large urbs nearby as far as I can tell. No one pays me much attention, so I join the queue at the counters and take a glass of mixed vegetable juice. It is all gratis. Most tables are big with benches and chairs at them. I find a seat at a smaller one facing the entrance. Five people already sit at the table, talking in the thicker dialect Kaet had used. A couple of them look up and acknowledge my presence. I concentrate on picking up the gist of the words. When David enters I stand to attract his attention.

"Ardel, I'll get a drink and be right back."

The five all look at me with interest. I smile at them as I sit, feeling exposed. I realise it's being Solo that's getting to me. As David heads across they get up and leave, greeting him affably as they pass.

"What can I do for you? It's very busy up top, so I can't give you much time, unfortunately."

"I'll come straight to what I want. One. I want to borrow some binos and a horse. Who's best at organising such things?"

"The Castellan. I'll tell him to contact you."

"Two. How do I get the cannion to work?"

"When you want to go somewhere you just say where and they'll deliver you. There's a mike at every set of cannion doors, but it's tiny, so you might not have noticed it. It's always on the left."

"But they sent me here without my saying anything."

"Because I told them. Anything else?"

"Three. I'll need to work on those files Faerachar had in his office last night. Do I have to see him?"

"Sorry, my fault. Everything is in a workroom, W7. Near your chamber, same corridor, towards the cannion. I'll send you the lock code."

"How can I get in touch with you when you aren't at work?"

"Use the service phone — I live in The Keep. Just along from here, actually. I'll let you know when I've got some free time. What are you doing today?"

"A bit of exploring around the area. That's another thing..."

A button clipped to David's shirt starts buzzing.

"Sorry, I must go. I'll be in touch." And he strides out.

As I pace round the main room in Coleridge while mentally sorting my priorities, I see the envelope on the desk. Slitting it open I pull out a neatly written note.

Regards to the Ambassador, Ardel Penaul,
this 23rd day of June, 2188.

     I apologise sincerely for what has taken place in the Reever's name. The abuse of an Ambassador of the League whilst in the execution of his duties, on my orders, is unforgivable, and I would not attempt to ask for your indulgence of my dereliction.

     As the Custodian of The Keep, in the Reever's absence, I can only say my zeal in trying to protect this place led to my blunder about your identity. I mistook the sign the Rider gave, on no less than four occasions between the far side of the river and here by The Keep itself, as a clue to your identity. It was only after some investigating on the part of the Reever that the true nature of the sign was realised. I had not thought the Rider would feel so strongly about evil-eye with one who upholds the good.

     I have offered to resign my post as Castellan, but the Reever refused in high dudgeon, saying you would not demand such treatment of a faithful servant.

     I trust we may bridge any chasm your treatment has opened between us. If there is anything you require, please ask it of me and I shall try to see your wishes fulfilled.

Yours in faith,
Castellan of The Keep in Derwent, in Wark-in-Alban,

Jonat MacLachlan

Refolding the paper, I put it back into the envelope. Then I think about the cistern. I doubt I'll ever get an answer from Faerachar. I lift the phone.

"Ambassador."

"Yes. I wish to speak to the Castellan."

There is a pause, then I hear a heavily accented voice, similar to David's, but clipped in delivery.

"Castellan."

"This is Ambassador Penaul. I have just read your letter. Thank you for your apologies, which I accept. I am sure we can work out any differences caused by my treatment. If it is possible, there are a couple of things I would like to achieve today."

"I'll try to help, Ambassador. The Communicator has already spoken to me about a horse and binos."

"Ah. Right. I wish to go riding in this locality as soon as possible."

"No problem. I shall get you a map."

"Thank you. There is one more thing. I would like to know what is in the water in the cistern, or whatever you call it, where I was detained."

There is a significant silence before the Castellan speaks.

"I shall come to your chamber directly." The line goes dead. Only a few minutes and there is a loud knocking at the door. The Castellan greets me with a swift bow.

"Have you everything with you that you require for the day, Ambassador? I will take you to the stables after we have seen the life in the water. Take a waterproof for your ride, the clouds can rapidly enfold the fells."

I gather what I need — rapidly.

"If you will follow me Ambassador, I can do better than tell you what is in the cistern. I can show you."

He leads me at a brisk pace along the corridor, away from the cannion. We go down a spiral ramp with four exits onto other floors and continue along a lower corridor for some distance.

"How old is this Keep?" Even with my longer legs I have difficulty keeping up with the Castellan.

"This part, about one hundred years. The lower levels were built about sixty years earlier to protect the population in this area from the airborne dangers while the work went on at Calda. That, and any manner of other threats. The upper stories, where you are staying, they were added roughly seventy years ago."

We go through doors onto a stairway, and descend six steep flights. As we charge along another corridor the Castellan stops suddenly and flings open a door. A dozen people are sitting at control panels, watching a series of screens.

"This is our control room. From here we can watch areas inside and outside The Keep. As far as we can make it The Keep is secure."

"Can you see into the chambers from here?"

"No, Ambassador. Despite appearances and this spying system here, we value privacy very highly. In your room you are completely alone — no audience watching down here. Once in the corridor, and we can follow you if we so wish. However, you wish to see the creatures in the water." He leads me into the next room. There are more control panels, though no one is at them.

"Yes. I'm hoping the nightmares I've had since my incarceration will stop after I've seen them."

The Castellan shoots me a raised eyebrow look.

We go through another door, along a short corridor and down two more flights of stairs into a whitewashed room with cement floor, in the centre of which is a large central drain. Tanks of various designs and buckets stand around the floor. There are a couple of workbenches and a small overhead crane. A round cannion cage sits in one corner. Through the window in a second door I can see down a corridor with pipes and valve chests on both sides. A man in a boiler suit waits with a scoop-net by a large container filled with water.

"The cistern is under us, through that hatch in the floor. I do not know exactly when it was built. The water is salt and the creatures are hagfish, living on carrion. I believe they were an abiding interest of one of the earlier Reevers. There are other animals in there as this connects to the sea. The water level is just below the high tide level on the coast north of Haven."

He nods to the man who fishes the net around in the water. He flicks the net up and dangles it in front of me. Sinuous pink forms are twisting violently around each other, and slime is dripping through the mesh. I recoil with screwed-up face.

"They make slime particularly so when they are stressed, for example being out of water." The Castellan nods again and the man dumps the creatures back in the container and empties it down the drain.

"Their main purpose was to get rid of carrion from the kitchens. Everything left from our consumption in this place is recycled by composting. But some carrion is more difficult to deal with, so we have maintained the hagfish, who thrive on it. Now. You want to go riding."

"Yes." I can't dwell on what I have seen because the Castellan leads me briskly back to the main control room.

"Get a cannion here. Me and the Ambassador are going over to the stables."

"Right." One of the operators taps at some buttons. When we leave the control room the cannion is waiting around the corner with open doors.

I choose a gentle mature grey mare from those on offer. Once I am mounted the Castellan pats the front saddle-bag.

"In here, the map, the binos, a compass, a radio: your phone may not work everywhere. The rear bag on your right has refreshments. This side has a survival pack in the larger section: it is changeable weather on the fells, Ambassador, and I do not know how long you plan to be, nor how good you are at finding your way. In the smaller pocket a hand-gun and a little extra ammunition. This longer canister has a stun-lance."

I look askance at the mention of weapons, and go to protest.

"We know Ambassadors never carry weapons, but I must look to your safety. You may need them if you meet dogs or boars. Or whatever. I assume, given your nationality, you can use a gun."

"Yes, Castellan, I can and the lance. I accept your thoughtfulness in its spirit, and it will be noted in my report."

He nods slightly, and I put out my hand, surprising him. He responds vigorously.

"I trust we can now treat one another equitably, Castellan."

"I am certain of it. Have a good ride. And be careful of your way, Ambassador."

Tapping my heels to the mare's flanks, she moves down the tunnel and out of The Keep.

June, 24th — Derwent & The Three Houses — Ardel

A light breeze fails to cool the air as I ramble beside the marshes along the river to the lake shore ahead. Unlike Derwent, this northern lake has cloudy water, and I can see a tow in the water, causing the surface to churn. The water level is well below the floodline debris left on the shore. I presume the winters might be cold enough for snow.

Some distance along the lake I notice sunlight reflecting from something amongst the trees. At the next pathway I trot the horse into the trees and come to a double roadway, metalled and a good height above the lake shore. My attention is drawn above one roadway by an overhead monorail. The sunlight is reflecting off a numbered indicator on one of the supports. Checking the map, only a single roadway is shown, I assume the monorail goes near to The Keep with it. The map is detailed as to the topography, but otherwise sketchy.

Moving back through the trees I let the horse pick a slow way along the grass flanking the floodline. Halfway along the lake the western hills recede further from the shore. Deciding to climb the contours rather than follow the shore, I set off on a steep diagonal up the nearest hill. My hope was to get a clear overview of the route of the monorail, but the slope gentles out, and from this hill's summit I see eastwards only from the middle of the lake. The stone circle is just visible through the binos — of The Keep there is no sign. Around me outcroppings of rocks are surrounded by short grass. Of the animals keeping it so, I see nothing, except their droppings.

We move northward along the broad ridge to the next hill, to look over the valley where the river leaves the lake. Beyond the river two broad low sheds sit just below the crest of one isolated hilltop. Winching machinery is positioned outside them and in two places right at the lip where the land falls steeply away. The screen of scrub on the hill is emphasised by an inverted vee of verdant short grass cut into it, leading from the sheds to the lip. Sheep are munching their way immobilely along the arms of the vee. A glider field, I guess, though the site seems wrongly sited for them to attain adequate lift. I check the map — again — no enlightenment. The track and monorail loop through the shallow pass between the hills and the river, following it westwards towards the sea.

Delving into the front bag trying to find the compass, I discover a sketch-pad and pencils. Dismounting, I open the refreshment saddle-bag to find some packs of food and two flasks, both with water. I take a swig — numbingly icy. I sit on the grass, making quick sketches of the puzzling vee in the scrub, the horse standing close by. Occasional clouds saunter over from the west; the sun will not last the afternoon out. I strip off and lay down on a flat rock, sunning.

The clouds are gathering in earnest when I wake an hour later, the horse nudging at me, the sun already behind a thin layer. Having dressed and eaten, I walk with the horse along the ridge, the lake at my back. The wind is blowing from the west, cool but not too strong. The ridge heads towards still higher ground. From its peak: to the west a small valley, its stream caught in flashes amongst the trees, descends into a larger valley from where a river twinkles light back at me when the sun breaks through the clouds gathering in the near distance. On the horizon I can see an island with two peaks, dark against its backdrop. To the east, the stones of the circle stand on a brow. I lean against the rocks marking the summit; the horse moves round them into its lee. My hair, caught by the wind, tugs at my scalp and I close my eyes, thinking of Dahqin.

"In such a place as this — my spirit rose, and flew to thee."

204

A couple of lines from a poem learned at school comes to my mind. The thought of Dahqin being close by — near enough to reach out to and touch — makes me jolt.

Descending across the hillside I walk the horse through a plantation of pulp trees and soon reach a track beside a stream, from where I ride around the foot of the steep-sided fells, looking down into a valley with cultivated fields and scattered houses. The track joins a road that passes between a sheer-sided mountain and a small lake. In a little settlement sited where the land opens out I see the first humans since leaving The Keep: I dismount to ask if there is a café.

"There's a pub," the youngest woman of the three says. A small terrier dog with them comes and looks up at me. The other women turn away.

"You come wi' me." We set off towards a group of houses by the river. "Tetchy!" The dog runs to her.

There's a man standing in the doorway of a single storey building; a small sign sports a red lion rampant.

"He's an outsider, Ted. Staying at Keep. He wants som'at to drink."

As I look for somewhere to hitch the horse, she is petting the horse and saying that Megan will be fine left to herself.

"She knows where you are and where she is. She'll not leave you. I'll get her across the lane into the meadow and just slip her bridle a little."

By the time I'm comfortable with Megan being loose, the woman is sitting at the tiny bar, the dog at her feet, its erect ears turning towards whoever is speaking. The man is looking enquiringly at me.

"Do you have something hot to drink?"

"We have good tea, fruit and herbal teas, all usual milk drinks, or coffee. But that's on the expensive side. Which'll it be?"

"I'll try the coffee, please."

The man goes through the list of coffees — exactly as I can get at home. I reset my pre-conceptions and ask for a cortardo. Unruffled, he goes behind the bar and starts making it.

I circle the room before sitting in an upright chair at a table by the largest window. I can see Megan across the road on the open field. The dog has followed me and is tapping at my leg. I put my hand down, but with no food on offer it goes back to the woman.

"Are you heading for The Keep now?"

She is medium height, mousey haired, a bit overweight, chubby-cheeked, and friendly. She smiles sweetly at me.

"How do you know I am staying at The Keep?"

"It's no secret. Everyone knows you're an Ambassador. You're only outsider round here. I'm Mary. He's a bit of a crack too, ent he, Ted?"

He looks at me quickly and mumbles, "If you say."

"I do not understand what you say too well."

But I catch her drift. She takes the coffee from the man and brings it to my table. Smiling all the while.

"Do either of you wish for a drink also?"

"I will. Ta, Ambassador. Gi'us a beer, Ted." He gets two bottles of dark beer and pours them into glasses. She brings hers back to my table — the dog lays across my feet. Ted holds up his glass and nods to me.

"Here's to you." She raises her glass.

"Salut." It's a very good cortardo.

"How long you staying for?"

"Some time yet. Which is the best way back to The Keep?"

"Depends. Shortest is by Keska. Easier by Seatola from here."

She is looking speculatively at me.

"How long have you got?"

I pull out the map, indicating she show me where she means. She looks at it closely.

"This the best you could get? Wait here."

She gets up and leaves the inn. The dog sits up, leans against my leg, so I stroke its head. It moves to sniff my hand, then wanders off to the entrance and lays in the doorway. I look at the bar man who smiles and shrugs, then I look at the map again. I can see exactly where I am, but of the places she mentioned the map tells nothing. I hear the dog's claws on the floor and look up as my drinking companion refills the room with her presence.

"This one's better." She slaps her map onto the table. "An old copy. You can't have it."

"Where are these places you told me about?"

"Here and here. This one's Keska."

I note the gradients and pass heights. Scribble the names onto my map. I ask her if she knows where there are three large houses close together that look north across Derwent.

"Know 'em well enough, it's here. The Three Houses. Only way from here is going out by Seatola — south of Derwentwater."

She points to the left of the window and finishes her beer.

"Got to go. Busy, you know."

And together with her dog she leaves me with the two maps and the watching barman. I study her map a while longer, then hand it to him and pay up, complimenting him on the coffee. My horse has wandered further into the meadows, but when I call her name, she comes to me. It is late in the day and the sky is decidedly stormy by the time I cross the Derwent valley.

Loitering by the lower waterfall I get jitters — I don't want to commit a social gaffe by arriving uninvited. The mare shifts under me, not prepared to settle. Eventually I face down this fear and ride up to the houses. Kaet is by her painting, but does not see me dismount. I put the mare in the paddock, then wander to the other houses. The oldest house is firmly shuttered; I peek into the windows of the middle one, but there is no sign of life. I return to her door and take off my over-breeches.

In answer to my timid knock, Kaet shouts down for the visitor to enter and come up. I put on the felt slippers, climb the stairs to the living room and pause in the doorway. She has her hair held up with pins, wears a work-coat and stands by the easel and paint table on the canvas sheet. The painting is finished, I think. She smiles at me.

"Ardel." She says it with warmth. "This is a really wonderful surprise. I hadn't thought I'd see you so soon. Business dealt with?"

"I have spare time for now."

Crossing the room I give her a genteel kiss on each cheek. She leans her head forward to keep her paint-spattered coat away from my clothing, twitches her nose.

"Please, I didn't want to disturb you."

"Horsey. You are planning on staying?"

When I nod, she tells me to take the saddle and harness off and put them into the shelter.

"I've got about fifteen minutes more. I should have finished by now, but I got held back by your visit yesterday. Don't take that as it sounds. Nor this: take a shower when you're done. It's the door at the end of the hall downstairs — there's towels on the shelf, and a neutralizer bin. Put your clothes in there for about four minutes. Leave the over-breeches in the porch."

Back in the house and smelling fresh, I sneak a look into the kitchen. It is as big as the living room above. Glass-fronted cabinets, set against a short wall between doors, display sets of old china-ware. This end there's a table seating eight. Towards the far end there's a couple of small sofas either side of the doors leading to a terrace behind the house. A couple of extra chairs sit next to a small table. A run of prep surfaces along the longest wall with a frige one end and an oven array at the other, two large sinks in the middle, and there is an island unit with hob. The perfect set-up — I'm envious.

"I'm finished now." Kaet calls.

As I turn to go upstairs I notice alongside the door a small shelf. A rotund, modern earth mother with a benign smile, in front of a beautiful little box lined with red silk, sits next to a bottle of wine. Alban Fastness Estates Dornfelder 2181. I climb the stairs.

"It's going to pour down. Yesterday was an amazingly dry day." As she speaks she dabs her brushes in water.

"I'm awfully messy when I'm applying paint." She sniffs at me. "That's a better ambience. What would you like to drink? I'll be doing something quick for dinner. Duncn's coming over for it later. Do you like him?"

"Why does everyone always ask so many questions at once?"

She laughs at me.

"We like to sow confusion. I noticed you don't do it. So, will tea do? And," she pauses. "You are staying for dinner."

"Okay, I'll take tea, as you made it yesterday. Can I help? You are ordering me to stay for dinner, so I have no choice now. Yes, I have an idea I do like Duncn. Why do you ask?"

"Not so innocent curiosity. I know you didn't have much of a conversation with him."

"I'm not sure he is really interested in me."

"Not interested — I'm not letting you get away with that. I saw what Duncn did while holding your hand. And your reaction."

"Faerachar is the one who bugs me. I don't know how to read him or to react to him. He seems to be so many different people all at once."

"You know that Faerachar has been playing with you. I take it you've seen the information you two were talking about yesterday. You'll work out how to handle him."

"But he's been flirting with me."

"You are attractive — he finds lots of men attractive. But it's not sexual, he just likes male company. And he sees you are easy to play. Ignore him: Siobhagn is the only one for him. Come down with me."

She leads me into the kitchen and gestures towards the sofas. Taking off her coat she goes through to the washroom, returning a few minutes later drying her hands.

"Are you looking for a flirtation?"

I shrug as I sit on a stool at the island unit. She makes the tea and sets some small savoury pastries on a plate.

"Who is Shivawn?"

"Siobhagn. Not quite what you said, but close enough for now. She's the mother of their children. They live in the Township."

"Who lives in the oldest house?"

"No one at the moment. First House belongs to Faerachar. Second House is Briged's — that's where Duncn lives."

She stops what she's doing, looks at me with a searching look, and doesn't say what she was going to.

"As you are interested in a sexual fling, why not try Duncn? My sweet young brother. I despair for him at times. Don't look at me with that mock-shocked expression. So I'm his sister, but that's no reason why I shouldn't be arranging such things. You fascinate him. Just be easy with him and his emotions."

"Are you saying Duncn is easy, but needs looking after?"

"Neither in the ways you mean. Just remember, aside from your casual flings, you've got someone at home, who loves you dearly. What's his name?"

"You mean you don't know?"

"I wouldn't ask if I knew. Sarcasm is unnecessary."

"I'm sorry, Kaet. It's Dahqin."

There's a strange look crosses her face, and she flinches like she's moved out of the way of something.

"I assumed as you knew my name, you'd know his. I thought Faerachar had told you."

"Darkin ... Darknin ... Hmm. Dah-qin. Finally got it. Is he dark-haired with dark brown eyes?"

I nod. She hands me the tray, walking ahead of me to the sofas, setting a trestle ready.

"Faerachar didn't tell me your name. I just knew it."

A persistent, gusting rain is falling by the time we settle ourselves for tea. Kaet lights candles, the flames reflecting off her dark hair.

"You came here to ask me about Faerachar, didn't you? Forget him — you know more than enough to work constructively with him without needing an edge."

"Yes, I did. But now don't want to implicate you in the politics."

"Political implication? If I was Briged I maybe wouldn't have told you anything. But I have other reasons for telling you about Duncn. Mine are all emotional, all to do with love and lust. Actually mainly lust. Duncn fancies you, and is in need of some physical passion."

"Doesn't he have a partner? I mean, he is beautiful; surely there is someone here who he can get to bed with. There's at least one person in

The Keep who is attractive and — well — just the sort I would make a play for in slightly different circumstances."

"Dark hair, fair skinned, your height, fearless gaze. Answers to Regin. His circumstances are complicated. And he's deeply in love with only one person. So don't."

"He did look boldly at me."

"And you look boldly about you. What's the time, please?"

I hold my wrist towards her and tap my timeband.

"Don't tell me. I don't want to know."

She frowns at that.

"When I get back to The Keep there is bound to be a message from Genève. I don't want to think about the implications."

"In that case we must make tonight special."

"Tell me about David."

"David? You find him attractive, don't you? So that's three."

"Of course, who could not. He took the appraisal I gave him with a certain pride."

She laughs, and throws a cushion at me.

"So you know. What else do you want to know?"

"Well the body language of you two at that meal ... I thought there's no way you are connected. He told me you discussed me and Duncn. Yet he lives in The Keep."

"I squeezed your interaction into seven words; he just laughed. That's not a discussion. It's true we are very private with our affections. Duncn knows most about us. Briged approves. Faerachar's a nosy parker and takes the micky too much, so we try to keep him in the dark about us. Which is why David stays in The Keep."

"Nosy parker?"

"It's slang — means he pokes his nose into our affairs too far. What can I tell you about David? He's very funny when he isn't working. He's from Falkirk, up in Scotia — hence the accent. Anyway, I met David while climbing near here, the stars sparkled and that was that. It was very romantic. We see enough of each other to fulfil our needs. I'm saying no

211

more. And you can keep what I've told you all to yourself."

"Met on a mountain top. Dahqin's the one you should talk to about romance."

"Yes, tell me about him. You've hardly mentioned him amongst these men you're lining up for seduction."

I shift to a more comfortable position, and begin to tell Kaet the story of my involvement with Dahqin. I would have got us out of Paris as far as Genève, but Duncn arrives.

As Kaet starts preparing the meal, she sends us off to settle the horses for the night. We are in the small stable between Second House and First House.

"I don't suppose you need to use the gym much, do you?"

"Never." Duncn grins and postures.

"I work-out four days a week. If I don't my body lets me know it."

"I'm usually too whacked at the end of the day to think of much except food and sleep. Pass me that bridle." As he reaches up to hang the tackle, I move around the horse, trapping him.

"Don't you have anything you really like doing? You know, things outside your work?"

Duncn's smiling slightly, swallowing and looking directly into my eyes. "I like to go rowing on the lakes, or sailing. What about you?"

"I like doing this." Our faces are so close I can feel his breath.

"Being in a stable?" I gently squeeze his biceps and smile again. Turning away I head outside. It's stopped raining.

"I think we'd better return to Kaet. She'll think we've left her." He's light on his feet and I'm not sure he's following me, but I'm not looking back. "Where's Briged?"

He's so close to me, I jump when he speaks, making him laugh.

"She's here tonight. She'll be at The Keep tomorrow, and then she's off on a tour for a few days."

"What happened to your father?"

"Went back to Skane. They were good in bed, according to Faerachar.

She never saw him again. Faerachar is more like a father than a brother. Kaet's the one I love most. They all tell me I only have to look in the mirror to see him."

At the porch to Second House I stop, turn and soak up his image.

"So I do that as often as I can," he says, slowly moving against me, looking up into my eyes. Though the light is failing, I clearly see the narrow brown surround of his green irises. I melt into his kiss.

"I need to clean up and change, Ardel." He sends me back to Third House.

Kaet is whisking egg whites. She tells me to keep an eye on the julienned courgettes being sautéd in a large frying pan, in oil and butter with a seasoning of thyme and marjoram.

"Eight eggs for the three of us. There needs to be watery juices left from the courgettes, it steams the egg mix, so don't let it dry out."

She folds the beaten yolks, seasoned with pepper, back into the peaky whites. Nudges me aside, checks the liquid is just so, and pours the soufflé mix evenly over the courgettes. Then she flicks thin pieces of halloumi cheese into the foam, re-closing the holes with a spatula. Little vents puff out bursts of steam, and the dome rises. She has a broad grin on her face as she gently touches the surface of the egg mix.

"I call this a souflette. When I'm happy with the stiffness of the eggs, I'll top it with Gruyere slices and brown it off under the grill. It'll deflate a bit. Meanwhile, can you get that pan of sprouting broccoli on the go. Simmer until bright, bright green. Okay, don't roll your eyes so much — I accept you know what to do."

"I love cooking. Getting green stuff cooked just right is my forte."

"Get out two wine glasses for you and him. They're in the top cupboard next to the frige. I sit at this end of the table. I'm not drinking alcohol at the moment. So water too, please."

Duncn arrives with a bottle of Alban Fastness Estates Dornfelder 2181, opened to breath. Talking about the wine leads me to discover Duncn is the Estate Manager that Regin talked of. I ask if I might accompany him to see the vineyard — he says he'll make that happen.

Kaet and I sit at the table, the meal over. Duncn has gone to check on the horses.

"Why would Faerachar tell me Duncn was Briged's paramour when I first met him?"

"All part of his playing with you. He likes to shock people; I'm guessing he was pleased by your reaction. He would bet on you falling for Duncn's beauty, so when he introduced you properly before dinner the other night, your reaction would have pleased him even more."

"He says he is the spitting image of his father."

"Not quite, Axel was closer to your height. He was on a windship into Edinburgh – we lived there then. Not much to tell really, it would have been sexual attraction pure and simple. He couldn't know he was a father. I don't know if she deliberately took the risk, hoping. I think it's the Taran blood driving through them, Duncn included."

"And you?"

"I was saved by an excess of my father's bloodline, I guess. Whatever, I am happy enough with what I have with David. Sex isn't everything in life you know, even if you young bucks act as if it is."

A buzzing sound comes from above.

"Damn! Now what can that be for?"

She runs up the stairs and her footsteps thud above the ceiling. Listening intently I realise Faerachar is on the phone, asking about the horse and me.

"He's annoyed you didn't let the stables know the horse is okay. I told him you are staying here tonight."

When Duncn returns I steer the conversation round to Briged and her itinerant life travelling the Fastness. It is through this chatter that I learn she has an important job in the maintenance of the ethics of government and society in Alban. A job with a title she does not use unless forced by circumstances. She is The Good Sounding Counsel: I will ask her directly to explain this role when she returns. Right now I have pleasure on my mind.

We move upstairs to settle on the settees, us with a glass of watered whisky each, Kaet with a herbal concoction she makes herself. Soon after, Kaet decides she will go to bed, but then chatters on with us for over an hour.

"Duncn, show Ardel where to sleep," she announces breezily when she does leave. For a few minutes we sit at opposite ends of the large settee, contemplating one another.

"What time do you rise in the morning, Duncn?"

"Just after dawn. Usually. It depends what's happening. You?"

"I must get back to The Keep first thing in the morning."

I slowly extend my hand along the back to touch Duncn's fingers. We slide together and linger over kisses.

June, 25th — The Keep — Ardel

Returning to The Keep I find Faerachar slightly cold in manner. He lectures me about his responsibility to the League for my safety. In future I am to carry a radio on me at all times. I politely refuse, but give him my phone number.

Back in Coleridge I find a message on the HiSec from Grandy acknowledging receipt of my report. It does not leave any room for reading between its single line. I spend the rest of the morning in room W7, looking through the material gathered from the illegal faxplex.

After a lonely lunch I take a public ferry from the Boathouse jetty and spend the afternoon walking on the fells east of the Township.

That night I spend with Duncn again, in Second House. We agree this is a nice interlude for a few days in our lives. But I can't believe he is so solitary in his life. We are entangled, in the afterglow of our romp — not yet tired.

"Can't you find anyone to love round here?"

Duncn shifts to look up at my frowning face.

"The man I look to will give me that, and make me as horny as you do, Ardel. But the right man isn't available round here right now."

As I wind my fingers through his hair he pushes my hand away.

"So I go looking for sex instead. And in the right time for that – you appeared."

I sit up, look down at the beautiful body stretched out in front of me. My frown is back. I can feel the growing excitement caused by the idea that I have a few nights to spend with this one man. This has never been the case before with all my other dalliances, which have lasted only hours. I shall have to be careful how I explain this to Dahqin.

"And what about you?" he asks.

"Well, you can tell I like you a lot. But there is someone else."

Duncn sniggers. "Called Dahqin. I can tell you're no saint."

"I suppose you heard from Faerachar today." He shakes his head. "Overheard me talking to Kaet, or she told you?"

Again Duncn shakes his head.

"You talk in your sleep – you were dreaming I guess. Dahqin was said quite a lot. You stopped when I cuddled you."

"I've had a few nightmares since I got here, but I don't remember anything from last night. Maybe I'm getting over it."

"Come on," Duncn draws me back down. "Cuddle up. I understand about Dahqin. I want that sort of relationship with someone. Well, I think I do." He kisses me around my lips, then pulls away and smiles. "Meanwhile ..."

June, 26th – The Keep – Ardel

When I return to The Keep next morning I find a message on the HiSec satcom. I should have taken it with me last night, because it is more important than the phone. Decoding the message, I am horrified to find it is from Bartouche. It required an immediate response. I am to hold fast, and only respond to communications from Bartouche. I send a signal confirming receipt, and for the rest of the morning I ponder what the message says behind the string of plain words. Finally I decide that Grandy is coming to The Keep. I have no idea how or when, nor where she will enter Alban.

I make an appointment to see Faerachar this evening — we are to meet over supper — then I spend the afternoon poring over the information in Room W7. Two hours before I am to meet Faerachar I go to the gym. Feeling primed, I relax with half-an-hour of meditation before heading along the terrace.

Faerachar is leaning against the parapet, a glass of beer in his hand, looking across Derwentwater

"Welcome, Ambassador. Or are you Ardel?" He is being officious.

"This is primarily about official business. What have I done that you find so upsetting?"

"I was worried the other night — more about the horse than you. I was annoyed that I had to go chasing after you. You had not thought about the stable staff with your lack of communication, because you were safely in the arms of another."

"Are you jealous?"

"Of course not. That game is finished. Anyway, enough about your domestic arrangements with Duncn. I'm happy we can move on."

"To return to your original question, I am getting used to being Ardel. How much longer that will be for I do not know."

"You have news from the Cantons, then."

I spell out what I have read into Bartouche's message. When I finish Faerachar changes the subject.

"Ready for food?"

"Yes. I'm starving."

"Regin's cooked for us again, that's a privilege he doesn't extend very often. What'll you have to drink?"

"A watered beer, please." Faerachar serves the drink from the butler-trolley and sits down. I remain standing for a while looking across the lake towards the stone circle, abashed at my real lapse about the stable staff. When I sit down we chink glasses.

"I don't think it will be a problem for us to get an inkling of her presence once your boss gets here. There aren't many ways into Alban — and all of them watched."

"Faerachar, what is the monorail for?"

"It allows people to move in volume to and from The Keep and the towns between here and Haven faster than by the roads."

"And the trackway beneath the one here?"

"When the restructuring of the Fastness took place after the Upheavals a transport link was needed between the main centres of population. The trackway was the first such system built in Alban, before we went back to railways. Speed was not so important, the need for weight and volume meant building something robust. An electric power supply drives heavy vehicles running on rubbered wheels on the concrete trackway. It follows an older road. We added the monorail later. The two use one power source. It's a handy compromise. As the urbs have regrown the system has become inadequate.

"We are investing more resources into the transport system, and are negotiating with the transport body in France for help in building a tgv system. We hope to join the Civitas rail link at Birmingham eventually. I am not a total introvert."

Our conversation stalls for a while. We both seem distracted.

"So much will depend on the outcome of what we are tackling," Faerachar eventually says.

A gong sounds. Faerachar leads the way through the Butlery, down a spiral stair, into a small dining room. A large Belle Epoque painting almost covers one wall. We sit looking through a large window across Derwentwater.

"I felt what you had to say would be for us alone."

"It is. Is there no secure way we can call anyone in Genève?"

Faerachar shakes his head.

"Not totally safe. But aren't you overreacting to the danger of contacting Dahqin? After all, you are known to be here on official League business. And he is your consort."

I ignore what he implies.

"I don't think I should talk to Dahqin right now, my calls will be logged in Genève."

Another silence descends on us. I have never been out of contact with Dahqin for so long. I don't know how to reassure him that all is well. He will find it doubly strange with Grandy not there. She usually phones him regularly when I'm away. My thoughts are broken by the arrival of dinner.

"It's simple food, isn't it Bess?"

"Yes, Reever. We hope you like it, Ambassador."

"It smells good and looks beautiful, Bess."

She inclines her head and smiles. "I'll let Regin know."

The main dish is a beetroot, carrot and chickpea curry, made scarlet by tomatoes, I can smell coconut and tamarind. It's served with sticky rice. After Bess leaves, we eat for a while without talking.

"What do you hope for from Grandy?"

"More experience in dealing with the things you dream up than I have, Faerachar. I have almost nothing to balance against you. Grandy trained in the Middle Zone Bureau, she's used to convoluted shadow-plays. She'll be able to help me counteract your manipulation."

"Isn't that a bold statement to make to the man who's manipulating you? It gives me one hell of an advantage. Except, you underestimate your capabilities. You have served me with a Notification of Censure."

"To be verified by the Jurisprudence Court, Faerachar."

"It will be upheld: your judgement was solidly based. You impressed me with your knowledge and grace."

I keep my face neutral, but am pleased to have his praise.

"Faerachar, I don't know why you've been doing the things you have. But some of them seem counter-productive to me."

He laughs, with the tone that causes my nape hair to prickle.

"I'll ask Grandy what she thinks when she gets here. I'll be interested in her reply. What do you think I'm doing?"

"Trying to make me think, maybe even act outside the rigidity of my training. From the moment I met comic Fred things have happened to make me question my assumptions about the way people react to me — particularly with my role as an Ambassador. We are trained to take account of these things. But maybe we remember clearly only that which is used frequently, retaining a folk-memory of the rest. Maybe you wish to awaken that memory ... If what you've done was premeditated."

"And if it weren't?"

"Then it was meant to be." I drink half the glass of watered beer.

"You seem to think it wrong of others to want to control society. Yet you ..." I leave it hanging.

Faerachar looks at me sharply.

"Are you implying double standards?" I raise one eyebrow slightly and continue to eat.

"I am aware of the delicacy of my position in this matter. I am not blinded by my power, and I do not have all the answers. But I do believe in something paternal overseeing society, and a brotherhood and sisterhood." He wags an index finger at me.

"A siblinghood, within society. The strong and the weak combining to make society a cohesive force. It is in my blood to want to control the way this society develops over the next generation or so. Beyond that I shall be dead, and it will be my successor's problem."

He pauses to eat.

"I hope whoever comes along will continue the way set by my predecessors. I think it is noble. I told you before, I do not think the aims of the men who colluded to get their hands on the League files are so thoughtful of the good for others. I think they are thoughtful only of their own selfish schemes."

He pushes his plate away, watching me finish.

"I do not doubt your sincerity." I move my chair back and relax. "But can you be really objective when you feel such responsibility?"

"I have to hope I can be. And I have to hope my advisers will continue to be open with me, Ardel. And that I will continue to accept their criticisms when they feel it necessary to voice them. There is fruit and yoghurt for dessert. Do you want some?"

"Yes, whatever is served." Faerachar gets up.

"Regin and Bess are probably busy. Come with me if you wish."

We go through the Butlery and swing doors into a cool prep room.

"Actually there are catering staff here all day and night, but every now and then I prefer to fend for myself."

He washes his hands and starts rummaging in a frige, pulling out bowls and tubs.

"I've got used to your informality. Grandy may take another view."

A smile spreads slowly across Faerachar's face.

"What are you smiling at now?"

"You might need to do some explaining to Grandy if you develop this flirtation with Duncn into an affair."

"Why should that be necessary? I won't be here long enough for that to happen — and Duncn knows it."

"Does she know your relationship with Dahqin thoroughly?"

"As much as she needs. But it's our business, not Grandy's. And not yours either. Anyway, these passing dalliances we each have do nothing to dim the feelings between us. She won't say anything to him."

But she will to me, and probably harsh words too. She doesn't know our relationship as well as she thinks.

"And how would you feel if he took another to bed as you are?"

"It wouldn't bother me." Even so, I know despite this denial, that Dahqin finding another attractive enough to have an affair of some length would be worrying. "It's not very likely to be different than others in the past."

"Here, take these dishes."

He picks up a large bowl of soft fruits and berries into which he has poured a tub of yoghurt, some soured cream and dark honey, and propels me through the kitchen doors.

"Go. Back to the table."

The light outside the dining room is fading now. He places the bowl between us, folding the mixture together with a big bronze spoon, and indicates I should help myself.

The subject shifts to Grandy and her arrival. Faerachar wants me to call Dahqin right now — that's not going to happen. He does not accept my reticence about making the call, and I can't understand why he is so insistent — unless it's his joy at meddling. We argue back and forth for too long, but my blank refusal ends the matter. Faerachar assures me that, in any case, Grandy's arrival will be noticed right away by the ever-vigilant Boundary Patrol. I want to know more about this force. I get a vague answer which re-awakens my suspicions of him. His phone buzzes. Whatever the problem, it makes Faerachar swear.

"I have to go. There is still time for you to get to Duncn."

"I am staying here tonight."

"Duncn will be disappointed."

Back in Coleridge, I try phoning Dahqin, but leave a lack-lustre message. I will try again in the morning. Grandy must have left word with him; she would not let him worry needlessly about her disappearance. I wonder whether to ask Dahqin to contact Bartouche, but decide against it. Happy with the prospect of speaking to him, I go to bed and drop into sleep.

Waking from a dream is merciful; I was in a pit with pink hagfish swarming around me, covering me in slime. I get up and sit on the window seat. The moon is still filling, and the cloud cover patchy. A boat is powering towards the boathouse from the south. Something to do with Faerachar's business no doubt. I go back to bed.

... I am falling sideways down a cliff-face in slow motion but land with a jolt next to Dahqin, who kisses me.

"I couldn't stay away," Dahqin says ...

Then I am awake. Duncn is holding me.

"What are you doing here?"

I feel a blithe happiness. He leaves before midnight, promising I can accompany him to work in the morning.

June, 27th — Grange & the Fastness Estates — Ardel

Amazingly I slept soundly; no more dreams, and no sudden awakenings.

I am perplexed to find Dahqin still out, so leave a message assuring him I am okay, but very busy.

Briged left yesterday heading to Leeds, another urb not mentioned before. That leaves Duncn alone. Making sure to pack my HiSec and enough clothes, I take Megan, the grey mare, and ride to meet Duncn in Grange — I'm a bit earlier than he said. His horse is inside the garden of the first house in the village. He's not in sight, but I hear him talking. I dismount and am about to tether her to the gate post when she pushes past me and goes to his horse. The noises of their greeting brings him round the corner. He looks very happy to see me.

"You're early. Come and have a mug of tea. The horses are fine; just shut the gate. Huw! we need another mug!"

Regin greets me well enough and signals for me to sit at the table, Duncn pours their tea; an ease clearly exists between them, but there's a dynamic I can't grasp. A boy lollops out of the house, only one shoe on, holding a clean mug in one hand and a shoe in the other.

"Dad, I can't undo this knot." He gives it to Regin and hands Duncn the mug. "Who's this man, Dad?"

"He's called Ardel, Huw," Regin says, giving me a friendly look as he undoes the knot. "What do you think his job is?"

He shrugs, pushing the shoe on, and lifting his foot to Regin. When I answer his politely asked question the boy gets excited, running back into the house calling to his Mum about Ambassadors.

"Make sure he takes you to the vineyards, Ardel."

"I promised him I would when we stayed at Kaet's."

"Okay." Regin says slowly, looking from me to Duncn.

Huw runs out, backpack on. "I'm ready to go, Dad."

As he gets up Regin smiles at both of us, but not with his eyes.

"Later," he says to Duncn.

"It's time we went," Duncn says to me, rising.

I look back from by the horses. He has one arm round Regin's back, who nods a couple of times as Duncn whispers something.

"I'll see you soon, Ardel." Regin says, looking squarely at me as he passes. "Have a good few days." He raises his hand in parting.

Duncn shows me parts of the Fastness Estates in the locality, including the controlled environment houses for the intensive and exotic plantings. These are set in various locations, including old quarries in other valleys on all sides of Derwent. He explains the extent of these holdings all over the Fastness of Alban. He tells me that wherever necessary there are methane gathering areas, feeding into a network of pipes down to local electricity-generating stations. A by-product of that process is carbon-dioxide that is used to enrich the atmosphere for the plants, beyond what humans can survive. It is very effective, as together with the artificial sunlight and heat, growing cycles can mostly proceed year-round. The infrastructure is seen as a necessary part of the investment for social cohesion of the Fastness.

There are crops they don't grow in massive quantities, like pawpaw and pineapples. These are supplemented by imports from tropical areas.

"There's just over a hundred of us, who manage the estates of the Fastness Regions south of the Scotian border, and another seventy odd up there. We work together making sure any problems are overcome and solutions passed on. We are employed directly by the central Fastness Administration, but are answerable to the needs of the Districts, where the political power base is. I'm the only one round here. There's a section based in The Keep to run the North-West Fells District. It's their long-term and day-to-day plans I follow up on. There're plenty of other landowners and growers, so we don't have a monopoly. We have to be commercial like them, but we all work together, exchanging good practice across the board."

"Why do you call it the Scotian Border?"

"Ah. Faerachar really has kept you in the dark. Well, there are two parts to Alban. Engeland and Scotia. They are really separate Fastnesses, not one entity. But the administration of some functions are run for both of them by the bureaucracy the Reever heads. Faerachar has political bosses he answers to, in Leeds and Edinburgh. And then there's the Ethical Code they all must adhere to, and we citizens aspire to. He's not like the ruling politicians in Mercia or Éire, for example."

I add this information to a growing list of items for raising at an appropriate moment, once Grandy does appear.

After a hectic, and frankly exhausting, day we return to Second House. While eating our evening meal I try to get answers to my questions about the life Regin leads, but Duncn tells me he has no right to say anything; if I want to know more I must ask Regin directly. It's his life.

June, 28th — The Fastness Estates — Ardel

This morning's focus is the vineyards. It feels so familiar yet he knows so much about viniculture, well beyond my meagre knowledge. The geology of the area is fractured, the vines are sometimes on scattered terraces. We visit four terroirs.

Lunch is taken in Loweswater village; a recipe using fish from the nearby lake with wild herbs, at his recommendation. The wine is a Riesling from the Fastness Estates. There's no denying the wines I've been sampling are good. Regin is right, Duncn knows his subject.

In the afternoon I see how fish stock in the western meres is nurtured and controlled. Riding over Honister and through Seatola he leads me along bridle paths to reach a small tarn high above The Three Houses. It's refreshing swimming in the cool water and we lay sunning ourselves, getting amorous. Only storm clouds dropping over the tops above the tarn make us head home. At Duncn's, we lustily shower before an early supper, and go to bed amidst the shriek and howl of gale force winds.

June, 29th — Derwent — Ardel

It is calm on the third day. After work is finished we go back to the tarn. As we splash around, Duncn's phone bleeps. He stands naked and erect on the bank, talking to Faerachar. He turns to me, holding out the phone. Sploshing to the bank, I take it and lean against Duncn, who lazily moves the fingers of one hand in circles on the left cheek of my butt while kissing the nape of my neck and tickling first one then the other nipple with his other hand.

"Where?" I raise my voice. "When?" I pull away from Duncn's attentions.

"Do you want to meet them ... Oh, of course not. Duncn, how long will it take us to ride to Haven?"

"About two hours if we set off right now, given the distance the horses have already travelled today. So we'd get there after nightfall. What about first thing tomorrow?"

Putting the phone down I turn to face Duncn.

"Faerachar says Grandy is here with a small retinue. He doesn't know who. He says tomorrow will suit."

"What makes him think it's Grandy?" Duncn asks absently, intent on sex.

"Who can tell. Maybe she's told someone. Will you come over to Haven with me? Apart from not knowing how to get there, I'd rather go with you than someone else."

"Of course I'll come with you." We kiss and press against each other, moving round until we are lodged against a smooth rock.

Book Four – Part 2

Meetings in Derwent
Everyone counts for something

June, 29th — Haven, Cumbria, Wark-in-Alban

The Blondyn is moored alongside the tidal harbour's south quay. The bottom is mostly firm sand with a coating of mud in places. At low tide it will dry out.

"You need to go to the Harbour Master's office as soon as you're settled. Ask for the Duty Controller. It's by the swing-bridge on this quay. You can't miss it. I hope you enjoy your stay."

The Pilot waves from the top of the ladder set into the wall and sets off in that direction. Kirus follows hard on her heels to get the formalities out of the way. He soon comes back.

"They want a crew list and IDs, Grandy. What shall I do?"

"Use our own names, and show them our IDs. There's no point us being clandestine anymore. And make some enquiries about The Keep while you're there."

He leaves them preparing food.

"What did the Controller have to say?"

Kirus places a town map on the counter and returns their IDs.

"We can stay as long as we want. I know where to get water and provisions. I asked about getting to The Keep, she said nothing until she got to your ID, then she became very friendly. She's been in touch with them. Seems they were expecting you. Someone will be down tomorrow morning. And a lot of people I met stared at me. Do I look okay to you?"

"Maybe Ardel worked it out and they are expecting me. As to them staring — there's probably no one quite like you living here."

"So, what's your plan?"

"A plan will form very quickly, once I know what Ardel faces."

She is rapidly chopping vegetables.

"What do you want doing with these?" Peran pushes a dish to her.

"I'm on holiday, still. And we are going to rest tonight, because after that voyage I need to."

"I've been thinking, Peran and I should hang around for a few days, in case you and Ardel need a quick exit."

"I don't think you can be of more help. Better to head back to Brittany to help Alun and Dahqin."

"We can't get back and be in time to help them. Peran's found out Dahqin is on the HiTail-it, but not where. It can go double our speed — they could be anywhere. Until he calls us to let us know they are out of danger, we're staying where Dahqin knows we are."

"I want to get a map of this area. Will one of you come with me?"

Leaving Peran to finish the meal they go ashore.

"Aaahh. Terra firma." Grandy stamps her feet on the quay.

"What?"

"Solid ground. Just right for me."

They walk briskly into the hub of the settlement. It doesn't take a lot of searching before they find the map they want. Kirus buys some fresh bread.

The map laid in the middle of the deckhouse table, they eat as they study, washing down the food with bottles of zero beer.

The higher hills start about eight kimetres to the east, and the roads split long before that. The northern road follows the river Derwent. A shorter route cuts towards a low pass, crosses a valley then climbs a higher pass before descending towards the same point near The Keep.

"What's this?" Grandy points to a black line running close to the northern road.

"Some sort of railway," Peran says. "The maps are similar to the ones in Kernow. There'll be a station." He moves his finger over the map. "It's here, look, a line running through along the coast. They have to be able to move the stuff from that dock on the other side of the river. This is a branch line."

When they climb off the Blondyn and head towards the town, maps in hand, the moon is rising over the fells to the east: the sun still heading down in the west. They easily find the station. A timetable tells them trains travel each way every hour and lists names that are not near The Keep.

"I should have seen this."

"We were in the covered market, Grandy. Behind those shuttered doors — right under the tracks."

They pass a bar from whence comes the sound of singing.

"That's not up to Dahqin's standard," Grandy says.

Continuing eastwards through a small park a group of young people obstructs the path. They are in uniforms marked with Boundary Patrol badges, and armed. They are facing a notice board, and discussing with an officer the slogan 'For every right there are obligations' — she admonishes them.

"Okay! This is the last time I'm telling you without consequences. Be aware of what is happening around you. Don't get in the way of civilians going about their business. We're here to help, not hinder."

As they pass towards the gates the older women calls to them, causing the whole group to look round. Kirus quietly swears.

"Just a few questions, please. Ma'am, gentlemen. Where're you from?" the woman asks, looking at Grandy.

"Brittany via Kernow," Peran says.

"Let me see your IDs, please." She glances quickly at theirs, but studies Grandy's before handing them back. "You've all come a long way. Where're you staying?"

"On board our boat," Kirus says, pointing back towards the port.

"Have you registered at the Harbour Master's office?"

When Kirus confirms they have, she turns to Grandy.

"You are on our watch list, ma'am. Does The Keep know you're here? I'm to report to them, if not."

"They do. What is the right way to address you? And may I ask, what is the Boundary Patrol? I saw police earlier in the day."

She points to her name badge. "Either one. I'd prefer Ruth, as this is a friendly situation. Patrol the Boundary is what we do. We're also a bit of a civic help force — if there's emergencies. The police deal with crimes, and we back them up. These characters with me are new recruits, joining after their Civic Service draft. I'm just teasing out their understanding of the Ethical Code."

At the top of the list on the board Grandy notes the slogan 'Everyone counts for something'.

"What do you know about my visit, Ruth?"

"That you are a friend of Alban, and we are to show you respect and courtesy, ma'am."

Grandy gestures to Peran for the map.

"Thank you. Can you show us where The Keep is, please. I cannot find it on this map. I believe it is very beautiful there."

"It's here," she points to the headland overlooking Derwentwater. "You take the monolink, from the railway station to Keswick. The country's beautiful, but not The Keep — it's like a carbuncle. You cross the river to get into Keswick and the Township."

Bidding them to go safely and have a good time, she lets them continue on their way. Grandy looks back from across the road. The discussion has restarted. Kirus breaks their silence.

"They're not like our Guard at all. Never seen such a bunch since I've been doing charter work. She sounds hard."

"Probably her accent," Grandy says. "She was friendly enough, but I don't like this feeling of being watched. Alban has been adrift from the mainstream in Europa for a long time, even though a member of the Confederation."

Soon they reach the eastern edge of the town. Apart from some widely separated dwellings, where light spills from unshuttered windows into the gloaming, fields lie before them. They walk to the divide in the roads, passing a couple who greet them cheerily.

"Well, boys ... That didn't take us long. Now what?"

"Back to that bar with the singer," Kirus suggests. "We haven't anything else to do, so we might as well do that over a drink."

The singer is taking a break. A few people give them cursory glances. Peran brings three large glasses of beer to their table.

"I don't know if you'll like it, Grandy. It's like the bitter in Mawes, Kirus. We can at least try it."

"Grandy, what do you think Ardel will be doing?"

"Having philosophical dialogues with the Reever, Kirus."

She sips at the beer; is undecided about its flavour and lack of fizz, but cracks a grin at Kirus.

"He's about your age, got time on his hands, and is attracted to other men. I wonder ..."

After hearing two songs and finishing the beers they leave the bar and wander back to the harbour. Outside a large building at the head of the quays they see more people in the uniform of the Border Patrol.

Instead of boarding the Blondyn they continue down to the seashore where they spend the rest of the evening. In the pale moonlight they swap stories of good times they have had in the past. At midnight a troop of four from the Boundary Patrol stops, asking what they are doing. Grandy elicits the information they are known locally as BeePees. They are older than the group in the park, and after a few minutes easy bantering carry on in a southerly direction.

On returning to the boat Grandy wishes them a good night's sleep and goes to her cabin in the port hull. Kirus opens two beers, and they sit in the deckhouse leaning against each other.

"I hope he is alright," Kirus says, not specifying who he means, but looking unhappy. Peran drags him to his feet and leads him to their cabin in the other hull.

"You're not alone with me here." He kisses Kirus. "They'll both be alright, I'm sure." He hugs Kirus tightly and will not let go.

"I realise I'm only a substitute, but I do love you both, you especially."

"I know you love me more, how could I not? Don't you ever think of yourself as a substitute. You hear? You look so like him, and hooked us both so hard, but you have much more to offer me that he can't. I love you very much as you are."

He falls back onto the bunk, pulling Peran with him.

"I hope one day I'll prove it to you."

June, 30th — Second House

Ardel wakes early with Duncn moving against him, the birds outside loud in their greeting of the day.

"Hmm?"

"We'll leave soon."

"Yeah... Okay." Ardel puts an arm across him.

Sunrise finds them on the road over Seatola looking down into the western valley. Riding fast alongside the small lakes, Duncn indicates they go to the west through a low pass. From its summit the coastal hills roll out in front of them.

"Only another eight kimetres," Duncn says, as they canter the horses downhill on the roadside bridle path. "What's Grandy like?"

"She lives up to her name in manner. I just cannot imagine her having roughed it in a small boat to get to Alban. Somehow it doesn't seem right."

"What does she look like?"

"You'll find out soon enough. Will they be easy to find?"

"Of course. They'll be in the port. And Grandy so noticeable."

"I hope she doesn't tell me off too much."

"About the reason for getting her here?"

"No, about you. I don't want her to know, but she'll pick it up."

"It's not her business. And it's not a problem. Is it? We're just enjoying one another."

June, 30th — At Haven — Ardel

At the Harbour Master's office, Duncn asks where we can find Grandy Emembet. The Duty Controller is suspicious of him.

"On what authority are you asking?"

"You should have a message from the Reever's Office in The Keep saying to expect us."

"Aye, we might have. You're not an Ambassador. Who are you?"

"I'm..." is as far as I get. Duncn pushes me back with his elbow.

"This is the Ambassador. I am from the Reever's Office."

Duncn lays a metal pass-badge for The Keep on the desk.

"Do you want further proof?" He sounds just like Faerachar. The official looks from him to me.

"No. Mind, I'm just making sure. If you go along South Quay you'll see a bright yellow windboat with black marks on its mast-foils. There's nothing else in the harbour like it, so you won't miss it. It's called Blondyn. They're all on board a while back."

Riding beyond Blondyn, we tether the horses at a water trough, stuffing the over-breeches into saddle bags.

Standing at the top of a ladder inset in the stone-faced quay looking down at the boat I take a deep breath, then climb down.

"Hello!" Hearing no sound from the interior, I look around the deck, then at Duncn, now sitting by the deckhouse entrance.

"Whoa! Hello, you. How can I please you?"

I swear the voice is Dahqin's. How can I deal with both him and Grandy while ... Duncn's posing.

"We come from the Reever." Such a wide grin.

"Wait a moment, Perfection." Duncn nods, yawns and blows a kiss towards the speaker. I relax a bit, that is not Dahqin.

"Thank you. Ardel, I'm glad you have come to greet me."

"Grandy. Are we going to be let in? We've been riding for well over an hour, and refreshments would be most enjoyable."

As I speak a perfect gem of a man, my age maybe, my height, appears and slides open the panels at the aft end of the deckhouse.

He surveys Duncn with a leer, then turns to me.

"I'm Kirus. I've heard things about you, Ardel."

He puts out his palm. Wondering who has said what to this stranger, I grasp it, turn it and shake it, Alban-style. Much to his amusement.

"You've been here a long time."

"Obviously he's been here long enough," Duncn says. There is a tinge of ownership in his tone, which buoys me.

"I am sorry we could not get here last night. We arrived as soon as possible this morning."

"Doesn't matter, Ardel. We needed the rest anyway. Come in. We can get you something to satisfy your hungers."

He and Duncn are eyeing one another. We follow him into the main cabin and sit where he indicates.

"Peran, our guests need feeding."

A crop of hair, the colour of Dahqin's appears from below — his face too similar. Kirus is smirking at my reaction. When Grandy joins us, Kirus and Duncn are in animated conversation; Peran and I, silently eating. I feel such relief and pleasure at seeing her.

"I hope what you have to show me warrants my presence, Ardel."

"I'm so glad to see you, Grandy."

"And I, you." But there is no smile.

"I never realised a Solo diplarg could feel so lonely."

Careless words — Duncn shoots me a hard look and she sees it.

"I think the information I've been shown is very important. Though quite what we are supposed to make of it, I do not know."

"Why does it feel so dangerous?" Her voice is neutral. They are all looking at me. I look questioningly at Peran and Kirus.

"I have not been introduced to you," she pointedly addresses Duncn. "So I do not know if you know of the diplarg or this matter."

"Duncn is the Reever's younger brother. This is Grandy, my patron. She has come to handle the other matter." Duncn nods.

"I am not privy to any of this, Ardel, and I have no wish to be made so. Though I know when not to repeat things, so talk on."

The emotion of rejection rises through me, stomping through my guts — I manage to swamp it.

"The danger is in something that was shown me, which has nothing to do with the diplarg as raised. You will have to see for yourself to understand. It is not something I felt able to discuss back and forth with you, as I hinted. How is Dahqin?"

"He was fine. When we last saw him."

"When was that? Do you know if he has another contract?"

"Two days ago. He hasn't got another contract, but he is busy."

"We left a problem behind." There is annoyance in Kirus's voice.

"Oh?" The only thing in my focus is his face.

"Dahqin was with us until two days ago, heading up here. Then we got a message from Alun saying he had been attacked by someone who followed Grandy and Dahqin from Genève. Dahqin went back to help him. We've heard this morning they have left Douarnenez, presumably heading here. But we can't raise them."

I am flummoxed.

"Who's Alun? Why did Dahqin go back?"

"Kirus's twin brother. I would not have got here so easily but for Dahqin and his friends in Brittany." I blink at her. "He insisted on going back. There was very little option."

I feel on trial, and glance for a brief moment at Duncn, wanting to feel the support of someone. But Duncn is watching Kirus. I stand up; adrenalin is pumping through me.

"Can we talk privately."

"We don't need to, these two know the bare bones of it."

I look between them, take a breath, feeling annoyance at her dismissal.

"Does his aunt know Dahqin is involved, Grandy?"

"Why do you mention her?"

"There is much more information like that for you to see. I can't fathom how the information was taken from the League. Faerachar has lots of theories and ideas. This is why I wanted your guidance. You will understand more when you meet him."

She nods.

"Duncn, what is the quickest way for us to get to The Keep?"

"The monorail shuttle, Grandy. It takes less than half-an-hour. I will organise it now, and get a time for you to be at the station."

"Thank you."

Duncn rises, moving towards the open deck. "I'll just get my phone from the horse." He looks straight at me.

"I need to get my saddlebag," I say to no one in particular.

"No mistaking Grandy," Duncn says as I climb off the ladder. Then adds with a leery smile, "He's a ride."

"Which one?"

"Which one do you think?"

"Well, Peran looks a lot like Dahqin."

"Dahqin must be good looking then." Duncn says it sweetly, striding towards the horses.

"He reminds me too much of a young Dahqin."

"So?"

"Dahqin is in danger and that reminds me of fidelity. I didn't think anyone could be so sharply reminded of that by another."

"Did you not?"

"What's got into you?" Duncn does not respond. Instead he vigorously pulls at the straps on his saddle bag and withdraws his phone.

"You should look at yourself more closely, Ardel."

He turns away from me and speaks into the phone. I take my saddlebag off Megan; I hate being lectured on myself, and am uncertain what actually caused the sudden anger in Duncn.

"The shuttle is leaving soon. Get them to the station by half-eight. I'll take your horse with me. Say my farewells. I'll see you later, I know."

As he goes to mount, I drop the saddlebag and grip his arm.

"Just because Dahqin's young ghost is here it doesn't mean I feel any different about you."

"I don't suppose it does."

"What about you and Kirus?"

"Fffh! Kiss me goodbye. I've got work to do."

The kiss is long, and extends into two, then three. I stand by the water trough watching Duncn and the two horses amble away, then go back to the Blondyn.

June, 30th — Haven

"Grandy, we must be at the railway station by half-over-eight."

"What do you want to do?" Grandy asks Kirus, surprising Ardel by her diffident tone.

"The boat is safe here. We'll come to The Keep with you, if that's allowed. Because until I know Alun and Dahqin are safe ..."

"It's allowed by me, Kirus."

Securing the Blondyn against intruders Kirus follows the others ashore. The little conversation between them does not make Ardel feel positive as Kirus only gives a garbled version of events. He feels better after giving Grandy a brief outline of the problems raised by the lost faxplex. They are still discussing that when the shuttle arrives at the monolink platforms. It is a single driverless carriage with seating for twenty. The Steward has come to meet them.

"Ambassador Miriam Makda Grandy Emembet, please allow me to introduce to you Margot Salkeld, the Steward of the Fastness of Alban." Ardel says it exactly as prescribed in the Protocols.

The Steward bows, shakes Grandy's outstretched hand while saying she will answer any questions from Grandy on the way to The Keep. Grandy introduces Kirus and Peran as her special aides.

"It will take us about twenty-five minutes," she tells Grandy, as she ushers the others on board.

"Shall we see the Reever upon our arrival?"

"Naturally. He was making ready to give you his full attention, Ambassador Emembet."

This makes Ardel snort. Grandy smiles at Margot, both of them ignoring Ardel.

"I think we had better be consistent. From the little Ardel has mentioned, formality is given cursory attention in this Fastness."

"Not by me," the Steward says stiffly.

She guides Grandy to a seat, and sits facing her. The shuttle leaves the settlement following the line of the river. Sitting next to Grandy, listening to her and Margot discussing things he thinks he knows about already, Ardel drifts. Dahqin is in trouble becomes the only thought filling his mind. He now recalls Alun was Dahqin's first lover, but he had never known about a twin brother. He goes to sit at the front with Kirus and Peran.

"Kirus, how did Dahqin get back to Brittany?" He tunes out the Steward's voice.

"Let me tell you about the people you are to meet, Ambassador. At this first meeting it will be only Faerachar Strachan, the Reever, and myself. He is the accredited Ruler under Confederation Rules. Later you will meet David Floriot, the Communicator, for he is the one with the means to handle the data from the faxplex. You will at some stage meet Briged Jardine, she is the Good Sounding Counsel, to whom all of us can turn when we are faced with dilemmas, or must answer if she thinks it pertinent to ask a question. She is not scheduled to be at this meeting, though she may attend at some point. I shall try to keep to the Protocols as closely as I can, but we are not familiar with them in the way you will be. I hope this does not offend."

"Thank you for your concerns, Steward. I understand the need for formality in tense situations. I will adhere to the Protocols. But I shall not take offence when others slip on the formalities, unless they are doing so to undermine the necessary seriousness of the matters we shall be discussing. Please explain to me what your duties entail."

June, 30th — The Keep, Audience Chambers

It has been a difficult afternoon for Ardel. He and Kirus had barely touched on the problems Alun and Dahqin might be facing. Kirus had kept going back to how he and Alun had always felt about Dahqin and still did; Peran had moved away to sit near the women. The anxiety Ardel feels about this information interferes with his concentration on the discussion now taking place.

Grandy had immediately got to grips with the problems arising from the stolen faxplex, and before looking at Faerachar's ideas on handling the crisis, she sketches out her own. There are few discrepancies when they compare notes. Lunch is taken during the discussions, Ardel picking at the food. Mostly he is wondering how Dahqin is and what he is doing, but now and then Duncn flashes into mind. And he doesn't know that Duncn has come to The Keep just before lunch and taken Kirus and Peran to Kaet's.

"So", Grandy says, "we are agreed we shall follow these lines of investigation. I do not doubt there is someone in the League who has passed this information across for personal reasons. The problem is finding that person. They would need to be fairly high up, and very assured of their position. What do you think, Ardel?"

June, 30th — The Keep, Audience Chambers — Ardel

She is looking at me through narrowed eyes.

"Are you are thinking of other things than the topic to hand?"

"No. I haven't the faintest idea how we find out the identity of our adversary. What about checking on any links with the trading house?"

I see Faerachar's amused eyes.

"We covered that about ten minutes ago. I think you had better sort out your domestic arrangements before we involve you any further, Ardel." He turns to Grandy. "What do you think?"

"I shall take the extraordinary step of saying this in front of Faerachar."

I am heading for disaster, my blood prickles my skin.

"Bartouche did wonder if it was a bad idea to involve Dahqin. I'm afraid she may well have been right."

"I didn't expect to see him." I look at Faerachar accusingly, and without any subtlety change the subject. "We all know what the Rules are. How they must be observed. After all we've already broken most of them ourselves, haven't we."

"Practically all of them." Grandy is savage in her manner. "Who have you been playing around with?"

She asks me, but looks at Faerachar, who tries to show her a blank face. This is not his battle, even though Grandy is suggesting his culpability. She notices something in his face, for he turns away, then all her attention is on me.

"You might as well get this over with now. If there's to be a problem caused by your rampaging libido, I would sooner know."

She gestures for me to move outside. I go out onto the terrace, leaning on the parapet, looking down onto the lake and lower terrace. Three boats are out on the water, sailing for lucky people's pleasure. For once I wish myself out on them, away from the reality I have to face.

I am torn between disappointment that Dahqin has not come, and relief his absence will not complicate life further. Flirtation with Faerachar had been a stupid idea. As for Duncn, well, if I'm really careful we can continue. But I imagine trying to ignore Grandy's watchful eyes boring into me, her knowing me so well. She approaches me, leaning on the parapet almost touching me.

"You had better explain things to me." Grandy says it gently, and quietly. "As a friend, I'm not here to pass judgement on your escapades. But how convoluted you've made things ... that will decide whatever I say professionally. I'm here to help you work through your personal problems as much as your professional ones, for in our job they are dangerously interlinked."

She touches my arm with the tips of her fingers. I turn a big sad smile towards her.

"I don't know exactly where to begin."

"It's not Faerachar – but I guess he wound you up. Tell me of Duncn."

I tell her of the growing feelings I have for him.

"Are your feelings for Dahqin diminished because of this?"

"I don't think so. I have to hope not. But realising that but for Alun he would have been here, and seeing how good looking Kirus is, and Peran so like a young Dahqin ..."

I tail off, caught by an inability to explain the conflict I feel, and certain it is wiser to leave it so.

"What are you going to tell Dahqin?"

"Little more than the bare bones of it about Duncn. We always do that, but he will know something more has happened. We'll deal with it, but I don't know exactly how. I've never before been off with someone for days at a time. I can't let it be divisive to us as a couple, Dahqin means too much. It caught me unawares. Anyway, I'll be leaving here in a few days — and that'll be an end."

"Maybe it's because you're men. Maybe there's even more of a difference between men and women than I imagined. Kazzia and I believe deeply in the feelings we have for each other. There's no question we each find other women attractive, but we don't give in to that lust which you men seem to succumb to when you see someone you fancy. If there's the opportunity, you take it. With both hands."

She lapses into silence, still focused on me.

"You realise, for a first shot at a solo diplarg you haven't been very restrained. It is not prudent to consummate any flirtation during a diplarg. And certainly not on your Solo."

"But I never did anything with Duncn until after I'd finished with the diplarg. In ordinary circumstances I'd have been back in Genève before the opportunity arose." Grandy raises one eyebrow.

"It's true," I defend.

"Grandy, can I introduce you to David?" They are standing by the open doors.

"He is our Communicator. We have a way for you to contact your patron without going through the usual channels."

Grandy and David touch palms.

"Hello, David," I say flatly.

"I thought you were on holiday," David says lightly.

"He's back working again," Grandy says.

David nods, then asks, "How's Duncn?"

"He doesn't know," Faerachar says. "Kirus will be able to tell you better at dinner tonight. Oh, we have another guest joining us for dinner. Briged thinks she may be useful to our investigations."

They look at him questioningly. I want to drop through the floor.

"From Cymru, she's been on a trip with Briged." Off he goes inside.

"What does he mean by that?"

"You know him better than us, David, and if you're asking ... Well. What is this method for getting information to my patron."

"We have a commercial agent in London, who does discreet business for us. We can get a message to him almost instantly, Grandy, by line-of-sight microw. Then he can send a messenger on the tgv to Genève, or wherever. We can get a message to her directly, and an answer back within twenty-four hours. Slow but secure."

"Then we'll use it." He nods and leaves us leaning on the parapet.

"Why has Faerachar only brought this method to light now? He must have been aware of it before." All my suspicions are back.

"It was part of our discussion that you zoned out from, Ardel. I asked for a solution to the lack of security in communications."

Most annoying for me is the way they had answered the questions David put to me, as if I was an errant child. I realise I deserve their assessment.

"Why did Dahqin have to go back for Alun? Why didn't Kirus?"

"Do you know who these friends of his are?"

"Not really. Though I've remembered he mentioned Alun to me as we were getting to know each other."

"His reaction wasn't based on any facts, just feelings. I can understand and condone Dahqin's return. The more I've got involved in this strange digression the more my feelings have influenced my moves. Who to trust?

To wait for facts to be proved will take too long, and may cause us to be too late. It isn't the way we are taught, is it?"

"No, but so little could have been foreseen. I have to tell you what has happened to me since I arrived. I take it Alun knows where we are."

"Yes, Ardel, and Dahqin knows exactly where you are, too."

I slide down to sit on the floor, my back to the parapet. She stretches.

"I must admit I wasn't at all sure you were acting properly in what you did – the disinterested guidance bit. I can see now you were right to raise the alarm in such a way. That was well done. If only we could get some inkling about where that information came from."

"All my verification searches drew blanks. How high up do you think the person is?"

"I don't know, but that information can't simply be drawn out of the registry."

"I feel like a pawn, Grandy, on the losing side of an awful chess game." I get up. "Can we sit at one of the shaded tables."

She chooses one sited away from the doors.

"I wonder if Faerachar and David are being totally honest with us. David certainly has the capability to play with faxplex. I checked out some which passed the verification check as if originals, before I realised they had to be copies. A secondary identifier was missing. As for Faerachar, he has been manipulating me since our first meeting."

She listens carefully to my recounting of the first few days in Alban. Understands perhaps how I had become disconcerted. She counsels I must now focus on what we need to find out about the stolen faxplex. And says we shall be working together on that. I am no longer Solo.

I walk her back to Coleridge and invite her in.

"I'm going to do some thinking about this other matter. I suggest you do some about your own affairs."

She walks on to her own door.

June, 30th — The Keep

Ardel is on top of the bed asleep when Duncn enters Coleridge. Peeling off his clothes, and still smelling of sweat he slides alongside Ardel, undoing the fastening of the bodysuit Ardel wears. Sleepily Ardel rolls towards him, and promptly forgets his guilt-caused indecision about their affair continuing. Neither of them speak, their mouths and tongues exploring in the same manner as their hands. But if Ardel pushes Dahqin to the back of his mind, Duncn does not forget Kirus. He squeezes Ardel's nipples just the right amount, the right combination of pleasure and pain, which has not yet failed to lead Ardel into what Duncn suggests.

"Does Peran really look like Dahqin?" he murmurs.

"Uh-huh," Ardel sighs.

"Does that interest you?" Duncn's fingers glide across Ardel's abdomen, causing his skin to goose-bump.

"Not at all like you do."

He can have Peran for a while, Duncn thinks, as he moves his mouth in a series of light kisses down Ardel's neck and across his chest. As he gets more excited about what is happening between the two of them, he forgets Kirus.

It is after dinner and Ardel is with Peran on the terrace outside the Audience Chambers, watching the moon's reflection on the rippling water. He is well aware Kirus is off with Duncn for the night, though only now realising he has been left Peran as a sop.

"Have you two decided when to head back to Brittany?"

"No. Kirus says things are going to change quickly once Dahqin and Alun get together. So we are staying here until they turn up."

"Have you been given a room yet?"

"I suppose we have. Why do you ask?"

Ardel looks at his face — so innocent looking and yet so knowing.

"Just curious. Why did you leave your home to go to Brittany?"

"I went there on a charter boat from Fal, as a crew member. We went into Douarnenez and I met Alun in one of the cafes. He looked at me like I was something tasty to eat. Hungry, is what it was."

He swigs some beer.

"We got talking, and a bit later Kirus came in. I couldn't believe it at first. Not only one tasty guy drooling over me, but two of them. I'd never felt so adored before. I guess it went to my head. I fell in love."

Ardel looks into the audience chamber. He cannot see Duncn or Kirus — feels hurt that Duncn has so easily swapped to Kirus.

"Ardel, what's the matter? You look glum."

"It's nothing really. I was just thinking about Dahqin again. I hope he and Alun are alright."

Kaet comes outside and smiles at Peran, then holding Ardel's elbow she says, "Do you mind? I'd like a quick word with you."

Before Peran can move, she drags Ardel along the terrace.

"What's the matter?" He asks this irritably, not wanting to discuss Duncn with her right now.

"Dahqin and Alun are on water, but I don't know where. There are no shadows." She is digging her finger nails into his elbow, but he barely notices the pain. "I don't understand any of that."

"Does it mean something has happened to either of them?"

"I don't know. But there's a female involved somehow."

The hair is twitching across the back of Ardel's neck.

"How do you get this information?"

"I just pass it on. I can't explain it, Ardel." She lets go of his arm, and he absent-mindedly rubs it. "Give Peran a cuddle, he needs it."

She kisses him on the cheek. "I'll see you soon."

She waves to Peran and goes back inside. Ardel mutters a parting, and rubbing his elbow walks back to Peran. Inside the Audience Chambers he can see Grandy, Faerachar, Briged and Gwyneth, the Cymric woman, sitting in armchairs, animatedly discussing something.

"Peran, where's the woman who sat next to Faerachar?"

"Shivawn? Why?"

"Oh, no reason, just she isn't in there now."

"Nor are the other two. They left when she did."

"It's been a bit of a strange day," Ardel says sorrowfully, putting his arm across Peran's shoulders and giving him a squeeze. Peran looks at the hand on his shoulder and turns half away.

"You don't need to worry. That squeeze doesn't mean anything has got to happen. In any case, where else will you sleep?"

"Oh! I didn't think *you* would get involved like this. How do we manage to creep away without drawing attention to ourselves?"

"We go through here," Ardel says, going inside.

The moon has set. Its light gone from the bedchamber. Ardel sits up in bed trembling. It takes him a moment to realise where he is. From the darkness Peran asks him what is wrong.

"I don't know. Something has woken me." He reaches towards where Peran is sitting up, on the other side of the bed, and feels the fine hair, so like Dahqin's.

"Are you okay?"

"I am. But you haven't been sleeping very well."

"What do you mean?"

"Muttering and tossing about. When I tried to cuddle you, you thrashed about all the more. That's why I'm over this side."

Ardel gets up and goes into the main chamber, Peran follows him over to the oriel window seat. A dim light comes from the terrace.

"What are you looking for?"

"A fire."

"I can't see anything." Peran's voice is calm and matter-of-fact.

"There's a stone circle up on the hill beyond Keswick. Sometimes there are fires up there. They only last a few seconds."

"Sure it wasn't in your dreams?"

"No my dreams are about other things. Not nice things."

Taking Peran back to bed he pulls the coverlet over them, and curls protectively around his back.

July, 1st — The Keep

Barely gone midnight, Ardel being soundly asleep, Peran slips out from the bed. He pulls on his shorts and grabs at a vest on the floor. He is relieved that Ardel has acted kindly, and he had needed to be cuddled more than he expected. As he pulls the vest on he realises it isn't his, but doesn't care. In the Butlery, he can't find the makings of a warm sleep-inducing drink and is about to go through the fire doors to the kitchens when one swings towards him and Regin comes through.

Sitting on a sofa in the inside lounge of the Butlery, sipping a mug of creamy, rum-infused Spanish chocolate, Peran tells Regin of how the night has unfolded since dinner.

"Did something happen you didn't want?"

"A change of partners without consent. I'm so angry at Kirus. Don't know if he still wants to be with me. It's Dahqin turning up in Douarnenez that's unsettled everything."

"Bit like Ardel turning up here. Believe me, for Duncn it's a fling, nothing more. No danger to your relationship, unless you two aren't dabblers."

As they chat Peran gradually snuggles into Regin's arms, and out come all his fears for the future of his life with the twins. They progress to Regin's office where, while he completes the shift paperwork, Peran sleeps on his rest-bed. Before the lightness of early dawn, he knows Regin's story. They walk from the office to the guest chambers on the floor above. As they near Coleridge, Regin hears the cannion doors open. He signals silence, and pushes Peran against the wall, sneaking to look round the corner at a small mirror sited at the ceiling-line, opposite the cannion doors. He sees Duncn entering. When the cannion is gone, he holds Peran by both shoulders, their faces close together. His voice quiet, he looks down at the wide eyes.

"Listen to me, Peran. Don't go back to Ardel's bed. Go to Kirus and make sure he knows how you feel. Don't walk away; listen to what his reasons are. Hang on to what binds you. He's in room B10 along here on the right — it's assigned to the pair of you. The first door past Ardel's is B12 — that's where Grandy is. Whatever you say and however loud you say it, she'll not hear. You have my phone number and rota. Call me if you want to see me again — I'd really like it if you do."

They pass Ardel's door, then windows looking out onto a small terrace, and round a bend in the corridor. Peran stands facing the door of B10, rising up on his toes. He looks across to Regin — blows a kiss.

"What's good for the Kirus is good for the Peran," he murmurs as he grasps the handle. He has dabbled; Regin is no longer celibate.

Book Five — Part 1

Dahqin's Discoveries
Falling into the trap of doing unto others...

June, 27th — Fal to Douarnenez — Dahqin

After the Blondyn rounds the headland, I go to the nearest pub on the quay, get a drink and sit outside in the sun. Even with the information from Peran, it takes an hour to make contact with Charlie, and agree a price for chartering the hifoil.

"I don't pilot it myself, Dahqin. I don't have time for that. I'll get my pilot over there and you can discuss the arrangements with her. If she says it's okay, it's okay. Go to Smiling Jack's, the last pub on the road down to the quay, next to the Old Custom House. She'll meet you there. You do everything else through her. Okay?"

"Sure. I'm sitting outside it now. I'll be inside getting something to eat. I suppose she'll recognise me. I'm the one looking desperate."

Charlie laughs. "You'll know her instantly."

Leaning against the wall at the end of the bar furthest from the entrance, I have a view of the whole room. The woman behind the counter comes over and silently waits. I order a watered beer and ask what's on the menu.

"You can have whatever you want, dear. So long as you tell me what it is. Here's a menu. What's a watered beer?"

"Pilsner and carbonated water. About half and half."

Nodding, she puts the beer and water in front of me with a cold glass. I look at the menu.

"Something light and cold is what I have in mind."

"A Ploughman's then, dear. You're not from round here." It is not a question, and I get no time to answer. "How are you going to pay for this?"

"Swiss francs in cash, or electronic euros." She nods, takes the euros and hands me a numbered slip of paper.

"Lots of people come in here for drinks and food and try to pay with their local credits. Your food won't take long."

I nod and pour the beer. I finish my food long before the pilot arrives. There is no doubting her when she enters. She looks round the bar at the dozen or so occupants, and comes straight to me.

"So you're Stiwll." Like she knows me.

I lightly tap my palm on hers. "Sure. And you are?"

She pulls up the next stool and sits down, leaning one elbow on the counter and studying my face. In the mirror behind the bar I note my bright pink hue, reflected from her bodysuit, which is unfastened to her waist with all the vents opened. Beneath it she wears some kind of cling suit. Her cropped sandy hair and grey eyes go with her puckish smile to complete the impression of an elfin creature. She takes time.

"Tozer."

"Can I get you something to drink, Tozer?"

"Sure. The usual, Dorra!" The bar woman raises a hand in answer. "So, what's the proposition? What's the hurry?"

A drink arrives, the same hue as her suit. She stirs it with a finger which she slowly licks as she waits for my answer. The woman goes to the other end of the bar. I lean towards Tozer, lowering my voice.

"I must get back to Brittany as quickly as possible. Douarnenez."

"Must. That's a tough word. What's the hurry?"

"It's too complicated to go into right now. It's important to me." She is sipping the drink, watching me over the rim of the glass.

"I know the weather prospects aren't the best, which is why I need to leave as soon as possible. How fast is the hifoil you pilot?"

She rattles the ice against the glass. "With me at the helm it's the fastest in this port, probably in any port along the entire coast. I can get you there real fast, if the weather's okay. You sound serious."

"I would say desperate, but serious will do. Are you willing?"

"Yes. How soon can you leave?"

"As soon as I sort out payment for the trip."

The bar woman has disappeared.

"Dorra! Can we pay now! You pay a deposit for the trip as soon as we get on board – the final settlement either way is sorted at the destination." The bar woman doesn't appear.

"How much is your drink?"

"How are you paying for this?"

"Swiss francs."

"Put down five. It's enough. Believe me."

I slap the money down on the counter, and picking up my small pack follow Tozer. Outside, she starts running.

"No time to lose! Come on! You're desperate, remember!"

She's very fit, I catch up with her up as she reaches the ramp down to the pontoons.

"What's your chosen name?" I am slightly out of breath. "Mine's Dahqin."

"Then I'm Inez. Know anything about boats, Dahqin?"

"A bit, Inez." She leads me down to the craft. Twenty-five metres long and moored stern to in a pen on its own. A slim central hull is flanked by two smaller outriggers barely touching the water surface. Underwater I can see the foils on which it planes, strung between the outriggers and a fin keel.

"Ever been in one of these?" She climbs on board.

"No, only the small ones we use on the lakes at home."

"How fast can this go in the conditions we have now?" I am excited by the prospect, despite the circumstances.

"Mid-sixties, with this wind, if the sea's not up. The wind is in the right direction for us. It's the seas that'll slow us down, still up from the last short blow." She points to the stern ropes.

"You can help me by singling up, then cast off the fore ropes."

Strapped into the co-pilot seat I watch Inez play with the controls. Clear of the marinas we are soon foil-borne. The wind noise across the opened top of the cockpit makes us raise our voices to hear one another.

"When we get the wind outside Pendennis the speed will come up quite a few more knots. We might even hit high forties with this sea. Could do Douarnenez in just over four hours, if we're lucky. So, hope the weather doesn't get any rougher." She grins at me.

June, 28th — The HiTail-it, Western Approaches — Dahqin

It is dark, nothing can be seen around us, and the hifoil is responding to automatic controls. Inez has dropped the speed to twenty-eight knots, from a high of forty-three. The cockpit is now fully closed.

"It's better to leave it to the autos. They don't need to see like I do. Do you want another drink?"

I nod into the darkness of the cockpit, then say, "Yes. Please."

"You're worried about your friend, aren't you?" She's making the caffeine-fizz.

"Yes." I had mentioned going to help a friend in trouble and immediately regretted it.

"What was in that drink you had?"

"That's a secret." She hands me the cups, sits back down and straps herself in. "We all need them, don't we? Let's just say it numbs my perception enough to take on this crazy job."

"Does this frighten you, then?"

"No, of course it doesn't. I haven't been this fast before at night. But you looked like a good guinea-pig to me, so I thought — why not?"

"You're funny. Maybe you're mad."

"And you're not? When did you leave Brittany?"

"Last night. At sunset. I didn't expect to be heading back so soon." The elements tug at my emotions.

"I knew who you were as soon as you came in." I need to talk about something, anything not to be left with the silences.

"There was no mistaking you either. But I have an advantage."

"Oh?"

"I've seen you before, in Genève, couple of years ago. A lot of you. Practically naked."

"You're joking!" I remember the place. Not the most staid of establishments. Once or twice, when I was feeling particularly raunchy, I took my act to the limits of acceptability. Ardel was not amused.

"I can recall every definition. You're neat. The night I was there you came down into the bar afterwards. Was he your boyfriend?"

"Don't remind me. My consort. He nearly had a fit. Luckily I can usually get him to forgive me. He doesn't understand artistic license."

"So if Genève is home, why are you going back to Brittany?"

"You are determined to find out, aren't you? What were you doing in Genève?"

"My question first."

"I come from Brittany originally."

"I go to Genève for my boss."

"Ahh."

"What does that mean?"

"Does he work for the League, Inez?"

"No. Why? Are you on the run from the Cantons?"

"Not so far as I know."

"Meaning what? Can you tell me about it?"

"I don't know if I want to, Inez. I have a feeling lives are at stake here, and I don't want any of them to belong to people I know."

"And you're dragging me into it. How did you get to Fal?"

"If you don't know you can't be dragged in. By wind-boat. Two hours before meeting you. Why?"

"The Blondyn."

"You know it?"

"Yes, Dahqin. Slightly. I saw it come in. It's owned by some twins from Douarnenez. So they were dropping you off. I wondered why they were in and out so quickly. They're like you, those guys. They've got a guy from Mawes living with them, called Peran. He's a friend of one of my brothers. The twins have been lovers since they were at school."

I manage not to react, but inside I'm reeling, about to drop into a personal chasm. Why didn't I know? How come she knows? Why on earth didn't they say anything to me? I leave it fermenting at the back of my mind.

"Where are they off to?" she asks into my silence.

"Somewhere up north of here."

"Well, unless you want to be dumped in Brest, I think you're going to have to tell me a bit more. I don't want a life history, but I may be able to help you more than you think. I have to decide how close to the wind to sail in more ways than one."

"It's difficult to decide what to say."

"Do you want to lift your friend and take him back to Kernow?"

The idea had crossed my mind. But I also want to get the identity of the Shadow before leaving Douarnenez. I take a deep breath, exhale loudly and begin to talk.

June, 28th — Douarnenez

It is still dark when the beeping wakes Alun. He has dozed fitfully, waiting for Dahqin to contact him. Every strange noise that could be heard around his parents' home woke him, had him listening and imagining. The constant checking of his time band only prolonged the hours of his tormented rest. The beeping is a welcome, if uncertain respite.

"Yes?" he whispers, talking into the radio under the coverlet. No reply comes, but downstairs the phone beeps on. He leaps out of bed, awkward in his movements. He hears his mother or father moving.

"It's okay," he calls through the door. "I'll get it." And hears the bass tones of his father's sleepy reply. When he sees Dahqin on the screen he joyfully presses the connection button.

"Where are you, Dahqin?"

"Off Brest. Where's the Shadow?"

"Last I saw of him he was watching the Tents. About midnight."

He glances at his timeband, three o'clock is staggering slowly closer. Only half an hour since his last check.

"Where can we pick you up? Is the harbour safe?"

"I don't know, Dahqin. Who are you with?"

"A friend." Alun looks doubtful. "She knows Peran. We could be in Douarnenez in an hour."

"Kirus said don't use the phone. How will you contact me?"

"I'll phone. He meant for Grandy and Ardel. How are you?"

"I'm shit scared and feeling on my own, that's all I know. Just get to Douarnenez and I'll meet you."

He goes back to his bedroom. His father is sitting on the bed.

"Who was it?"

"Dahqin."

At the end of the harbour's eastern mole, Alun, his father and Bran, a friend of his father, sit watching the still dark western skyline. From the north-eastern quarter early dawn colours the sea's shimmering surface, in parts green–blue, in others rosy–pink. They talk quietly in short bursts with long silences between, watching all the time for the Shadow.

"We could make him disappear now," Bran opines. "It's easy."

"But we don't want the people he's watching us for, to know we've found out about him."

"Alun, they probably already know."

"Leave it, Bran."

"Okay, Bedow. But Alun, you and Dahqin might not be able to handle this on your own." He adds in a mutter: "You're both good lads." They fall into another silence.

The hifoil speeds towards the harbour, then stops almost dead, sinking onto its hull. Inez puts it stern to at the end of the wind-boat pontoons and Dahqin sets up the stern lines.

"If anything happens to me ..."

She nods. "I'll leave."

He runs along the pontoons and up the ramp. Looks round carefully. Runs towards the market hall in the centre of the quay. Seeing the party on the eastern mole moving, he waits in the shadows between the building and the harbour. At the landward end of the mole they duck into the darkness cast by the harbour offices.

He sees Bran slip forward. Then he hears the sound of two objects meeting violently. He watches Bedow and Alun run forward and runs out to join them.

"Now what?" Bran says, looking at the prone figure by his feet.

"Did you have to?" Alun is white-faced.

"Leave it. He did," Dahqin whispers into Alun's ear as he hugs him.

"Hello, Bran. I didn't expect to see you." They tap palms.

"Not this time, nor the time before, hey?"

Dahqin shakes his head. "How are you, Bedow?" They embrace.

"I'm alright. We need to move this man. We don't need witnesses."

"Is he still alive?" Alun asks. Bran nods, but stoops to check again.

"I say we put him on my boat, find out what he knows and feed the fishes."

Alun is appalled by this and starts an angry protest. His father waves his hand to silence him. Dahqin wants desperately to ask Grandy for advice.

"So what are you going to do?" The sound of a female voice startles them all. "Well?"

"This is Inez. She knows Peran. Alun's Kirus's bro ..."

"I know which one he is. Hi, Alun. So you're the friend. What are you going to do? He's bleeding."

"He'll stir soon enough," Bran says as he checks him again.

"Get him onto the HiTail-it," Inez says. "At least then he'll be out of the way."

"No!" Dahqin turns to Bran. "Take him to your boat and make sure he's secure. Don't hit him anymore. I'll be over in a minute. I need to find out who he is working for."

Bran slings the prone man over his shoulder and disappears into the shadows. Dahqin leads the others back to the HiTail-it.

"He'll maybe need help with securing him," Inez says to Bedow, who shakes his head.

"Who needs something to drink?" Without waiting for any answer she produces a bottle of Éireish poitín and pours out four glasses.

"Dahqin, put the coffee on. I need some caffeine."

"Sorry, Inez, but you do that, I'm going over to Bran's boat. I need to make sure he doesn't go too far, Bedow. You know what he can be like when he's angry."

Dahqin watches Bran complete his handiwork securing the Shadow. The tape is around his wrists, his ankles, his chest and arms. It seems only the end of the roll will stop Bran. He had pulled a piece of rag over the Shadow's mouth and another across his eyes – they too are taped in place. He gets three snap-cords and passes them around the de-humanised bundle, snapping them onto strongpoints placed along the hull. The Shadow is now securely lashed into place.

Muttering, "That'll do," Bran stands back and surveys his work, then looks at Dahqin – flashes a wink and smile at him.

"He won't move easily." Bran is very cheerful – much more than usual. He pats Dahqin on the shoulder and goes up on deck.

Dahqin stares at the bundle as it twitches occasionally, testing the bonds. He looks away, steeling himself. This is the person who had tried to club Alun. He goes after Bran.

"Is he able to ..."

"He can breath through his nose, but he'll not move from there unless I do it." He is about to lock the cabin door. Dahqin stops him.

"I want a drink, Dahqin."

"I need to search him." He returns a few minutes later and shows Bran his haul. A bunch of keys with a local address tag, a cosh, a touchpad and an ID card. The Shadow is from the Cantons.

Dahqin keeps one thing hidden – he had also been carrying a League Warrant Card.

"I've left his other stuff on him. These are all I need. You can lock it now. Back to HiTail-it. There's coffee on."

"That'll do as a starter. I meant a strong drink."

They hear Bedow and Inez talking about the HiTail-it, one sailor to another. Silence comes as they climb on board. Dahqin goes down into the cabin and lifts the coffee pot from the stove, takes two mugs and climbs back into the cockpit. Bran is holding out the fourth glass to Inez for her to refill. He smiles heartily and refuses the coffee. Only Bran looks cheerful. Only Alun looks scared. Dahqin sits between Alun and Inez, facing the two older men.

"What now?"

Bran is about to say something, but Bedow puts out his hand, silencing him.

"You are the only one who knows what this is about. You should be the one to make the decisions." He looks steadily into Dahqin's widening eyes, then turns to Inez.

"I recognise you, Inez. I am the father of Alun and Kirus. This monkey with the big eyes is like a son to me also. He once spent so much time in our home I thought I had three sons. Now they only come to the Nest when they are in trouble."

Alun and Dahqin glance quickly at one another. Bran helps himself to another slug of poitín. Bedow takes the bottle from him and hands it to Inez.

"My sons are behind you as always, Dahqin, and I will help you do what you need to. But you have long enough been an adult now. For this you must act as one."

Bedow looks through the shaded windows of the cockpit. "Where are the other three who made up the Bagad, I wonder?"

"Sensible and settled down, Mam tells us," Alun says flatly, then he curses. His father reaches over and pats his head before looking back to Dahqin. Inez sits quietly, sipping at the mix of poitín and coffee in her glass. She too watches Dahqin.

"Well, I know who he is and where he has been staying." He lays out the items taken from the Shadow.

"Was there anyone else that might have been with him?"

It is answered with shrugs and shaking heads.

"He had a bag!" Alun is excited, he picks up the keys. "He had a black bag. Don't you remember? I thought he was a day-tripper as he only had a small bag. It must be here." He leans against Dahqin.

"I wonder what he's kept on this? You were always better than me at using these things." He hands Alun the touchpad.

"This could get us into a shit load of trouble," Inez says.

"I can't think what are we going to do with the Shadow. Maybe we should hand him over to the Guard and let them deal with him. But I want to keep his touchpad and ID as proof of him being here."

"You leave what happens to him to me and Bran. We'll land him in one of the blind coves on Kab y Gavr - you know Alun — eastern side right near the point. Then I'll tell the Guard I've seen him when I go sailing later today. He'll be safe there until they rescue him. With no ID — and not being local — and us speaking Brezhoneg he'll not have a clue. Bran's boat is like half a dozen others round here. Electronic identity. No name to give the game away. Nor will he know how you left here."

Bedow stands up and turns to his son. "Now, I have to organise someone else to take the ferry to Brest. You are leaving with these two. That's as close to an order as I've ever given you since you went to high school. And you'll take it." He looks at Dahqin.

"I'm putting this commitment onto you. For the love you have for them and they for you — take Alun — get him back to Kirus and Peran. And you keep them three and the Blondyn safe away from here until you hear from me. I don't want to hear from any of you four unless things get bad. And then only so I will know. Otherwise I'll contact you, either one, when this matter is old news here. And that won't take long. You know how it is. Don't worry about your business, Alun — I'll cover the lost income from the Blondyn."

Bran has picked up the cosh and is slapping it against his other palm. He rises to go with Bedow, slipping the cosh into his pocket.

"Success in your enterprise, Inez." Bedow says. "Despite this, they are dependable."

Alun hugs his father. "I'll see you before we go."

As Bedow is climbing off the vessel Dahqin leans over the rails.

"I don't want my parents to know I'm in town. It will raise too many awkward questions. I need to call someone in ..." he stops himself.

"Come to the boatyard office, any time after eight o'clock."

Although the key tag tells them where the Shadow is staying, Alun and Dahqin are convinced there is no way they can get by the owner of the house. The Bagad having played too many tricks on her in the past.

"I'll get his bag for you," Inez says. Dahqin is not so sure.

"I can do it," she insists, going below. He draws a map so she can find the boarding house.

"I've got to find out who he might have as a contact in Genève," Dahqin says, for the third time since Bedow left.

Alun gives up on the code for the keypad.

"It keeps asking a question. I don't understand what it says."

Dahqin looks at it.

"I recognise it, but can't understand it. It's some old language the League uses."

"What if this guy really is with the League?" Alun said.

"He is. I've got his League Warrant."

He gives it to Alun to examine.

"There seems to be two sides. It's just most of the League doesn't know that yet. And he's on the other one to us."

"I'm going to get his bag," Inez says, returning to the cockpit.

"I'm going to the boatyard," Dahqin says, standing up.

"I'm going to sleep," Alun says and goes into the aft cabin.

They walk up the ramp onto the quay, Dahqin scanning people, hoping no one he knows is around.

"Why didn't you say you knew them well, Inez?"

"Why didn't you say Alun was the friend, Dahqin? I know where you fit their story now. I'll not mention it again."

"I'd appreciate that, Inez. This is a mess. Aren't you worried by what we've got you caught up in?"

"Not particularly, Dahqin. I assume they'll do what they say with the

Shadow. I didn't know Bedow was their Dad. Bran said he'd feed him to the fishes — and he seems the sort who might."

"Bran will do what Bedow says. He likes to appear more menacing than he is. But if friends of his are under threat, he'll do all he can to defend them." They walk to where the main street reaches the quays, where Dahqin stops.

"Maybe I should wait until you get his bag before I contact ... I'll wait until you get back before I try." He turns back towards the hifoil and Inez goes on, map in hand.

When Inez gets back to the HiTail-it she finds the two men curled up together, fast asleep in the aft cabin. She drops the bag by the bunk, leaving them asleep and goes to get iced peach tea.

"Dahqin, have this." He rolls over and sits up.

Alun shifts in his sleep, then rolls towards Dahqin, opening his eyes as he hears Inez talking. He focuses on a hand holding a glass of something in his direction, then sits up and sleepily takes the drink.

"I've got everything that was in the room. He was booked in for another two days. Kept very strange hours and seemed to be grumpy. She didn't tell me any more about him and I didn't ask too much."

Dahqin nods. After a few minutes he says, "Bran's already sailed."

"Bran frightens me. He always did." Alun speaks through a yawn.

Inez picks up the bag and dumps its contents onto the bunk. She and Dahqin sift through the articles. Only the phone is of use, but being code-locked, it doesn't add to their knowledge.

"That was a waste of time."

"Not true», Inez counters, "now the Shadow has left Douarnenez. All anyone will find out is he sent his girlfriend to pick up his things and left two days early. If anyone bothers."

"Yeah, but they'll have a description of you."

She laughs at him and pulls an auburn wig out of her body suit pocket, fitting it over her short hair she puts on a pair of glasses.

"What description?"

"You've done that before. Cunning little Inez."

"Listen, sometimes I feel it's better to look different. This hifoil is faster than the others because I can override the auto controls. It was something Charlie had done ages ago. Besides there's an air of excitement to being hidden in the open."

She gets up and stuffs the wig and glasses into a locker.

"You'd better make that call Dahqin, and afterwards we can get on and do something positive."

"Alun, are you coming with me?" He reaches for his mouth fresheners. Alun slides off the bed and fumbles with his shoes. Dahqin hands him a tablet.

Alun soon returns alone.

"He'll be on the phone a while yet."

They settle down to wait. To pass the time she challenges him to a game of backgammon for very small stakes.

Dahqin comes back looking very serious. He does not say who he had spoken to, nor what they had said. He sits in the cockpit making thumbnail sketches of something on a scribblepad. After half an hour, Inez pushes the backgammon case aside, and leans across the table taking Dahqin's scribbler out of his hand.

"Well?"

"I still don't know." He shrugs his shoulders.

"Surely your contact must have given you some advice."

"Carefully worded. She thinks all her calls are being listened to, even at home. She doesn't trust the phones."

Dahqin pushes the scribblepad away from him and sits upright.

"We have to do as Bedow says. Go and join the others. There. Positive enough?"

"Okay, Dahqin, where are we heading now? I'm assuming you can pay for this."

"Of course I can, Inez. Second deposit coming up. Head north-north-west, go round the end of Kernow, and carry on northwards. I'll need to see what faxcharts you have."

"Before that, I need a kip. We'll leave in eight hours."

June, 28th — Douarnenez

The weather forecasts are good. If the local wind is a little on the light side for maximum speed, by the time they are passing Cymru the storm presently lashing the Blondyn will have blown away. Steady medium strength winds are forecast for when the hifoil reaches that area.

"Are you going to tell us where we're heading?" Inez asks as Dahqin views the faxcharts already in the multi-viewer. She stands behind his seat, her hands resting on his chest. Her familiarity feels right, and he accepts the intimacy.

"Not yet." He shakes his head, then winces because she has grasped one of his nipples and is twisting. "Yoww!"

He pulls her hand away as she smiles at his reflection on the multi-viewer screen.

"Only teasing, Dahqin. I thought you'd like a reminder of your boyfriend."

"I can't forget him, and you doing that isn't quite the same as him doing it."

"Drink, anyone?" Alun asks from the cabin.

"Make some real coffee, Alun. Dahqin, does your contact know who this man is? I mean, what he does?"

"Communications section of the League."

"They don't know what is happening to him, do they."

"No."

Nodding her head from side to side she climbs out of the cockpit to get the boat ready for leaving. She explains they will run a three person, four-hour watch system, with a one hour overlap in the fourth hour. That way they are only two hours on their own.

"Which is long enough. And it gives adequate rest between stints."

She takes the first four hour watch.

In their cabin Dahqin explains his plan.

"So we are heading straight for Alban."

"Yes, Alun. But until I know exactly where the Blondyn is, I don't want to tell Inez. We might be able to catch up with them. We'll start calling Kirus in the morning, when we're near the Cymric islands. Use Brezhoneg."

Alun is facing him, watching his face as he speaks. When Dahqin falls silent, he kisses him – the first time like that in seven years.

"Alun, I'm so glad you're safe. Why didn't you ..."

The question doesn't get asked because Alun is faster and puts his lips back onto Dahqin's.

June, 29th – On the HiTail-it

"Inez, it's time for your watch." Dahqin shakes her awake. She sits up quickly, rubbing her eyes.

"Where are those other faxcharts I need?"

"In there." She points to a locker at the foot of her bunk. She stretches and yawns. "I'm pooped."

She yawns once more, lays back and is asleep.

He lets her doze, opens the locker and stares into the jumble inside. Faxplex and faxcharts are haphazardly chucked into it. He pulls everything out and starts sorting – quickly able to separate the faxcharts because of their different colour cases. Finding the charts he needs, he wakes her up and goes to the cockpit with them. When she climbs into the other pilot seat he hands her a caffeine fizz and an energy bar.

"Just finishing the course. Have you sailed up here before?"

Still stretching she glances down at the chart.

"Alban! All your friends have gone to Alban? They must be stark-staring-bonkers."

"Translate." Inez taps the side of her head.

"Oh, I see. Well, Alban's where we're heading. Is it okay to tidy up that locker in your cabin so the faxcharts are easy to find?"

"Help yourself, Dahqin. I've never had to load any extra charts before this trip. I leave that space to Charlie."

He puts the faxcharts in alphabetical order in the box that is there to hold them. Then he continues methodically arranging the faxplex. As he picks up each one it shows the date and names of sender and recipient. A name on one of them makes him stop. His interest heightened, Dahqin pinches with thumb and finger to view the document. To his surprise there is no blocking code.

30-04-2188. Charlie Trelawn.

Dear Charlie,

Thank you for the information you gave me last period. So profitable for me. It is amazing how easy it is to make huge gains even within the strictures placed by the sang-real.

Your assistant is charming, as ever, a pleasure to be with, though whether she really finds me delightful company, I have to leave in doubt. However, she is a most suitable courier.

I have procured the goods mentioned in our last despatch. I am arranging for them to be shipped to a secure destination from your Hamburg Depot. One of my other contacts will be handling that side of things. You traders — so full of promise. If only the conditions were right.

I look forward to our next meeting.

Yours in league,

Yves Penaul
Sion, Valais, Confederation Helvetica

He checks the link-names again. There is no doubt in his mind that the person involved is Ardel's uncle. The family name Penaul being unusual.

He puts the rest of the documents into the locker in neat stacks behind the fiddles that he has refitted, and puts the letter from Yves at the front. Closing the locker he goes back to the cockpit.

Until he goes below nearly two hours later, he lets Inez tell where the HiTail has taken her.

June, 30th — On the HiTail-it

With little trace of the violence of the storm twenty-four hours earlier, the hi-foil races on. Though it is sunny they don't open the cockpit because the wind noise and buffeting at high speed is wearing. Alun has tried to raise the Blondyn, but though the number connects there has been no answer.

"They've already left the boat, wherever it is." Dahqin surmises when he gets up. Inez makes some rehydrated soup for them before going to bed. Dahqin moans about the packaged food.

"Tough! I never carry anything else aboard. I seldom spend more than ten or twelve hours at sea."

He grimaces, eating steadily until pushing away his empty bowl.

"I didn't think I'd ever feel so strongly about returning to the Cantons. I thought this was going to be a bit of an adventure, but not anything like it has become. I wonder what the punishment is for assaulting and kidnapping a League employee in a Fastness."

"Alun would have been the victim if he'd not been fast enough. Don't start softening on the Shadow. I know we must never fall into the trap of doing unto others what they would do unto us, and all that stuff, but every now and then a case arises where you have to ask what happens if you don't." Dahqin is about to respond when she continues.

"And remember, he was already outside the law when he was kidnapped."

The course takes the vessel close alongside two big islands, Ynys Môn to starboard, and Mann further north, to port. Isolated clouds throw large shadows across the landscapes. It is now early evening and they head north-east, gradually picking up the outline of mountains ahead.

"Running before the wind is more exciting when the waves are bigger. You'd love it." Inez checks the chart. "Another hour and a half, max."

"When were you last in the Cantons, Inez?" She flicks switches and presses buttons. The hifoil leans to starboard and seems to decrease speed. It is an illusion.

"April, I think." She frowns. "Yeah, late April. Why?"

"Just wondered. I'm going to see if Alun's okay."

In the aft cabin Alun is hard asleep, but his face is twitching in and out of frowns. Dahqin curls up to him, awake in contemplation.

June, 30th — Arriving at Haven — Dahqin

However impartially I try to think about it, I am put out by the revelation Alun and Kirus were always lovers. When we were young teenagers it had been normal to sleep three to a bed, we'd started that so long before. I had always hoped to remain part of a triangular arrangement with them, but since the first sexual encounters of puberty I had only had sex with one or the other. Nothing other than a bit of horseplay happened when all three of us were together. I wonder why they were unable to tell me about what they got up to.

Inez is calling me. I'd dozed off. I unwind from Alan and jump up into the darkening cockpit.

"They're calling us on the radio. I don't know what to tell them."

"What's the call sign or name of this thing?"

" HiTail-it. It was Charlie's idea of a joke."

"What vessel?" The voice is strongly accented.

"HiTail-it."

"Where from?"

"Brittany."

"Brittany? Another one. Aren't we lucky. What is your business?"

"I am Dahqin Stiwll, Aide to the League Ambassadors. I can divulge my true business only to them or the Reever."

"We shall get a pilot out to you, Sir."

The radio falls silent. I mute the mike and sit down, taking a gentle poke at Inez with my bunched fist.

"You blagger." She laughs.

I smile back, but need to be serious.

"You might not understand why I ask some of the things I'm about to. I'm not trying to corner you, believe me."

"Why are you softening me up, then? I'm already on your side."

"I know that. But I need to ask about some things you've done."

"Why do you say that?"

"I don't really know what might come from what we've done."

"Fucking hell! What's going to happen?"

"What's the matter?" We've woken Alun.

"You'd better ask your fuck-buddy here!"

"Inez." She glares at me, nostrils flaring, and her lips a thin line in the angry rigidity of her face.

"There are some faxplex in that locker with the faxcharts. Do you know what's in them?"

"No! Unlike just about everyone else, I mind my own business."

"I need to take them ashore to be looked through."

"They belong to my employer. He'd mind. But don't let that stand in your way. I can tell you won't."

She seems to shrink into the seat and the anger tails out of her voice. "What questions?"

"Did you ever go to the Cantons for Charlie with faxplex for someone in the League?"

"In the League? I don't think so. The contact I had was youngish. But what he did I don't know, something similar to Charlie I thought. Why are you asking?"

"What do you mean by youngish?"

"Low-thirties, I think."

That doesn't fit. "Wait a minute." I get the faxplex from Yves and hold it out to her. She reads it, drawing it very slowly towards her.

"Oh ... Yves ..." She looks at me, putting fingers to her lips, a puzzled frown crosses her features.

"Yves — always flirting with me. He tried to be outrageously witty but was over-familiar. Oily. I never gave documents to him, ever. I went there five times for Charlie. The first time was before I was working full time for him. That time Yves wasn't there, but always afterwards he was. The last time this must have been in the bundle. What does he mean by me being most suitable?"

"You don't ask questions." I say it quietly, looking at my feet.

"HiTail-it, HiTail-it." I flick the mike switch.

"Station calling HiTail-it. Receiving you."

"This is the pilot, we are heading your way now. Where shall we board you?"

Inez gets into a lather about the pilot boarding. I let her sort it out; we follow their launch in.

Inez goes off to complete the arrival formalities in the Harbour Master's Office. Alun has gone to check on the Blondyn and as it has better accommodation than the HiTail-it we have already arranged to meet back there. We invite Inez, but she'll be happier on board her own boat, she insists. She's not at ease with the berth; she needs a good sleep; and finally she says we need our own space as well. I haul the faxplex off the hifoil, in a canvas bag, and head over to the tidal harbour. Leaving the bag with Alun I walk to the Harbour Master's Office, to speak to the Duty Controller. I lay the Shadow's League Warrant on the countertop — partially obscuring the photo.

"My name is Dahqin Stiwll. I am Aide to the Ambassadors. We shall be going to The Keep in the morning to join them. My pilot and crewman will travel with me. We need to travel early."

She's listening very carefully, but leans forward to look closer at the Warrant, so I cough and deftly switch it for my Helvetican persID, one of the few magic tricks I am good at. Her eyes flick towards me, then she looks again at the card on the counter.

"That can all be arranged, Sir."

"As we must not impede cargo ship movements, I would like the HiTail-it lifted out of the water and placed on trestles for safety of the foils. I take it security is sufficient to guarantee it's safety ashore."

"We shall get the boat lifted once we have suitable trestles in place. It will be later in the day. The Boundary Patrol barracks is at the head of the wet dock opposite. I can make arrangements to site the boat between these two buildings. You've had a good voyage. We were told to expect you tomorrow."

"Oh. Really? Well, that is efficient all round. We had an exceptionally good run, and my pilot is very experienced. Can you tell me — are there arrangements in place for us to travel to The Keep tomorrow?"

"I shall make them tonight, Sir."

"Inez Tozer is staying on the HiTail-it tonight. We other two are staying on the Blondyn." I shake her hand and bid her goodnight.

I find Alun sleeping in the largest cabin. I deposit the Shadow's phone, Warrant and persID cards in with the faxplex and go back to him. I undress and climb into the berth. He wakes with a start.

"It's me. Are you okay?"

"I am now." His arms fold round me.

Book Five — Part 2

Things Come Together
We need to counter guile with probity

July, 1st — The Keep in Derwent

Faerachar is awake at his usual early hour when staying in The Keep. There's a report from the Castellan's office: the Aide to the Ambassadors, Dahqin Stiwll entered Haven on a fast wind-boat last night, with two companions, and asked for certain things to be done. As they were expecting him, the things he required have been organised. What further actions does the Reever require? Faerachar laughs to himself. He sends back that they are to render every assistance to the Aide and provide an escort to get them all to The Keep, and specifies the time when they are to arrive.

"So," he tells his reflection as he shaves. "Dahqin has arrived."

He taps his razor on the mirror, smiling. "This will be interesting."

Faerachar rises to greet Gwyneth as she comes out to the breakfast table. Grandy is right behind her.

"You're expecting a lot of people," Gwyneth says.

"Yes, and a lot to achieve today. Bridget will be at that end, can you sit to her left, please, Gwyneth, and Grandy, you to her right. Ardel will be next to you."

"My journey with Briged was a delight, Faerachar."

"I'm glad of that, Gwyneth. Some sort of compensation for us not being any help to you in the case of the unfortunate man found in the river where you live."

"Ah. It is as it is. I've had an interesting time here. But you ..."

271

She wags a finger at him as she sits. "You'll be a conjuror today. I can see mischief in your eyes."

He reminds himself Briged has seen something in this woman.

When Briged appears he doesn't rise, but waits for her to come to him. She lightly touches the top of his head. At the arrival of the three men, Faerachar rings his little bell, at which the first course of breakfast is brought out. But before the food can be served, Dahqin and his companions appear at the Butlery door. Only Briged and Gwyneth notice his entrance — and so short the distance, that he has grabbed Ardel's shoulders before the others realise, making him jump half out of his seat, much to Faerachar's amusement. And because of Alun's presence it is some time before Peran and Kirus realise Inez is there too.

As breakfast proceeds, Dahqin, sitting opposite Ardel, holds forth on the exhilaration of travelling on the HiTail-it.

"There is some information I found on board, it might prove useful. I've only glanced through it, but see what you think."

Dahqin has somehow taken over the conversation and, though noticing Ardel's tension, he digs deeper.

"Bartouche would only speak in Brezhoneg on the phone from her home in Lausanne, Grandy. She was adamant HiSec is not used. We carried out the whole conversation as a Breton riddle game."

"*She* realises the need for caution," Grandy says, slightly raising a hand.

"I guess. We've got the Shadow's touchpad and phone, Ardel, maybe you can open them? Peran, your uncle Charlie knows Ardel's uncle Yves. They've been exchanging faxplex."

Faerachar pushes away from the table and lounges back in his chair, a fixed smile on his face.

"So, Dahqin?" Grandy says sharply. "What's that prove? Lots of us know people from other places and walks of life." Her hand is fully up.

"Yves mentions valuable items being shipped and making riches. I realise this doesn't tell us much, but it is in a missive from Yves to Charlie which suggests a link between them that is not strictly honest."

"Can it be proved?" from Briged.

"Well — the documents have to be authenticated, but I'm sure it's worth chasing."

Grandy looks briefly at Inez.

"We must walk before we run, Dahqin." She slices her hand horizontally, and he finally understands he has over-stepped his position.

"Sorry, Grandy." Embarrassed, Dahqin flashes an apologising look at Ardel. Slowly niceties and little tales are exchanged. But there is tension in the air.

❖

"How can you think that of Yves? And how come you're suddenly involved in *my* work?"

Ardel is angry with Dahqin; he has meddled where he has no right to and breached secrecy. For the first time, he is annoyed that (as ever) Dahqin is the centre of attention; miffed because his arrival impedes the liaison with Duncn; scared because he is faced with the latent relationship between the twins and Dahqin, as revealed by Kirus. And he is angry at himself. He should be glad and happy his consort is with him, and safe.

They are stood away from the table with their backs to it, and are speaking very quietly. But the body language is taut, and a hurt silence develops between them.

Dahqin does not ignore the anger, but chooses not to rise to it. He had acted indiscreetly at the table, and will need to work hard with Ardel and Grandy to recover from that. Once things are settled, he will be able to tell Ardel about Alun and Kirus. Hopefully without any of the guilt about the reawakened deep-down feelings. Ardel takes hold of his hand and says something so quietly, he asks him to repeat it.

"Come to my chamber."

Faerachar waits until they are out of sight before ringing the bell, gaining everyone's attention.

"I had planned many things for this morning, but it seems we have to make new plans once more. I shall meet those of you who need to be there – including you Gwyneth, if it please you – in the small audience chamber above, in an hour. You will be met and escorted there, as The Keep is a bit of a warren." He stands up.

The twins and Peran head off to room B10. This leaves Inez wondering what she should do. She leans on the parapet, occasionally looking at Faerachar and the three older women talking, not taking in anything being said. When they leave the terrace together, Gwyneth comes over to join her.

"Nothing and nobody are what they seem, are they?"

Inez shakes her head.

"How about a walk along the lake shore? Beyond this Keep."

Gwyneth is naturally friendly, and Inez succumbs. They get escorted to the lakeside.

"Where are you from?" Inez asks, as they wander across the lawns, towards the paddocks.

"Cymru, luvvie."

"Why did you come here?"

"To report the death of a stranger. What about you?"

"Oh, I'm being paid by Dahqin to be here."

Gwyneth stops at the first paddock and calls her horse. She lets it nuzzle at her, petting its cheeks and upper nose. Then she turns away and resumes the walk.

"And how does this sombre mood of yours tie-in with Dahqin finding the information on the boat, Inez?"

Inez exhales sorrowfully.

"He was looking for something else and noticed it. I'd never looked through the documents. See-no-evil-hear-no-evil-speak-no-evil, that's me."

"Doesn't always work out like that, does it?"

Inez shakes her head. As they reach the first headland Gwyneth sits on a seat facing across the lake, in the shade of a tulip tree.

"I can tell you are not here willingly."

Inez sits on the grass, half-turned towards Gwyneth, and gestures her resignation with a half-opened hand. Looking at Gwyneth and seeing the kindly face of an old woman, Inez plucks a piece of grass from the ground and starts pulling it to shreds. Concentrating on the grass she tells how she feels about being fooled by Dahqin.

"He's so nice in a lot of ways, but he's got sneaky."

"Tell me about Charlie."

After an hour Gwyneth leaves and wanders back to The Keep.

With help from one of the grooms she gets back to the audience chamber. Faerachar looks up at her as she enters.

"I thought you'd decided not to come."

He is sitting with Grandy, Ardel and Briged discussing some of the faxplex, a large jug of iced peach tea and glass cups to hand on a waiter's trolley. Dahqin, Peran and the twins are talking outside the open doors, lounging on steamer chairs.

"I was with Inez. Love does strange things to people."

"So true." Grandy glances at Ardel.

"She's in love with her boss," Gwyneth says, pitching it to draw Peran's attention. Momentarily their eyes meet before he looks away.

"She has her own picture of him, perfectly innocent in itself. But she doesn't want to be here."

She pulls an upright chair from a nearby table and sits down.

"Peran."

"What do you want to know?" He looks cagey.

"How long has Inez worked for your uncle?"

"On and off since she left school. About four years I s'pose."

"Do you know how she feels about him?"

"Well, not exactly. I'm friends with her brother really. And I haven't been living in Mawes for a couple of years, so I'm not up to date."

"Peran," Grandy interjects. "Do you think your uncle could be involved in something underhand?"

He frowns for a bit.

"If money is to be made I guess he might get involved. My Dad always says his business is legit, but he can be a bit shady. He's only using Inez anyway. She never asks questions, and always gets hurt when he dumps her. He's done it to her before, but she always goes back to him after a bit. Can't leave him alone."

Faerachar stands up.

"I'll notify the Boundary Patrol. She's bound to head for Haven and try to get the vessel away."

"Um ... I don't think she can." Dahqin is standing by the doors.

"Why not, Dahqin?"

"Well, it should be on a trestle on the quay, Faerachar." He gives Ardel a penitent little smile, and sees Briged turn to look at him.

"You ordered the boat out of the water?"

"Yes, so it wasn't damaged by the larger vessels in the wet dock."

Briged's gaze is intense, so he looks away to Grandy.

"After finding out the Shadow works in Comms. And knowing Yves is in charge of them. Well, and that faxplex. I thought it best."

"Did you ask Inez about her role in this exchange of documents?" Briged is still focused on him.

"Yes, Briged. She wasn't very happy about that. Swore at me. I think she didn't like to hear criticism of Charlie. It took a lot of persuasion before she agreed to come to The Keep. She won't trust me after this."

"Briged, can you look after our guests. Suggest something for them to do now. I'll check on that, Dahqin. I have to get back to the necessary business of Alban. Until Grandy hears from Genève I can see no reason to waste the day indoors."

He bows slightly and leaves the chamber, heading for his office.

Briged loses no time in finding a solution. But the group of males is gone before she realises, which suits the three women very well.

"I suggest we take a picnic and go to Saints Island in the middle of the lake."

"Where do you think Faerachar has gone?" Dahqin asks Ardel, as they lead the other three to Coleridge.

"To trap some poor sod and hang them in the dark," Ardel says, and shudders. Dahqin grabs him by both arms.

"What are you on about?"

"Come on, you and your Bagad, I'll get us a boat for you to sail and tell you when we're afloat."

"She has gone, Reever." The Castellan's voice chunks the air.

"Do you know where?"

"No. We only know she did not come back to The Keep with the Cymric woman."

"Keep looking. And notify the Boundary Patrol, especially the post at Haven. Watching only. Unless she does something desperate."

"Certainly, Reever."

Faerachar goes to his private chambers. In the shower, he temporarily sluices away the cares of office in a torrent of pulsating water. Wearing a beach-wrap he climbs the shallow stairs leading to the most private terrace, encircling the black dome. Siobhagn is lying on a thin mattress, naked. He lays down beside her and kisses her shoulder, teasing her auburn hair as he does so.

July, 1st — Haven & Buttermere

Inez leaves the gardens of The Keep following a throng of people who are on their way home. She buys a ticket to Haven and boards the monolink train with the rest. It stops at various places along the way, and despite two or three people smiling at her she manages to ward off their friendliness.

At Haven she retraces the route they had taken from the dock that morning. She is close to the enclosed dock when she sees the hifoil sitting on trestles. Inside she screams in frustration. Nimble as she is there is no way of reaching the deck. Two BeePees are lounging against the wooden structure. She notices the Blondyn down in the drying harbour and goes to have a look, but it is locked down and no solution to her needs.

She wants to escape — get home to Kernow. She sits on a bollard, refusing to examine her feelings about Charlie. Instead she thinks about her feelings towards Dahqin, which had grown strong in a short time, only to be tempered when he took the faxplex ashore and started casting Charlie as a villain. She wants to talk to Alun about this; she's known the twins for years and they are sound.

Wondering what to do next, she notices the same BeePee officer who had led them to the station that morning, standing in the Harbour Master's office doorway. He smiles and waves. Her first instinct is to run, followed immediately by a feeling of sickness. At the edge of her field of vision she sees the officer move. She gets up and walks quickly in the opposite direction, across the swing bridge and towards the town.

Her resolve to accept Dahqin's ideas about Charlie — which felt like treachery — had dissolved when Grandy had said that friendship with someone who might be a criminal was no cause for being branded a criminal yourself. And that's what she feels is happening with Charlie's reputation. Dahqin doesn't know him; he is conflating facts with suppositions. She knows he is a fun and loving person. He isn't the sort who sets out to cause chaos. She accepts he is a bit thoughtless, but he has a complex business to run.

She finds herself on the outskirts at a fork in the road. Here the houses are set well apart, unlike the large dwelling blocks that spread out from the covered shopping area around the station. Her mind is in a whirl; she doesn't remember getting here. She sits at the edge of the road, halfway to tears.

She needs to find somewhere safe to stay. Somewhere that will allow her time to find out how to leave the Fastness. She checks her time band to get a compass bearing and chooses the more southerly of the two roads. After walking for half an hour she hears a vehicle moving along the road behind her. She ignores her first instinct to climb over the wall alongside the road, and hide. Instead she turns to face the battered electric truck that comes around the bend. Inez waves at the driver to slow down, which happens, the truck not stopping but crawling at a slow walking pace.

"Where you going?" The woman asks in a strong local accent. Bright brown eyes in a chubby smiling face framed with mousy hair watch Inez through the open side screen.

"I know its daft, but this way."

"Best hop in then." The truck stops, Inez slides into the passenger seat, and they are moving again. Just once the woman turns to look at Inez, but then ignores her until they approach a crossroads.

"Which way're you heading?" Inez admits to being lost.

"Tell you what. Come home with me and have some'at to eat. Then you can decide on a full stomach."

"Thanks, I don't know what to say."

"Which means yes." Her companion decides. "You're not from round here are you."

Inez shakes her head.

"I can tell. It's your clothes. They're very jazzy — never see any of 'em round here in stuff like you. I'm Mary. I should have said."

"I'm Inez."

Half an hour later they are inside her new-found friend's home. It is simply furnished, though it does not at first occur to Inez it is all that can be afforded. She comes from a reasonably wealthy home, knows wealthy people, and, since working for Charlie, has quite a lot of wealth of her own. There are poorer people she knows of in Kernow, but she has barely noted their real circumstances. For the first time ever she finds herself with someone who does not have much, but is happy to share what they have with someone only just met.

"Calm down, Tetchy. I'll get you som'at." Mary fusses the dog that has already inspected Inez, and found her wanting.

"Right, Inez, I'll make a cuppa tea. You do drink it? Then you can tell me all about it." She bustles away into her small kitchen.

"What do you use your truck for? I mean for transporting."

"There's four of us own it. I was taking hay down to Haven. The price were not the best, but it'll do, like. Are you hungry? I'll do a bite to eat anyhow."

Inez wanders around the small room taking stock. Two books on a wooden chair next to a ceramic stove, one spread open. Small trinkets sit incongruously with books and an old multi-viewer on the shelves to each side of the stove, a kneeling Earth Mother sits prominently on top of an ornate box. A table and stools by the window, the centre of the room filled by two large armchairs. She peers at one of the watercolours hanging on the wall opposite the fire. It is a bumblebee sipping at, probably, sugar water, the detailing amazing. The delicacy of its little hairs and of the hooks on its feet astonishing. Mary bustles back into the room carrying a teapot and mugs, her dog in tow.

"That's my bumblebee you're looking at. I'm proud of that. Them other two are by a friend of mine."

She goes back to the kitchen, returning with some bread and cheese, a bowl of small tomatoes and young pea pods, and two big chunks of a light fruit cake. She sets it all on the table by the window, pours the tea, then changes her mind on where the food should be.

"Sit in that armchair."

Inez takes a mug of tea and sits where she's told. Mary puts the books onto a shelf and the chair between the armchairs, setting the food onto it. The dog sits facing it, looking from the plates to Inez, his erect ears turning slightly towards whoever is speaking.

"Help yourself to that. Ignore him, or he'll be getting on your nerves. He's not needing it. He just wants to know he can control you."

She plumps down in the other chair. Curling her legs beneath her, she puts aside the mug of tea, before turning her attention to the bread and cheese.

"So", she eventually gets out between bites, "what were you doing at Haven?"

"I went to see if I could get my boat out of the harbour."

"Ooh. Making money where you live, are you?"

Before Inez can answer Mary is taking a slice of cake.

"I love this," she says, screwing up her eyes with pleasure. "I made it meself."

"Oh, it's not mine really. I only pilot it." She stops, but Mary is sipping her tea — watching Inez wide-eyed — in expectation that tales of great interest will flood forth.

"Yeah?" Mary finally says by way of a goad.

"Well, I brought two men up here from Brittany."

"Hey! There were some of them blokes yesterday. We're getting lots of outlanders round here just now." She nods her head, encouraging Inez to continue.

"Anyway, they're all at The Keep now. I don't really know why they're all here. I left there around lunchtime with the workers going home and got the train to Haven."

She sips at her tea, it is really too strong for her taste, but she does not want to upset her benefactor.

"When I got to the harbour I found they'd lifted my boat out of the water and there were some of those Patrollers guarding it."

"You mean BeePees. What's wrong wi'that? At least it's safe."

"But they won't let me go on it."

"What did they say?"

"Well ... I didn't actually ask them if I could."

Feeling able to talk freely to Mary, she tells all about her long one-sided affair with Charlie. Mary produces copious quantities of tea and plenty of comfort food, listening to the unfolding story with her feet tucked under her and wide-open eyes peering over the ever present mug. When Inez had started to talk Mary had remained silent except for muttered *Ohs* and *Ahs*. But as the tale of four years of heartache goes through its repetitious cycle Mary becomes more vocal.

By the end of the evening Inez half–believes she might only be convenient for him. That his repeated confessions of love for her might have more to do with her insistent demands for such confessions than with any feelings he might really have. With her pragmatic approach to life borne from low expectations of circumstances and of men, Mary cuts through to the essence of the romance. The want is all on Inez's side and the convenience all on Charlie's. She is throwing herself against him, as Mary puts it, like the sea against the rocks.

"But the sea can't cling to the rocks after it's flung itself, can it? Difference is the sea don't know what it's doing, and you do. Don't be a tit for any man. They aren't worth it. Tell you what we'll have a beer."

July, 1st — The Keep in Derwent

In late afternoon Faerachar and Grandy listen to Gwyneth explaining her reason for entering the Fastness and how the trip went. They are sitting at a table outside the Butlery on the lower terrace. Having already denied all knowledge of the matter, he does not want to be drawn into any discussion that might develop with Grandy. He excuses himself and goes to his office.

He rejoins the conversation with some papers in hand, just as Gwyneth concludes her very factual account of her travel to Derwent. He asks her about previous journeys into Alban, then about her journeys closer to her home.

"I suppose you must know the Dyfrdwy valley very well."

"I love that valley. Upstream from Wrecsam it is so beautiful, but I avoid certain parts of it now. After they started building that trading base. Up near the source." She looks at Faerachar over her glasses.

"You know, when we first got married, me and my husband did a long tour on horseback around the northern Cantrefs seeing where we liked the best. Y Bala was high on the list. The area around Yr Whyddfa came top, but he had this idea about working in Mercia, see. Which he eventually did — better wages. So we moved to the third choice, Wrecsam. Since his death I've gone back regularly to those places. I've never really let go of him."

She folds her arms across her chest and massages her elbows. Faerachar is looking over to the fells.

"What you really want to know is what the trading house base is like, isn't it?

He turns back to face her, surprised by her incisiveness. She grumbles about how the trading house is tainting the society in the area, with its credit notes.

"SJ Trading Entrepot. Big black letters on a deep yellow ellipse. It can be seen from way down the valley. I've a feeling that body is connected to the place; to those rough-cut characters that Rhys Parry brought into Wrecsam."

She sighs, looking down with a hand across her mouth.

"Given the river was in spate for a couple of days before the body turned up, the weirs would have had plenty of water to carry it downstream. It's a place surrounded by high wire fences and there are guards and dogs. At night it's lit up, really bright. The gates are guarded all the time. I've been told some of them are armed. Nothing can be that valuable."

"Where is it exactly?"

"Up a dead-end road. I can draw you a map."

"No need I've got a map here. It's a bit out of date, but it's the topography of the place I'm interested in."

Grandy leaves them poring over the map, and heads for the door midway between the Butlery and Coleridge, that leads to the guest accommodations.

In room W7 Ardel is reading through the records the Shadow made on his touchpad. Dahqin, allowed to participate and keeping quiet, leans against him reading through the same text. They look round as Grandy enters.

"Being in this Keep with Faerachar is perplexing."

A horrible image comes into Dahqin's mind. He is still digesting what Ardel had told them while they sailed the lake.

"Dahqin, regarding what happened to the Shadow in Douarnenez on your second visit, I've made sure there is a record of the whole episodee. I'd like you to go through it to ensure accuracy — any time in the next couple of days. I'll leave a copy in Coleridge. It's for the authorities in Brittany to investigate the incident itself."

"Grandy, I am really so sorry about this morning."

"You were out of order, but you have apologised enough. Little harm is done, luckily for you. You need to remember my warning signs."

She changes tone.

"A huge thank you for getting me here by an interesting route. I have enjoyed the company of your friends immensely. You have been an invaluable help, Dahqin. But as this is a highly sensitive matter, you will need to leave Ardel with me to do our jobs. Follow what the twin's father told you, and treat this as an unexpected holiday. The other three should keep you busy. We'll see you in the evenings and on rest days."

As Dahqin turns to go, Ardel pulls him back and kisses him.

"Faerachar is scheming something, Ardel. I feel superfluous."

"Whatever I have achieved, I only managed if Faerachar wanted to achieve the same result. Hardly any of the questions I asked have been answered squarely. Things have altered since you arrived. But Faerachar told me he believes it is alright to use any methods to thwart one's adversaries, however such methods affect what comes after."

He returns his attention to the screen.

"I don't think I've seen such a full touch-pad before, and so much about incidentals. It lists two visits to the toilet. When did you first spot this character?"

"At Genève in the station, but not on the train or in Paris."

"It's academic anyway. Grandy, you know Yves in a more objective fashion than I. Do you think he's capable of a heinous act like this?"

"Anyone is capable of anything if the circumstances are right."

"Ah–ha! Instructions. Maybe these will tell us something."

❖

July, 1st — The Keep — Dahqin

I like the feel of the Coleridge suite and glad I can share it with Ardel. The doors to the terrace are open, as are the windows in the oriel, the breeze is fitful. Lounging on the seat looking out across the lake, I take stock. I deserved that dressing down from Grandy, and the one earlier from Ardel. I've got away lightly on that score, but I'm embarrassed inside, and it's washing up in waves. I shouldn't have ignored that little voice nagging at me to calm down, but I was buoyed up by the completion of the escapade, and anxious knowing Ardel met Kirus without me controlling it. But Ardel has said we need to talk — that's a hanging sword.

Staying on my own is not good for my mood. I go to B10, the room the twins and Peran are using, and knock.

I can just hear Kirus shout, in Brezhoneg, "Come in, if you're Dahqin and on your own. If you aren't Dahqin, go away."

Alun is not with them. They are completely at ease, sitting up in bed, looking sleepy. It's one of those with a high head board at both ends, the one at the foot acting as a back to an ottoman.

"He's told us what Pap said about us taking a break. He's gone to the Blondyn. He'll be tidying up, and there's a few small jobs to do. He'll stay down there tonight, and probably one more. You've sated him — you know how he is after that. Recluse."

Kirus moves the cover down and pats the mattress between them; Peran looks happy for me to join them. I sit on top of the cover with my feet their end, needing to talk about feelings.

"I know my arrival in Douarnenez caused upsets. I was a jerk during our first conversations, Peran. Alun hadn't mentioned you, and your looks threw me. But that's no excuse."

"It was a shock to me too. We've just talked about that and what we both want, Dahqin."

From under the cover he pulls out my vest that Ardel had taken — I tell him he can keep it. They are open about the upset between them the previous night, how Kirus had gone with Duncn without care for Peran.

"But we know where we are with each other now, and it's good."

Peran does all the talking. He is worried about Ardel's troubled sleep and nightmares. He assures me nothing sexual occurred between them. My relationship with Kirus is a worry for him, which he insists he shall overcome, given time.

"Peran, I'm in a good relationship with Ardel — despite that hiccup this morning. And I have a good career in the Cantons. I'm not coming back to Douarnenez to live. Not even for my love of Kirus."

"Told you, Peran."

That night the four of us eat together. Grandy is with Briged and Gwyneth. Regin serves us. I like him, he's self-assured, witty. He is so attentive to us, the food is really good, and the wine excellent. Peran's very relaxed, Kirus is happy, and Ardel gets on with them both. The conversations flow smoothly. He thanks Regin in a nice easy manner for the special food he has cooked us, and invites him to join us for a last glass of wine, which is accepted. He's back in his professional stride and feeling confident; I love seeing him like this. My anxieties drain away. Ardel serves an after-dinner drink, in Coleridge, and declares a need for sleep. We all need a peaceful night. I know Alun is okay — tucked away in his own space on the Blondyn.

July, 2nd — The Keep

Ardel and Dahqin get up early and after a workout head down the terrace for breakfast. The table by the Butlery is empty.

Regin comes out, greeting them cheerily. When they enquire about everyone else they get the news that Faerachar is away on Fastness business; that Grandy will be another hour and have breakfast with David; that Briged is eating with Gwyneth before she heads home.

"Oh, and Duncn came over late last night and moved the twins and Peran to Second House. What can I get you?"

That news distracts both of them. Ardel has not spoken to Duncn since they sat down for dinner on opposite sides of the table the night before last. He plays with his cereal, having eaten only a few spoonfuls since it arrived.

"What's the matter, Ardel?"

"Nothing. It's going to be a full day's work in W7. I think I got a bit too relaxed over the last few days."

July, 2nd — The Keep — Dahqin

I munch my way through my muesli, and finish my coffee. There is something eating at Ardel. It's connected with what Regin's just told us. Selfishly, I'm not happy because now they aren't just along the corridor. Also I can tell Ardel wants to do something without me, but is afraid to ask. There's not been a hint of any encounters in our conversations. But it has to be that. Could be Regin — there's a very easy interaction between them. I've not met Duncn yet so it might be him, given what Kirus has said. I'm not going to let this fester, because I haven't told him everything about me and the twins.

"I was thinking, me not being employed by either the League or the Fastness. And with Grandy, you and David's people hunkered over the faxplex from the hifoil. I might as well go over to where Kaet lives and Duncn takes everyone. It's time I met her."

"I can't believe you've only been here one day. I'd take you over there, but I'd have to clear with Grandy first."

So, studied coolness. Got what he wants, whatever it is.

"Actually, I don't mind riding over to meet Kaet on my own. The others are over there anyway, and I don't think you should push your luck with Grandy. I could do with some time to myself."

A frown flits across Ardel's face, but he doesn't seem too fussed.

"I've been cooped up with people in small boats too much lately. I'll see you later. Let me know when you'll finish for the day."

July, 2nd — The Keep

In a private interview room near his office Faerachar sits silently, as the Castellan disagrees with what he has just proposed.

"That is not good for any one of us, Reever. You. Me. The Fastness itself. Nor the hard-won changes in our society. You know it is a Transgression of the most serious kind for such an operation to be carried out. So I urge you, do not take up this idea of sending a surveillance team into Cymru to find out about this base.

"Your last order to me of this outlandish kind was highly questionable. Based as it was on that arcane legal ruling regarding the defence laws — from the time of the Upheavals. And that was carried out within this Fastness. I understand the gravity of the threat to the Confederation. The man was dead by accident. But it was not decent. I do not see how it can be squared with the Ethical Code. I feel I am being put in an indefensible position by your actions. It is out of character for you to even suggest these things.

"With the high drones stationed above the dome we have all we need to find out anything we want across the Confederation. Without recourse to putting our people in jeopardy of being arrested and everything that would entail.

"I have to be able to look the Steward and the Communicator in the eye. I have to be able to look into the eye of the person I admire most for the solidity of her ethics. Your mother. It is with good reason she is the Good Sounding Counsel. I am employed by the Fastness on the strength of my personal ethos. You are in danger of making it impossible for me to do my job. It is finally your decision, but you must recognise the limits of your position. If you decide to go ahead I will have to inform the Council of Counsels in Edinburgh of my personal decision to leave the post of Castellan. And the reasons.

"You are going wild, Reever. In unsettling the young Ambassador you seem to have unsettled yourself. And these hagfish are a curse now. It is time their purpose here was reconsidered.

"The Security Section is being corrupted by what you are asking of us.

The threats we face do not need a force to meet force. This must not be. The role of the good people in the Boundary Patrol is under discussion at the next quarterly session. Hopefully to move it to more civil pursuits; to meld it with the Civic Service system, is my hope."

On the edge of anger he slams his left fist into his right palm.

"We need to counter guile with probity."

He pauses to calm his temper.

"Reever, because of the time I have served with you; because of the respect I have had for you since you worked at your father's side, I shall drop all rank with what I say. Faerachar, you should ask your father for disinterested guidance. Listen to it, take heed, then go and tell your mother everything you have been hiding. You will face her wrath, and you deserve that. But if you do not do this you will destroy everything. Everything she and those who've worked with her have achieved. Everything those who came before her strove for across the decades since the Upheavals. You will destroy yourself.

"You have been a good Reever, but the next Scrutiny will have to know of what has happened in this last period. You must reorder your thinking, or you are a spent force, instead of one for good. You have to think of an Official Confession to the Court of Counsels and afterwards ask for a Redemption Hearing in the combined Governing Council and Parlement." He looks hard at Faerachar.

"I have advised you as best I can."

Faerachar shifts in his chair, chin resting on his left fist, bearing the Castellan's scrutiny. For near fifteen minutes, occasionally glancing at the watchful Castellan, he silently weighs his situation.

"You are right, Castellan. And I know it. Thank you, Jonat, for bringing back me from my role. I have turned this into a game, fighting this conspiracy. Whether that is because it is so grave a thing to contemplate, I don't know. You are a valued advisor, as well as an honourable person and it is unforgivable for me to have asked of you what I have, yet you are allowing that forgiveness to me. I have not treated your ethos with its due respect. So twice I ask your forgiveness.

"I must not dream of fighting these malcontents on my own, as if in a childhood game. The League must alert the Confederation, for it has been compromised, and they working together take on this struggle. My purpose all along was to get the information into the right hands in the League Secretariat. This path I have stumbled onto unthinkingly would undo everything we have managed to achieve so far. It will take me a while to stand back into my normal persona. I must handle this rightly. I crave your forgiveness a third time."

Faerachar asks the Castellan about Inez. The girl had been sighted around the harbour at Haven, but disappeared back inland before nightfall. They have not seen her since. After the Castellan leaves he calls David. The new faxplex inspected so far have contained no further incriminating evidence, they will continue their search.

❖

July, 2nd — The Keep

Momentarily frustrated by having to rely on others, Faerachar wanders moodily onto the upper terrace and looks down in time to see Dahqin, on a horse, heading south. He goes to his office, makes a couple of calls, then signs out for the rest of the day. From his official apartment he goes to the boathouse and takes out the traditional lugsail dinghy prepared for him. Slow and elegant it is just the boat for a relaxing afternoon. He has a half-bottle of rose-hip wine with him, and settles into the stern of the boat letting it head where it will.

He now has to wait; it will take patience helping the League to reach the same conclusion about this conspiracy. True, he has information that allows him to see clearly what is afoot, but he dare not use it, for his working with Charlie has been ensnared by other associations of the man. Sure, Charlie had warned him in time, and they had managed to intercept the faxplex heading for SJ's safekeeping. He had failed to realise; he believed himself in control. Believed everything would go exactly as he wanted it to. When had he lost touch with his probity? With his ethics — his link to reality.

Ardel and Grandy will not see all the information he has. They will be affronted if they do, and he would be an outcast from his own mother. They'll find what they need soon enough, when the extra pieces from Charlie complete the jigsaw. And maybe there is still something in the material Dahqin had brought. Pity that letter from Yves to Charlie was there.

He wants humane endings. He had not meant Jarnie to die. He had needed him alive as a messenger to the conspirators, telling their plans were blown. One leg over the tiller, he sips the first glass of wine, trailing the other hand in the water.

Watching plump clouds drift by the peak of the sail, he thinks of the airship leasing company he had part-owned. Luckily his part was already sold to Charlie. SJ Letrap is suspicious — only a matter of time before he connects Charlie and Faerachar. But their insider in SJ's Birmingham depot is already gone. Putting the faxplex on that particular airship had removed the need for the interloper. In fact he had only agreed to have the man there as a stupid bet with Charlie. By thinking it was a bit of a joke; he had corrupted himself.

His mind changes tack. Imagining what is developing at the southern end of the lake, he smiles. A veritable orgy will be the result if Duncn has anything to do with it. And he wagers on Kirus being in the throng.

"Oh, Ardel, I was indeed toying with you — so unbefitting of me in this dangerous situation."

He's sure Kaet has intervened to get Ardel and Duncn together, but can't understand her end-game. Ah, end-games. Facing Briged is not a good prospect. Her ethos is more rigid than the Castellan's. She can remain ethical and yet intrigue so.

Soon he must tell Bridged about the family information he has kept from her. Kaet knows; she made good guesses and caught him out. They are both worried how she will respond to the news.

A ripple of wind skitters across the lake surface driving little waves in its path. He senses its approach and sits up in time to use the wind to full advantage. It lasts but a few minutes and he watches it blow on its way eastwards towards the township, leaving him ghosting again.

It is time he acknowledges Siobhagn and makes the two bairns secure. Life, like the wind waits for no one. Either take it fully as it comes and survive or lose out in the struggle to correct the aftermath of yesterday. He pours another glass of wine and settles back to the comfortable position he had been in before the flurry distracted him.

He recalls a riddle put to him by his daughter a few days before.

"What kind of bird with wings can't fly?" She'd asked him.

"An ostrich," he'd said confidently. She'd shaken her head.

"Emu?" She'd laughed, pirouetting.

"No, Silly ... A Bird Shadow."

Shadows. A thought comes — he voices it.

"What we see is illusion, only the shadows are real."

Poor Shadow, wherever he is now. The youngish man who had given the orders to follow Grandy, and thus Dahqin, was the secretary to Yves. He lay wondering what the outcome of the investigations would have been if Dahqin had not chosen that hifoil. He'd chosen it because Peran was Charlie's nephew. Dahqin only went back because the Shadow got desperate and took a shortcut in order to gain knowledge for Yves. And Dahqin only found the letter because Charlie is untidy.

"Poor Charlie, I like you. Easy–come, easy–go."

He wonders where Inez is, but lets the thought go, she cannot affect anything now. Charlie has to sink, at least a little way, for a short time, when the rest of them go under. His lifebuoy is obtaining the faxplex for them. The most pleasant thing to Faerachar's set of mind is fate casting Ardel as the cog completing the machinery turning to knock down the greedy uncle and his associates. Dahqin coming in as a detective is a sweet bonus of lubrication.

He pours a third glass of the pink liquid, looks lovingly at it, then decides to head for the jetty nearest his emotional home, and rapidly drains the glass. The Keep is never home. His family memories are tied to the Three Houses above the southern end of the lake, but Siobhagn refuses to live in too close a vicinity to Briged and Kaet, and in an isolated spot too. So he maintains for her and their children a home in the Township, which she finds more convivial.

He goes south to the Three Houses.

July, 2nd — Third House

Briged is living and working from her apartment in The Keep, to give Kaet the use of Second and Third Houses for the menagerie of young men gathering around her. When Faerachar arrives he finds Kaet listening to music. She lies on the larger sofa her eyes closed. Her living room is cool, the windows open. Two book cupboards are open, Dahqin sits cross-legged in front of one, in the act of pulling a book out and opening it. He creeps up to her and kisses her forehead. Startled, she puts a hand to her belly, then sits up.

"Faerachar! I didn't expect you to give me any of your time. Will you stay for lunch? One more won't make the slightest difference."

Dahqin looks up and nods at Faerachar's tilt of the head, but remains sitting on the floor, reading.

"I have nothing better to do with my afternoon. Though I have to confess to imbibing a little strong wine before landing here."

"Nothing new in that. Has Siobhagn gone back home, then?"

"All the birds from The Keep are flown. I was lonely. I will go to her when my head is clear."

"You'll always be lonely, you always have been, and its not relieved by the company around you. It's inside you, and you know it. Learn to live with it and you might — just might — get rid of it."

"I'm thinking of acknowledging Siobhagn."

"That will make Briged happy. Why so suddenly decide this?"

She takes his hand and leads him to the kitchen. Dahqin can hear their voices, just audible above the music.

"I only found out because of those faxplex. And then Ardel turning up. It has finally made me realise I should do it. The kids are mine. And while that was a long time ago — I still think it best for all of us. But it will bring up her past and I don't want Briged unsettled at this moment."

Dahqin pricks up his ears at the mention of Ardel; he creeps over to the open door, taking the book with him.

"Faerachar, the more delay, the more it will cause trouble between you and Briged. And Ardel needs to know."

"She must know first; so it must wait. Stopping this conspiracy is more important. There is something else. I have stumbled badly on my path, sister."

"Oh ... you have had critical advice ... But you will make it right though ... Don't tell me any more, Faerachar. You must go to Alastair."

"Let me help you prepare lunch. Where are they all?"

"You can scrub those potatoes. They're in Second House."

"Is Ardel with them? I saw Dahqin coming this way on his own."

"Ardel has gone off to meet Duncn. Dahqin doesn't know anything about it yet. He thinks Ardel is at work with Grandy. I can't read Dahqin, he's very good at hiding inside himself."

July, 2nd — Third House — Dahqin

So now I know. Huffing a sigh, I have heard enough. I creep back to where I'd been sitting, put the book back into the cupboard and noisily shut the doors. Turning the music up just slightly I go heavy-footed down to the kitchen. Faerachar and Kaet greet me casually, and I ask to help them.

"Chop these." Kaet gives me a knife and a bunch of chives. "Put them into that yoghurt when you've done and add a bit of salt. Where're the other three?"

"Peran's sitting outside the front of Second House. The other two are fornicating. Peran said earlier about taking a short break for himself. I think that's thrown Kirus a bit. They seemed settled last night."

Faerachar wants to know more, and I regret saying it. The chives done

I indicate a bowl of small tomatoes. "These?"

She nods. He rephrases his query.

"One answer's in front of you, Faerachar." He looks blank. "Peran thinks he's only a substitute for Dahqin."

Making an 'Oh' face, he goes back to scrubbing the potatoes.

"What do you think?" she asks me. "They do love him."

"He knows. Kirus made a bad move with Duncn that first night and I think he's making a point."

"Can you tell the others the food will be served in about an hour. It'll give them time to clean up. Are they really fornicating?"

I laugh, rinsing my hands. "I doubt it."

"Kirus with Duncn?"

"Stop asking questions Faerachar, and finish the potatoes. Would you rather I called the others?"

I shake my head.

"Get Kirus to tell Duncn fifty minutes-ish."

I suppose Ardel will arrive with Duncn.

July 2nd — Second House — Dahqin

Peran breaks out a smile when he sees me. I ask him how he's feeling, and he says really happy.

"Regin is calling through on his way home."

I tell him lunch will be ready in about fifty minutes, and go seeking the twins. They are in their assigned room, relaxing on the bed. Alun cuddling Kirus, who holds out his arms to cuddle me. I crawl into his embrace, feel his lips on the back of my neck.

"Why didn't you ever tell me you were playing with each other all the time I was with you both?"

Kirus holds me tighter. Alun clears his throat, moves his right hand onto my shoulder — a slight squeeze.

"We were scared. We thought we'd lose you if you found out. You gave each of us something that we needed — that we couldn't have together. We are so different in our tastes and you fed each of us. Our love, yours

295

and mine, is not so hotly sexual, Dahqin. Not like you have with Kirus."

"And then I frightened you away." Kirus whispers it, his breath hot on my neck, his tongue licking at my ear. "I've never told Alun why."

I twist round, kissing him, over and over and over, the tears seeping silently across my face. Yet I feel light, and happy.

"What are you saying, Kirus?" We stop, he twists to look at his brother.

"We were exploring things. I got too dark. Dahqin wisely ran like a hare. Let's not dissect it, Alun."

He starts kissing me again, but I cannot get enough of him, because he pulls away. We are gazing at each other, our eyes a hand's breadth apart, breathing each others breaths.

"Since then Peran has made me realise how unwise I was, and I will never go there again. But I still love you the same as I did then, Dahqin. I want you as much. Just I love Peran a bit more, and right now he's holding me away."

As we kiss again. I hear Alun sigh, and we both turn to look at him.

"Is the Bagad reviving, Dahqin?"

"I hope, Alun." We are about to start kissing again when I recall why I had come over.

"Kirus, Kaet says can you tell Duncn that lunch will be in — better say forty minutes."

He reaches for his phone. When the call is answered Duncn is bare-chested and clearly in ecstasy.

"H-h-hi, Kirus ..." I see Ardel's bodysuit and pants on rocks in the background, and a few wisps of his hair at the bottom of the screen. I lurch off the bed and head out of Second House.

Outside, it takes me a few minutes to calm down, and I turn to see Peran and Regin watching me, both slightly flushed.

"Are you coming to lunch too, Regin?"

"No, I've got to get back home. I'll catch you later, Dahqin."

As I go round to the front of Third House, I see them kissing.

❖

296

July, 2nd — Derwent and the Rigg

In The Keep, Grandy is visited in W7 by David who has finally found a list of people who appear to be linked together across the Confederation through secret trading deals that break the rules on monopolies and cartels.

"That's a relief, David. All of the faxplex in this room are now scanned and there's only that one letter between Yves Penaul and Charlie Trelawn. So we might as well tell Faerachar what we have found between us. I hope he'll be glad."

She tries to get him on the phone, but is told the Reever is away and all matters are to be left in the hands of the Steward. She puts the matter into David's hands and leaves W7 for her own chamber.

She had given Ardel the day off so he can spend it with Dahqin. She found his note and map, telling her that he and Dahqin have gone to see Kaet. She has no desire to spend her time in the company of a group of young males, so decides to explore the area around The Keep. She gets a bike from the stables and heads east across the suspension bridge and the water-meadows. Her time of exit, and direction taken, are entered into the Castellan's Office log-book.

She had never paid much attention to the stone age remains she had stumbled across in her travels in Europa — until Dahqin had told his tales of Karnak and the other remains in Brittany. Now she heads towards the circle at Rigg, as the stable-hand called it. Despite the low gearing she finds it easier to carry the bike on the pathway through the woods, remounting as she reaches the open fields.

She drops the bike outside the stones and takes a drink of water, nibbling on an energy bar. While cooling down she paces out the dimensions of the circle for a reminder of this moment. Then notices the upper parts of The Keep in the distance. With the binos she finds the oriel of Ardel's apartment and further round the small enclosed terrace of her apartment. The upper small apartment block and terrace she takes to be the Reever's.

At the smaller inner group of stones she leans back against the one nearest her, at first unaware of the sensation tingling into her body, but as the seconds pass she recalls Ardel's story, and like him, she feels the skin touching the stone warm up. From deep within her a sigh rises to her mouth and is gone into the light wind. She feels certain they are on the right path. Ardel had told her and Dahqin about the fires he had seen which he thought came from the stone circle.

Moving into the precise centre of the stone circle she sits on the short grass; drifts into meditation, and in this state sees the flames.

There is no heat, and no sensational noise of fire, yet the flames are all about her, filling the circle with golden-yellow. It lasts only a few seconds, and she finds herself facing the smallest stone in the circle, her hands almost in contact with its surface. Some force seems to be willing her to touch it, but she feels an even greater reluctance to do so. After a few moments those feelings go. She returns to the original stone and gently places her hands on that once more. Feeling the tingle crawling through her she feels secure.

July 2nd — Third House

Dahqin has barely re-entered the kitchen when Kaet suddenly goes rigid, dropping a bottle of wine. Faerachar goes pale, but does not touch her.

"What's the matter?" Dahqin goes to help her, but Faerachar stops him, and he gets no answer.

"Fire is tasted ... No! No! No! Mustn't!" Kaet's voice is distorted. Then she falls towards the smashed bottle and Faerachar is catching her.

"What was that? What just happened?"

"Can't you guess? You're Celtic too." Faerachar carries his sister from the kitchen, Dahqin following him up the stairs. Lowering her onto the large sofa, he arranges her hair about her pale face.

"She'll be alright in a while." He looks up at Dahqin standing in the doorway. "So is whoever was tested."

"It's the stones, isn't it?" Faerachar nods. "Who was being tested?"

Faerachar shakes his head, looking down at Kaet.

"I have no way of telling. She may know the answer now, but that doesn't mean she'll remember it when she comes round." He feels her neck pulse.

"Won't be long. Don't tell any of the others, okay? She'll know if she ever meets the person who was there."

"Do you know what has happened?"

"Yes, someone took force at the mother stone and drew out the flames. Anyone who does might be tested on the contra-stone."

He looks sadly at his sister. Turning away from Dahqin, he leans down and kisses her.

"If they fail the test ... I've never known anyone who has failed."

"You mean it's pointless because everyone passes?" As he asks the question, Dahqin realises the implication of what Faerachar has said.

"But what happens to them?"

"I don't know, Dahqin."

"Ardel could have ... You made him touch that stone!"

"But I was there too. He didn't touch the mother stone for very long and I distracted him. It can only happen if the person does certain things. I needed to know his spirituality was sound. I couldn't think of another way ... We should leave it now. She's coming round."

Dahqin glares at him, goes back to the kitchen and clears up the mess.

July, 2nd — Buttermere

"Come on." It takes Inez a moment to realise Mary is talking to her. "It's near midday."

Inez sits up and wonders what difference it makes knowing what the time is. There was nowhere to go and nothing to be done.

"Here. Have a cuppa tea." The chubby hand enfolds a mug.

For a moment Inez thinks the evening's conversation is still in progress, but it is definitely daylight outside.

"Are you hungry?"

Inez shakes her head, she feels bleary from the beers.

"I could do with a shower."

"Right. I'll get you a towel." Mary says and disappears.

"So what're you gonna do?" she asks when she returns and throws a towel onto the bedding.

"Don't know." Inez looks up at Mary. "What would you do?"

"I'm not you."

"If you were me, Mary."

"But I'm not. I don't know you, but even if I did, I couldn't be inside your head." She turns away, going down the stairs.

Inez sits sipping tea and blinking. Eventually she goes to the shower. The shower cubicle is small and Inez wonders how Mary fits into it, but then realises she is not being fair. Mary seems larger than she is because she has a zest for life that leaves no room for dejection. If life gives less to her than it gives Inez, she is not letting it worry her. Mary takes what is possible. She means it when she says there is nothing to do in the village, but it does not mean her life is empty. There is nothing except the multi-viewer and the books with which to while away the evenings, just life itself and gossip with the neighbours. Mary always accosts the outlanders, vicariously gathering others' experiences.

Dressed and downstairs, Inez tells Mary she wants to get back to The Keep, but does not know how. Mary says she will take her in the truck. There seems no point in trying to escape from the Fastness. And although she is not totally convinced by Mary's view of the relationship between her and Charlie, it is because of a reluctance to face the inevitable and accept he is perfectly capable of using anyone for his own purposes.

"Four years," she says, as they set off for The Keep, Tetchy in the cab with them. Mary offers her a toffee to chew, but Inez declines the gift. The dog settles between them, leaning against Inez.

July 2nd — Meeting on the Seatola road

When the call comes to tell Duncn about lunch Ardel continues to race him towards a climax, and feels extra pleasure when Duncn tries to sound normal on the phone. There is a sharp stab of guilt, however, when he learns Dahqin was in the room with Kirus.

"You'll get used to the idea of how this is," Duncn says, when Ardel tries to play the romantic in love as they are dressing.

"I told you before, I admit there's a strong draw, but I don't love you, Ardel. Not in the way you're on about. And you'll be gone soon."

"What will you do?"

"This place isn't a desert. You've noticed that. I'll do what I've always done. Forays into the orchard to pick out the choicest fruits. I always go for the best."

"I shall want to have you again."

"With the surfeit of beautiful bodies at your disposal? Aye, I suppose you will. If it's any consolation, I shall flirt with you in front of this Dahqin of yours." He teases Ardel's nipples through the bodysuit.

"I might even borrow him from you." He bites Ardel's neck, leaving a red outline visible on the tan.

"Ow!" Ardel rubs the spot. "It'll mark."

"I know." Duncn sniggers and starts getting the horses ready.

Clattering onto the Seatola road they meet up with Mary's truck.

"Duncn! How's your butt?" Mary yells out as he trots up alongside. She slows down and Duncn matches the truck's speed.

"Hey! What're you up to with a tasty bit of rumpy right here?"

"I got him at Kaet's, my butt's fine, Mary! Found any good cocks lately?"

"What! Let men's little dinkly-danglers near my prize possession? I'd rather have a cuppa tea!"

Ardel closes up alongside Duncn, peering across the rump of his horse into the open top of the truck cab. As Duncn and Mary gossip about mutual acquaintances, Inez glances up at Ardel. There is a mutual shock of recognition.

"I know him," Inez tells Mary, as Ardel reaches over to touch Duncn's arm. Mary looks round at Duncn's companion.

"Ambassador!" She laughs. "Naughty!" She wags a finger at Duncn. She stops the truck and they both get out.

"Faerachar's after you," Ardel says rather primly. Inez climbs onto the back of the truck to meet Ardel with level gaze. The dog barks twice as he speaks, looking at him and wagging its tail.

"So fucking what!" Inez snaps.

"Seems BeePees're watching Inez," Mary says. She goes round to Duncn's horse and pets it, squeezing his thigh and winking at him.

"He's a bit of a crack. Might of known you'd get 'im."

"Mary, he could never replace you in my affections."

"He'd better damn well not either." Whipping her hand from his leg, and grasping both hands together in front of her breasts she assumes a hurt air.

"Come on you two. Stop bridling. You're both alive you know."

"Come to Kaet's with us. Have lunch," Duncn says to Mary. "I think she's beginning to suspect you aren't going to be my bride."

This sets her laughing again. Inez clambers back into the cab through the open top. They set off, the two men pacing the horses alongside the truck. All the time Mary keeps talking to Duncn. "I can only hear half what she's saying," Duncn says to Ardel. "Not that it matters."

"Who is she?"

"Mary. You've obviously met her."

"Yes, she loaned me a map. But, really, I mean, who is she?"

"Mary. That's all there is. Just Mary. She lives here. She does this and that. She's ever ready for a drink, whether beer or tea. She's always ready to eat. And when not just talking — taking the piss. Always taking the piss. That's Mary. Additionally, Tetchy likes you, which means so much to me."

"Hey! Wharra you talking about? You're meant to be listening when I'm talking to you."

"See."

❖

July, 2nd — Third House

Kaet is still on the sofa recovering when Duncn and his companions arrive in the living room. There is a flurry of introductions.

"Mary. It's been so long. You'll have loads to tell me. We'll be eating in a little while. There's plenty here. Hello, Tetchy." He wags his tail at her and taps her leg with a paw.

"No! No food for you."

"Yeah. Nothing for him. But I'm hungry."

"You always say that, Mary." Faerachar says.

He greets Inez in a friendly enough manner, but she glares at him and goes to sit with Peran. Dahqin follows her in with a tray of wine glasses, which he hands to Faerachar. Duncn is smiling, but Ardel is nervous as he makes the introduction, for Dahqin looks livid.

Dahqin is fully aware of the expectation of the audience. He sees raw sexual desire on the face of the man Ardel has introduced. As Duncn opens his mouth to speak, he pulls him into a tight embrace and kisses him deeply. As his hands slide across the muscular back he feels the tension loosen in Duncn's shoulders, and gets a response from the exhibitionist's tongue in his own mouth. From the pin-sharp silence in the room Dahqin takes his cue and closes down their kissing.

Slowly standing away, he lets his right hand slide down across the taut chest and off at the navel. They hold each other's gaze, until with real tension mounting, Dahqin looks carefully at each face in the room, starting with Kirus and ending with Ardel; who is struggling with his response, because of all the things he had imagined happening, this is not amongst them. Around them the murmur of conversation starts. Faerachar begins handing out glasses of wine. Before Ardel can say anything Dahqin steers him out onto the top landing of the stairs.

"Dahqin, I ..."

"Don't say anything. Don't spoil the moment. Okay?"

"But ..."

"Oh, and don't worry about explaining that." He pokes at the love-bite on Ardel's neck. "Duncn is beautiful. What's he like in bed?"

As Ardel is about to answer, Dahqin kisses him in the same manner he had kissed Duncn.

"Tell me about it later," he says pushing Ardel away. Then he grabs him and kisses him again.

"When we're alone." He drags Ardel back into the room amidst a short pause in the conversations.

"Are you alright, Kaet?" As he bends towards her, she nods and reaching up touches his cheek. He goes over to Inez and Peran, leaving Ardel with her.

"What?"

"Now, did I say anything, Ardel?"

"No, but I know you're thinking it."

"I think many things. Do you know where Grandy is?"

"Last I knew she was with David. Why, is anything wrong? You're very pale."

"Unlike you. He is very like Peran, isn't he?" They turn to glance at the two sitting one on each arm of the chair Inez occupies.

"Like brothers."

"Yes ... brothers." Then he continues distractedly, "I've never seen him kiss anyone like that. I can't think clearly about it at the moment. I'd rather talk of something else."

He looks across at Duncn, who is talking to Kirus, over whose shoulder he is watching Dahqin. Kaet follows his gaze.

"How will you travel back to Genève?"

He drags his attention back to her; it is something that has to be thought about. Mary's laugh envelopes the room as she responds to something Faerachar says, Alun joining in the banter. With food being eaten, Tetchy tries his luck. The afternoon progresses, mellowing the jagged moments that had peppered the meeting of Duncn and Dahqin. The tide has risen and covered the rocks, as Mary might say.

Before sundown the party starts to break up. Mary leaves first, having the journey back over the passes and the old truck being what it is, she wants to make sure she is home before it is dark. And Tetchy needs to eat better than the titbits Alun has been feeding him. Faerachar also leaves early, as soon as his head is clear, wanting to get to the Township to spend the night with Siobhagn and the kids. No one sees him go, striding off to the jetty to pick up the boat. He doesn't even say goodbye to Kaet.

"We should go back to The Keep. Come on let's say our goodbyes and get our horses."

Ardel drains his glass and puts the other hand to Dahqin's cheek.

"You aren't sleeping well — Peran told me you had nightmares the night before I turned up."

Ardel goes to proclaim his innocence, but Dahqin puts a hand over his mouth.

"Peran's explained to me the circumstances. He appreciated your care for him. He said it felt nice to be cuddled by you."

As Ardel rises he can't resist adding, "Oh. And he said he'd never before slept with anyone as old as you."

"Old!" Ardel says it so loudly the room goes quiet. "Sorry ... Didn't mean to make a big exit. We're off now."

Ardel crosses the room to Kaet and hugs her.

"Duncn, are the horses still in the paddock?"

"Yes. Your saddle's on the second pole in the stable. I don't know where Dahqin's put his. Do you want me to come and find it?"

Dahqin has just reached Duncn, after embracing and kissing everyone else on both cheeks.

"I always know where my saddle is. I can find it, even in the dark," he quietly tells Duncn, kissing him on one cheek and sporting the shortest glimmer of a smile he can manage.

"We'll catch up tomorrow." Then he turns to Kaet.

"It's been a great afternoon. Thanks, Kaet."

She hugs him and and they air-kiss. Ardel waves at the rest of them, including Duncn, and leads Dahqin out into the cool of evening.

July 2nd — The Keep — Coleridge

Back in Coleridge, showered and relaxed after the ride back, they settle onto the oriel window seat. Dahqin sits more upright, his back towards the window, while Ardel sprawls, his head in Dahqin's lap.

"I'm so drained," Ardel says, his eyes closed. "I've been very foolish. I was absolutely sure of how I would handle the diplarg. Had my plan. Knew the protocols inside out. The questions and answers of greeting ... It was going to be really easy. And in one sense it was." He blows a sigh through his lips.

"But the manipulation ... If I had not been so annoyed with the lack of deference ... So angry at being made frightened." He falls silent.

Dahqin watches Ardel's face, he slowly moves his fingers through the blonde hair.

"Such a fool. I was arrogant, so sure I would easily get my way because of my training and background. And you, coming here to help me, are so brave, and loyal to your friends."

He slowly rolls his head from side to side, pressing against Dahqin's thighs, feeling them tense against his head and shoulders, his neck joints crinking. He opens his eyes and sees his lover's dark eyes taking him in.

"I've never told you exactly how much you mean to me, Dahqin. It is very, very much." He closes his eyes again. "But I can't find the right words to describe it properly for you."

Outside the sunlight is going from the high tops to the east. They sit on in the encroaching darkness.

"Are you angry at me about Duncn?"

"Not about Duncn, Ardel. I can easily accept him. I would have even accepted the younger version of me — Peran."

Ardel feels a deep breath being taken.

"I am boiling mad at you. There's a little niggle inside my head, and a little warble in my heart ... You let them in this morning ..." He takes another deep breath.

"Well I aided and abetted you doing that. But I truly don't want them to be here."

Ardel tries to sit up, but Dahqin pushes him back onto his lap and massages his shoulders until Ardel gives in.

"You weren't honest with me this morning. And I felt it, and it hurt, but I didn't challenge you. Because I haven't been open with you about what has happened with me since I went back to help Alun."

Ardel opens his mouth to speak.

"Shush! You need to hear what I have to say first." He is again slowly moving his fingers through Ardel's hair.

Ardel can feel his heart thumping more heavily. Then realises he can also feel against the back of his neck, Dahqin's thumping slightly slower. They stay in silence for many minutes, still pressed against one another — the unsynchronised beats a fateful drumming in his head. For the first time since they have been together, Ardel knows he has to work to make sure he will keep Dahqin by his side. He has always been able to rely on Dahqin making that happen, but something has shifted. He had manipulated the situation this morning in a way he had never done before. He hasn't respected Dahqin enough — rather, at all — in this instance. Taken his presence for granted. Why did Duncn feel so important this morning? And it had led just to sex.

"I know I love you as I have never loved another," Dahqin says, making Ardel alert. The fingers start massaging his head again — it is so relaxing, but his heart pounds faster.

"And I want that to continue. Yes! You can be an arrogant arse, but that is a tiny part of you. No, you *never* have said how much I mean to you. Though I often see on your face and by little actions, I do mean a lot to you." He stops moving his fingers but leaves them in Ardel's hair touching his scalp.

"And I feel joyful it is so. But not so happy you shy away from expressing your feelings." He moves his legs slightly.

"When Grandy said she had not had the expected number of messages from you, I went into the worst kind of fantasy regarding you. Then in Douarnenez — knowing we were being followed I was a bit scared — though Kirus and Alun buoyed me up. But when we got that call from

Alun, things in my head changed." His fingers start moving again.

"I suddenly knew, if Alun was not alive, nothing would ever be truly joyful for me again. And I believed at one point even you being in my life would have made no difference."

He holds Ardel's head lifting it off his legs, shifts himself, and lowers it back onto his lap.

"Now I know that may not have been true, though it might have felt like it for a long time." Slowly the fingers are moving again.

"But in the relief of Alun being safe, we became lovers again, which I hadn't expected. And that has not happened to you and me with other people, who have always been just passers-through."

His pause makes Ardel hold his breath.

"My love for Alun and Kirus grew into me from childhood and was there right through to me moving in with you. It is still inside me now — it was merely resting. I only ever mentioned Alun to you because I thought the triple-love in my history would scare you off, and it became buried — something not to drag out. I was more often with Kirus than Alun. I thought we three would live together in some way all our lives. But no. I left them behind because of a rift between me and Kirus. And I carried the guilt of betrayal of him about that. But they never told me the whole story of we three. Until today — so now I know it."

Dahqin drops his head; his chin on his chest.

"That guilt is fading. And it has changed what I was otherwise going to say." He is silent for what seems an eternity, making fear rise in Ardel.

"I need a drink."

"Let me get you something, Dahqin."

Ardel puts one of the lamps on very low. Gets the jug of nettle beer from the frige and brings it back with two glasses. They drink in mutual silence. Ardel tries to get Dahqin to lie down, but he resists, so he lays his head back in Dahqin's lap and closes his eyes. Putting one hand on Ardel's chest, right over his heart and the other across his forehead, Dahqin takes a deep breath.

"I would ordinarily have told you about any sexual encounter with another, as you do with me. I know we both feel the same about that honesty. But this of Alun — I couldn't tell you, because a deep-down love different from mine for you is involved. And on my arrival there was an anger in you I couldn't fathom. I thought you would be overjoyed on seeing me, but you were annoyed."

He lapses into silence for a few minutes. Ardel slides a hand over his chest and places it on top of Dahqin's hand.

"And you said nothing about Duncn to me. This morning you implied you would be with Grandy and David. I knew you were not being upfront about something. Then, I heard of you and him when I was upstairs at Kaet's and she and Faerachar were talking in the kitchen. Which is why I could made such a show of greeting him like I did ... Do you think you feel some kind of love for Duncn? Different from that you have for me."

Ardel tries to sit up, but Dahqin holds him down and takes a deep, deep breath.

"I need to know what you feel in this. I need your honesty in this. I need you to be honest with you. Without that, the strength of my love for you is of little use. So tell me how it stands — with your blue eyes open."

July 2nd — The Keep — Coleridge — Ardel

My eyes snap wide open, fix to Dahqin's gaze. My head throbs heavily and my heart thumps hard against the pressure of Dahqin's hand. Absolute truth. It has to be. Anything less and Dahqin will feel it both in the words I speak and what my heart will do. This is not time for a rapid easy response. Every sound will count with a weight greater than any other I have ever made in this life.

Why was I so tetchy with him when he arrived? That was partly because of what Kirus had told me on the way from Haven. Dahqin had not been open with me from the start about Alun and Kirus. But in that moment it had mattered no more to me than the fact of his arrival complicating the burgeoning relationship I was hoping for with Duncn. What did I feel for Duncn when compared to how I feel at this moment, for Dahqin?

But I must not compare the two. That is not what he has asked me to do. Nor can I start with excuses; appeals to forgiveness. Nor rancour because of Dahqin's lack of can'dour in the past. This is about me and Duncn, in the now. And Dahqin will make a decision about our relationship, dependent upon my response.

The absolute truth. No more gliding aside from the questions he asks me from time to time. No more glibness about my absolute need for freedom of activity.

I pull my thoughts together about my feelings for Duncn. All of them, the straight-forward lusts, and the trickier ones I piled aside as too difficult to face. And in this process I keep tripping over the ones I piled aside about my feelings for Dahqin. I'm trying to keep focused on Dahqin's eyes. But mine are skittering all over the place and I'm blinking too much.

"They took me by surprise, the feelings I have for Duncn. I went into it with lust foremost. You are right I cover my emotions, especially those about this amorphous thing called love." I can feel the ruckle in my brow; this is so hard.

"I feel a bond with Duncn unlike that I feel for you. I'm trying not to compare things, but I've never looked so closely at these bits of me until now — tonight. I'm so scared I'll fuck it all up."

I grip hard on Dahqin's hand, trying to repress my catching breath.

"I know I don't want him not to be part of my life — and that's not about the sex, enthralling though it's been. It's about something else, something intense. I usually run away when it's like that. And I don't know what would have happened if you hadn't ... No, I can't say it this way — it will be a comparison, and it isn't that. Really, it isn't. You are something else, so ... so ... You're vital to me, Dahqin. You dovetail with me so snugly. You buoy me up in a way that no one else does. Certainly not Duncn. I can't describe the attraction for him — it's like I'm steel caught by a magnet. It's like we are joined somehow."

"I don't even know if Duncn feels anything like this for me — he is so dismissive in his words. But I am sure there has to be something in him that answers what I feel for him. It has to be some kind of love, it's too intense not to be. And I know I don't know where it fits. It isn't like what we have."

I am shuddering with emotion in a way I have never known, I try to calm it, but it hits in waves. I'm suddenly in tears.

"It's only possible to get this out because without saying it you would go, not knowing how much I love you. I couldn't bear it if you leave. Oh fuck! Fuck! I'm comparing and that's not what you asked for. Fuck! ... Fuck! ... Fuu-uck."

July 2nd — The Keep — Coleridge — Dahqin

Ardel is twisting his head, splashing his tears on my torso and legs in the process. He has answered me fully, without seeming to realise it. The dilemma he's facing, I recognise, it's the same as mine over Kirus. But for time and place, it would be so much harder for either of us to deal with. He has looked inside himself at his repressed emotions. Those clumped nuggets of love that are never completely smooth — the little crevices in their surfaces jagging with sharp edges at the gloss of happiness. Now I need to make sure he doesn't bury them again.

I massage Ardel's scalp, slowly moving my fingers through his sun-bleached blonde hair. Duncn is no threat to our relationship, anymore than Kirus is. But from now on the four of them are going to be a constant in our lives, for we must include Peran. I can't imagine exactly where this will lead or how any changes will come about — I have to let it happen organically, not manipulate it.

"You are my love in life, Ardel. But honesty is the key to our future. Our honesty with ourselves and with each other. I will always love Alun and have a need for Kirus; I do love you at the same time.

"Realise why I live with you, not with them. The loves are different. You must try to make it work the same for you — with me and with Duncn. We six are bonded for whatever reason. For our own sakes we mustn't make it either-or. Even without us, deep friendships are starting. And I am happy with that. There is room for us all to breathe within this six-way entwinement. But we must make sure fidelity is our touchstone."

Still trembling, Ardel presses his wet face against my bare abdomen.

"We have had an open relationship — encounters with strangers, which we have not found threatening, and often not as satisfying as we hoped. Why not contemplate instead a safer, less open situation, Ardel, amongst close friends who we are drawn to and see from time to time?"

July 2nd — The Keep — Coleridge

They talk about their lives together, from now into the future. Ardel tells of what Kirus said on the shuttle; how fear and jealousy crept in, which had fed some of the anger Dahqin felt on his arrival. This allows Dahqin to talk openly about the twins. When Ardel explains where the rest of his annoyance came from, it leads Dahqin back to Duncn.

"So, is he best in bed, or better outside in the sunshine? When Kirus phoned to tell him about lunch I knew you were just out of shot, down below his chest. Your bodysuit and pants were on the rock behind him, and a couple of times a wisp of this hair I hold, appeared. I was so angry with you."

There is a long pause. Ardel tenses.

"And yet — it — was — so — damned — horny. He's got a body shouting, I've done hard work for this. He is so beautiful."

He rests two fingers over the love-bite on Ardel's neck.

"I know you can feel how I feel, now you've finally relaxed with your head in my lap." He curls down and kisses Ardel's forehead.

"Now ... Let's go back over your morning on the fell."

Book Six

Verification
Without knowing the full answers

July, 3rd — London

SJ is unhappy with the way events are developing. He has heard nothing from the voice behind the death-mask for days. The last conversation had been cryptic and the death-mask had hinted at problems in Alban which SJ had not understood, however he tried to configure it. The connection with Alban worried him, because there had been no solution to Jarnie's death, other than the finding from the Doctors' Committee in Cymru. It had said death was caused by his neck being broken — most probably from a violent fall. And he had been in the water considerably less time than he had been dead.

"Get Gabri to come in and see me," he tells his secretary.

He is determined to go to Denbigh base and check out the faxplex for himself. He wants to get a good look at the data, not just check the coding strips, as Gabri had done. He can combine the visit with a hands-on audit of how things are shaping up there. He has not yet found a replacement for Jarnie, nor told Gabri of his death. The last thing he needs is an angry psychop on the loose drawing attention to this operation.

After organising the visit to the base — leaving later in the day — he feels better.

"It's secret. No one there to know. No one here to know. Right."

"Got ya, SJ."

He tells Gabri that Jarnie is still out of contact, but it is nothing to worry about, that bothers him. While they sit talking SJ's desk terminal lights up. The brightness of the screen overwhelms SJ's natural colouring. Gabri gets up, silently indicating he will go, but SJ waves him back into his seat.

"Wait a minute," he growls. The screen goes blank, leaving the room in comparative darkness. SJ opens the blinds and swings his chair to face out onto the square.

"Shit!"

He remains in that position for some minutes, then turns to face Gabri once more.

"There are a number of things I need to check on before I go. I'll let you know when I'm ready."

With a curt sweep of his hand he dismisses Gabri from the room.

As soon as he is alone he presses the playback button, once more reading the dismaying message. Reaching for his touchpad, he transfers the information. Once done he obliterates it from the multi-viewer's memory. He is now out of contact with the mastermind; informed he will be kept up to date from time to time, but nothing is scheduled.

"I'm going out for the afternoon," he tells his secretary. Picking up his touchpad he leaves via a private entrance.

It is late when SJ leaves his family to travel to Birmingham. He is in a foul mood, and has let everyone know it. Gabri is travelling with him from Birmingham, but right now he is alone in the back of his private cab, working on estimates for a new venture, and frequently cursing. In the front compartment SJ's driver casually glances at the data screen, then returns his attention to the puzzler he had found in the cab, probably dropped by one of SJ's kids. They are on schedule, the busbar between London and Birmingham being uncrowded at this time of night.

"What's our time of arrival?" SJ expects an instant answer. "Well?"

"Twenty-three forty, SJ. Our slot's clear."

"Mix me an orange-soda." A couple of minutes later a glass of drink slides onto the tray in front of him. He chinks the ice cubes against the heavy glass. At least things are still going well with the Denbigh operation. Which is more than can be said about the Great Enterprise.

Unperturbed by SJ's anger, his driver pours himself a drink and returns to the puzzler. The cab speeds on its programmed way north-west.

Having a private cab is an expensive luxury, but SJ is a vain man, and likes to be ostentatious with his wealth. There is another advantage — private cabs have power packs allowing them to get right to the destination — whereas public cabs are confined to the busbars and sidelinks. Sometimes that leaves inconvenient distances to be walked. He takes the platinum toothpick from its sanitised case and teases an offending lump of nut away from its resting place between two teeth. His attention returns to the documents in front of him — tapping the toothpick against the tray as he reads on.

The hotel at the airship depot is less luxurious than its name and management seek to imply. There are others, of much better class in the centre of Birmingham, but this time SJ wishes to remain out of the gaze of acquaintances who are all too prone to gossip. He meets Gabri in the bar. It is uncrowded even for this time of the week. The driver hovers in the background; awaiting orders and making sure there are no snoopers while Gabri and SJ talk tactics.

"Make sure we're both up at 0600," SJ orders his driver, as he and Gabri leave the bar for their rooms. The driver nods, finishes his drink and retires to his own room two floors and two prices below theirs.

Once he is alone SJ takes out his touchpad and goes through the list of tasks he has prepared for himself. Aside from the faxplex he is going to make the most of this surprise visit. There's stirring to be done. He makes a few alterations and additions then goes to bed.

July, 4th — Travelling to Denbigh

SJ is awake and dressed when his driver knocks.

"Gabri is waiting in the foyer, SJ. Should I order breakfast?"

"Don't bother, we're having it on the flight. I'll update you on my arrival time back here. Make sure you get everything I've asked for from the warehouse."

"Yes, SJ."

They drive the short distance to a moored airship – the trading house logo emblazoned on the nacelle sides. SJ climbs into the cabin followed by Gabri carrying the cases. The co-pilot latches the door and soon they are lifting away from the field, heading west. The sun is already well into the sky; another dry, hot day starting. The co-pilot acts as steward – leaving Gabri and SJ alone as soon as he has served their breakfast.

It is a long time since SJ has been in an airship. He watches the panorama passing beneath the windows, all the while ploughing through the myriad things on his mind that have to be sorted out during the day. He pulls out his touchpad from time to time and works on it. The main urb of Birmingham is by-passed – it looks so similar to London.

He looks at the uniformity of the over-roofing of the suburb. Streets between the blocks of homes show as straight lines under the vast canopy, with zigzags and curves denoting pathways between individual homes. It is a wealthy suburb, rather like the one he lives in. The climatslats are already inching open over the gardens of the houses, and the shading-panels around the homes will soon begin to darken. The batteries of focused solar-panels resting above the roof of each dwelling are aligned to catch the little energy on offer from the early morning sun.

Hardly anyone can be seen moving along the streets. Those that are, doubtless being employed in some sort of service industry. The western edge of the dome-roof curves away towards ground level, and the fields begin. Staggered rows of wind generators stand idle – the vertical scoop-blades waiting to catch any slight breeze.

Animals are feeding in the grass strips around arable land. Hedgerows follow neat drainage ditches, outlining the intensely farmed area around the suburb. Farther west the land use changes, fields are less regimented, hedges squiggly rather than straight. Orchards spread around isolated pockets of houses, each with its cluster of wind generators and solar-panels. The higher hills are coming closer.

Away to the south a short line of hills rises abruptly between two river valleys. Closer to their route an isolated lump of hill stands to the east of the Severn. It is nearly 0800 when they cross the river and pass over the marcher lands of Cymru. To the north Wrecsam is barely visible. SJ has no idea where they really are, so he gets up and walks through into the control cabin. Telling the co-pilot to get him another drink he settles into the vacant seat, and questions the pilot on the areas they are passing over.

As soon as he emerges from the airship SJ is issuing orders.
"I want to see the latest shipment figures."
"Available in my office," Rhys Parry answers.

It is late in the afternoon, the base is buzzing with tension. In a small meeting room SJ flicks through the coding sequences he has been given to check the authenticity of the faxplex. Everything clears without any bother. As he watches the multi-viewer click through different faxplex the content surprises him; it is all personnel information. He can't see a direct use for such material. As he loses interest, he ponders on the how of Jarnie's death. He will probably die without knowing the full answers, but somehow can't let the matter rest. It is just too coincidental and dangerous to the Great Enterprise.

He stays at the base until it has already lost the light of the sun.
"Those faxplex stay in the strongroom for my use. Only mine. Understand?"
It is his parting shot to Rhys Parry, out on the landing strip, as he climbs the steps to the cabin.
"Yes, SJ. Understood fully." Then the cabin door is shut, and the airship lifts away from the base.

In the strongroom the faxplex are slowly melting into a congealed mess, his entering of the authentication codes having triggered a chemical change in the material. Over the next few hours it will turn to dust.

Book Seven — Part 1

Faerachar is missing

Throw away your gloom

July, 4th — The Keep

Grandy had last seen Faerachar on the day she rode up to the Stones. She had expected to see him the next day, but he was not available. And today he is still missing. Briged too has gone away. No one is certain exactly when she will return.

Now Bartouche has sent a message as she has organised a Runner to collect the Shadow's belongings. She calls the Steward.

"Good morning, Steward. A League Runner is coming to collect some of the evidence we have. With the Reever out of communication, I do not know where to turn for permission."

"Good morning, Ambassador. In the Reever's absence I deputise. My apologies this was not explained to you. Tell me, please, what is the role of Runner?"

"The Runners are trained to convey securely documentation and other small items necessary for the Ambassadors to operate effectively throughout the Confederation. They are mentioned in the Protocols. Obviously, to enter a Civitas or Fastness, as a minimum they must have tacit permission from the relevant authorities."

"Where are you at this moment, Ambassador? I shall come to you directly."

"I am sitting outside the Butlery."

"A few minutes." The phone clicks off.

When Margot appears at the Butlery door, she is carrying a tray with cups and a cafetière.

"I thought it is time for coffee. I know you like it, Ambassador Emembet."

"That is so thoughtful, Steward, thank you."

She places the tray on the table and sits opposite Grandy, pouring the coffee. She produces a touchpad and places it in front of her, scribbler at the ready.

"Explain to me what the Runner will need us to do to speed their way here. How will they travel from the Cantons?"

"Rather precipitously, my patron has already despatched the Runner by tgv to Birmingham."

"Then they will come into Alban at the crossing point to the west of Nottingham. She needs the items fast, your patron?"

"Yes. Are you aware of all we have to hand? It is more than one Runner can take. At the moment it is only the four items which Dahqin Stiwll brought to us from Douarnenez, and a couple of faxplex."

"Yes. I have seen the list. Despite appearances on the surface, the Reever had fully briefed us three lesser mortals about the conspiracy. I have not met Dahqin Stiwll, but I appreciate his role in getting vital information to help the League and Confederation. I will go to the Castellan and discuss the use of a powered-glider for this Runner. How will we recognise the person?"

"The Runner will get to Birmingham on the midday arrival today, Steward. At the ID check — when they produce their Warrant Badge — they will say they need to speak with Franz Stiwll. They don't of course, he will know nothing of this, but his real name is a useful low profile cipher. Strangely, given his public profile in the Cantons."

"There is a shuttle service direct to the crossing point from the central station in Birmingham where the tgvs arrive, Ambassador. The Border Patrol at the crossing will be informed to seek out the Runner."

"The Runner will have information on the shuttle service. We are ignorant of what happens in this secretive place. And I trust you can arrange a smooth and fast passage here. Not like Ambassador Penaul endured."

"One of the Castellan's Special Agents will escort the Runner here. There are weaknesses in our laws, which allowed a single person to order such an event. We are already working on changes to the relevant laws to ensure nothing like that can re-occur. Those recent events added up to a shameful episode — even if intended for the right reasons."

"Let us leave it for another time, Steward. The League, too, must learn. I shall send a message to my patron confirming the Runner will be recognised at the crossing point. Please let me know as soon as the Runner has been met and when they are likely to get here."

"I shall do that, Ambassador. I have noted Franz Stiwll as the identifier and I have your phone number already. Are you still working with the Communicator's team?"

"Yes. More seems to come in every day. I would like to know the provenance of this latest information. It has to be known. Or the case is likely to fail."

"I will discuss this with the Castellan and Communicator, and my Deputy, who is acting as Steward. As soon as we are sure of our position, you shall know."

When Margot leaves, Grandy sends the message to Bartouche.

By late afternoon the Runner had handed documents to Grandy, had refreshment, taken the evidence, and a secure phone from David for Bartouche, and departed.

July, 5th — The Keep

Grandy is happier having confirmation that Ardel had properly handled the Diplarg and that the Jurisprudence Court has accepted his Notification of Censure.

They can now concentrate on the information about the conspiracy. Verifiable proof is needed for the League to prosecute whoever has taken and passed on the stolen data. The League can then approach the Confederation, which must deal with the members of the conspiracy.

David has a team of his specialists, working alongside Grandy and

Ardel. But there is an air of uncertainty within the team, some seeming to believe that Faerachar has disappeared.

July, 6th — The Keep

Grandy and Ardel, with Dahqin in tow, are about to have breakfast with David, when he tells them that he does not know when Faerachar will return. She understands they have no right to know why, but the lack of explanation rankles, and David picks up on it.

Dahqin decides to give breakfast a miss. He heads to Three Houses much earlier than usual.

Each morning Grandy and Ardel have been making sure every piece of evidence is recorded correctly in their records. Anything looking like a new avenue of interest is highlighted, discussed with David's team, and either followed up immediately, or left pending. The whole body of evidence being secured for future use.

In the afternoons she encourages Ardel to use her presence as a training opportunity to improve and strengthen his diplomatic skills. She is a proficient mentor, and he an eager pupil. She presents him with classic scenarios of Digressions, and makes him work out how they had been actually solved, not letting go until he gets the right solution. Thus she has kept him busy every day — and in the last three days until late.

It is mid-morning and they take a break out on the terrace.

"We still have fifteen days before we must return to Genève, Ardel. Going to Sion within forty-eight hours for debriefing. I have spoken with Bartouche — that phone is a blessing."

He nods, but says nothing.

"The Reever must provide a formal response concerning your treatment on arrival."

He sighs. "And what am I to be told about my behaviour? I expect to be admonished for some of my actions. My judgement should have been better in most of my dealings with the Reever. I thought I was being clever, but he is older and — well, more skilled — anyway."

"Ultimately, I must be guided by Bartouche as to how she sees your work on the Diplarg and what comes out of that. You know the procedures. I will be exacting, but I will not be harsh. Your record keeping and attention to the diplomatic details will easily stand external audit."

She points her index finger towards him, then bunches her hand and brings it back to cover her lips — though he feels the silent *But!*

"I will think long and hard about what I write concerning your demeanour when away from the actual task of diplomacy. We both know you were pushing against the edge of the guidance. I expect you to reflect very carefully on how to impose self-restraint when your libido tries to take your reason."

He nods again, showing embarrassment.

"Dahqin can travel back to Genève with us if he wants." She turns to study his face. "Have you asked him what he wants?"

"Not exactly."

"Then I recommend you do. Just to be certain."

"I will ask him this evening," he says, frowning.

"I'm feeling caged here right now. We'll take the rest of today off. Both of us have frustrations caused by this place and its ruling family."

"Yes, the ruling family. Good phrase. Faerachar discusses so much of his work with Briged. Doesn't she influence his decision making unduly. She is the Good Counsel, but she is his mother. Is that healthy?"

"Ardel! She advises, but he makes his own choices. In any case he must answer to the Councils and the Courts for those."

"Another failing in my understanding. Grandy, I need your mentoring skills more than ever. Let's go where you can talk me through this failing."

"It's not a failing, but you're still distracted. How do you feel about Dahqin and Duncn and the twins all in one place together? Having just lectured you on your need for restraint, this will sound odd. Why don't you join in with Dahqin if you feel so left out?"

He shrugs his shoulders.

"It's okay. We have discussed what is happening. About me with Duncn. I just don't feel it's ... Oh, it's just too weird. Seeing him kiss Duncn in front of me ... It's ... it's ... Well with them all together ... Him and Kirus. It's ... I don't want to talk about it."

Grandy laughs, because along with his serious tone he is blushing furiously. He cannot be honest as to why he shall never put it into words for her, so he changes the subject.

"Let's get a drink." They head for the Butlery. With zero spritzers and olives served, and a few sighs released, they begin to relax.

"I wouldn't mind going back to the stone circle. I want to try something," he says. "What are you looking at me like that for?"

"I've just remembered something that happened to me, at least I think it happened." She is quite still, trying to recall.

"That memorable day when Dahqin met Duncn, which you hadn't mentioned until just now, but I had heard about."

He nods, grimacing.

"I went up to the stone circle. Actually my priority was for some time on my own away from all you young men. Well, like you I leaned against one of the stones and felt the area of contact getting hot."

She stops again, a puzzled look on her face. "And then ... and then I meditated ..."

"And?" Ardel encourages, spinning both hands in front of him.

"There were flames. Flames all around me. I was walking towards the flames and they sort of moved with me. I don't recall any feeling of heat, but the shimmer was in the air above them. I felt myself drawn to a stone on the other side of the inner circle, like I had no choice." She stops again, her brow furrowed.

"There was some compunction on me to touch that stone, but inside me something very strong made me resist."

She is rubbing her hands one over the other.

"I did not let my hands go down to it, but it was very difficult to turn around and walk away." She focuses on one of his eyes.

"The flames were gone as soon as I turned." She blinks a few times.

"You ... Ardel, you have an aura. I have never seen that before – and it is fading now as I say."

She lets out a long breath, her head sagging slightly, and she blinks a few more times. Ardel feels his shoulders aching. He puts his hands to the opposite shoulders and brushes them down his arms, flicking them away as the fingers part. And the aching is gone. Grandy sits up and shakes her head.

"That was a weird feeling. And what did you just do?"

"It just seemed right. My neck is still a bit stiff, but the other aches that built up across my shoulders as you told me your story, are gone. I can't explain why I did that with my hands."

He flacks his fingers into his palms a few times and pulls at his fingers. "What colour was this aura?"

"It was silver, Ardel. You said Faerachar encouraged you and then stopped you from doing something? Is that why you want to revisit?"

She stops talking as a memory flashes in her mind.

"The thing is I leaned against the first stone for a considerable time before I went into meditation. I know this is a fanciful notion, but had I taken too much of the earth force they talk of in these Celtic Lands?"

"Don't know. Dahqin was with Faerachar and Kaet when she went into a strange trance, and said someone was being tested. He told me Faerachar was almost panic-stricken. I think that was you. Grandy, how did you get back to The Keep?"

"I don't know, but it was with the bike, and very late. I checked with the Castellan's office. I did sleep very soundly."

She shakes her head and splays her hands then drops them. An expression of inexplainability for all she does not know about those lost hours.

"It's too weird," Ardel says. "We should hike on the hills to the west. Above the trees there are some good views of the surrounding peaks and country. And they aren't as gloomy."

Within the half-hour, having got a packed lunch each, they are crossing a small stream over a clapper-stone bridge heading away from The Keep up through trees towards the nearest fells.

Ardel points across the valley. "The powered-glider used by the Runner is based on that hill. They use a hydrogen engine."

"David told me they are fast, "

"It's probably what Faerachar used to get to the Poisoned Lands. He told me they have the means to move around very fast. Then in typical Faerachar style wouldn't tell me what or how. All the way through he's been testing me in a far harder fashion than have you. At least with you I know why it's being done. With him, I don't have a full understanding of his motives."

They trek up to Lord's Seat with a view out to sea. Grandy settles against the low rocks, facing west.

"We sheltered in the lee of that island, on the night before we landed in Haven."

"It's called Mann," Ardel says. "It's on the Confederation register as a Fastness, though with even less information than Alban. We need to gather better information ourselves, not rely on them providing it."

"A change in the protocols governing the League's interactions with the Confederation? That's a radical idea."

"I think it would be of enormous value to both organisations. Isolation reinforced through myth is not healthy — though it has advantages for those doing it — up to a point."

"I like it, as an idea. Develop that into a thesis ready to present to Bartouche when we go to Sion. It bolsters the promise we think you might ultimately fulfil."

Nodding, he takes note of her tone. He lays back and at some point feels himself drifting into a snooze. When he wakes Grandy isn't with him. Looking around he sees her on the next peak, to the east. She is doing tai chi exercises. He strides off to join her. She has finished and is waiting for him, eating an apple and holding out one for him.

"Grandy, does Briged remind you of anyone?"

"Your mother. She is an older vision of her. Why do you ask?"

"I think I'm getting confused by the visual, I feel a connection with her, like I've known her for ever. I'm sure it helps she's so warm in her manner, which my mother sometimes isn't."

"Your parents are like mine, Ardel. Not liking to expose their inner selves to their offspring. Briged is the very opposite of that."

He eats the apple.

July, 6th — The Three Houses

Dahqin meets Duncn for the second time as they both ride up towards Kaet's from the lake.

"Dahqin, I thought you might be avoiding me."

"Well, Duncn, I've been up here every day since that gorgeous kiss you gave me, but you're never here. Who's doing the avoiding?"

Duncn's face creases with the cheesiest grin. "You leave too early in the evening to see me coming back home hot and sweaty. Someone's got to do the work when Faerachar and Briged are missing."

Near the bridge they stop the horses in the lane, the noise from the beck in background.

"Any idea why Kaet moved the twins and Peran into hers?"

"Briged said she needs peace and quiet for a few days when she gets back," Dahqin says, studying him carefully.

"Has Kirus been forgiven by Peran?"

"Why do you wonder that, Duncn? None of us five is a youth. Peran, hardly still. Now, I'll let you off your own hook — Kirus and Peran are fine. And I've got round to forgiving you. But the more important question for you is: has Peran forgiven you?"

"You?" Puzzlement shows on his face. "Hmmm, Peran."

"Yes, me. At least you told Ardel you were going off with Kirus, but then you pushed Peran at him. It was not decent of you, nor of Kirus. Peran's the only one who can give himself. I think Ardel has mostly got over your leap away. And even though Kirus enjoyed watching your exhibition on the fell, he thought your rapid back and forth between him and Ardel greedy."

"Harsh! So you did watch. Wait a minute, weren't you aware Ardel was with me?"

"Not from him. What little I saw was a shock and made me angry. What did you expect from me when you came in with Ardel? It looked like you thought you could twizzle me round your little finger."

"I braced myself for a slapping — you looked primed for it. You took the wind out of my sails, and my breath away too. I like your spark, Dahqin. Are we friends to be?"

"I think we are already friends — we tasted very good together — but for the moment we are each off the other's menu."

"Are you proposing to me for the future?"

"What do you feel for Ardel? Are you another who flippantly slides away and hides their emotions deep inside?"

"Oo-hh-ff! I am drawn to him, but I'll not pull at Ardel so glibly now I've seen how things go with you two. You drive straight into my weaknesses, Dahqin. I don't speak to anyone I play with about my emotional desires. That doesn't mean I bury them away. Round and round they go in my brain. Yet with you — desire you though I do — I'm ready to tell you all. If you have the time for me to start, we'll put the horses in the paddock and come back down here, where the babble of the beck cloaks our words."

"Sure. I've got the time. For the sake of the three who are dear to me already, and Peran — me and you need to understand each other well."

"The twins? As well as Ardel."

"You telling me will entail me telling you."

Settling on the bench by the bridge, they view the valley.

"You start your tale, Duncn. How was it you first met Ardel?"

"I'll start my tale, as you call it, way before I knew of there being

327

an Ambassador in The Keep. The politics of this realm I leave alone, other than in the votings, where I mark my choices on the ballot. Right from a young age, we, the ordinary population, are made aware of the responsibility we all have to maintain the equitability of this Fastness. Making ourselves knowledgeable on the rights and obligations and imperfect laws by which we govern this realm. It sounds onerous, but it's second nature in us now. Briged and Faerachar breath politics in and out all day, every day, so of course I hear things and am aware of what goes on through their conversations. But I don't get involved with politics at home, and I have no feeling of deference for the likes of Ambassadors, and why such exotics are here.

"Oh, I knew an Ambassador was at The Keep. It was on the grapevine as soon as he clattered over the bridge with the Riders, but the rest of what happened to him; nothing came out. The Keep is tight on such things. And I'm glad I'm not part of that."

He stands up and circles round, stretching his legs.

"My focus is on the estate management I do for the Fastness in this area. I'm good at it. I like the freedom my job gives me. The exercise it gives me. Most especially the body it gives me. I can own to a huge dollop of narcissism. It has an advantage — my fantasies can most often be fulfilled.

"I was a few years younger than Peran, and already aware of being a fit beauty. Those lads in this vicinity who met my standard were gone through, and left behind, because I was Briged's son. Couldn't escape it, and Faerachar was by then the Reever."

He stops in front of Dahqin, puts his hand out and tweaks a lock of Dahqin's hair.

"While there is little deference in our society, there is a social ladder. Anyone who got close to me was ribbed by the rest for only being there due to the rung I stood on. Climbing Duncn's ladder was the cry. So, having drained them, I shut almost every one of them out."

He sits down heavily, leaning with his elbows on his thighs.

"I tried to do it to Ardel, that day — just before I bit his neck. Mark my conquest and ride off." Rubbing his brow, he looks up at Dahqin.

"I told Ardel I would do what I always had done. Scrump from the orchards for the best fruit. I didn't tell him how far away those orchards are — Glasgow, Edinburgh, Liverpool, Manchester, Leeds, Nottingham. When the feel of my hand becomes too clichéd. When the need for another body to feel and cuddle up to gets too pressing. I take the trains and go where no one knows I'm related to the office of Reever. And no one here can see what I get up to."

He breaths noisily and sits up.

"Physically it is usually satisfying, but emotionally not very fulfilling. Sometimes it makes me sad."

Dahqin puts his right arm across the back of the bench and rests his hand on Duncn's shoulder.

"It's okay, Dahqin, I'm not going to get maudlin. But you need to know where I've set my own prison boundaries."

He glances over and smiles wickedly.

"So imagine my delight when my brother and the Ambassador hove into view in the gloaming one evening. Suddenly the class and style of fruit'd improved in this area. Well, I like my siblings. But some things become habit. Back in my youth I'd try to hide from Faerachar who of my friends I bedded. And him being him, always wanted to know the fullest picture." He laughs.

"When I met them, and Faerachar didn't introduce us, I knew instantly I would pique Ardel's interest. But I was damned sure I wasn't going to let my brother know how this vision had piqued mine. So I never once looked directly at Ardel — a dead giveaway."

Dahqin laughs. "Ardel would have been so annoyed you didn't look directly at him. He would have picked up that Faerachar was deliberately not introducing you. I wonder what was said after you were out of earshot."

"Best left alone, Dahqin, don't you think?"

"Yes. But the thought is lodged. Go on ..."

"When Ardel met me later that night — I was summoned by Briged to go to The Keep for supper — I knew he wanted me. When holding his hand I just hung on, for there was no need to speak. I know what I saw in his eyes, and he in mine. To break the silence between us, Faerachar made one of those harrumphing coughs, which are annoying and draws everyone's attention to the point of focus." He shakes his head.

"I didn't know about you then. He didn't say, and I didn't ask. When we spent the second night together, you got a mention or two during his tossing and turning. Does he talk in his sleep a lot?"

"As a habit? Not that I'm aware. I can be a heavy sleeper, Duncn. But I do know he has been, because Peran told me, and that he's had nightmares. I also know from Peran he was a perfect older friend when they were snuggled together at your doing."

"Ah ... Aye, well ... He has been disturbed by what happened to him during that first day at The Keep. I can't but think maybe at my brother's behest. Do you know about the hagfish? For us, who've grown up here we all know why they are there, and know they're harmless to us. We get to see them as a curiosity on school visits. They aren't necessary anymore to the functioning of The Keep, but are left over from when they were. It's like a practical joke that's been played for too long."

"Yes, Ardel's told me. And while understanding what they are, wish to forget them. What do you mean — at your brother's behest?"

"Look, it's okay to spend short periods of time with Faerachar, he can be very entertaining. I understand enough to know he would try to throw the Ambassadors from the rigidity of their protocols. We are taught about the League in school, so I have some inkling of how it is. And maybe he doesn't realise anymore how affecting it can be on the mind, when the hagfish are seen for the first time."

"That's interesting in its way, Duncn, but you ... I want to know about you and Ardel. Don't balance what you say against what you think I might feel. I need you to be as truthful with me as I shall be with you."

"In those first two nights I felt like I had something really special, Dahqin. Something, even knowing you were in the background, I couldn't make go away. And it grew stronger in those days and nights when we were together. And even with you sitting here beside me now, those feelings are still here. I've lived long enough keeping such feelings in check. Now the taste of them is too sweet in the mouth to push away. But I won't intrude on your relationship any further, Dahqin. I respect what you have, and myself, too much. But I do like Ardel very strongly."

He pauses.

"Which brings me to Kirus. He is so sexy, more so than Ardel. Will he forgive me? He's right, I'm greedy. When I met him on the boat — I drooled, but so did he. I also thought he would break me out of Ardel. But he didn't. Hasn't."

He looks Dahqin right in the eyes.

"Okay! And yes... I've been avoiding you. Don't leer. You and Alun arrive and suddenly my own home is overflowing with five tasty men who are going to be around for a while. The thoughts spinning in my head were and still are mad. Honestly. Mad." He goes wide-eyed, and whoops out a breath.

"I know you are all going to leave soon, so I'm making hay. The worst thing is my best friend seeing how I act when I go away. I don't know the price I'll pay for all this hay."

Dahqin's face is as neutral as he can keep it.

"I can't tell you what Kirus will and won't do about you. We are going to enjoy our time together, the three of them and me. You will have to find your own way through our relationships. I know Kirus — the so sexy — well enough. He wants to play with you, but is wary of the impact it will have on Peran. You need to stop avoiding him, and ask. There'll be a direct answer."

"You know, after you dragged Ardel out the other day, I went up to Alun thinking he was Kirus. Luckily — before I made a hash of it — you came back, and it was Alun's reaction that showed me the difference. But he got crappity with me for talking to Kirus about meeting up, because of the way I was looking at you while asking. He seemed serious about it. Can I ask about the three of you?"

Dahqin nods. "Anything. Everything. This is our one chance to be uninhibited and wide open."

"Explain where things stand between you."

"He was annoyed at you — crappity sounds right. Only a little while before you'd been enjoying my consort while talking to his brother, who you'd been with the night before, on a phone I could see as well. You pressed a lot of buttons in the little group watching your performance. By the time you talk of he would have been only on low simmer, now he'll probably give you a peck on the cheek.

"When we were younger, we three shared a bed at their home more nights than not. I was happy. I had two lovers. I had been so sure of my allure to each of them separately, I missed the fact that they had their own love affair going on.

"Which I never knew about until Inez said it a few days back. It threw me quite badly. Peran understands them so much better than I did. The fact is I have a love for Kirus, maybe in the way you feel about Ardel and he feels about you. But I had to leave Brittany to gain what I now have."

He looks up into the trees and laughs harshly.

"That's what you saw on my face. The person I really wanted to slap was me. And then Ardel. Because he lied to me to go and see you. Making me question what I do have. Though slapping is no relief to passionate anger."

"So how do you feel about me?"

"Firstly. You dismissed what he tried to tell you about his feelings, so he is unsure how you feel about him. Secondly. Ill-placed respect is as poisonous as jealousy. Particularly if you are ignoring emotional forces you cannot quell. If it's a game we start playing, setting it up for winners and losers, all of us lose. You will both be diminished and I will have lost part of the person I love so much. He has not felt like this about another since we have been together."

He taps Duncn on his arm.

"I was not honest with Ardel about my life with the twins. He found out from Kirus when they were on the shuttle. That must not happen with you two in my life. If we look honestly at the feelings each of us engenders in each of the others, perhaps a mutual benefit is possible so we all get more than we otherwise would. But finessing emotions is a dangerous manoeuvre, Duncn. Unless we all strive to retain our own probity and articulate it to each other."

"Okay. It'll take me a while to think through all that clearly. But now you know what I feel for him. Thirdly?"

"It is not my place to pass on what you have said to me. You have to do it directly. Now *fourthly*. How do I feel about you? Hmm ..."

Dahqin grasps Duncn's chin and turning his head so their eyes meet.

"You are the embodiment of something dangerous. You could be a firework on top of an open box of them, and I could be holding a box of matches."

He lets go of Duncn, who continues staring into his eyes.

"I do not own Ardel any more than he owns me. We are together because we want to be together. If I tried to control what he is by allowing my need for him — my anger at him — my annoyance when his mood does not accurately align with mine — to restrict him: or him try that with me ... It would destroy everything we are. So ... I think you and I have burgeoning desires to spend time together in the company of my consort and those lovers who came here to help me rescue him from the Reever, in a formulation yet to be devised. Is that enough of a proposal for the future?"

"And I thought I was temptation."

"You're both temptation," Peran says as he approaches from behind the bench. They face his cheeky grin.

"Ooh! Worried! I only heard that last bit you said, Dahqin ... Honestly. I won't repeat it ... I know when to keep quiet, and when the truth is needed."

He turns round to look back at the house.

"Kaet's made some tea, and sent me out to get you. The other two are just getting up." He scratches the side of his nose.

"You do have a very fine chin, Duncn. You've been under her observation since you got here, but she won't have seen that little bit. I was in the way."

He walks round the bench and quickly leaning in, kisses Dahquin on the forehead.

"What's that for?"

"I want to thank you for what you said the other day. About you, Kirus and me. It means a lot to me." He steps back.

"And you ... You've got to talk to Kirus, Duncn."

"How long have you been behind us?"

"Honestly, Duncn, only seconds. Your confidential chat — I could sense it from the house. I paced it."

"So not only the looks you share — you're both matchmaking."

Peran's cheeriness disappears.

"I'm joking, Peran, not angry. Come on give us the smile again."

He pats the seat between them.

"I want and need to apologise to you, Peran. It was selfish of me to drag Kirus off like I did. You're a really nice young man who deserves more respect from the likes of me. I didn't think about your feelings for Kirus."

"I can accept your apology now. In the time since Dahqin appeared on the doorstep in Douarnenez I've learned a lot more about what Alun and Kirus mean to me, and what I mean to them. It's been a bit turbulent in here." He taps his chest, then accepts Dahqin's outstretched hand.

"It was a bit of a shock to me, what Kirus told Ardel on the shuttle. And I want this to be just from me to you two, I don't want them to know." He pauses.

"Please." He checks they understand.

"If you hadn't said to Kirus what you did, Dahqin, in front of me, it's likely I'd have gone back to Kernow. When I first realised who you were I thought I suddenly had very big shoes to try and fill. I really did think I was just a substitute for your looks alone. But now I know I only need to keep the shoes I already have. And I thought you didn't like me at all — now I know that's not the case."

He noisily sucks in air, and shifts to face Duncn.

"When you went off with Kirus, you took away someone I love very much, and needed to be with at that moment more than I ever had. We didn't know what was happening to Alun, and Kirus going off with you to distract his pain hurt me more. Suddenly I wasn't sure where I was in his affections. So it's not all your doing."

He narrows his eyes.

"I might be just twenty, but you handed me to Ardel as if I was a juicy peach you'd bought. I was appalled. If Ardel had acted differently towards me that night, as I thought he might, I would have felt badly used by both of you, and hatred might have come up. But he made me feel protected. He was scared something bad would happen to Dahqin. He and I needed each other emotionally that night." He sits back and addresses Dahqin.

"He doesn't know how much I know from his night-talk and I want it to stay like that. He kept saying he wanted to stop spinning. Is he sleeping better yet?"

Frowning, Dahqin nods, squeezing his hand.

"You ..." He leans against Duncn. "Mr Beautiful Tempter. I know you aren't all the way through as bad as you came across then. Play with Kirus, please. We need you to — I know your phone call off by heart — especially the Aah–Uh–Uh–Uh! bit."

Dahqin bursts out laughing, setting Duncn off. He looks from one to the other.

"I'm really glad you haven't fallen out with each other over Ardel."

He stands up and looks with a worried face at Dahqin.

"I didn't mean Ardel isn't attractive. It's just not like that for me."

"We're fine, Peran. I'm glad you feel ok with Ardel. And what you've said stays only with us. We know when to keep quiet too. Let's get the drink of tea from your sister, Duncn."

And alongside Peran, an arm draped across his shoulders, they head for the house.

July, 6th — Third House, Derwent & Haven

Following the lunch party at Kaet's on the 2nd, Inez had kept away from the men. Not too difficult when they were in Second House. She is angry about being captive, and feeling helpless. She tries a few times to contact Charlie, but is never able to get through. Faerachar had said Charlie knew she was safe, and would not be out of pocket due to the impounding of HiTail-it. As if he knew Charlie, she'd thought. She stayed with Mary one night, but became quickly bored of the slow pace of life, and returned to Kaet's. At least she could sound off to her, and feel she was heard. On the evening of the 4th Kaet had moved the twins and Peran into Third House, since then she's stayed in her room rather than mix.

This morning, as they sit alone in Kaet's kitchen — the remains of breakfast on the table — she is moaning to Peran, the only one with whom she feels an affinity. She needs to sail away, back to a faster life. He starts to clear the table and she rises to help him.

"Why don't you borrow a bike from The Keep and do a bit of exploring further afield."

"I don't want to go back there. I don't trust anyone there."

Peran stacks the dishes in the sonic cleaner, while she puts the rest of the things away.

"You don't have to go into it. Go to the stables entrance and ask one of the grooms to let you borrow a bike. The other three are busy planning something for today; if it's really interesting I might go. But I've already got something else planned. If you want, I can come over there with you now. We're fast walkers, it'll take us about one hour-ten." He cleans his hands.

She's huffing, now unsure about confronting Faerachar.

"Kaet says he only comes here occasionally, so you need to go to the Keep if you want to see him."

Agreeing to his idea and his company Inez grabs her backpack. As they cross the footbridge over the Derwent, Peran hands her a map centred to the south-east of The Keep, covering a square of country one hundred kimetres a side.

"You can borrow this. I bought it a couple of days ago in Keswick. I was really surprised at how big the place is. It goes right back into a side valley. Ardel said there wasn't much over there, but it's busy. Any ideas what you want to do?"

"I want to check on the HiTail-it, and get some personal things from there. I'm still angry with Dahqin for being such a shite. He tricked me about putting the boat into the wet dock. I really liked him until I found out he organised that. At least he told me to my face. Maybe if this gets sorted out and Charlie is okay about things, I'll find him funny company again. If I get to the radio on the HiTail-it I might be able to raise Charlie. I don't understand why I can't on my phone."

"Why don't you go over there and ask the BeePees to let you get your stuff? If they say yes, you'll be happier, and if they don't you'll feel like you do now — but with extra endorphins from the bike ride."

It is another bright, almost cloudless day, the wind slight, the temperature climbing. The Keep comes in and out of view as they follow the well marked path along the western shoreline.

"Do you want me to find out if we can see Faerachar?" Peran asks, as they round the final headland and The Keep is fully in view.

"No! I've decided not to do that. I'm mad at Dahqin — who I can't help but like. Him! I don't like him at all. I don't trust him. I've realised as we walked it is a stupid idea. He'd just dominate any conversation."

"Then I'll head back, once you sort out a bike. So, is it Haven?"

"Yes, it is. You're right. I'm normally good at getting what I want. I'm going to pick myself up and make that happen. Thanks Peran. Give me a hug. I'll see you tonight."

"Okay. Cycle well. Be brave again. Throw away your gloom."

He watches her ride away, then heads for his rendezvous with Regin.

She sets a fast pace along the trackway to Haven. When she gets there, she sees The Blondyn has been moved to sit right alongside the Harbour Controller's Office. The HiTail-it is still on the makeshift trestle. Nobody is guarding it. At the Boundary Patrol barracks she marches into the Guardroom, looks the duty man in the eye and smiles.

"Hi! My name is Inez Tozer. I'm the owner of the HiTail-it, the boat that's on the trestle over there. I need to check it over, especially some of the equipment inside. Have you got a ladder I can borrow?"

"Certainly have, Inez. We've been keeping a good eye on it. Hang on, I'll get a couple of the troopers to help you get on board safely."

He taps at the phone on his desk.

"Mark, get a ladder long enough to reach the deck of the foil boat. The lass is here to check it over. Get a couple of the troop to see her safely on and off." He looks up at her.

"Can they give you a hand with anything on board?"

She shakes her head.

"No, Mark, just to make sure her and the ladder's safe."

He walks over to stand outside the doorway.

"They'll be out in a while. It's a fast looking craft. Bet it's fun to sail."

She joins him.

"It is, but only when it's in the water. It's no fun for me or it, sat up there on the trestle."

"I have a boat in the tidal harbour, nothing like yours. A small cat. I love it when the wind is right and the speed comes up. Exhilarating. What's beyond exhilarating?"

"I have no idea, but this boat gets you very close to the edge of fear when it's flat out. Six days I've been away from it, up near The Keep. Feels like a lifetime."

"I can imagine. How much longer are you up there?"

"What I had to do is finished. I'd love nothing better than to get it in the water for a bit."

"What's stopping you?"

She regards him — from the insignia he would seem to be an officer.

"I mean, where it is, it'd be easy enough to drop it into the tidal basin by the harbour office. It's high tide in about four hours. It's springs, so there'll be plenty of water for those foils."

"Yeah, I s'pose." She feels tingly. This is not possible, surely? She needs to make certain. «Um, don't I have to get permission from The Keep to put it in the water?"

"I haven't seen anything about that in Daily Orders. I'll just make sure." He goes back behind the counter. She hears him talking on the phone. A woman comes round the side of the building carrying a ladder, a younger man just behind her.

"Where d'you want this setup?"

"Either side, but in line with the front of the cockpit. It'll only need one of you to hold it while I'm going up. I can tie it to the railings then."

The man raises his hand and leaves them. She is up on the deck, the ladder secure, when the duty officer comes over.

"The only entry in the Logbook is from the night you arrived. About it being kept out of the way of the cargo boats, and not to damage the foils. I've also checked with the Castellan's Office, they say it's your boat, and you can do with it what you want. I can arrange with the Harbour Controller's Office to get it lifted in."

"Yes! Please." He wanders off in that direction.

Inez is feeling sick. It all feels too neat. She quickly checks around the inside of the boat. Everything is as it should be.

She opens the cupboard to get out the faxcharts she needs. The cupboard Dahqin had tidied up, and from which he had taken everything but the charts. It looks like it always had — a mess of jumbled up items of various kinds. And frighteningly, sitting upright in front of the rest is the faxplex from Yves to Charlie. She dashes for the sink and pukes, then sits on the bunk, trying to calm down.

"If this gets me out, I need to be focused," she mutters.

Faerachar. It has to be his doing. He had spoken as if he knew Charlie. In her head she accepts one thing for certain, she knows him less than she has claimed.

"Hello! Inez!" Going to the cockpit she looks down.

"I've arranged everything. The port dues are paid already, the Duty Officer says, and the lift-in fee. He's been told from higher up the chain of command it's all in order for you to depart for Kernow, when you want. Is that wise? I thought you were just going out for a sail locally."

She holds up her hand, then indicates she's coming down.

"Are you okay you look very pale?"

"Yeah, I'm fine, thanks. I've just puked. I probably ate too much before cycling over here."

"Oh, can I get you anything to help?"

"No, I'll be fine. Well I did think I'd go for a quick turn round the bay. But if the Ambassadors have finished with my services, I might as well go home. I'm used to handling this on my own. It's so fast the passage times are short. I just dial in the courses and let the auto-controls do it all."

"Everything is manual on mine. But I only go as far as Mann or Éire." He turns away, then turns back. "Oh, the Controller needs your passage plan before you go in the water."

"Okay, I'll get it done. And I need to get the bike back to The Keep and a map back to a friend near there."

"Come over now, and we'll sort that out. The bike is easy we all know it's from The Keep by its markings. I'll get a trooper to drop them both back for you. It's a good day for sailing."

They enter the Guardroom.

"I'll mark it on the map. Can I jot a note to go with it, please?"

"Sure. Do you want to leave as soon as you're afloat. On the peak?" He hands her paper, an envelope and a pencil.

"Yes, exactly then."

He taps on the phone, talks to the Controller. She scribbles a note to Peran, tucks it into the envelope, carefully sealing it. When he is finished she marks the map as he watches — folds it, gives it to him with the envelope and shakes his hand. Thanks him for all he has done for her and walks out.

She checks all round the outside of the boat, making sure there is no damage to the hull, outriggers or foils. She writes the passage plan and delivers it to the Controller. She can make Fal easily in ten or eleven hours, given the wind and the sea state.

The riggers go through the lift-in arrangements, particularly regarding the foils. The pilot launch will lead her out to the fairway buoy and she will be off. She completes the departure form. Just her name. She shakes hands with everyone doing things to allow her to escape, and thanks them for their help. Back on board, she settles into the pilot seat and lets herself doze.

She is woken by banging on the cockpit window. By half-four she is clear of the fairway buoy. The HiTail-it is up on the foils and getting faster. Fal will be reached, all being well, when the summer sun is rising over the north-eastern horizon.

She makes a caffeine fizz and reaches into the drawer where the protein bars are kept. There is a package with *Inez* scrawled on it. Inside, a bundle of euros, wrapped within a handwritten note. Nothing else.

Charlie is waiting for this. 9 days hire balanced with the deposits.

She counts the notes. Balanced with Dahqin's deposits, exactly right for nine days.

❖

July, 6th — At The Keep

Briged meets Grandy and Ardel outside the Butlery. Ensuring they are free for the rest of the day, she serves them a white wine, and lifts her glass in salutation.

"I had hoped we would be able to enjoy each other's company more frequently than we have up to now," she says to Ardel.

"And it is with great pleasure I again spend some time with you, Grandy." She pauses. "Oh! I must tell you — Gwyneth is safely back home, and sends her greetings to you both. I am so glad I took her with me on my last tour of duty."

"How far did you get in the time you had together?" Grandy asks.

Briged laughs. "Up to the Great Glen, so, far to the north. At least when we got back her horse was well rested here in the stables, and pleased to see her." There is another silence.

"How far did you get on your trek this afternoon?"

"We were only away for a few hours, Briged. Ardel led me to a good viewpoint, called Lord's Seat. We've had a lazy walk, rather than a trek."

"Ah, I see. And is the investigation going well?"

"I suppose it to be. Having Faerachar away has left us rather rudderless." Grandy says. "We are thankful David and his staff are so diligent, but I know he cannot, within his position, answer the questions we wish answered. I think they are political rather than administrative."

"Ahh ... uh." Briged sighs.

After a few minutes, Ardel asks, "How long will Faerachar be away?"

Briged looks hard at him, takes a sip of wine; holds the small etched glass up so the lowering sun is refracted through the wine, and studies it for what seems more time than it actually is. Then she focuses on him.

"I have no idea, to be precise. And I am annoyed at him. I fear he is up to something of which I shall heartily disapprove."

She lowers the glass.

"There are moments in the past when Faerachar has not been entirely honest with me. When he tries so hard to keep something from me. Well, I feel we are in another of those moments. But as yet I cannot fathom what it might be." She sips at the wine again, looks from one to the other.

"But enough ... Each of you in your own way has gained something rather extraordinary from your stay here. It seems you are both blessed, as it is said, with aspects of the innate intuition, that some call sight. It is a gift, but it is also a curse if not used carefully. It takes time to gather to yourself the necessary filters to deal with all the oddities that will present themselves to you. You should not fear it, because all that has happened is you are now aware of a deeply buried animal trait. You will not have to deal with the manifestations Kaet has. I can see your auras, and for each your spirituality is clear." She focuses again on Ardel.

"Don't worry, it will not impede your in-built venatorial proclivities."

"My what?"

"Hunting urges. No need to be prudish here — with Duncn you rather overplayed your hand, after Dahqin appeared. Fear not, there is time yet to temper what happens next. As for Faerachar he is very good at pretending, but played you wrongly; he has felt my ire. Too late to say beware. Goodness knows, if you and Dahqin are here for too long this family will go to pieces."

She breaks into a broad smile, relishing his reaction.

"We like you both a lot. And his wild friends too."

"Th-thank you, Briged."

"Now, I want to talk about something else, entirely. Having Gwyneth with me, I realised, we must use the opportunity of your presence to take a leap forward, and become more open to the rest of the Confederation, and the League. We are moving too slowly out of our isolationist past. This need for isolation was engendered by the savagery of the break-up of the single political entity existing on this island before the Upheavals. Alban is not so straightforward a Fastness as the League has been told over the years. And with you here it is time for us to change that."

Grandy and Ardel exchange glances.

"I have talked with sufficient members of the Governing Council and the Scotian Parlement to see what they think of me taking you both on a tour of these dual lands. There is broad agreement that it is a good idea. Because of this the Court of Counsels, who must co-ordinate or smooth, had no need to more than nod. So, I propose to take you, over the next week, on a tour of this beautiful land — warts and all."

Ardel looks to Grandy to take the lead; she takes time.

"What do you think of this prospect, Grandy?"

"I agree in principle, Briged. I was wondering if it will be breaking protocol for Ambassadors to go tramping round the country without permission from Sion — but I am officially on holiday. Ardel must come with me to broaden of his experience. Our presence here in Derwent is not necessary on every day."

"Grandy, there is another, who absolutely must come with us."

She sips more wine. "Dahqin."

"Ah. You are right, Briged. Well, Ardel?"

"Of course I agree with the proposal. Thank you for allowing Dahqin to be with me on this tour. Though it may unduly raise his expectations for the future."

"Ardel, he needs to be kept busy. His other friends will not cause any lasting mayhem, but a bored Dahqin ... left with them and Duncn."

She shakes her head, still laughing. A buzzer sounds at the Butlery door. Briged goes in, returning with an extra glass.

"No, couldn't be. He must be with you, at this time." She pours a good measure of wine into the glass.

"He has just put his horse into the stables, and will be up. I suspect he will need calming down after he hears, so you should discuss it in Coleridge. Grandy and I can then proceed with a more civilised conversation. We'll regroup here at seven o'clock, and discuss it in more detail over supper."

❖

July, 6th — Third House

The twins are helping Kaet prepare the evening meal, when Peran wanders in, sweaty and in need of a shower. He drops his backpack by Kirus's feet.

"Six hours is longer than you thought, Peran. You look exhausted." Kirus tries to pull him into an embrace, which Peran resists.

"Have you had a good ride?" Kaet asks, but not waiting for an answer, announces that David is coming for the meal.

"The way you say his name tells me you're in love," Alun says. "Why hasn't that surfaced amongst all the gossip round here."

"We keep a low profile." She laughs easily. "We've been together for a couple of years. He's so lovely — just right for me. And because it will come up in conversation — I'm pregnant. Faerachar does not know. I'm trusting in you three."

There is banging at the front door.

"No one uses the knocker up here. Kirus, bring them in."

Following a BeePee trooper into the Kitchen he points to Peran — who looks aghast.

"Good evening, Mr. Trelawn. I have this note and map for you, Sir. The Duty Officer said to tell you Inez Tozer is heading back to Kernow on the HiTail-it. She left just over two hours ago."

"What? But she said she'd be back later."

"No doubt, Sir. But she has left the Haven. We all watched it go." He bows slightly to Kaet. "Sorry to intrude into your home, Ma'am."

"No need to apologise. Thank you for dropping off Peran's map and note."

He salutes Peran, calling him Sir, again. Kirus follows him back out of the kitchen. When he returns he flips a mock salute in Peran's direction.

"Well, Sir, that's a surprise. Do we salute you enough, Sir?"

"Not really, Kirus. But you're showing an improvement." Peran turns the envelope over a couple of times, frowning.

"Just open it." Alun laughs.

"It's making me edgy, Alun. Why did she address it just to me, why not to all of us? We all know her."

"You've known her most of your life, Peran. And you are the only one of us who knows Charlie."

"Charlie?" Kaet asks.

"Oh ... He's my uncle. He owns the boat Inez pilots."

He tears the envelope open and pulls out the note.

" 'Peran, something spooky is happening. The BPs and harbour people are helping me get the HiTail back in the water so I can leave. Everything's paid up. Tell Dahqin the faxplex he took off have been put back on board. I'm a bit scared by that, but am going anyway. I'll let you know when I'm safely home. Maybe Charlie does have contact with Faerachar. Love to the twins. Tell Dahqin I'll forgive him at some point, cos I know he's on the right side. I hope you get back to Douarnenez soon so we can catch up. Take my other gear with you, please. Thanks for loaning the map. Thanks for being you. XX Inez X' ."

He glances at them and looks back at the note. "So she did it."

"And everyone was helping her get away. But why are those faxplex back on board?" Alun is frowning. "How did that happen? That's weird. I'm calling Dahqin."

"Wait, Alun." Kaet says. "I want to talk to Briged about this. Can I have the note, please, Peran?"

He hands it over. Kaet goes upstairs to make the call.

"Briged says to leave it alone, it's Fastness business. David and I never talk of politics and the governance of the Fastness. I do not want his work brought into this house. This is our home, where we can relax together, and I want it kept like that. So, if you want to discuss it further, please go out of my hearing. Tomorrow she is taking Grandy, Ardel and Dahqin on a jaunt around Alban for a week. It seems Charlie and Faerachar do know one another quite well. Charlie sometimes comes up to the western isles and they meet up. Does he sail himself, Peran?"

"He's a good sailor. He owns a couple of boats like the Blondyn. He takes my cousins on sailing holidays, and I've gone a few times. Him and Faerachar are of similar age I think, and of a piece, if you know what I mean."

"Yes, I can imagine. Well, they have known one another for years. He has been helping Faerachar rather like you lot have Grandy. Now, I don't want to hear another word about it. You are to be on your best behaviour about this, or I'm banishing you."

She starts to check through the prepped food, making little noises of notation for the recipe she is concocting.

"Your father told you, Alun, to take this as a break. So you don't get bored by what is not happening round here when Dahqin is away, why not go sailing to the western islands and sea lochs. It's beautiful and wild up there." She beams a big grin at them.

"Kirus, no need to frown like that, Duncn might want to come with you. Did you tell him Peran?"

"Tell who what?" he grumps. "What are you up to Peran?"

"No 'Sir'? You and he do need to talk, Kirus. Seriously. Please. Love you as we do you'll need to sleep in another bed if you keep playing Duncn's call. I've got perfect timing on word, sound and action. I'm even getting snatches of it in my dreams. You've even called me Duncn. Yes, Kaet. I told him this morning." Laughing he goes to Kirus — allowing the embrace.

"Kaet, your brother is so tasty. And so difficult to leave be."

He's sniffing around Peran.

"You're hooked, Kirus. Admit it."

"Hooked, Sir. Yes, I am. There — said it. Does that count? Sir."

"It's a start. Just ask him. He's sleeping on his own over there."

Kirus swings Peran round so they are both facing Alun, and hugs him tight.

"And there's love all round me. Especially from you, Alun."

He nuzzles Peran's ears. "And you, Sir." Then as a whisper, "I smell a stranger. When will my punishment end?"

"And how do you feel about Ardel and him?"

"That's between them, Kaet. Him and me? It's best we get it over and done with as quickly as possible."

"Honestly!" She rolls her eyes. "You two are a match, just not sure what kind. At least he's agreed to come to dinner. He's been avoiding me since you three moved in here. It's either because of you, Kirus ... or ..." She focuses on Peran, but he looks down concentrating on the floor.

"Or Dahqin. You three had quite a chat this morning."

"I'm going for a shower," Peran says, pulling out of the embrace and clumping up the stairs. When he has got to the top, Kirus follows noiselessly, carrying his backpack.

July, 6th — The Keep — Coleridge — Dahqin

I am so excited. We are going to tour a Fastness together. Exactly as I wanted. Admittedly, under supervision by our Guardians, because I can't be trusted not to cause mayhem with Duncn if left behind — as Briged took pleasure in telling me. As if Duncn doesn't cause enough on his own.

"Adventure! Adventure! Adventure!"

I grab Ardel and twirl him round a few times.

"Let go of me, or I'll throw up. You are really horsey. We need to get showered and you definitely need it. Even the over-breeches haven't killed the smell. What have you been doing?"

"Helping Duncn all afternoon clean out the small stables up at Three Houses. He took the afternoon off. It gave me time to persuade him to talk to Kirus. How do you feel about them getting together? We were planning on going to the Roman fort at Hardknott, but Peran went off with Inez, and didn't let us know when he'd get back."

He tells me it is something he can ignore, as he has to concentrate on his career. He's had his fun with Duncn for now. He believes that together we will work out how to deal with what has started here. Then he changes the subject.

"Grandy asked me if you want to come back to Genève with us. It'll be on a League airship, I guess from Birmingham. You don't need to answer right now. Just think what you want to do next."

"I can answer right now, with a great deal of certainty. I would love to travel back with you, officially, as your consort. I can't imagine why I wouldn't. Why did you ask with such doubt in your voice?"

"Fear. Grandy asked the question in a particular way. I had a bit of a wobble about my capabilities of perception. I hate getting things wrong, as you know, and I don't know what you want to do."

"That's sweet. Just one more thing about Duncn and you. You've got fifteen minutes left to discuss what you both want, before he joins the others. He's expecting your call. I'll start showering."

Ardel goes out onto the terrace to phone Duncn. I slyly watch his body language. He's relaxed completely by the end of the call. I'll find out later what they agreed. Heading into the washroom he passes my pile of clothes, and ignores my naked body. I hear the shower come on.

"Do you think Grandy will say this is the holiday you asked for?"

"No! Get in here and I'll scrub you down. You're so horsey. Put those clothes out on the terrace. And close the doors. This room will turn into stables else. We need to be back out there in thirty minutes."

July, 6th — The Keep — The Butlery

There is no wind as they head along the terraces; the evening is as warm as the day has been. Briged and Grandy sit at a round table by the parapet, across from the Butlery door. A large map of the Fastness of Alban acts as a tablecloth. Alongside is a covered butler-trolley.

"Good. Right on time." Briged says. "We can eat and at the same time I can show you what I propose we do, if you agree."

Getting up she grasps Ardel's proffered hand, gaining his attention by taking his other elbow.

"You'll hear of things that almost certainly will make you angry. With good reason, given how your entrance into this Fastness was manipulated. It was one of the bitterest disagreements I have ever had with Faerachar, once I found out about it. Ardel, I know I have expressed my regret that you were dealt with as you were, but perhaps you feel my apology was not as it might have been. Understand, please. I have nothing to apologise for. It was not done in my name, and I will never make hollow apologies on behalf of others or communities or this Fastness. Such things are meaningless grandstanding. Apologising means taking actions to redress the situation, not puffing hot air. As we go through this tour, for your sake and mine, please say how you feel; do not let anything linger. Then we may all deal with it, and this Fastness can learn and adjust."

"Thank you, Briged. I accepted the concern you showed me in the best spirit, and with respect for you and your ethics. Faerachar has time and again apologised, and I have accepted those too. What he has not done to my satisfaction yet, is tell me exactly why he did not have me removed from the cistern until a couple of hours after he had returned. That cannot be easily dismissed. I fully accepted the apology given me by the Castellan, which I deemed to be heartfelt and honest. I shall take your advice and raise my concerns as we travel. We are both looking forward to this tour of Alban very much. Let us four set off in harmony."

"Thank you, Ardel, for such a wish. I have one more thing to do before we eat." She opens a bag hanging from her chair and withdraws three slim books from it.

"These are titled *How Alban Works*[3]. I present one of these to each of you. They are given to all students when they leave secondary education and go from young adulthood, through Civic Service and into the next phase of their lives. Into the world of adults and the education that comes from living in a society where everyone counts for something.

"How everyone, either through labour of learning, to give to society later on, or through pure labour, works together. All with the aim of maintaining an equitable society. This book explains the democratic rights and obligations of the citizens. The need to participate. The importance of taking part in the votings. It explains the democratic principles underpinning the society we have. It is in plain language. There are clear diagrams. It does not patronise.

"It sets out the strengths and weaknesses of all democracies, including how it is here. There is an explanation of how power sits with the people in these joined Fastnesses. It includes the Ethical Code. I could go on, but won't. The point is you can refer to this book to understand how we work with one another here. It is easy to digest for most people. It points to more wordy documents for those who wish to see a dot above every *i* and the crossbar on every *t*."

She hands the books across.

"Now, let us fill our plates, and. I'll serve a good wine and a shot or two of akvavit from Skane. And as we feed we can talk."

She opens the trolley revealing a chilled Smörgasbord. She serves the iced akvavit in frost-covered shot glasses.

"Help yourselves. This section on the left is for those who like piscatorial foods." Picking up a plate she gestures along the trolley, and reaches for an oyster.

3 *How Alban Works – extracts from a lecture – page 472*

"The purpose of this trip is to allow you to observe life in this Fastness at first hand. It is my hope it will allow us as a people to move forward from where we have stuttered these last few years."

She places her plate on the table, and stands waiting for the others to be seated.

"A good appetite, with new friends." She raises her akvavit and downs it in one. "You don't need to follow my lead."

Then she picks up a pointer and traces a line across the map, it illuminates in red.

"Ardel, this is the route you were taken on to get here from Newark. We'll come back to it at some point on the tour. And you shall have this faxplex map as a keepsake of our journey."

She tells them the border between Mercia and Alban came into being during the Upheavals in response to an idea — that everyone should count for something.

"But you do not need a history lesson at this moment. What I say is a simple view of the governance here. The rest is in that book."

The meal passes with Briged giving them an overview of how Alban functions, broken into manageable chunks by trips to the trolley. After an hour she calls for a break and a proper stretch of their legs. Ardel and Grandy walk further along the terrace, talking quietly. Dahqin opens the book he has. It is inscribed by a strong hand in flowing script.

Dahqin, Enjoy the adventure of discovery in Alban. You will always be welcome here. You will succeed with your Bagad. My blessings. Briged.

Before he can close the book, she is pouring wine into his glass.

"You are the linchpin, Dahqin," she says, smiling down at him.

"You have good emotional wisdom. The six believe in what you say and who you are. You have risen to this only lately. How close you came to stumbling here, for there is a personal cost to your desires. But it is a small price paid now, that will bring you all you desire in the future."

She turns to look at the other two, then back to him.

"I hope you realise I was joking earlier about your presence here being a maelstrom. Ardel needs you with him."

"I realised as you said it, Briged. I like that type of humour. Ardel is okay for now, and I will see him through whatever else comes at him. Duncn and I spoke of such things only this morning. So I hope I do achieve for us all what I want to be. Love and friendships are tough bedfellows. Literally."

"That's true. Kaet said you worked with him all afternoon in the stables. Just know — you six shall become seven. He thinks he will be alone here because of complications he does not control. He will not. He is not — the time is coming."

"You are very perceptive, as is Kaet."

"Though she and I are sighted, it is no easier for us. Now, on a more practical note. In your washroom are some laundry bags. Put your clothes from the work today in one, and leave it on the terrace outside the doors. I'll make sure Regin takes it for cleaning."

As she heads to Grandy and Ardel to top-up their glasses he opens Ardel's copy. *This is a start on your quest to know more about the Fastnesses, Ardel. I hope it is a good start, for you will always be part of our family. Much love and blessings, Briged.*

Dahqin is deep in thought when Ardel puts a hand on his shoulder.

"Are you worrying about something?"

"No. Thinking through what we've been doing here, those of us who have no specific purpose. I've been enjoying my time. I'm glad you are taking a break."

"Not sure about that. That's what we've been discussing. I've got a project to outline before I get home. This will be a working trip most days. It'll interest me."

"Then I'm going to request my own itinerary."

"Well, fellow travellers, it is my intention to let you decide what your priorities of this tour should be. I have put forward those things that I believe will best explain this Fastness to you, but you must dig into that which interests you most. You must meet ordinary people. We have

closeted you for long enough here in Wark-in-Alban. So, here's my list."
She hands across a sheet of paper to each of them.

"Tomorrow is fixed, I'm afraid – but I can arrange things at quite short notice for the other days.

"I'll be cheeky. Briged. Can I have some introductions to people who are involved in the arts, theatre, education of the arts, in film. Anything which enhances the essence of enjoyment of life, outside the necessary structure of being able to live. I don't mean to sound or be dismissive, for the underlying stuff is your bread and butter. So I want to leave the discussions of that to you three – while I enjoy myself."

He bows to her.

"Of course, Dahqin. It shall be as you wish."

"Thank you. Where do we go to first?"

"We start in the north-west, on the main island of Na h-Eileannan Siar where a form of Gaelic is spoken. Then on to Orkney. Both of these have a small population, but are distinct each in its own history. There are lots of ancient stone sites and the views of some are humbling – but only if the weather is with us. From there we come ever southward. A couple of days in Edinburgh before heading back into Engeland."

"How long will it take us to travel so far north?"

"We shall fly from here, so just over two hours, Dahqin. It is about five hundred kimetres."

"Fly? And at speed. Is it those powered gliders we've seen based north of here? That's going to be amazing."

"You guess right."

She folds up the empty bag. "If there is no dissent, we shall have an early breakfast and leave immediately after. We should meet here at seven o'clock, ready to travel soon after we are fed. I bid you three a good night's rest."

As the Butlery door closes, Ardel and Dahqin sit back down.

"The idea of flying has flummoxed you, hasn't it?"

"Yes. I mean, you know I sometimes daydream of learning to fly gliders. But it's both an exciting idea and too frightening, so I'll never pursue it.

Now, we are going to be flying at the same speed as the tgvs, but high up. I am so excited."

Regin appears, asking if they are finished. Grandy says they have, and thanks him.

"I am away to my bed. Good night to you all. Be here at seven sharp, the pair of you."

She strides off along the terrace, calling back to them.

"No loitering in the morning over that one hair, which just won't go exactly as you wish it. You'll both look fine."

Regin laughs. "I like her sense of humour."

"She knows us too well."

"Come on, Dahqin, best drink up. Packing for six days to be done. Thanks, Regin. The food was gorgeous, as ever. You really judge the flavours so carefully."

"I've only just come on duty, Ardel. One of the day chefs prepared this for you. Briged has told me you are all off on a tour tomorrow. You'll be able to see whether the people who gave you information at your formal dinner knew what they were talking about." He swings round checking the area.

"I'll be serving breakfast here, at seven, as Briged ordered. Right! That's me done out here. I've picked up your horsey clothes, Dahqin."

"Thanks, Regin. I appreciate that very much."

"It's nice to be appreciated, gents. Nice to know everyone counts for something, including me."

Book Seven — Part 2

The Tour of Alban
Without you we are merely ordinary

July, 7th — Derwent to Aberdeen via the islands

The first day goes by so fast; the route is a zigzag spectacular. The country below them seen as a slapdash throw of greens and yellows in the cultivated lands, huge dark forests, with purples, pinks, greens and browns on the higher lands, interspersed with spangled bodies of estuaries and enclosed waters. River valleys with birch woods and beaver ponds dot the remoter parts. The colours of the seas and beaches in Na h-Eileannan Siar and around the inner islands dazzle.

Dahqin sends Alun a series of short bursts of their flight, suggesting they explore the area on the Blondyn, while he and Ardel are away. He gets the reply that they are preparing to do just that, Duncn in tow. Alun also sends a photo of Inez's note, adding she is back in Fal and had been met by Charlie. When they land at Stornaway he shows this to Ardel.

"I'll talk to Grandy. What do you think about it?"

"Me? I'm not sure I should get involved, Ardel."

"But I want to know what you think. You are a good observer of people, Dahqin. Better than me, I think."

"Thank you ... Okay. When I mentioned Yves and Charlie at that breakfast, Faerachar physically pushed his chair away from the table. Like he was distancing himself. His smile was fixed and he over-relaxed. And in the faxplex I was able to see, Charlie's phone number is in a lot of places. One day you said as an aside to Grandy, the amount of detailed stuff coming in suggested a leak in the conspiracy. I know a little about him from Peran and Inez. While he might sail a fine line where making money is concerned he doesn't come over as a sociop. He sounds too haphazard. Maybe he's the leaker and Faerachar is trying to protect him."

He met Inez on arrival. I bet that locker on the HiTail–it only has charts in it now."

Dahqin is about to mention what he overheard at Kaet's. After all, Faerachar had said he'd stumbled badly on his path, and it wasn't a physical act he had described. To Dahqin, it ties in with him not being available, but it might not be any business of the League. He decides to say no more.

"And? ... You were about to go on, weren't you?"

"Yes, but it's my suppositions – not based on facts; so it's not appropriate for me to say. Briged must know more about Faerachar's links than we can guess. Come on, she's calling us over to our reception committee."

In both islands they are introduced to small groups of locals who have been chosen by lot from volunteers. It gives them a good look at how the smaller communities are free to make their own decisions. The Stone Age remains in both are spectacular in their settings, but more sparse than those at Karnak. The discovery of a cache of ancient earth mothers at one site in Orkney had occurred not long before the start of the Upheavals.

"Your earth mothers are so much prettier, Briged."

"They are made by women, Dahqin."

From Orkney they follow the coast to Aberdeen, the major urb and port in the far north of Scotia. It spreads westwards along a high ridge sticking out into the sea to the north of a large harbour. There are suburbs on the higher lands to the south side of the estuary. As they spiral over the city before landing, Briged explains that as the inundations of the lower lands proceeded the buildings had been demolished and the dressed stone re-used. New breakwaters and quays were built on the site of the old harbour, giving very deep water. The harbour is much larger than Haven; the ships too. Trade is mostly with Skane and Europa.

Next day Grandy and Ardel will meet with business people from the region. Before the Upheavals the main industries here had been focused on the extraction of hydrocarbons from undersea reserves. As the climate changed quite rapidly, brought on in part by the role methane and carbon dioxide played in heating the planet, that industry had withered and all but died. But the skills learned and innovations made had been redirected into finding solutions so humans could live with the changes while mitigating the past mistakes.

As they sit for dinner, Dahqin turns to Briged "The people I met in both places were so enthusiastic about the arts as a channel for social cohesion and interactions between the generations. It was exactly what I hoped for. Thank you so much."

"I'm glad, Dahqin. About tomorrow — I have seen a clip of you on stage, and so I have taken the liberty of arranging for you to take part in an impromptu workshop with a group of final year students from Dramusica, an entertainment industry school. Ardel tells me you are quick on your feet with improvisation. In my imagination you will think of something from your experiences that will quickly help them get to grips with improvements to their techniques. You blush. Is this too much to put on you?"

"Er ... Blushing, yes." He looks under knitted brows at Ardel.

"If I knew what you saw, I would know better if such a blush was needed. Ardel keeps part of a very early performance to hand. But of course I will do whatever helps with the promotion of the arts across the Confederation. Especially if it could lead to me getting bookings this far north."

"It was your signature song, Dahqin. Three shows back. Though I was tempted — for Briged has a broad sense of humour. And you are not noticeably the shrinking violet."

"Aah. The blush is worthy then. I have taken another liberty, Dahqin. I have invited the choreographer, Magda NcFarlan, to join us for this meal. She lives nearby. You two may then have a discussion about what to do tomorrow at Dramusica. We meanwhile shall discuss our bread and butter."

July, 8th — Aberdeen

It is nearing noon when the final run through of what Dahqin has improvised is put to the test. He had arrived early to meet the chosen students, and they have been quick on the uptake. The finished routine, using the music from one of his songs, is energising. An audience from within the school fills the seats, joining in a rousing applause.

Magda thanks him for his efforts, and calls on the students in the cast to do likewise. They drag him on stage from the wings — begging to let them do it again, with him singing the common language version. He says he is unsure if there is time, but Magda knows there is. She says they are recording the workshop as future teaching material; surely it is a fitting end to the experience to have a performance with him in it as a spur. He will have the rights to it, she says. He counters that his time in this is given freely, and for his own enjoyment. That some feeling for music and acting is as innate to all humans as breathing. As drama students they should know the need for endless improvement.

He is in his element, and it shows. He has been impressed by the students, and wants to add to their confidence, something he knows is vital for them. The ovation at the finish means more to him than many had. He takes two bows with the rest of the cast, then Magda comes on stage to wrap things up.

"There is little I can say to adequately thank Dahqin for his input today. But I can praise you all in the cast for the efforts you have put in. You have shown me and everyone watching, that you have gained from the time you've spent this morning. It has added a polish to your performance by working alongside him." She smiles at him as he laughs.

"To bring this surprise workshop to a close, I would like to ask someone who has been an encouragement to decades of students here at Dramusica to say a few words. You all know who she is, so please show your appreciation for her."

As the clapping starts Briged walks out of the shadows at the back of the auditorium, down the central aisle, and onto the stage. Dahqin's surprise at her presence is clear. Magda's voice soars above the clapping.

"Briged Jardine."

"Dahqin, you are an amazement to behold. You have engaged with these youngsters showing an enthusiasm that is affirmation of the life we try to promote. I am told by those here who can judge you professionally that you have achieved so much in one morning. You were right — this is sweetness on our bread and butter."

"Briged, this has been so exhilarating for me." And because it feels natural, he hugs her.

"After I have said my piece, I think you should say something to consolidate what these young people have seen and heard today."

She turns to face the audience.

"You have all seen me before. Some are aware of what role I play in this society. But I am not important here. You are. You are part of the future of this Fastness of Alban Scotia. For what you shall do will strengthen our society. It will ensure our saying, *Everyone counts for something* is a reality for everyone. Not a collection of words strung together to make the one saying them sound good. You will help embed this into the next generations. They have been in his company for four hours, and you just a few minutes — but I assume you all know his name." She cups her right ear and turns her head slightly.

"Dahqin!"

"Well, I am merely a tour guide. Dahqin said to me at the beginning of this journey he wanted to meet with people involved in the arts, in drama, in singing. Anything, he said, that enhances the essence of enjoyment of life. Outside what he called the bread and butter — the necessary structure of being able to live. Entertainment is so important for it makes us more humane. I am glad I was able to witness what you have achieved between you. Bravo."

She turns towards the cast with a sweep of her arms and begins to clap. The response from the audience is immediate. She turns back to the audience and after a suitable pause signals for silence.

"Dahqin ... your turn."

"Two things. One for the audience first. Always remember we perform for an audience. Today you out there are that audience. Always bear in mind — without you we are merely ordinary. Today it was you, as an audience, that fed us the buzz. What a buzz of sparks you have engendered. Someday it will be you up here. Feed your audiences. Send out those sparks. Get back the buzz. It has been a privilege to have performed in your company today.

"To my fellow cast members — what can I add? You are amazing. You have picked up and gone with this routine to a high standard. You made it your own. It helped a bit that by some fluke this song is known by some of the cast. It has been humbling and gratifying for me to work alongside you. Briged is right. We who work in the artistic world — whatever role we take — have a vital job to do."

There's a pause as he swings round, his arms out, smiling broadly.

"Enhancing the essence of enjoyment of life. That is our goal. It takes a lot of work. Make sure your mind is in the right frame and you will succeed. Life is drama, and the world can be a stage. Make use of it. But remember too ... I said to Briged, what we do is outside the necessary structure of being able to live. Well. The important word is necessary. Because." He drops his arms.

"Without that necessary structure there is little to enhance."

He brings his hands together and bows.

"Thanks for the time we've had. Success to you all." He starts clapping the cast and audience, setting off another round of applause.

Briged hugs him and kisses his cheeks, then she motions for silence. She signals that the cameras stop recording and only resumes once she knows they are off.

"I said I am a tour guide, and so I am at the moment. You are taught about the Ambassadors' League, and will know something of its role in our part of this world. Well, there were two more guests hiding in the audience than Dahqin knew of. I would like to introduce to you two League Ambassadors. The first ever to visit Alban. I am showing them the necessary structures that allow us to live decently. Without them being here we would not have met Dahqin. Please join us Grandy, Ardel."

They emerge onto the stage from the wings. Dahqin takes Ardel's hand, drawing him into a hug.

"He is worth that praise, Ardel, wouldn't you say?"

"Indeed Briged. I am a bit intimidated finding myself in the lights next to Dahqin. This is a first for me, and not my natural habitat. But I have worked out the audience is friendly."

"Ardel has never been on a stage with me before. He usually stays in the shadows until I'm ready to leave the venue."

"Grandy, you have a few words to say to our young people."

"Thank you Briged. To the cast I want to add Ardel's and my appreciation to that already expressed. It has been a joy to watch the enthusiasm you all put into that fantastic performance. To you in the cast, and those in the audience who still have more to do in your studies, your skills are an important asset to the society in which you live. I have travelled in parts of this small planet where such skills are not appreciated, sometimes not allowed, and their lack makes the human condition drab. You live in a society different from most I have visited. A major part of the difference is the practice that makes everyone count for something. We are heading south now, to Edinburgh, then into Engeland. But this moment in time will stay with me. I have known Dahqin's repertoire over a few years now. Yet I believe I have never seen him so carried by the enthusiasm of his collaborators. Success indeed."

"Thank you Grandy. As I said earlier you are all important to the future of this Fastness. We have enjoyed watching both of your performances today. I'm not sure how much praise to give Dahqin. Though as every one of you counted in those performances you can all afford to swagger for a while. Our time here on stage is at an end.

"We have a train to catch in ninety minutes. But in the canteen there is a buffet to which you are all invited. Make the most of this event to reach out to our visitors — all three of them — not just the star of the moment. I know you will share with them the best of what this establishment produces. So rise and go to the canteen. Eat. Talk."

They leave Dramusica, Magda leading them through an excited, clapping throng of young people.

"That will have them chattering for the rest of the week, perhaps the next period, Dahqin. I am so glad to have met you."

"And I you, Magda. I'll be in touch."

"I shall be back in two periods, as usual," Briged tells her, and gets into the cab.

"Briged, I cannot express enough how enlivening this morning has been. I thought the flights yesterday were exciting, but the mechanical marvel can never top the human spirit lifted high. I'm so buzzy."

Ardel squeezes Dahqin's hand, which he has held since they left the canteen.

"I love seeing you so happy, Dahqin. It is your vitality that grabs me. I can say in front of these two witnesses you make my soul sublimely happy."

July, 8th — Edinburgh

The route down the coast from Aberdeen takes them through small ports, places with views out between cliffs to the sea, then the city of Dundee. It is late afternoon when they arrive in Edinburgh.

Briged has arranged for Dahqin a tour of Edinburgh on arrival, in the company of a professional City Guide. With Grandy and Ardel she takes them to a meeting with her colleagues from the Courts.

"We still say City as a title for these large urbs. Hence — the City of

Edinburgh. It came through the Upheavals with hardly an injury. Kaet has told me it compares favourably to the older urbs in the Cantons. Does it?"

"Aside from the paucity of busbars and sidelinks, it is remarkably similar in its feel to me," Ardel says. "Cobbled streets are all the same, in essence. My perception of the Fastness will have to change. Briged, are there more of these urbs of similar size in Engeland?"

"At least six as large and a couple larger."

"Which implies there are trains or other transport links between them. I could have been in The Keep within the day, having travelled comfortably, very quickly."

"Yes, Ardel. Tomorrow Dahqin will be travelling by train between the various venues on his tour. There are frequent train services across this central belt. Do you wish to discuss your journey to The Keep?"

Ardel shakes his head. "Time for dinner. Did you say it is a short but steep walk?"

"Yes. Across the gardens and up the stairways. Let us go."

On their return to the hotel they settle into a pair of settees farthest from the bar, with a view of the floodlit Castle across the gardens.

"One of the Counsels said the role of the Boundary Patrol is being discussed – a proposal to change its purpose." Ardel says. "Can you tell us a bit about what its current purpose is, and how it might change?"

"I am aware of the discussions, but not involved. The Governing Council in Leeds and the Scotian Parlement have been discussing this matter since the turn of the year. I told you the other day the southern boundary was an ideological divide. It is time for a short history lesson. In the preceding political entity governing these islands as an unequal union, the population's multifaceted social beliefs were not fully represented in the parliament of the day. The population in what was then England was so large compared to the other two nations of Scotland and Cymru. True there were devolved governments, but the state was run with a highly centralised administration, which increasingly ignored and overrode the local power.[4]

"There was a moment where a particular government tried to foist huge ideological changes on an unwilling populace and used lies to push their ideas. There was unrest; it was dealt with badly. For Scotia this led rapidly to an independent political entity. In Cymru it took longer to stabilise.

"Anger escalated in the English areas and there was a civil insurrection in the north. The Upheavals as they are known. This happened to coincide with the gradual inundation of the lowest lands, making conditions worse and leaving communities isolated. Local militias sprang into being, some driven by a rabid nationalism, just the same as elsewhere on the mainland of Europa in the past. When men are in charge with their angry entitlement in full flood it always ends thus. Things are worse when women tacitly support them in it. Scratch the skin; the Beast is out."

She stops talking, the emotion evident in her voice.

"I am glad I was not alive in such a turbulent time. Thankfully we are now part of the Confederation and the League is the neutral arbiter when there are differences. As there always seem to be.

"Getting directly back to your question Ardel. The Boundary Patrol was a product of joining like-minded militias together. But now we no longer need such a force to protect the boundaries of the two parts of this Fastness. Our neighbours are members of the Confederation, and the interactions are through dialogue. The need for defence is no longer by military means. Now the Boundary Patrol is less important in keeping us safe against the outside than is the Communicator's unit.

"One of the guiding principles in the Ethical Code is everyone counts for something. To that end there is a period of three months immediately before we reach eighteen when we all spend time in Civic Service — seeing the Ethical Code working in society. The Boundary Patrol has always got involved to help society in times of natural disasters or other emergencies.

4 *The Slide into Chaos — page 471*

One idea is that the troopers will become a unit of the Civic Service with permanent employees. In any case, there is likely to be a rump of a security force of some kind. The various councils will meet to reach a commonality about the change."

"Even so, you are not worried by what comes from this?"

"It is not up to me to influence those decisions, Ardel. My role is within the Court of Counsels, which has to make sure what is decided does not compromise the Ethical Code. I am a sounding board for those making decisions when they need to have a disinterested talk with an expert on the Ethical Code.

"The Boundary Patrol has had a particular influence on the society in this Fastness. It ensured our isolation, allowing changes to our education system and our political practices to become embedded, free from outside interference.

"It is also true during the early days there were fractures in our society about where to head. The important outcome was that the extreme elements were kept in check, allowing a centrist commonality to rise as a philosophy. I know from what was written at the time that luck played a big role; a group of like-minded personalities coincided to drive the changes."

She sits for a few moments, looking serene.

"The education of our youngsters is a never ending task for this society. While a particular generation may come to regard the situation as thoroughly embedded it may not be the same for the next. It is so easy for lessons learned in the aftermath of such an event as the Upheavals to be forgotten by the generations moving away in time. The real lessons must be perpetually taught.

"Above all people must be taught to think for themselves. To accept that the best answer, is not always clear. And the glibness of one — seeming easy — solution can be startlingly destructive to the stability of a society." She frowns, her face hardening.

"In oligarchal and quasi-democratic societies power and control by the apparatus of governance shapes the humanity of that society to serve its own ends. We, the citizens of Alban should be aware of the dangers such systems hold for everyone."

She has a drink of water.

"Of course, we also control, but to maintain an equitable society. In setting up the new structure all those years ago, the source of power was to be turned on its head. Power would come from the population as a whole. But steeped as politics were in various brands calling all the shots something radical had to be done to reawaken critical thinking. The management of the political parties was very corrupting to the workings of democracy. Fear and cronyism are not good bedfellows for democracy.

"With the theory of commonality the governance is different. Some will say there is no sparkle in our politics, but things do get done. Things that command the approval of the greater part of society. Leave the sparkle to the arts and entertainment.

"Of course it does not allow every voice to carry equally into the final result. Almost everyone has to give up something of what they would like on the path leading to whatever seems to be best for an equitable society. We must make sure vacuous slogans or catchphrases are not allowed to drive down the voices of reason or give space to a mob mentality. It is not always a smooth road we take, but we are well down it now to having most of the population accept readily this concept."

Briged leans her head back and closes her eyes.

"My dears, I am tired of my voice. It is time I went to rest, before you are too. It has been a very busy day. At least it started with a good burst of energy. Thanks for that Dahqin. I hope what we three discuss is not too dull."

"No, Briged. Only a few weeks ago I would have been looking around for a distraction, but I realise now my world can only exist and prosper if the society in which it sits is well founded. It looks to me like here in Alban it is almost so. In the Cantons and even in France, it is easy to believe it existing somehow in isolation, but it never is."

"Never. Music, acting, drawing or painting, all are innate human activities, whether fulfilled or not." She stands up.

"Is eight o'clock for breakfast too early? Your escorts for tomorrow will meet you in the foyer one side or other of nine, Dahqin. I chose them for you with care. Luckily for us three there is a slightly later start to our day."

"This is a good time for me to withdraw too," Grandy says, as they all stand. Briged bows her head and leaves.

"Are you enjoying yourself, Dahqin? I mean you aren't just being polite to Briged, are you?"

"Oh, come on, Ardel. You know me better than that. I'm having a fantastic time with these people she has introduced me to. Especially this morning ... No, I'm thoroughly content."

"So what is the niggle? Grandy and I both know you well enough to sense something is being kept back. You've picked up on something. Are you worried about the others?".

"No. It's not them ..." He looks around, they are the only occupants.

"Can we sit down, please. That conversation we had in Stornaway, when you said I was about to say something, I was. And I can't get it out of my head. When I overheard Faerachar and Kaet talking, he said '*I've stumbled badly on my path, sister.*' She told him to go to Alastair — whoever that is — and he, Faerachar, would put right that which he should not have had done.

"Briged is definitely not as bright-eyed as she has been. I think she has an inkling of what it is he's done, and there's a big black cloud hanging around that she wants to deal with. But she's taking us three sightseeing instead. I feel a bit guilty, because I'm having a good time."

"It could be anything Faerachar has done, and not connected to why we are here. But you are right, Briged has concerns other than this tour. She is also tired." Grandy has taken hold of Dahqin's hand.

"We've heard a number of things we need to talk to her about in private, Dahqin. And some are to do with Faerachar. I actually like him, and I think he has been an able administrator, but he has been a bit flaky about a number of things on which I've worked with David."

She lets go his hand.

"That way of his of deflecting from giving an answer is defensive, though he passes it off as jokey. Something is brittle within him. I suspect he's doing what Kaet advised. Alastair is his father, by the way."

"It is possible she has taken us three on this tour to distract her at a time when she cannot help him. I mean so as not to allow her position to be compromised," Ardel says.

"Possibly true. Listen, Dahqin, Briged is too formidable an operator to be acting with politesse. She genuinely wants us to be here. If Faerachar is wobbly: as his mother she is affected, but maybe not in her position as the Good Sounding Counsel. It is not something we three can get involved in. Ardel and I must be disinterested at all times. You can feel empathy, or sympathy, or both, but do not offer your help. And make sure the empathy or sympathy you feel is not about things in you. As an actor of some ability you should know that."

"Yeah. Thanks for the words of wisdom, Grandy."

"We'll make the most of the next few days. When we get back to The Keep we have only a few more left in Alban. By the way, we shall be departing by League airship from the glider station near The Keep. Margot has already arranged it. Never been done before. Let's go on in a hopeful manner. Briged will deal with her own woes, Dahqin. I really must get to bed."

July, 9th — The Tour — Edinburgh

Briged takes the Ambassadors to Holyrood Palace where they spend the morning with members of the Scotian Parlement, including the Speaker and Cabinet, who are elected by a vote of all members.

In the afternoon she takes them to a community discussion club in an outer western suburb, where people from the locality can meet up to thrash out any differences on budding issues. She warns them meetings can get noisy, though always in a structured way; attempting to forestall the difficulties that always arise when dialogues do not reach consensus and neighbours become estranged.

July, 9th — The Tour — The Historian, The Actor, The Educator

For Dahqin this morning is a whirl through places and people. Falkirk, Stirling, Cumbernauld and Paisley. The focus is on how the arts help enhance life for people of all ages. Briged has chosen well, and they gel comfortably with Dahqin. The Actor and Educator take him to places they visit regularly, introducing him to people who matter — their audiences; at schools and care homes, in discussion clubs and theatres. While they rove from one venue to the next the Historian takes them to historic sites — palaces, castles and odd corners of towns — where he weaves stories of the part played by each, in shaping society over the centuries.

By late afternoon they are at Dumbarton Castle, against which the high tide slaps, on a viewing platform atop the highest of the two hills. There are a few clouds casting shadows on the water. The Historian is pointing out landmarks and explaining their historical importance. As they turn to face the far western coast of the Firth, Dahqin interrupts his flow, pointing down to the estuary.

"I know that boat." Sailing towards the castle, unmissable amongst the shadows is the Blondyn — sun gleaming off its glossy black sails.

"Sorry, but this is so weird. Four of my friends are on that boat. I hope it's not rude to call them?"

"Not at all, maybe they'll want to join you for the rest of this tour," the Historian says.

"Get them to land on the jetty here," the Actor says.

"They can come to the clubs in Glasgow with us," the Educator says. "They can take us to where we get the train."

Dahqin calls, and to the jetty they come.

Dahqin and his escorts get a late train back into Edinburgh, and he arrives at the hotel just before midnight. Ardel is sitting watching the multi-viewer. He switches it off.

"I can tell from that smile you've had a very good day, Dahqin."

"Yes, Ardel, the funniest yet. How was yours?"

"Technical. Interesting, but sometimes overly serious. You were right on the button last night. Briged is an amazing woman so strong in her certainty; though appearing sometimes vulnerable, I have a feeling she isn't. So, give me a kiss, then lighten my mood and tell me of your day."

"Kiss, hug and I'll shower. I'll tell you in bed."

"Briged did choose my escorts carefully. They are good friends who spark off one another. Easy guys to be comfortable with. During the day it was all as I expected until we got to this place called Dumbarton. It's the site of an old Celtic stronghold, now an islet off the north shore of the river. We were on a viewing platform, and I saw Blondyn in the river. So, like in a corny joke, I told the Historian, the Educator and the Actor of my like-minded friends on board. They jumped at the chance of fresh faces." He giggles.

"Our night in Glasgow was a riot. We went to three bars and two clubs — all heaving with exuberance. They rival the places at home. These guys know how to let their hair down. Duncn was recognised in one bar. Peran is a really good mimic and caused confusion by introducing himself as me — and the twins as his minders. We three Bretons with our accents and him with his burr were treated royally. Such fun. It's a pity you couldn't have been with us. But I'll stay in touch with those three, so next time."

July, 10th — The Tour — Into Engeland — Leeds

They fly from Edinburgh along the coast as far as the River Tyne. Turning inland they follow the river, crossing the Tyne conurbation; flying low over the bridges before continuing upstream until they approach a small town with a large church still dominating its centre.

"This is Hexham. We turn south here." Briged says above the propeller and wind noise. Fifteen minutes later she points out Ripon.

"That's where I started across the fells, Dahqin. Over that way."

He leans across Dahqin, hoping for clues, but it all looks the same.

The glider banks out to the south-east. Flying over Lincoln on its island. Briged remarks on the cathedral, as they turn westwards, landing soon after at Leeds.

Leeds is Engeland's equivalent of Edinburgh. Here the Governing Council and Court of Counsels meet and the Council of Laws Peculiar sits. Briged takes Grandy and Ardel on another round of the bodies of governance. She also takes them to the local barracks of the Boundary Patrol, encouraging them in an informal meeting to seek answers to how both the longer-serving members and the younger recruits view the likely changes of purpose of the service.

"They are certainly forthright in their views," Ardel tells Briged, after they leave.

"Most of them think there won't be much change in the service they give to the community at large. A lot of them say they'll be happy to leave the weapons in the armouries. Some of them think they'll be combined with the police force in some way."

"That may well end up being the case. As I said the other night, I do not know how the members of each governing body will pitch it."

"From the book of *How Alban Works* — in the section on the Ethical Code, for every right a citizen has there are balancing obligations that attach to it. Then there is the section on what sort of acts by an individual will limit their rights. It's not like that in most of Europa."

"That is true, Grandy. The principle is this, individuals who commit a minor infraction sometimes do not set out with that intent. They deserve a chance to be given help to overcome their weakness or other cause for their action. But there is also the Law of Accumulation. Individuals who think they can repeatedly commit a minor infraction find themselves in a different regime, because of the accumulated bad behaviour.

"The serious or major offences listed in the criminal codes, mostly these are premeditated by nature, it means redemption is a difficult thing to contemplate. For example, violent physical acts against the body of another, or emotive coercion of another, carry the most weighty sentences. Whilst everyone is treated equally in justice, those guilty of such crimes must work harder to be considered responsible citizens in the future. But there are circumstances where the whole picture of a crime against another switches the perpetrator into the victim. Justice is sometimes found to be contrary by those who do not think clearly about the facts. Procufisks must have a strong moral ethos. I was once one for a few years in my early thirties."

For his entertainment Dahqin has been introduced to a team of six young adults who have completed their twelve weeks in the Civic Service and are now attending the School of Art in Bradford. They are assigned a suitably large cab, accompanied by one of their tutors. Their task is to take him to six pieces of art in cultural sites in the vicinity. Each has chosen one piece. They have ten minutes allowed to describe the meaning of the piece and why they have chosen it, and twenty minutes allowed for a discussion to develop within the group. He too has chosen three pieces he wants to see, and would have to do the same. The tutor was the judge of how well they had fulfilled their task. It was a challenge from which he emerged having learned a lot more than he passed on. All in all, he had a thoroughly enjoyable day.

July, 11th — The Tour — Nottingham

The crunch point for Ardel comes in Nottingham.

They travel down from Leeds by train, a quick journey. They are having a rest day; tourists with Briged as their guide. After lunch taken as a graze at stalls in the food hall of the covered market, they walk through the centre of the shopping district, and follow the switchback lanes up to the castle. In the city it is not obvious the river is close by. Only when they stand on the esplanade in front of the part-ruined castle, can they look down on the river and across the broad valley to the south, into Mercia a few miles away. The lines of wind generators on each bank are turning slowly in the early afternoon breeze. The river is already curving in its course to flow in a more north-easterly direction towards Newark.

"Briged, how many hours is it from here to The Keep by train?"

"About four hours. Whichever way you go there are two changes."

"More than one route, then?"

"Yes."

He walks away from them, facing eastwards over the valley. His shoulders rise up as he breathes in deeply. Noisily exhaling, he drops them. Then he sits on the nearest bench, his jaw clenching and releasing. Dahqin wanders across and sits on the bench with him, head turned to face Ardel, who half-turns his head in response.

"Fucking Faerachar." He says it quite softly. Dahqin reaches over and massages the far side of his neck.

"I hate him at this moment. I know it'll pass. Why did he think that game was needed?" He puts his hand up to grasp Dahqin's.

"T–ch–ooh! There's a bit of me thinks *How dare you* and another part says *I'm actually glad you did*. You would not be sitting here with me else. I'd not have met Duncn. I would never have told myself how I feel about you — let alone told you — if I hadn't been so unsettled."

He lets go of Dahqin's hand.

"I have to stop being angry. It's not good for me." He stands up, pulls Dahqin up, and they return to the women.

"I apologise for my moment of anger, Briged. It was aimed at Faerachar, but it is also nuanced. There are positive things for me and Dahqin that have come out of what happened through his actions."

"There is no need to apologise, Ardel. Anger must be let go at the right time, or it builds up too strongly. Do you wish to continue with this tour? We can go back to The Keep early. It is no disaster if we do."

"We continue, Briged. You have gone to such efforts to arrange it, particularly with Faerachar's absence on your mind. If I am to succeed in this role I have chosen, I must master my ability to exude equanimity in the face of all adversity. I must drop all sense of entitlement to deference in my role as Ambassador. And I'm beginning to realise, from just being male and born into privilege. The Protocols do not award such deference to me — ultimately they are to protect me against its adverse influences. If I do not learn this fully it will block me from acting disinterestedly."

"On my mind, he is, Ardel, but not impeding my thoughts about what I want to achieve — as the Sounding Counsel — with you and Grandy. Nor as friends on a journey. As to Faerachar, he is of my loins, and, exceptions aside, a birth mother cannot easily expunge the inner love for the child she has carried and borne. He must answer to others for any action he is responsible for, and be judged accordingly. But I will remain his mother, and love him in some fashion. However angry, or maybe even devastated, I might get in the moment I find out what actions of his have driven him to go to Alastair."

She turns her focus to Dahqin. "I am glad you are here to distract us from these dry crusts we have been nibbling. Come, let us move from this lofty viewpoint."

"What is next on our list, Briged?"

"Your discipline, Dahqin. We are headed to a very successful cinema complex, exhibition space and film school, Broadviews. It has run almost uninterrupted since before the Upheavals, even though this city was on the frontline. It's back across the centre, beyond the market. Twenty minutes stroll at most."

There is a big surprise for Dahqin, for when they enter the foyer a teaser of him performing at Dramusica is running on the screen.

"Most of the teaching establishments in Alban involved in the arts are in contact with one another, collaborating on teaching methods. And due to your efforts in Aberdeen, you are now part of the teaching material. The filming up there was done by students enrolled in Aberdeen, but actually doing a course in film and media run from here," Briged says.

"Magda has been in discussions about this with people here. You mustn't waive your rights as you seemed to."

"I will get in touch with my agent and Magda to arrange something, Briged. I'm more than happy to allow the use of my image to any of these teaching establishments. This is good publicity material for me. I'm thinking to a future where I am not on stage so often. As to that future, I've not discussed this with this man holding my hand, but I know we will be back here as visitors, maybe also for my work. There are a lot of exciting things happening here in this Fastness. The scope for me is huge."

·"You make whatever arrangements you like, Dahqin. I'll come back here with you whenever I am able to fit it in. You know that. So long as we travel in comfort."

Two women standing near the reception desk are watching them, and wave to Briged. After a few minutes conversation she returns.

"Well, Dahqin. My motive for taking you on this tour was simply as Ardel's consort. I was focussed on using the opportunity of these two Ambassadors being here to liven up the political discussions in the various Councils."

She smiles at him.

"But the little speech you gave to the students at Dramusica was uplifting to hear and so pertinent to the ethics of our society. And you opened my eyes to a strong link that will help make a big difference out in our society at large. Tomorrow we are in Manchester, the city in Engeland where the main broadcasting organisations are based. Are you willing to give a live interview during the evening topical programme broadcast tomorrow night? The slot is just over fifteen minutes. You'll know how the lead up and leaving add to that time. If you choose to do this, the theme is on the importance of the creative arts in helping a society become more humane. I shall not put words into your mouth — what you choose to say must be authentically yours to own. Think on this proposal, please."

He nods, looking to Ardel.

"You know the protocol you have signed up to as my consort, Dahqin. You have done such interviews at home. You know we cannot be mentioned. Go ahead. It's an opportunity for you and a help to Briged. Do it on two counts. First, to bolster what you said and did in Aberdeen, and second a promotion of your craft here in Alban."

375

"I'm happy to do it, so long as you are holding my hand, Briged."

"That's a given, Dahqin, they want me on the programme too. Look boldly at the women I was talking with, Dahqin. They know me well, but I did not know they would be here. One is the producer of the program in question. This film of your performance with the kids in Aberdeen drew their attention — your face is shown a lot. And then you appear right in front of them. There is one more thing — as Ardel and Grandy cannot be part of your story; what has brought you here? I mean the reason you are here in Alban."

"But they were on stage at Dramusica." He looks at Ardel.

"The cameras had been switched off before we went on stage, Dahqin. Say you came with friends from Brittany on a sailing holiday. That is a good facet of the truth. Could the link to you, Briged, be through Duncn?"

Agreement reached, he turns to Grandy, a broad grin on his face.

"Shall we get a coffee and explore the venue, while these two stars promote themselves?"

After an hour of discussion, and a confirmation call to his agent, Dahqin has the spot sorted.

Going in search of Grandy and Ardel, they find them viewing a photographic exhibition. They spend the rest of the day at Broadviews; watch some short films on one of the small screens. Get side-tracked into a discussion with students about the Dramusica workshop film and how it can best be edited to send differing positive messages. They wander out into the nightlife around the city centre. Occasionally people speak briefly to Briged as they pass. She says her appearances on television and radio give her a certain public profile, which she likes. For their evening meal she takes them to one of her favourite restaurants, selling Chinese style food. It is busy and noisy — just what they want. Walking through the alleyways towards their hotel Briged tells how she loves this city more than most. She can never forget it was one of the pivotal cities when the Fastness was being formed, and its people are rightly proud it was so.

Together with Manchester, Liverpool and a couple of others, these cities are why the border rests so far south.

July, 12th — The Tour — Manchester

Up early again, they catch a train to Manchester.

Due to the broadcast that evening, they spend the morning in similar fashion to their day in Nottingham, soaking up the atmosphere of the much larger city. They have a light lunch picked from street stalls along the canals.

Briged apologises profusely to Grandy and Ardel for abandoning them to a team of constitutional lawyers for the afternoon when she and Dahqin go off to the Broadcasting Campus. They assure her it will not be a dusty and dry affair, as these are members of the Councils of Laws Peculiar whom they had met already in Leeds and in Edinburgh. On both occasions they had run out of time in their discussions, hence them asking for her to arrange this meeting. It is their intention to tease through the differences in the Laws Peculiar, because mostly it had not been clear to them. And it seems the members are looking forward to the joint meeting.

When the four of them meet up for their late evening meal, it is not immediately clear who has had the most entertaining time. Grandy and Ardel had enjoyed an incredible discussion across the group of lawyers. Dictionaries had been pored over to ensure the words meant exactly what they were meant to mean.

"That is what happens when you put twenty lawyers in a room and ask a simple question, with no clerks present." Grandy laughs. "I don't think I've ever seen a set of people get so passionate and yet still be so humorous throughout a four hour session. It really was funnier than anything I've seen in film or on stage."

"Did they get to a clear explanation of the differences you had found?"

"Yes, Briged," Ardel assures. Then he raises his right hand and chops the air. "And. No."

"What? How can that be?" Dahqin shakes his head, laughing.

"Well. In the end they did agree to accept that in Engeland and Scotia the same word could carry a slight difference of emphasis depending entirely on what words were supporting it. They definitely had fun reaching that conclusion."

"It was a very constructive meeting, Briged," Grandy says. "We did get some clear explanations of how the two differing systems of law have grown up and are applied. They were pleased the Laws have been cut in number, and that clarity is better than it once was. But emphasised it remains an on-going operation."

"How do they ever get new legislation written, Briged, if these arguments go on all the time?"

"I think, Ardel, they were intent on having a good raucous time. It is much calmer than you've described when they are making sure the Law says what it must. The passionate arguments are heard in the Governing Council and Parlement and are about what the Law should cover. These lawyers have to write the words to fulfil those needs. The emotive arguments are over when their work starts."

"And your afternoon, Dahqin? How enjoyable was it?"

"Have you watched it, Ardel? I'm glad you were there, Briged. Those two were really tough on me."

"Of course we did, Dahqin, so don't try to paint a different picture. You had them eating out of your hand. The pair of you were good together. The message was clear and concise, and you both have a nice turn of comedic delivery. There, how's that for a critique?"

"Thanks, Grandy. I've never heard you say anything so praiseworthy about my stage performances."

"We watched it in the hotel bar, Dahqin. Grandy said we should have a cocktail to ease my tension. A waste of money, if not of effect, as you both came across very well. The message is powerful. I mean that with a straight face, even though I can't make mine stop smiling."

"Briged, how do we go tomorrow morning?"

"By train via the western route, Grandy. It is slightly quicker that way. We should be back at The Keep by noon. I have to ask this. Are any things awry about this trip? Things we should speak of now?"

"Not on my to do list, Briged. You accommodated my wishes so well. And how can we beat our last appointment. I'll forever be associated with you in this Fastness. And I'm happy with that." Dahqin claps his hands twice, and points to Ardel.

"Thank you so much for arranging this, Briged. My eyes are opened wide about how different this place is compared to how I thought it was at first view. Other than what you know, I have no complaints."

"Thank you, Ardel."

"Briged, I have thoroughly enjoyed myself. I am amazed at how poorly the League is informed. Ardel has a proposal to make when we get back to Genève about a survey of the various Fastnesses in Europa. I wonder how that will fare with the Confederation."

"I hope it is accepted, Grandy. I have gained so much from this tour. It has been a very pleasant and amusing trip. There have been some difficult moments too, but not enough to spoil the overall effect, I think." She drains her glass.

"Reality will come back to haunt us tomorrow."

Book Eight

Briged Jardine's Story
It's not perfect, but it's better than pretending we live perfectly

July, 13th — The Keep — Dahqin

The return to The Keep puts me in a subdued mood. Briged leaves us on arrival. After having a quick lunch on the terrace, Grandy and Ardel disappear to meet up with David. I call Alun, who says they plan to be back in Haven late afternoon. I'm about to head over to see if Kaet's at home when Regin comes out to clear the table.

"You've made a name for yourself since we last met, Dahqin. I saw you last night. That little chat you and Briged had was entertaining. I didn't realise you're a singer. Love that song."

He apologises for making me uncomfortable when I colour up. I tell him praise right after a performance is easily accepted, but out of the blue, from someone I get on with, it catches me.

"Do you mind if I sit and chat for a bit? After I clean these away."

"No, of course not. I'll help you." We carry the dishes away to the kitchen, and Regin wipes the table.

"Do you fancy a drink?"

"Yes please, Regin. Something long and cool would be nice."

"I'll whisk up a strawberry soda with lots of ice. Back in a few minutes."

I pull my chair further into the shade of the canopy over the table. Regin is so affable and my mood begins to lift.

"Here you go." Regin brings out a jug and two glasses of a bright red fizzy drink garnished with mint leaves, and sits opposite me.

"Cheers!" he says, raising his glass.

"Salut ... Mmmm. This is a good blend. Slightly peppery?" It brings a smile to my lips. "So, Regin, you think I have a fan here?"

"Of course. How could I not be? You actually quoted me from the night before you left. Briged says you all enjoyed yourselves, but she didn't go into details with me. Did you get to see much of Alban? Did Ardel find out if he'd been given the right answers?"

I go through the list. Flying was amazing. I had a fantastic time. I can't say how the others feel, nor if Ardel got any answers at all, that's for them to say. Briged organised such a variety of things for me to see and do, all connected with my business. No politics for me.

"What you said before we left — about how you like it here because everyone counts for something including you. I had to quote you. It's really inclusive, and I like the idea a lot. Has it caused an issue for you? I didn't mean to, but your name popped out before I could stop talking."

"Flying — you lucky bugger. My workmates'll keep calling me *Raygeen* for a while yet, but they can't make it sound as sexy as you do, and they'll soon stop when something else comes along to amuse them. Anyway, I really believe in making happen what those phrases on the public notice boards say."

"What happens, do you know, to those with less natural ability. I met so many talented people, but what happens to the ones I never saw. Those in the shadows?"

"There's an amazing amount of support to make sure people are part of the community, whatever they are capable of. Everybody has a role to play in society, and they shouldn't be treated like a dog's turd that's left on the pavement, because they might not be as bright or quick as someone else, or completely dependent on others. We are expected to play to our strengths and help others along where we can. That's sort of the message from the twelve weeks we spend in the Civic Service when we're teenagers.

"We're given a lot of scope in our working lives to run our own jobs effectively. It's a general principle here in Alban. I mean, as an example, I'm sitting here chatting to you, using up some of my time in the day. But that's fine. As long as I do my job properly — meeting the needs of my employment — the number of hours I actually work for my money is not set in stone. It's up to me to make the day work for both those I serve and me. If it's done in less time and I'm not on a rota, I can go home; if something goes wrong I might have to stay longer. Making time for a chat with someone — that's fine too. If I'm given responsibility for me doing a good job, why would I do down my colleagues. Taking the piss is taking the piss, however we try to hide it. And it can't be tolerated. Usually we can deal with it up front, between ourselves.

"Here's another example — you helped me clean up. I appreciate that simple act and respect you for it. If I can help someone else I will. Even if it's not my job. I've worked in Birmingham, and when serving drinks to people in receptions or whatever, some of them only see what's on the tray. They don't see the person beyond. It isn't like that up here. Usually, there's an acknowledgement of the person doing the task. You certainly do that. Ardel too. Now — it could be because he likes to look at me."

"Ooh. Too much following with the eyes?"

"Hey! I'm not bothered — nice to know I can attract. It's the same with Duncn, even now. I realised at the formal dinner that Duncn fancies Ardel a lot — they were watching each other more than they watched me."

"Yeah, I know how they are. Attraction, it's a funny thing. You would attract Ardel. And then there's Per..."

"Let's get off this subject, Dahqin. Tell me where you enjoyed most. I mean on the tour."

"That is difficult. Each place brought something different. The performance by those kids in Aberdeen you saw a bit of last night; I was so happy working with them. But in Leeds the group I met there taught me things I didn't know and that was enjoyable too. I do like the confidence out there amongst you. I'll go with Glasgow. It was the partiest place, but I was with party people, so I might have misread it."

I describe the night out, including the bars and clubs; the Actor, the Entertainer, the Historian, and Duncn with the twins and Peran.

"Duncn in Glasgow — it's a long time since I went to clubs with him. Well, I have to go. What are you planning on doing now?"

"I think — going by horse to Third House, Regin. To await my friends getting back later this afternoon."

382

"Kaet's like a sister to me. She's a live wire and a good listener. And those lads and you are a good bunch for Duncn to be with. He needed it. One last thing. We try to make sure there aren't too many shadows for people to be lost in. It's not perfect, but it's better than pretending we live perfectly. I'll see you later. Enjoy yourself."

"You too, Regin. Thanks for the conversation." I sit on mulling over our chat; have another glass of the strawberry fizz, take my glass and the jug into the Butlery and head off to the stables.

July, 13th — The Keep

When Grandy and Ardel meet up with David they sense the tension in him. He assures them it is nothing to do with them. What he needs to do is formally hand over all the relevant documentation for the League.

"I'm allowed to say this — Faerachar is back from seeing Alastair, and is taking time out. You will be briefed before you go back to Genève. The day to day stuff you've been used to will continue. Regin will be looking after you just the same. I'll introduce you to Esme, my deputy. She'll give you any assistance you need. Let's go. Esme is in W7 now."

He leads them out to the cannion.

"She's got the completed catalogue to sign over. She's fully aware of what has been arranged."

After the introduction to Esme, David shakes hands with them.

"I'll definitely see you both before you go back to Genève. I still owe you a dinner, Ardel. It'll be over at Kaet's, not here. Bye, Grandy, Ardel." And he is gone.

She is methodical in her handover, leaving them after double-checking everything and promising to send someone to make sure they have all they need for transporting the documentation. They sit in silence for a few minutes.

"No point in speculating, Ardel. We will need to apprise Bartouche of our situation. I'll write a brief text on our findings from the tour, and about this turn of events. Then, I'll help you with checking the catalogue matches the documents. What did Dahqin say he was going to do?"

"Go over to Kaet's to await the sailors home from the sea."

"Let's see how we do. I've only met Kaet in passing, and I wouldn't mind catching up with the twins and Peran. You don't know them that well yet, do you?"

"Not the twins. Only when out sailing on the day Dahqin arrived, then that day at Kaet's. I know Peran better. He's visited briefly a few times to see how I am. I quite like him. He seems a caring soul."

"Those days still too painful?"

"I'm less spiky about them, and realise I deserved far worse from Dahqin."

He starts to go through the catalogue, then looks up.

"What's the latest on the Shadow? I'm worried that Dahqin will be in trouble for taking his ID and Warrant."

"Bartouche has said he'll be fine. She'll send confirmation. If we work quickly we can descend on Kaet. Or is that ascend? For once I'll ride a horse alongside you. These could be our quietest days here. But, we await the facts."

July, 13th — The Keep

After entering her official apartment, Briged goes to the bedroom and picks up her earth mother. For no reason other than it is a dispassionate object and won't throw words at her. After a few minutes she puts it back on top of its box and goes to the phone in the main room.

Standing, she rings Faerachar. There is an advantage in not being able to see one another. She speaks into his silence.

"I know you have been with Alastair and have much to tell me. I have spoken to the other three. Where and when do you wish to meet me, Faerachar?"

"First House, Mum. It can be nowhere else. I have a load that I must lower from my shoulders, to stand aside for a while. And I do not know how to proceed. Briged, I need your sound counsel. Alastair has been invaluable to me. But I need to hear your voice. Though you are my mother, so might need to stand aside."

He sounds teary. She feels the prickle of emotion in her eyes.

"At what time, Faerachar?"

"As soon as you can come. I will stay here now. I have handed out my authority to the other three as required in the Code of Conduct. Margot will act in my stead and her deputy step-up."

"Though I am your mother, you may still sound me out as a starting point. The other three know that. My ethos is strong and my shield. Afterwards, you will go before the Court of Counsels. And I will become a witness. I shall set off within the half-hour."

She pauses to steady her voice.

"Faerachar. Whatever comes out. Whatever the outcome. You will always be my son, and I always your Mother. You will always have my love. You will not lose me."

She puts the phone down. Stiff as a statue she looks with unfocused eyes towards the valley to the south — where nestles First House.

It was the male sanctuary to which Faerachar had always retreated when she and he had argued during his teens. It was where he had imbibed the wisdom of his father's ideals, and where the passion of his mother's beliefs seeped into his mind to mingle with that wisdom. What caused him to stumble, she wonders. Although it is a bright day outside, she sees a gloom in front of her. Sighing, she bestirs herself and goes to her small kitchen to prepare a calming herbal tea. While it steeps, she phones the Castellan, and requests one of the fast boats be readied for her with a boatman.

"I will be at the boathouse in twenty minutes, Jonat. I shall be at The Three Houses for at least the next thirty-six hours. You are the guardian of my communications during this time. Let Margot know, please. I will keep you informed as things change."

She calls Kaet.

"Faerachar is having an emotional breakdown of some kind. I do not know how serious it is. I will keep you informed of what is happening with your brother, in a general sense, not in the politics. And I will speak with Duncn on his return. If you already know from me the manifestations may not come at all, or if they do, not be as weakening to you."

"Do you want me to keep the visitors away? Send them over to The Keep, maybe."

"Goodness, no. First House is his safe place, but we need life to be bright enough in the other houses. No sense in all of us collapsing. Ardel and Grandy know something is going on, but are professionals, and will not ask anything of you. Dahqin and his friends can be with you and Duncn as they have been. I'll talk with you when I'm able."

She calls Siobhagn — learns that Faerachar has spoken with her every day since he went away. She wants to meet once they know what is wrong. It is an encouraging sign, Briged hopes.

July, 13th — First House

Entering First House, Briged calls out, but gets no reply. She goes through the rooms, finding him in the study in the attic space Alastair had always favoured. He is fast asleep on the daybed set on a dais, so the view down the valley can be seen even from the horizontal position.

She makes a pot of lemon and ginger tea, adds some honey and returns to the study with it, a couple of cups and a pot warmer. She sits in one of the reclining chairs, her feet up, sipping the tea, watching him sleep. His face unstressed, but now adorned with a straggly beard, grown while he has been missing. Just so had she watched him when as a child he had gone through a bout of fever.

Fifteen years he has been Reever. Twenty-five years old when he was first elected. She sighs. It was a young age to take on that mantle. And in truth he started working in parallel with Alastair when he was barely twenty. Is this the way it ends for him, as Reever? What is it he must say?

The only aberration she is sure of is his dealing with Ardel in that odd way. He'd thought it a bit of a joke. She'd told him they had been in isolation from the rest of the Confederation and the League too long. That he thought he could do whatever he wanted. Well, she'd said. There are consequences. You know that. And he had pulled up. She had relaxed, thought he'd learned all he needed to. But Margot and Jonat have noticed other things slightly out of kilter. She drifts into a snooze.

The cup slides from her hand and clatters on the floor, waking them both. She picks it up. She fills the cups, holding out one to him. He starts to shake his head, but then sits up, yawns and takes it from her. She sits back in the chair. Silently they drink the tea. He puts his cup aside, and looks at her, his eyes ruddy, lids puffy and tired looking.

"What can I say to you, Briged? I must say everything. I have done a number of foolish things over this last five or six periods. I thought they were all unconnected, but now I am enclosed by them, like a lobster caught in a trap-pot, and I don't see a way out." He pauses, silently crying, looking at her. She silently looks back.

"Ardel admitted being arrogant and foolish." He blows out a sigh. "Well as I always knew I would, I've bettered him, about a hundredfold. In entirely the wrong way. Who is the arrogant fool now?" He sucks in breath, whistling through his teeth. "All is at an end I think."

He rubs his cheeks dry. Slouches, his head down.

"What do you think is your mental state?"

He shrugs his shoulders and looks up.

"When I got to Alastair I thought I was okay, but he told me I was standing on the very lip of a precipice ready to fall. That I should go and seek help. Am I burned out? How am I to know?" He heaves a few sighs. Tears trickle down his cheeks.

"What must I do now?"

"Have you spoken to your doctor?" He shakes his head.

"You must see her for an assessment. Today. Make a call now. You don't sound so broken as you did on the phone. But that might mean nothing. I am going to make more tea. Phone her now."

She returns with two mugs of lavender and rose tea.

"What is her response?" She hands him a mug.

"She will be here in about an hour."

"Then I shall sit with you, unless you want me to withdraw."

"Please, Briged, I want you here."

His face creases into a grimace and he starts a thin keening as he sobs. When the bout passes he says "I ... I shall see her alone."

They drink in silence, and apart from Faerachar going to the toilet, neither leaves the room until the doctor announces her presence. Faerachar goes elsewhere in the house. Briged lies back on the recliner, her feet up, and drops into a deep sleep.

When the doctor has gone he comes back to the room and lies on the daybed, not waking her. It is nearing five o'clock when she wakes with a start, and rouses him.

"What is her assessment? Which must be sent to The Keep to the Directorate of Employment."

He is to remove himself from work and hand over to others.

"So I have achieved my first goal." It is said with a brittle laugh.

"She has gone to work out who it is best for me to speak with, regarding my state of mind. But I couldn't get her to understand what was necessary that I do regarding the Official Confession. She said if I was not careful, in a few days I would be no use to me, let alone the Court of Counsels or the Fastness. She was forthright and repeated it before she left."

He starts to sob again, gulping in breaths between them. When he can command a coherent voice, he asks "Oh, Mum, what am I to do?"

"You will take her advice."

"I can't yet. I must tell you what is in my mind first, as I need to sound out my follies."

"I'm not sure that is wise. What is in the front of your mind?"

"My thoughts are those of someone who has betrayed the trust people had in him. Your trust most of all, I think. You carried me and birthed me. You have seen me naked, you have seen me drunk. You have seen me in temper and in love, in merriment and in jealousy. If I cannot bare my soul to you and be open to the bone about my misdeeds to you, then am I from my ethics lost altogether. And I deserve neither your consideration, nor your pity. Maybe not even your love, my mother though you be. I do not know how far I am fallen."

Droplets of tears gather on the end of the beard hairs, dripping off as he speaks.

"Nor yet do I. Do you think you can regain that trust?"

"With genuine contrition, maybe. But I have breached the Ethical Code in thought and deed. How ca-can there be a way back?"

"Then do you want to tell me now what I do not know already? Or will you follow her advice?"

"I have ... I have to say this now, or maybe it will never get said. Then explain to me what I must do under the law. I cannot just dr-drop my hands to my sides and walk away from what I have caused to be. I cannot wait for the doctoring to unload into the open these st-stumbles of mine. I will be driven mad if I cannot tell the one person who is dearest to m-me." His sobbing carries through the whole of his words, a refrain of overwhelmed reason.

And so he begins to tell her what she does not know. Her responses, she keeps within her, pummelling her sense of who is her son, who the Reever is. She will weigh it all up at the end.

He tells of the deals with Charlie. She knows of these, for he had declared them in the Public Register. He tells of how Charlie spoke to him of the planned corruption of the League, learned from loud-mouthed business associates. Of the clandestine placement of a spy in SJ's base in Birmingham arranged with Charlie to gather evidence. Not an ethical action, possibly criminal under Confederation Laws. Of how, when Charlie heard there was important information being sent through his trading base in Hamburg, they had concocted the plan to grab the faxplex. Then he could approach the League with evidence of what was afoot. This is a confusing action, which she thinks might balance some of the lesser things he has done. But it isn't ethical. He reminds her of what happened to Ardel, and how he had thought it would not be so bad for the Ambassador to be left a little longer in the cistern. She had dealt with this idiocy, he knows it was unacceptable. And it wasn't ethical.

He tells her of Jarnie, and what happened to his body. She is mortified. He had also lied to Gwyneth. Doubly unethical. He told of his thoughts of sending people to reconnoitre the base in Cymru. Her mind whirls wondering how he could contemplate such a thing. A transgression if he had carried it out. He tells of the conversation with the Castellan, which had led to him going to see Alastair. She hopes he is possibly on the right path to redemption.

And then he tells her of the information about the family tie he has withheld from her and Ardel because he is worried how they both will react. It knocks her down. It doesn't quite sink in. Her anger from childhood rises bitterly to the fore.

"That is all of it, Briged, all of it. I have listened as I've spoken. It is a deep pit I am in."

He is on the edge of sobbing still. He lays down on the daybed, rolls onto his back and closes his eyes, taking jarring breaths. She gets up puts a hand on top of his two — crossed in the middle of his chest — and kisses his forehead.

"I need to go and think about everything you've told me. I'll be back before nightfall."

She goes to her own home, Second House.

"How can I be his sounding board?" she says to her reflection in the mirror next to the front door. "For that is my role, but ..."

She can't go and talk to Kaet about this either. Alastair is the only one who can let her talk her way through this dilemma. But can she fully trust his reactions, or her own openness at this point? Their son is involved.

She decides to take a walk up the hill to the little tarns. She needs to get air. She needs to get distant views into her mind to broaden her thinking. Put some space between the familial and the political. She heads towards High Seat.

July, 13th — The Little Tarns

As she walks, she realises Faerachar had been right not to drop the information earlier on either her or Ardel. Of all his actions this one is correct.

It's a pity he drops it on me now, she thinks. Right when she needs to concentrate on the Ethical Code and the process set out for an Official Confession. The revelation has made her angry at him for telling her in the worst possible circumstances, and then for what it drags up. The hatred she has never let go. Somehow she has to let go of it now.

Arriving at the bigger of the little tarns she is taking in the view and beginning to calm down when she notices Dahqin, sitting on a rock ledge seemingly doing nothing.

Should she backtrack and leave him in peace? She counters the thought and moves into his field of vision. He looks up slowly, not at first registering it is her.

"Hi, Briged ... I was drifting in my mind." He holds up a notepad.

"I've been trying to write some lyrics for a song, but there's too much going on around me in other people's lives."

She walks over and sits with him.

"I have a feeling you have a knack for putting into words what others need to hear, Dahqin."

She feels like crying, but fights it.

"I take it you are waiting for the others to arrive at Kaet's."

"Yes." He fidgets, looks away from her for a few minutes. She is still looking at him when he turns back to face her.

"Briged, I'm a bit worried about what the next few days might hold for Ardel. Well, and for me ... Are you ok?"

"Yes, and no, to use Ardel's words. What have you done since we arrived back here?"

"After lunch I had a talk with Regin, getting information about life here for ordinary people. Especially the people at the bottom. Someone always is, aren't they." She nods.

"I like his way of explaining, I think he's an open-minded man."

He checks the notepad.

"He said ... *It's not perfect, but it's a lot better than pretending we live perfectly.* He wound me up a bit about me dumping him into his moment of fame last night. He said Duncn and he are friends from school days — but I think it was more. Is Duncn important to him?"

"Yes. They were a couple from their mid-teens until soon after they both had finished their time in the Civic Service. In his twelve weeks with the Service, Regin had impregnated Perdie. Regin wanted to be a father and part-live with her when the child arrived. That didn't suit Duncn. Though Regin was the love of his life, children were not in his plan. Instead of working out some middle way, Duncn pushed him away completely." She shakes her head, tutting.

"It took nearly three years for them to reconcile. Too long a time for them to get back together then. Now they act as friends, but anyone who spends time with them cannot miss their turmoil. Anyway, neither has taken another lover in all those years. And they watch each other longingly. Duncn always goes away to sow his oats; Regin is no fool, so ignores it. But now has watched him cavorting with Ardel and Kirus right under his nose. Something is changing in Regin."

She sighs, then peers at Dahqin with a slight furrowing of her brow.

"Are you truly happy to bless their loves? Kaet has told me about it."

"On that question — I truly am. Honestly. When I told Duncn it was better that, than him walking away, I meant it. And with what you've just told me I'm really glad I said it. I don't know how we shall work it out exactly, but we shall over time."

He taps the note pad against his leg.

"That's where the lyrics'll come from. Regin's the seventh, isn't he."

She pats his arm and barely nods.

"Then I'll wait for Duncn to realise, before saying anything to Ardel about them." He turns his face into the gentle breeze.

"Briged, I need to ask you something else. But this probably isn't an okay moment for you."

"It is an afternoon for talking of worries, and filling in gaps. Does this follow on from your talk with Regin? Or what I have told you?"

"Neither... On the day I met Kaet for the first time, I overheard her and Faerachar talking in the kitchen. For me the biggie was Ardel had gone to see Duncn, when he'd told me he would be with Grandy. I didn't know about the two of them then. But they also talked about something else, something found out from the League faxplex. They mentioned it might affect Ardel badly. I hoped it would have come out by now, but with Faerachar out of circulation it might not. It wasn't found by Grandy and Ardel, because I'd've known if it was upsetting. He's mentioned nothing."

He pushes the notepad and pen into the leg pouch on his shorts.

"Is it ethical to ask Kaet? I feel guilty for eavesdropping. I feel feeble for not asking then. I feel scared of how it will affect Ardel."

"You missed out how it will affect me too. Did they say that?"

Dahqin nods.

"You don't have to protect me. Faerachar has now told me what it is. It fired up my anger." She lets out a long breath.

"It's why I came up here to clear my head. I need to tell Ardel myself — it is not bad for him. It might even be good for me eventually. I am emotional and angry about my past, so when I have a simple version clear in my head I will tell it to you and he together."

Her face lightens.

"But I cannot leave you with a mystery eating at you. They were alluding to Ardel being related by blood to my brood and I. Where is he now, do you think? He and Grandy were in The Keep when I left."

"They were there when I left. I can call Ardel and find out. You do look just like a version of his Mother. He must have said."

"Yes, he did. When first we met, but looks can deceive. I need to clear this from my head ..."

Her voice breaks. She looks at him directly, her eyes moist; her determination visible.

"Dahqin, right now I need a Sounding Counsel of my own." She stops again, looking round. "But I can talk this through with no one."

"You can, Briged. Talk it out to me. How else will you endure? I can listen, which might help you. I'm not wise enough to do more. And I can and will let it go afterwards."

She pulls out a kerchief and dabs at her eyes.

"Sorry, Dahqin. This is about Faerachar, and has caught me out. You saying that is enough. And you are wiser than you believe." She rolls her shoulders and moves her head through a couple of gyrations.

"Faerachar is not in a good frame of mind at the moment. He has his own self-caused situation to sort through. He is my son and I must speak harsh truths to him. My ethics will let me do this task, but I am his mother. I have never felt this alone."

She looks at the mountains in front of them.

"I need to tell this family news to Ardel today. Tomorrow I must be the Good Sounding Counsel; helping Faerachar get his stumblings out in the open." More deep breaths.

"Stumblings. His word. What a euphemism. Please call Ardel, and ask if he will meet us in Second House."

He makes the call, standing up as he talks.

"Ardel has Grandy with him. They are coming over Cannon Dub, on horses, to see Kaet."

She gets up, nodding.

"They'll be there by the time we arrive, won't they?"

"Probably. Come on, we'll walk fast."

"She will need to know, as his patron, for it will affect him. Is it alright if she is there?"

"She can be there. Did you come by horse?"

"Yes, but I walked up here. It's in the paddock. I put my saddle in the nicely cleaned stable. Duncn was a hard taskmaster."

"I'm glad you both like Duncn." She smiles at him. "My paramour, as I call him. He looks so like his beautiful father."

"We both are drawn to him, Briged, in some way. We are in each others lives now. When we go he might see a way back to Regin."

July, 13th — Second House

When Ardel and Grandy arrive at Second House she leads them into her sitting room. Dahqin, already on the settee, pulls Ardel close to him. Grandy sinks into an armchair. The windows are open — a gentle waft of warm air passes through the room. She pours her favourite white wine, chilled Fastness Estates Fendant, into small glasses and hands them out, then sits in the other armchair.

"I am more emotional than I have been for many years. So please bear with me. It is something personal."

In her usual manner she raises her glass.

"Ardel, Faerachar has been hiding some vital information from me and you. I am angry at him for playing in this way."

She tuts, breathes out through closed teeth.

"It was not right. It was not honourable. Not ethical."

She pats the arms of the chair.

"I can understand what he thought he was doing, but it has left me almost ... I can't conjure up the right word to explain what I feel. I don't think there is one. It is both emotionally painful and yet joyous at the same time. With time the feelings, I hope, will shift more to the joyous than the other way."

She pauses — sips at her wine, puts the glass down.

"Did you ever meet your grandfather from Éire? You are old enough to have done."

"My grandfather? No, Briged. I never met any of my relatives until I went to Éire for the League. I remember him dying, because my mother became so upset she was ill for weeks. She was unable to travel for his funeral. Since I was born, I believe my parents have never been there."

"Well, we are related, you and I, and my brood. My father was also your grandfather. I expect your mother will be somewhat shocked to find out she and her older siblings have an elder half-sister. Though now I go by the name Briged Jardine, my paternal name was Muirdeag. He had been with my mother for some years before I was born, 'but she was not from the right bloodline' was the little told me in my teens. I was born a few weeks after my father officially acknowledged your grandmother as his consort, is what Faerachar has told me. I was shipped off by him to a distant aunt, first in another part of Éire, then moved on again to more distant relatives over here in Scotia. Though I was visited by my father in those early years, I never saw him again after the age of two or three. I remember only his square florid face and his loud angry voice. My mother ..."

She falters, and stops talking, picking up the wine glass slowly and taking a sip "... I cannot recall."

She puts the glass down, giving Ardel a thin smile.

"I hope your mother, the youngest of my half-siblings, will be happy to know me, so I might feel joyous." She closes her eyes and breathes very deeply, when she opens them, they shine.

"I see this shocks you, Ardel, your mouth is part-open and you are staring at me rather wildly. You are in the company of close friends, so please say something."

July, 13th — Second House — Ardel

I close my mouth. I can think of nothing to say. I look at Dahqin, who pulls me to him, nuzzling my ear. Rising, I cross to Briged's chair, kneel down beside it and reach out to her.

Thoughts crash into one another. I can imagine how Maman might react to this news — she might hide behind her hauteur and refuse to change things. When I met the uncles and aunts, in Baile Átha Cliath, they were so proud of the bloodline of the Muirdeags. Will they deal with this magnificent woman as their father had, or will they be more accepting? I don't know. I know Maman has a softer side. How can I present this knowledge to her so she will go to that side, smothered so deeply under the varnished layers of cold privilege. How can I prevent an ultimate rejection of Briged by our family if Maman does not uncover her inner self. I have to protect Briged from such devastation. It's an awkward hug given the chair arm is between us, and I need to get up.

I feel his hands on my shoulders, rubbing slowly. I pull back from

Briged's embrace, looking at her with a smile, aware of my wet cheeks. She smiles back. Looking up at Dahqin, I see he's smiling with a wet face. I get up and hug him. In our time together I have seen Dahqin cry just once. When his Gran, his Papa's mother, died.

"Are you ok?"

"Of course, Ardel. But with both of you weepy, I couldn't help it."

We sit back on the settee.

"Briged, I don't know what to say, because despite the tears, having you as part of my family makes me very happy. I love being in your company, and knowing you are my aunt means it is my duty to visit you as often as I can in future. Now I know why you look so much like Maman." I pause.

"Dahqin, we need to talk to Maman." It is one of our code phrases; it means *we must leave this until later*. This time I mean it literally.

"As soon as we're home, Ardel."

"Briged, when will you tell Kaet and Duncn?"

"Kaet knows already, Ardel. She heard in her usual way and badgered Faerachar into telling her the details, but he convinced her not to tell me. Do either of you know when the four of them return?"

"Kaet told me they are already at Haven, and will be here within the hour." Dahqin turns to Grandy. "Kaet's looking forward to meeting you properly. Are you coming over with us, Briged?"

"Of course, but only until I tell Duncn this news. Then I must go to Faerachar. Grandy, I beg your indulgence, and know you understand this is an internal affair of the Fastness, beyond your remit. But I can tell you that Margot is now acting as Reever for the near future, and you must deal with her."

"I fully understand our presence adds an unnecessary layer to what is happening. I want you to know this is a misfortune I hope is swiftly resolved. I am glad we are trusted to stay on in The Keep at this time. And doubly so you continue to extend your personal hospitality towards us up here in The Three Houses."

"Thank you, Grandy. It is the least we can do for the Fastness. And our personal hospitality ... with what you have just heard, how can it be otherwise. I have gained a nephew, and my offspring a cousin. Let us calm down somewhat, finish our wine, and go over to Kaet's." She stands up.

"There is one more thing I wish to do. This is an opportune time, Grandy. I will be a moment." She goes upstairs.

"It'll be for you, Grandy." Ardel says quietly. She stands up at the sound of Briged coming down.

"I hope you will accept this gift from me, Grandy." An Earth Mother box is cupped in her hands.

"Thank you, Briged. I accept it in the spirit in which it is given."

The box is lowered into Grandy's outstretched hands.

"I had noticed them in various places we visited on our tour. Is it the Mother of this Earth?"

"She is so — symbol only that she is. I hope it was not presumptive of me to give this? That there are no proscriptions on such gifts between friends on a vacation."

"None, Briged. And it is not presumptive either." She opens the box and slides out the figure, taking a sharp intake of breath.

"The tingle. Briged is this normal? I can feel the tingle from the stone in the circle."

"Very normal, Grandy. And your slight glow too."

Grandy puts the Mother and box on the small table by her chair, and embraces Briged.

"I would love to give one to every woman in the world, but I don't know how to do so with grace. Imposition is not the way it can be done. So instead I give one to all my female guests. Little by little, I can only hope."

Briged empties the few drops of wine from her glass, smiles broadly at them. "Come — off to Kaet's."

July, 13th — Third House

Walking between the two houses Dahqin asks Grandy if they can let the others go ahead.

"Bedow wants to know what has happened to the Shadow, Grandy.

The Guard in Douarnenez have said the case is closed. Is it okay for the twins and Peran to return home? And what charges will I face for nicking his IDs. It's a double crime to take them and not to hand them in, isn't it?"

"Ardel broached this with me this morning, Dahqin. You handed them in to me. They are why he was deported from Brittany into the hands of the League Security Office. I await Bartouche's advice on their return home."

In Third House, Dahqin changes from his shoes, and finds a pair of house slippers to fit Grandy. In the kitchen, Kaet is laughing, and dancing with Ardel, who looks sickly.

"They'll be here in fifteen minutes," she shouts, as she whirls him to a standstill; he retreats to a chair.

"I'm going to make some tea. Briged?"

"I better had. I'll need a clear, clear head." Kaet goes over to her seated at the table, putting her arms around from behind.

"I love you, my darling. And I wish you did not have such a hard task ahead. It will come out right if he does what he knows he must."

Briged reaches up and pats Kaet's clasped hands.

"I love you too, daughter. I told Gwyneth how sons are both a joy and a trial. And so it is. And you two — take note and do something for your own mothers to make it more joy than trial. But whatever happens we will get through it to live the other side. Now let us be joyful we can celebrate something else. Which is pleasing to me at least."

Kaet looks across to Grandy. "You were at Rigg. I felt it was you and now I know for sure. You are so beautiful and have such presence."

Minutes can drag so when there is a desire to see the effect of a piece of good news on someone loved, especially when there is also bad news to be told soon after. They run out of things to say to each other. Briged and Kaet sit at the table, on sides of the same corner, facing the door, mugs empty. Ardel is on the sofa at the opposite end of the room, Dahqin massaging his feet. Grandy, in one of the armchairs is either sleeping or meditating, her cup of tea untouched since she'd put it down.

Then Duncn bustles in followed by Peran and the twins, and the room is energised and smiling. Kaet shoots off her chair, grabbing him to her. Dahqin and Ardel sit up and Peran sits between them. The twins lean against the counter.

"You're very happy to see me, sister. More so than other times when I arrive back. Or do I misremember. Is it because I'm a sea-farer now?"

"Sea-*dog* maybe. What news do you bring us from afar?"

"Other than we have had a fantastic time, none that can be told you with Briged here." He slips from her arms and goes to Briged.

"Mum, what has happened? Why the waiting room atmosphere?"

"You only call me Mum when you know there is bad news, and have some idea what it is. So let's not talk of it." She smiles at him. "I want to tell you some good news. But maybe you know of that too?"

"No, Briged, I don't." He looks over as Ardel stands up. "And you look like a cat with cream. What's to be told me?"

"My father was also Ardel's grandfather. Faerachar told me earlier today. Enjoy having a cousin to welcome. I think it is in order for you to embrace him and kiss. I believe everyone has seen you do it before." They both redden. "Haven't they?"

"What have you heard, Briged?" He looks at Dahqin, who shakes his head and shrugs, hands out, palms up. Kirus chuckles.

"Told you it'd bite you." Kirus carries on chuckling.

"It was me," Kaet said. "I was telling *that* particular story but turned it into a kiss." Briged closes her eyes and shakes her head.

"They'll never let up, Ardel. Come here, Coz. Is this what I call you from now on?"

July, 13th — Second House

Inside Second House, Briged leads Duncn into the kitchen. Sitting at the table he stretches across to hold her hands.

"Faerachar is not in a good situation. I know how deeply you feel about him. He is ensconced in First House. If you want to see him and he is willing, go over. Though your older brother, he was father to you in your childhood. For him, you are both brother and son. Tomorrow is the start of a hard road for him and for me."

"I'll do that now. When I'm back, tell me what else I need to know."

She makes herself a liquorice and cinnamon tea, and listens to the noise of the wind in the trees. She stares into one of her favourite paintings. Dark clouds breaking up over fells, and a sun settling towards the sea lighting the landscape with its golden glow. It always reminds her of spring. Around her a storm is brewing. Spring is a long time off.

Back at the table, he reaches across and lightly squeezes her hands.

"He will call me when he needs to. Kaet is here, but I know who I shall talk to. Distance will not matter."

"It cannot be Ardel. This is a matter internal to Alban. It is not fair to put on him a conflict of interest."

"No, Mum. Not him. Our feelings for each other are not yet settled. Neither are his about Faerachar. It's Dahqin. He is wise to me and my ways. I can say anything to him and he will not turn away. He would not let me turn away from myself. We are matched, our feelings already sorted. Yet we have kissed but once, on the first day we met."

He looks away from her, at the painting. When he looks back there is mirth at his mouth and eyes.

"And I am glad Ardel is my cousin, for it takes the pressure off. You embarrassed us back there, unintended. That is a rarity for me with you. As we're alone I can tell you why Kirus laughed so. You will see the dark humour in it. That day, before I met Dahqin, I was busy with Ardel. I answered a call from Kirus. The twins and Dahqin could see me from the belly up, but not Ardel. I was in a mad rampant mood, and made him carry on while I was talking to them. I'd spent the night before with

Kirus. Dahqin was as angry as a marten, of course. When we met, his face was angry — I thought he would strike me. But he kissed me in front of everyone. In front of Ardel. No kiss with anyone has ever been like that was for me. We both know what it did for us; so bosom friends we are."

Shaking her head she squeezes his hands.

"Honestly, you young men. Dahqin knows the part Regin plays in your life. Do you mind?"

"No, Briged. How did that happen?"

"He picked up clues while talking to Regin after lunch. When he asked me, I could not leave his questions unanswered."

His countenance turns sombre as he looks at her.

"I sounded to him this afternoon, Duncn. Something I have only done with Alastair in the past. He allows people to be open with him in a way I've rarely seen. I hope he has let go of my need, as he said he would. I don't know how he looks to himself."

"He talks straightforwardly about emotional things. That's why I can be so open with him. I might have more loves in my life than I need, but I will cherish all of them. I hope Regin's love is strong enough."

"Let Dahqin be your guide."

He goes around the table and massaging her shoulders, lays his lips on her hair.

"Now I must get back to Dahqin's New Bagad. When you need a hug, Briged, I shall be here. I love you, Mum"

Briged finishes her tea, realises she is hungry and makes herself a bowl of raw shredded vegetables, spatters dressing on it, and wearily sits to eat it. Then she walks over to see Faerachar.

July, 13th — First House

She goes through the kitchen, and sees he too has eaten recently. She clears the remains away. Up in the study he is hunched at the desk, a thin ledger open, a pen in his hand, upside down. He is dressed in different clothes and has shaved. She sits in the recliner, but on the edge, moving the back upright. His eyes are red, and she can see the tell-tale residue of tears on his face.

"You look brighter, Mum. So Ardel and Duncn know."

"Yes, Grandy too. I understand why you didn't tell me earlier. It has brought such bitterness back into my mind, which I realise I must now let go. It will be hard. Voicing it to them is a start, I suppose."

"I know. I am sorry I have failed him so." He breaks into a bout of tears, huffing himself back into talking. "Says he is happy to add Ardel and Dahqin to our little family."

"It is a positive outcome. The family link known. Not part of what you must sound to me."

"I would add it to my list, Briged — that I withheld this from you. It wasn't ethical."

She shakes her head. "Faerachar it is a family matter. It is nothing to do with your role as Reever, or Ardel's as Ambassador. Nothing to do with my role either. It is discrete between a mother and her son."

"I am trying to complete the pros and cons of what I have done, but so far only one refrain comes out. Not ethical. Not ethical."

He turns to look north across the water towards the Keep. Sighs. Moves his hands into a joined fist on the desk.

"The things I add, you must parse them for alignment with the Ethical Code. I will put my complete draft before the Court of Counsels, whatever you tell me in the sounding. I have to be brutally honest about everything I have done and accept the full consequences. I must look you in the eye and be able to say I told everything. The more put in freely, perhaps the more understanding of where I turned wrong. And perhaps I will be redeemed. Even if not as Reever, at least as me."

His shoulders down, he slumps his forehead onto his hands.

"It is a start then. Is there anything else you need to say to me right now? If your answer is no, then in the morning I shall ask the Court of Counsels to begin the necessary processes for an Official Confession.

You have my services as the Good Sounding Counsel during daylight tomorrow."

As he shakes his head, she settles back into the chair.

"I saw you have eaten something. I will make a supper for us later, we can eat together. Unless the Court deems you to be a danger you will be left, to be with Siobhagn or here. Leastways, not on your own. Have you thought to go to her?"

He shakes his head.

"How can I appear in the township? I will see Siobhagn when I can. We have arranged to talk each evening. She will come here with the bairns tomorrow night, maybe stay over. I need the solitude here to fill my ears with silence, the better to hear my inner voice. Your company over food will be nice. But of what can we talk?"

"Of our family, and not of the Fastness."

"Then I have to tell you one more thing we planned but now I do not know if it will happen ..."

He tells her between sobs he and Siobhagn had agreed to acknowledge one another, for the sake of the bairns and for themselves, as well as for her. But would Siobhagn now go ahead? He had ruined the lives of all those he loved, including the bairns.

Briged rises and crossing to him folds her arms around him. There is nothing she can say to ease this fear of his. Only hold him against her, sensing his anguish. Siobhagn holds that answer.

July, 13th — Third House

Lively conversation is underway when Duncn returns to the kitchen at Kaet's. He stands in the doorway listening to the banter. Leaning against the kitchen worktop, Kirus is focused on Dahqin, both bright-eyed, speaking Brezonheg. The other three are on a sofa chatting in common tongue, occasionally laughing. Kaet and Grandy are sitting at the table, in quiet conversation in English. He sits next to Kaet, she pulls him over to lean against her; he tilts his head onto her shoulder.

"Sad?" He nods. "Faerachar will get through this, but it will take time. Things will be made right."

"Do you want to talk privily?" Grandy asks. They both shake their heads.

"I need to talk to one of those two, until I've got rid of this sadness. I think it's got to be Kirus."

"On what grounds?"

"Darling Kaet. He doesn't let anything get in the way of a good mood. I want his arms to hold me for a bit longer, so have to break them two up for a while."

Dahqin calls to Alun in Brezonheg, handing him a bottle of beer as he joins them.

"You need to let Bedow know you are doing fine. Tell him we will have a definite answer regarding the Shadow, soon. If it's safe, when would you go?"

"Within a day. Weather depending," Alun says. He looks at Kirus. "That's right, isn't it?"

Kirus nods. "We need to get back to earning money. This has been a really fun time, but we need to get bookings."

Switching to common tongue, he says, "Look out, here he comes."

He holds out his arm, and Duncn slides along it. A quick frown crosses Ardel's face.

"I was going to stand here and talk to you," Duncn tells Kirus. "But can't let frowns settle. I'm going to send Peran over to you instead."

He winks at Dahqin as he goes, sitting next to Ardel, putting a hand on his leg. He says a few words to Peran, who gets up and heads straight to Kirus.

"You didn't ask for me to come over, did you?" Kirus shakes his head. "Well give me a kiss anyway, I haven't had a real one since we left Glasgow."

"You've had as much as I could allow you, Peran When will my punishment end?"

"If you two have time for kissing," Kaet says. "You can help me put out a picking table for a bit of supper. Unless no one's hungry?"

"I am, for one," Grandy says. "Get the crockery and cutlery, Kirus, I'll help you lay table. When we sit down you two can tell me what you've been up to on that trip of yours. Ours wasn't as exciting as Dahqin's."

"He's bragged about it already. We were in a bar and his face was grinning out of the screen. But I'll forgive him everything, Grandy."

He looks across to Peran and Kaet as they put cheeses, vegetables, fruit, bread, biscuits and dips onto platters, then back to Grandy.

"Without him I know Peran wouldn't be here. You observe and don't comment, Grandy, but you know Peran is important to me – and I really messed that up. But Dahqin is too. Look at him now, is he really hearing Alun? Look how he watches the other two on the sofa. Hoping, but with a little fear tucked into his eyes and along the eyebrow line. He's a good actor and I know him so well. I want him to be very happy. With all of us."

They are talking very quietly, having placed out eight settings, ending up at the far end of the table, away from the others.

"Watching you six in close proximity, over these past couple of weeks has been an eye-opener, Kirus. You two and he live in unity, so much of it without words. Small looks, and things are understood. And you drop into Breton – a big barrier. No wonder Peran felt scared of his position. Have you ever seen Dahqin with tears?"

"Once, when he left us to move to Paris. I cried too, for hours that day and on and off for months after. Alun did too for a while, but he can live with the ïdea of love in his head. Me, he must be there by me. To look at, to touch. And he had gone. Even after Peran moved in it happened sometimes."

"I understand you about love. I saw him cry for the first time, today when Briged told us about her father. She was aiming at Ardel and it affected him deeply, but Dahqin too. Do you know what he has promised those two?"

"No. He balances what he feels for me against what Ardel is feeling for Duncn. The thumping of joy in my heart when I saw him with you at

The Tents — I had missed him so. Alun was right not to warn me. When Ardel introduced them here, I was niggled with Duncn, because of what that call did to Dahqin. But when they kissed ... I wanted to be there in it with them. I'm greedy, as I've told you. This is Dahqin's New Bagad. I feel it. And boy, am I happy. Especially as Peran is still here for — well, selfishly, for me. Little Dark One."

"Between you and Dahqin, how can it not be a success?" He shrugs and smiles. "Why Little Dark One, Kirus?"

"It's said to be one meaning of his name. It so suits who he is. Physically and surprisingly."

She is about to ask him what he means, when Peran claps his hands. "Food's ready."

"Come on, up to the table," Kaet says loudly, placing a second ewer of water, flavoured with lime zest, saffron and a little honey amidst the platters.

"It'll be dark soon, and some of you need to go back to The Keep."

Grandy sits at the end by the door, in the chair she'd been holding while they've talked and Kirus stays with her, motioning Peran to come and sit opposite. Kaet sits at the other end, her normal place. Dahqin pulls Alun next to him. Duncn and Ardel are still quietly talking on the sofa.

"You two, come here!" Kaet demands. Duncn shoots up instantly, getting between Kirus and Ardel.

"All with something in your glass? Then I call on Grandy, as the most sensible amongst us, to raise a toast to us all."

"Thank you, Kaet. I came here on a quest, to aid Ardel, with the help of Dahqin and his three companions. What unexpected times we've had. Those who are missing we add into this toast." She raises her glass.

"To Dahqin's New Bagad, nurtured by Kaet. May you prosper and find support in each others arms."

The sun lowers more in the sky. Dahqin is talking to Alun and Kaet, when she grasps Ardel's arm, but she isn't looking at any of them, she is looking up.

"Come with me."

She gets up, and holding his arm leads him out of the kitchen. Dahqin goes to rise, but Alun signals him to stay.

"Peran said she did this when he was talking to Ardel at The Keep, the night we left Douarnenez. Whatever it is you won't change it."

"True, Alun. So ... everything I've tried to do since arriving in Douarnenez has been about getting us all together in some way, without rancour. I know I can only control my own interaction with you all. The rest, you each have to do for yourselves."

"Dahqin, don't let doubt creep into your desires. We are back together when we can better understand the limitations on what we once thought almost limitless. There will always be little niggles between individuals, you know that. You are in love with each one of us five to some degree, even if you don't acknowledge it yet. Isn't that right, Duncn?"

Dahqin looks across into Duncn's eyes. Alun laughs quietly.

"At some point in time, you two may answer what is written on your faces when you look at each other. I will tell you this Duncn, my love for this man needs only the occasional kiss, cuddle and sweet words for me to be content. A night in his arms, or he in mine, bliss. And there is always joy in me whenever Kirus is made happy."

July, 13th — Returning to The Keep

It is still in the gloaming as Grandy, Ardel and Dahqin set off for The Keep; Duncn heading out with them.

"I'll see you across to the west side of Derwent."

He and Ardel ride behind the other two.

"Well, Dahqin, are you happy with this Bagad of yours?"

"I am happy with that, Grandy. But sad for Briged. I hope things sort out alright, with Faerachar."

"As you know, Dahqin, time is the answer."

"I like it you get on so well with Kirus and Peran."

He turns round to see the other two deep in discussion.

"Kirus told you lots of stories of our growing up together. I hope he was honest. I wouldn't like you to have gained a false impression of my saintly qualities."

"Oh, I certainly began to realise you were a different person to the demure Dahqin I know." She bursts out laughing.

"He made me 'laugh so much. You boys must have been a nightmare to your parents. Duncn's right to say he doesn't let anything get in the way of a good mood."

"Just between us two, Grandy, me going to Paris almost destroyed Kirus. I felt guilty about it a lot. When I used to go back, before I met Ardel, he wouldn't meet me. Alun told me he couldn't stand the pain of the separation, and me coming and going was like a wound that kept bursting open. I once thought they were very similar in temperament, but as we got older I realised Alun is just romantic. Kirus needs to express his love physically. The fact is the one who understands best what their desires are is Peran. He's good at it. He can wrap Kirus round his little finger. Which makes Kirus very happy."

"Dahqin, I'm turning back," Duncn shouts. "Wait up."

They stop by the bridge, the surface of Derwentwater glimmering to their right.

"Beautiful windless evening, on a horse who knows where it's taking me." Grandy says. Ardel moves on close by, running his hand along Dahqin's thigh as he passes, smiling at him.

"We'll keep going, Grandy. Dahqin can catch up with us."

"Give me five minutes," Duncn says as he dismounts. Dahqin swings down. They lean together against the parapet.

"I have a boon to ask of you, as my bosom companion." Duncn sounds light, but Dahqin hears through to the darker tone.

"Whatever you need from me, you shall have."

"That's a blank card, Dahqin. And thank you. Can I talk with you when I need, about how things unfold here? I shall be in need of a listener who I trust." He takes hold of Dahqin's hand.

"I trust no one with my life, more than Regin, Briged or you. I need to beg him to forgive me right now. I fear why he is so calm. So I need someone outside my family. And I fear for my brother and so for my Mum." He looks down. "Will you be that one?"

Dahqin squeezes his hand, and turns to stand in front of him, pressing tightly against him.

"I am here for you Duncn, wherever here happens to be. You call me day or night. You might not get straight through, though work about the only reason. But I shall mark your number with a priority, pick it up as soon as I can, and get back to you with urgence."

"Thank you, Dahqin. Thank you, so much."

Dahqin huffs breath across Duncn's ear, and lets the tip of his tongue lightly brush the lobe a few times, leaving it damp. Duncn relaxes, a smile forming.

"Wise." Duncn says, not letting go.

Breathing in the scent of each other, occasionally giving a squeeze in the hug then letting it go, they hang together for many minutes.

Eventually Duncn lowers his hands, and pushes Dahqin away.

"You need to catch up with the others. I'll see you both tomorrow evening, Kaet says there's a meal planned."

He pats Dahqin on the shoulder, and they mount their horses.

"Sleep well, Dahqin."

He sets his horse trotting up the lane, Dahqin watching until they disappear into the darkness of the trees. Riding at a trot he closes up with Ardel and Grandy halfway along the lake. They are ambling along, talking of what they must do in the next few days, their voices coming to him through the trees. He is still some distance from them when Grandy's HiSec breeps. He slows his horse, allowing them to move out of earshot.

He thinks instead of what might be with the Bagad. The important thing is to let each one find their own way through to what relationships they want. It is not his to try and make things happen. Especially with Duncn and Regin. Ardel is his love and consort in this life. Kirus, he will always love and desire. Alun, he has a deep affection for. Peran, is a good

410

younger friend. Duncn. He settles a thought; let him and Regin work out their need for each other, and time will bring some answers for Ardel. A voice intrudes.

"Dahqin, come on. Grandy has finished the call."

"Thank you for the privacy, Dahqin. That was Bartouche. Things have changed fast. When we are back in The Keep and are cleaned up, I'll join you both in Coleridge to explain what happens next."

July, 13th — The Keep — Dahqin

Grandy doesn't waste any time, she is talking as the door closes.

"We've got a lot to discuss, Ardel. Don't ask questions of me until I finish this bit. Dahqin, I trust your discretion. You will have calls to make, so your news first. The twins and Peran can leave for Douarnenez as soon as they want. Tell Bedow there will be no action by the League regarding what happened to the Shadow in Brittany. The airship is coming here on the 15th, so we are travelling back early. You can say —Charlie is with Inez in Genève, after going there voluntarily, and they are under League protection."

As she sits, I start to rise.

"Wait a moment, Dahqin, you need to know this next bit too. You have nothing to fear either. Bartouche says to give you this."

She hands him a faxplex.

"So, finally you are a Hero." She's laughing heartily. "Kirus told me so much."

"Kirus is in so much trouble, then. I was very young when I wanted to be a Hero." I read the letter.

"Wow. Is this for real? I'll need a frame for this, Ardel, look. Thank you, Grandy. Well, Great-Aunt Matilde. I'm so relieved about the Shadow stuff. I can tell them this?"

"Yes. All four of you will be presented with genuine articles of commendation when you meet Bartouche, probably in Genève, in a few weeks time. It will cite how you and your friends aided the League at a critical time. But they must not tell anyone else until the official letters arrive." She sips some water.

"You cannot pass on to the others what I now say. Faerachar and Charlie, you were right about them. Yves is under arrest, his Secretary too. This happened days ago, but she could only tell us today. Without the Shadow and his records, Yves would not yet be in custody. That's it, Dahqin. Oh, we are having a working breakfast tomorrow with Margot, I mean the Reever — I must remember to use their titles — David, the Communicator and Jonat, the Castellan. And the new Steward will be introduced. What do you want to do about your breakfast?"

"I'll leave here early and take breakfast with the others at Kaet's. The twins and Peran will probably be gone by tomorrow night, so I'd like to spend time with them."

"Right." Grandy says. I am dismissed, which is fine by me. I walk along the terrace, until their voices are a quiet murmur.

"Tomorrow morning, Ardel, during breakfast we need to cover a number of key areas. The first is the provenance of some of the evidence we have that is different from what Charlie produced. They have to tell us what they know. It seems that what we have accumulated here goes wider than what he sent Faerachar. With the airship there will be two runners to guard the evidence. Next, we need to pursue the promise Faerachar made about ensuring an Ambassador cannot ..."

There is no wind at all and not a cloud in the sky. The stars are bright, the moon not yet risen. From across the water comes piano music. There are lights against the cliff behind the Township. An outdoor concert is underway in its square.

I know the piece. Schubert, Four Impromptus. It's gentle. Perfect in the background. I settle on a double steamer and phone Alun.

"Is Kaet there?"

"We are all here in the kitchen."

"Okay, then. It is safe to return to Douarnenez. Alun, let Bedow know — better you than me. Charlie and Inez are now in Genève under League protection. They went there voluntarily. I'll be up tomorrow morning, early. For breakfast, if I may, Kaet."

"Just turn up anytime, Dahqin."

"Well, guess I'll catch up with you after work, Duncn. Hot and sweaty, wasn't it?"

"It's my job to get him through the shower."

"You said, leaving within the day, Kirus. So I'm coming over early."

"Dahqin, are you pushing me aside for him?"

"Don't I have a say here?" Duncn pipes up.

"No!" Kirus and I say together. There's laughter in the background.

I tell them we are to become heroes. After finishing the call I stay out on the terrace, enjoying the gentle rolling of the music, and close my eyes.

"All alone?" It is Regin.

"Can I get you a drink? I'm finished for tonight, I'm going to have a small beer before I go."

"I'll have one, please, Regin. We need to talk."

Coming back, Regin joins me on the double steamer.

"I like these summer concerts. I have no idea what the music is, but I like it, Dahqin." We chink bottles.

"It's Schubert, Impromptus, this is Opus 90 in C minor. I'd never be able to play like this, not my style."

"What's the talk we must have? Oh boy, your scent is really heady."

"I know you are why Peran hangs onto my tops. Kirus says there's someone else's scent involved. He said Peran was away for six hours the other day. And I saw you two kissing on the day I met Duncn."

"Who else knows?" He's wary.

"Nobody, I've said nothing to Kirus. I didn't want to start the chat like this. We are due to leave on the 15th. Peran and the twins will be away tomorrow on the late afternoon tide."

"Peran going."

"I've got a couple of big asks of you, Regin. What time do you finish tomorrow? And how badly upset will you be if Duncn spends a couple of

413

hours with Ardel tomorrow morning – really early?"

"I'm away from here when this beer is finished, I'm off tomorrow. I'll not be fatally wounded if they get together. Why?"

"Why don't you come up to Three Houses and see Peran openly. Kaet won't mind, will she? Duncn and Ardel will be working, Alun will already be on the boat. And I'm being selfish – Kirus and I need some time."

"You know how to bargain. I take Huw to school, so I can get there around half-nine. We'd planned to meet about eleven. When are you getting up there?"

"I'll cycle up for daybreak. I want to wake Duncn and get him to go see Ardel. You're the only person who knows."

"Has Peran told you anything about me and Duncn?"

"Not a word. I only know what you hinted at this morning, and what Briged told me this afternoon. You love him a lot, don't you?"

"Yes. Kaet knows I'm not celibate anymore. It's a first step to getting back with him." He suddenly sits up. "I have to go, Dahqin. I'll be there."

Such a quick departure – he's left half the beer. I sit up, yawning. They're still murmuring in Coleridge. That wasn't what I'd planned to say. I'd promised myself I wasn't going to get involved like that. And yet how else am I going to get time with Kirus before they go.

I try to make my mind go blank. It doesn't work – Kirus is too real.

It's gone quiet in Coleridge. The Fantasy has started and Ardel is looking down at me.

"Schubert, Fantasy in F minor Opus 103. One minute in. What are you thinking about?" Sitting down on the edge of the chair, he holds out a glass of chilled nettle beer. I take it.

"Grandy has gone to bed. I'd like to hear the rest of this."

"I'm thinking about what has happened to you and me since you left Genève to come here. And about the others."

"Shift over a bit and let me alongside you."

We chink glasses.

"How are you going to tell your mother about Briged?"

414

"I've got some thoughts. A mishmash of hopeful and worrying. We can talk it through properly after I have been to Sion and survived a grilling by Bartouche. I thought you must have known she was my Mâitre and kept it from me."

"I didn't know her by that name. She's Mam's aunt. She used to visit quite a lot until I was about fourteen, then she and Uncle Geraint fell out. He's Papa's eldest brother."

"And Charlie is Peran's uncle. Spooky connections."

"Relativity. I'm blaming the stones, Ardel."

"Dahqin, we should see the stones tonight. The moon is rising soon and it'll be full. It'll be romantic up there with you. We can get a couple of bikes. Please, Dahqin. I want to feel the magic of the place. And with you there, I'm sure I will."

"On a full moon night? What are you thinking?"

"You braved Karnak in fog, you claim, this should be a doddle."

"Okay, Ardel. But you promise me — we touch nothing in the circle. No testing of me."

"Absolutely. None. Promise."

I assume there is someone in the stables at this time of night.

July, 13th — The Stones, Castlerigg

They ride to the Rigg catching sounds of the concert. The still hidden, rising moon is lighting the highest fells to the north as they reach the edge of the circle. The stones are discernible in the darkness, blacker than the backdrop, and the night is cooling fast.

"What the ... what is that?" Ardel sounds scared. Ahead of them the ground is smoky, little white swirls just visible as the tip of the moon crests the fells east of John's in the Vale. They watch as the whole area inside the stones turns white. "This is too weird."

"It's mist lifting off the ground, Ardel. There's an inversion in the valley, look." He grasps Ardel's hand firmly. "Look down at your feet."

"They're disappearing." Ardel laughs. "It's like we're floating on clouds."

415

As the moon rises it lights the eastern sides of the stones next to them, a twinkle of crystals adds to the spectacle.

"I don't feel scared at all, this is wonderful."

"This is the magical part of the stones everywhere. Be in them but not part of them. Though I've never seen anything quite like this in Brittany."

The mist is rising slowly, now over their ankles. The moon floats free of the fells, big and creamy. The stones on the far side are black intrusions between them and the moon.

"I love you so much, Ardel."

Two forms become one — a solitary pillar amidst the stones.

"Now let's get back to a warm bed."

July, 14th — The Keep

Warm from a hot shower, Ardel goes to look back across Derwent towards the circle. Dahqin comes up behind him, touching him lightly on his lower back.

"Oh. What's happening? It's the flames again, Dahqin."

Ardel presses back against him, as the mist glows where the stones stand. He shivers. But the glow is the colour of moonlight. Then he realises, the mist bank is lit seemingly from within by the moon, and is creeping fingers over the edge of the hill towards the woods at the foot of the escarpment.

"It's magical," Dahqin says, putting his arms around Ardel. "Not magic. Let's watch the fingers prowl through the woods. Then bed."

July, 14th — The Three Houses

Dahqin arrives at The Three Houses as dawn is breaking. He goes to Second House and throws a couple of pebbles at Duncn's bedroom window. He is about to throw more when Duncn comes out in his shorts, and ushers him inside, indicating they be silent as they climb the stairs. Barefooted Dahqin follows him back to his bedroom.

"I need a good cuddle with you," he says in answer to the question on

Duncn's face. And taking off his top, he climbs in under the coverlet.

"Our farewell can't be just a quick hug as I board the airship back to Genève with Ardel."

"Of course not. We need a little pampering. Come on."

"But not for too long. Will you go and say goodbye to Ardel — he's not starting work until nine."

"Oh. Yes. I'll reset my alarm."

An hour or so passes, half in slumber, half in dream. Moving to snuggle against one another, feeling the sensuous delicacy of skin against skin, with nothing between to blur the skittering sensation of being touched by one's lover, immersed in their scent.

The quiet buzzing of the alarm wakes them fully.

"You can stay here, or go over to Kaet's now. It'll be unlocked, same as this was. What will you do today?"

"Time with Kirus. Then I'll help them with whatever they need."

"I said my goodbyes to them last night. I don't like the moments of departure to be crowded and prolonged. No watching the disappearing vessel for me."

He grins. "Besides, Kirus was here for a while. What would you have done if he had been here?"

Dahqin laughs. "That is such a descriptive smile you have on your face. I'd have cuddled both of you. It's all either of you would have been good for."

"I know we're each off the others menu — box of fireworks, box of matches." He licks his lips and brushes his mouth across Dahqin's neck. "But surely we can have a couple of kisses."

Dahqin crosses to Third House and dumps his shoes in the hallway. He creeps into the shadows of the bedroom where the twins and Peran seem sound asleep. He can make out where Kirus is, and pulling off his shorts and top gets under the cover behind him, passing his arm over him.

"Dahqin?" Peran rolls over against Dahqin's hand.

417

"I didn't mean to wake you, Peran. Sorry."

"That's okay." He holds Dahqin's hand. "I'm glad you want to be here." They remain in silence until the sound of Duncn's horse crossing the bridge reaches them.

"I'm getting up to make tea and coffee. Make him move over. What do you want, Dahqin?"

"Coffee, please." He watches Peran climb over Alun and pull on his pants and shorts. Hears the door shut. He is tight against Kirus's back. Moments later Kirus moves towards Alun, then turns onto his back looking towards Dahqin through half-closed eyes.

"Dreaming, am I?"

"Depends what you think you see."

"I know your scent, Dahqin."

"Just want to cuddle you, Kirus. I heard you've had a hard time."

"Finally been to see Duncn."

"Yeah. Getting a bit sad we're splitting up again."

"That's never going to happen. There's going to be photos of you out in the Tents after all these years. You'll be coming to Douarnenez regularly from now on. Promise me that, or get out of this bed."

He turns onto his side.

"Not getting out? So you are promising. Shall we let Peran catch us right now?"

"Don't listen to this devil, Dahqin." Alun yawns and stretches over, making Kirus turn onto his back again.

"He loves making Peran annoyed enough to tell him off. Just lay here cuddling up with us two and be happy, Kirus."

When Peran comes back with the drinks, that's how he finds them. He opens the blinds, letting in the light of the western sky. Undresses and clambers into bed, squiggling down between the twins.

"Kaet's up and busy down there. You need to sit up and drink these while they're warm." The twins start moving. "You too, Dahqin. Alun, hand them across."

Dahqin twists round and sliding down towards the foot of the bed, sits cross-legged facing the three of them. Kirus hands him a mug. They drink, smiling at each other. Finishing, Dahqin stretches and stands.

"I'll have a quick shower, then I'm going to help Kaet. Any towel?" All three nod.

July, 14th — The Three Houses

In Second House, Briged has not slept well. She was awake when Kirus left, and heard Dahqin when he arrived. When she knows they are in bed together she relaxes into a deep sleep, broken by Duncn's alarm. She listens until his horse has crossed the beck. Only as she goes through her morning rituals does she realise how early it is. She makes herself a strong coffee — not her morning drink at all — eating some fruit with yogurt and honey, while she muses.

She has a unique role in the Fastness. She is responsible for the work of no one else, is answerable to no one person specifically, but ultimately overseen by the Court of Counsels sitting in Session. She is the disinterested conscience of the Fastness holding fast to the Ethical Code, enabling those involved in the governance of it to stay on the right path. The act of Sounding seems a straightforward thing. But it seldom is, though plain-speaking Briged is good at it, especially with Faerachar as Reever. But as he is now, teetering emotionally, how far can she push at him?

Going to her workroom she calls the Clerk to the Court of Counsels. They know one another well, having worked together in different jobs over many years.

"Elspet, I hope you are keeping well. Your family too."

"I am, Briged, so are they. You look tired. Whatever is the matter?"

"I have not been sleeping too well of late. The purpose of this call is to broach a subject you will need to lay before the Counsels in Session. I will, as always, send written confirmation of what I am telling you, and I know you will get this call transcribed."

"What is afoot, Briged?"

"There must be an Official Confession to the Court of Counsels organised. I am passing this on in my official capacity as the Good Sounding Counsel. But the official involved is the Reever, Faerachar Strachan, my son. At this moment Margot Salkeld, the Steward, is acting up as Reever. The situation is complicated because he seems to be in the middle of an emotional breakdown. I have checked the rules, and there is nothing that adequately addresses the procedures needed in such an instance.

"He has been examined by his doctor, who has confirmed his mental state is fragile, but not the severity of it, or what treatment is appropriate. This is awaited. All this will be sent to the Directorate of Employment in The Keep for processing, which will deal with the employment safeguards.

"But it means the legal timetable in the regulations concerning an Official Confession maybe negated. There seem to be no exceptions applying in the procedures. He may not be in a mental state suitable to take the stand before the Court. Of course, I cannot judge that any more than another Counsel. Only the medical practitioners can do it. Today during the hours of daylight I shall be available to him, as the Sounding Counsel, as I would for any other person. This is as he has asked, and says he must do it to try to save his own sanity. I have discussed this with his doctor who has said it may happen, but I must judge it carefully. She has told me what to watch for.

"You know me well enough. I will ensure he knows which of his actions are ethical, and which not. I will not advise him on any other basis. The legality of what he has caused to happen is not for me to judge. Such things will have to be decided by the Court of Counsels and passed on to the Law Courts where necessary. Depending on the outcome of those cases shall he be able to appeal to the joint Governing Council and Parlement for a Redemption hearing. I will tread this line very carefully."

"Aah, Briged, I see where this leaves gaps. I shall put it to the Court this morning in the briefing meeting. It will, in all probability, have to go to the Councils of Laws Peculiar for ratification as a rule change within their purview, not having to go to the Governing Council and Parlement, except after the fact for their information."

"As you can appreciate, Elspet, this needs to be dealt with expediently. Of course the governance of the Fastness is secure and in capable and safe hands. There is continuity. The Reever, Margot Salkeld, will apprise all necessary bodies of this turn of events. This is merely a forewarning, and a request for guidance from me, regarding a possible postponement of the Official Confession."

"My best regards to you, Briged."

"We shall speak very soon. My regards to you, Elspet."

Inside the kitchen of First House she opens one set of shutters and cracks open the window, letting in a stir of wind allowing the sounds from outside to mingle with Faerachar's light snore. She makes tea for them both.

The bedroom door is ajar, the curtains wide open. He lays under only a sheet, though the night had not been warm, and then she notices the coverlet mostly on the floor, on the opposite side of the bed. Putting the mug on the small cabinet, she gently shakes his shoulder, withdraws, closing the door.

Back in the kitchen she sits at the table, cradling her tea, watching flecks of dust stir round in a shaft of sunlight. Upstairs she hears his feet on the floor, heading to the washroom. Minutes pass and she hears the cistern work, then the shower start to run. The shiny wings of two micro-moths jigging round one another occasionally flash, as the sun slowly changes the angle at which it enters.

He was a wee bairn, six, maybe seven when he first noticed a micro-moth. After that he sought them out. She had bought him a macro-viewer so he could record them, leaving them to fulfil their short lives. There are beauties in his collection of photos, two she remembers in particular. The first had lustrous green wings, which caught the sunlight, each wing with a creamy white stripe across it and the most amazingly long antennae; easily four times the length of it. It'd been twitching them as it sat on the rim of a glass. The other with feathery antennae had a hairy ginger topknot on its head. There was a sheen to the brown wings each decked with two white triangles.

"They are males" he'd told her, showing her the photos when he was thirteen. "See the horns on the second set of legs? They're for grasping the females during mating. There is no finesse in their sex."

The shower is shut off. She hears him go back to his bedroom, clump around; she hopes — to dress and come down. She wonders if he still notices the little moths, so tiny and easily missed when something larger displays its beauty. If we move too fast in life and miss the little details we do not understand the world on which we live, she thinks. She closes her eyes and turns in on herself.

July, 14th — At The Keep — Titles

Breakfast with the Reever, Steward, Communicator and Castellan is finished. The agenda for Grandy and Ardel over the next day and a half is drawn up. Margot has made plain her determination to be open when doing things her way. Especially things once left mysterious by Faerachar. She emphasises she has no wish to disparage the way he had worked, but it isn't her way.

"So, it is agreed, Ambassadors. The first item this morning is for the Communicator and Castellan to explain to you the equipment we have in the dome and how we use it to safeguard the Fastness. No one can miss the dome, yet no one acknowledges its purpose. I want that to change. I know you are aware of the various discussions underway in the Councils concerning the future of the Boundary Patrol. They can discuss this with you if more detail is required than the Good Sounding Counsel covered with you. Also the Communicator can explain the importance of his department's abilities to deal with any perceived threats from outside this Fastness. Anything which might corrupt the way we do things as a society. As agreed I shall meet up with you both over breakfast tomorrow morning before you proceed to the glider field when your airship arrives. Now, myself and the Steward will leave you with these two capable men."

The Reever rises, shakes hands with Grandy and Ardel, and the Steward does likewise. Both women nod to the other two and leave the upper terrace, heading towards the Reever's office.

"Well, Ambassadors," the Castellan says. "We will try to stick to the protocols as much as we can. It is more difficult for the Communicator than me, for I understand there is a link between you and Faerachar's family, Ambassador Penaul, and that now includes a growing friendship with David as Kaet's promised consort, which is wonderful. But in the professional sphere we shall try to use a little distance so as not to confuse what is being said."

"Thank you for those words, Castellan," Grandy says. "I agree the Protocols are there to aid our work with one another, not diminish the interactions, but to protect those involved. Knowing where the boundaries run is important. So, on that note... Who will take the lead in our tour of the dome and who spill its secrets?"

"I will be explaining the workings of the system, Ambassador Emembet. The Castellan will be explaining the way we use it to protect the Fastness."

"Thank you Communicator." She smiles at them both.

"Do you wish to say anything Ambassador Penaul?" Ardel shakes his head. Grandy raises her left eyebrow.

"Er... No, there is nothing I wish to add at this time, Communicator. Once explanations are given I'm sure I shall have questions."

"Then come this way please."

They are taken from the terrace through a number of secure doors and enter a cannion controlled from within.

"A lift. Like any other," Ardel says. David nods.

It opens into an operations room, brimming with electronic equipment. Very different from the Security Section Control Room Ardel had seen, low down in The Keep. As they pass through, the Communicator explains the equipment in the dome feeds information into this array of multi-viewers and other machines for analysis. They are taken through more secure doors to another lift taking them up into the dome. It is much larger inside than Ardel had imagined. The black glass blocks all external visible light from entering the interior, which is lit dimly. There is one big dish aerial and numerous smaller ones.

"We are standing in this faraday cage for our own safety. We used to have a satellite in geostationary orbit linked through the main dish. But it was brought down thirty-odd years ago. Now we use a number of high altitude drones travelling on circuits within the boundaries of Alban. The main dish is still used with them. These smaller dishes and other aerials on the framework allow us to capture any radio or televisual signals at any frequency within Europa at least, though some do come to us from further afield." The Communicator indicates different items.

"We analyse these incoming signals and can build a picture of what is out there. We do not, actually cannot, decode everything. We have very strict operational guidelines, tied in with the Ethical Code. For your peace of mind, Ambassadors, other than the one instance with the stolen faxplex, of which you are aware, we have never tried to decode League traffic. Firstly it is illegal under Confederation and League Conventions. Secondly it is not the purpose of our listening to intrude into the League's business, which requires probity. Thirdly, even if we were acting nefariously, I believe we would not be able to break the League codes because of the philosophy behind the coding. You and I have discussed this briefly, Ambassador Penaul, haven't we?"

"We have, Communicator. I do have a question. Much of the information coming into our hands seemed to be of uncertain provenance. Are you able to tell us if the source of any one piece of information can always be traced?"

"Yes, if it is from an external source and comes through here it is notated in the transcript with full travel string. A lot of what we got came directly from Charlie Trelawn, of course. I suppose that is all now in the League's hands, as he is in their protection. Did you have specific information in mind?"

"No, Dav ... er, Communicator. I am trying to build a picture of how you worked out which sources to concentrate on."

"I believe personal friendship had a lot to do with it. We also have access to our data records here. Do I need to explain further?"

"No, Communicator. I understand completely what you tell me. Do you need clarification Ambassador Emembet?"

Grandy shakes her head, holding David's gaze.

"Communicator, what assurances can you give me that there are no copies of the files stolen from the League left in this, or any other place? You were up front about making copies during our searches, and you tell us all are now handed over. What about the faxplex sent back into Cymru?"

"Ambassador Emembet, Ambassador Penaul, you and I have worked closely together here in The Keep. There is an empathy of belief in probity between us; I and the other officials in this Fastness believe in the Ethical Code which guides us. It is not just words on public noticeboards. Those words really mean something. Honour and trust can be lost through one little slip. As we have sadly witnessed." He stops. Looks at the Castellan, who nods.

"I can look you both directly in the eye, and say with absolute certainty that I have ensured every copy other than those you have secured and sealed in your boxes, has been destroyed. They are the pukka copies, nothing fishy about them. Unlike the ones sent back to Cymru, which have also been destroyed. I know they are dissolved into a pile of powder." David again looks at the Castellan.

"The Communicator can show you how that works, if you like."

"Yes, please," Grandy said. "Just for the knowledge of an experiment carried out. It is intriguing."

"If I might add some commentary here, Ambassadors." The Castellan clears his throat.

"Before we go back into the bustle below. I'll explain why we collect this information. It is for defending the interests of this Fastness. It is tied in with the idea that we do not need the Boundary Patrol as a militia force. As you are aware, this is being discussed right now. But we cannot be left naked to the intrusions of an insidious foe. A foe who does not move by capturing ground, but by capturing the psyche of us humans. Awakening the scavengers of envy and avarice. Making us believe what we need, want, must have, is more, more, more. More of anything. More money to spend on more of nothings. More leadership. Leadership honed on more of the fear of the other. So more fear. Keep it there as a goad.

"The economic ideas driving commerce in the societies before the Upheavals have never gone away completely, for within limits they are effective. But they cannot produce an equitable society. They rely on people being feared they might become the ones at the bottom. There will always be a bottom. But being there should not mean being in an awful place. People should still be able to live and enjoy humane existence. So we watch and monitor. Keep those with a rapacious bent under observation.

"We try to ensure our education system gives people the power of discernment. Keeps them aware of the dangers of being sucked in." He changes tone. "It is not often stated, though it is acknowledged, what we do with our education system is exactly what all these others do whom we oppose. The difference is the ideals in the Ethical Code. We use the same tools as other controllers, but we do it from a position of altruism so people are empowered to have a meaningful say in how their lives are lived. Not for our own selfish gain at another's expense."

The Castellan seems to finish, but then continues rather angrily.

"It is a crying shame that at the moment of winning one battle in many on this front, Faerachar Strachan has paid a personal price. I am letting my personal view surface. I hope you accept I am distressed by his situation. I trust your discretion."

He looks at Ardel.

"Ambassador Penaul, I am aware of what you have heard from Briged. Of your relationship to her and her offspring. I hope she has happiness coming her way from this discovery. I also hope what transpired here at the beginning of your time with us can be left behind you, and not taint your memories of us and Faerachar. He is at heart a decent man. All of us have feet with some clay."

He holds out his hand to Ardel, who grasps it.

"Thank you, Castellan, for those kind words. Once I got over the shock of my greeting, I began to warm to Faerachar somewhat. Knowing he is my cousin will allow me a way through to seeing him in a better light. I too am saddened by his current situation."

"Are there any further questions either of you want answering about our thinking on this communication shield?"

"No, Castellan. I think we understand enough for now," Grandy says. "If we have queries later on, even after we have left for Genève, I trust we shall be able to ask."

"That is certain to be the case, Ambassador Emembet. Now, Communicator, let's see this experiment of yours."

July, 14th — First House

When Faerachar fails to show in the kitchen, Briged sets off up the house. He is in the attic scribbling in the thin ledger. He doesn't stop writing.

"Hello, Briged Are you alright?"

"Yes. Do you want something to eat and drink?"

"A drink and some biscuits would be nice. Camellia tea, rather than coffee, please." He puts the pen down, gets up and quickly hugs her.

"I've got to finish this. I got up about two and back to bed about five. It's just short references. And I've had a message from my GP. I'm to be assessed over a six week period. She will come up tomorrow afternoon to see me."

"I'll get the tea. Short references are good."

When she returns he is still scribbling. She puts the mug and a bowl of biscuits on the desk. He puts the pen down and hands her his phone. It is showing the message from the doctor. Sitting, she reads through it twice. He dunks a biscuit in the tea and bites off the soggy part.

"You will be visited by this counsellor every third day over the next twelve days."

"Yes." Another dunk. He swigs from the mug. "That's a lot, isn't it, Mum?"

"I don't know." She puts his phone back on the desk. Sips her drink. Faerachar noisily finishes his tea and takes a third biscuit.

"I have put down twenty-five things I should not have done over the past six periods. I am putting some of my reasons why I did things. Eleven of them I know. The others, mostly more recent, I have no idea why I did them. Do you want to look at them now?"

"No. I will look at it when you have put in all reasons you can think of, Faerachar. When do you think that will be?"

"By lunch or a little later."

"Then we shall go through it together this afternoon."

"I need to know what my position is with the Ethical Code, so I may face Siobhagn this evening."

"You said they would be staying the night here, didn't you?"

"Yes, she still means to come."

"Faerachar, you can hold your head high with her. She loves you, or she would not have had two children with you. When speaking to Siobhagn do not cage yourself in with the actions you have taken recently, talk of yourselves and love. She will talk with me tomorrow."

"I can think only of me being held tightly in her arms tonight." Tears start, heaving sobs. As he calms she rubs his shoulders.

"I'll leave you to get on, Faerachar. I shall bring food over at one."

❖

July, 14th — Third House

Kaet laughs loudly when Dahqin says he's come to help her with breakfast. She puts some bread to toast and points out the various options for him to have with it.

"I'm not making anything for breakfast, Dahqin. Never do. Making the second hot drink of their day — that's me done. Peran always makes the first. They get food themselves. And go off shopping. Sometimes I do dinner, but they have done far more than me. So you don't have to help me at all. Thanks for the offer though. I've had a bit of a holiday on that score, which has been nice. These three are practically domesticated. And tidy. Peran, very. Kirus is a bit more ... well, he will tidy up and make a good job of it too. But Kirus gets easily distracted, I've noticed."

She looks him up and down.

"Bet he's been very distracted up there this morning."

She gives a low chuckle. "Dahqin, you're embarrassed. Oh, that's lovely."

"Well, I'll not break any habits Peran must have taught them. I'll just take this last slice of toast you've made and remove the evidence of your largesse. Will you be glad to get peace back with them gone? Especially with your pregnancy."

"No, if I'm deep down truthful. These are large houses. We don't make them live properly as they should. You and those three have brought a joyousness to them. I'll miss that a lot. Especially as ... you know." She puts a hand on his arm.

"I'm sorry it was through my thoughtless gabbling that you found out about Duncn and Ardel. I did wonder when you came into the kitchen, but there wasn't a hint of it on your face. It must have hurt."

"Yes, it did, very much, because he had lied to me. But it would have been much worse if the first inkling of them had been what I saw on Kirus's phone. At least I was half prepared. That was a traumatic day for my love of Ardel. Thank goodness Alun and Kirus were here."

"Let's get back to today's practicalities. I'm taking Alun to the Blondyn with their stuff. Does he always spend so much time on his own?"

"More than I remember, but he's always been quieter than Kirus. He doesn't like goodbyes, either. Kaet, when I was with Duncn this morning I noticed some drawings he has on his wall — of him and Regin. One's very erotic. I've invited Regin up here to say goodbye. Will it be alright to get him to explain them to me? I'm being nosy for all the right reasons."

"And all the naughty ones, too. Are you to blame for Duncn leaving ninety minutes before he usually does? His horse crossing the bridge is my alarm."

"Sorry. I sent him to see Ardel."

"Setting the opportunities, Dahqin? I see Regin a lot, he's told me enough about Peran for me to read between the lines. Those drawings are by me, I did wonder if Duncn would hang them. Make sure Regin tells you about the third one he has. I should sign them, they are my most dynamic works. Briged will be happy to see him in Second House heading for their bedroom, though you might be a surprise. It's nice you are looking out for them all — close to romance for you young males. But please, don't take Kirus over there, spend your time with him upstairs. Those two can cuddle up in the bedroom behind here, next to my studio. Regin uses it when Perdie has Sam to stay over."

"Do you know what's in my mind?"

"No. It's clear on your face, Dahqin, and in his yearning when Kirus mentions you. Your guard is down, sweet man. I'm trying to be helpful. And now I can feel the heat from your face." She touches his cheeks.

"I won't be back till close to one. I need to get some bits and pieces for this meal David has asked me to prepare. He says he promised he'd cook for Ardel, so I'm covering for him already." She laughs. "Do you know about this?"

"Sort of."

"Well, it's all of us. Including Siobhagn and the kids. It'll be special. I hope Faerachar is up to it. Grandy is coming. David confirmed with me just before you came down. He'll bring them over to the landing by boat. You're being trusted to take it back to The Keep. Think you can cope with that."

"With my eyes closed."

Six feet thud down the stairs.

"Finally. Get to work. Dahqin's starving. There'll be coffee in a jiff, and tea, Peran."

Kirus is sitting on the end of the bridge parapet, arms round Peran. They are watching Dahqin leaning against the truck, talking to Alun. Earlier than he said, Regin arrives as Kaet is walking over the bridge. He has a large canvas slipcase slung across his back. She pecks at his cheek.

"Regin. So, you've brought it."

"I'm leaving it here with him, Kaet."

"At last. You're just in time to say goodbye to Alun. I'm off to Haven, back about quarter to one. Look at Peran's sweet, flushed face. Use the time well, darlings."

She gets in and Alun closes his door; they watch it until the rattle of the cattle grid.

Peran slowly smiles as Regin approaches them.

"Regin, you are the stranger with excellent good taste," Kirus says, then laughs, and pushes Peran forward. "My punishment ends."

He moves towards Dahqin, who heads inside.

"Wait, Kirus. It's not too early for a beer. I'll bring them over to the seat by the beck."

Returning with the beers he sits on the ground leaning against Kirus. In the middle on the bench, Peran's eyes are bright, a sheepish grin fixed on his face — one hand on Kirus's leg, the other on Regin's.

"We sit at the bench of the formulation yet to be devised, to make a proposal for the future. Right, Peran?"

He opens the beers and hands them out.

"The other two have had to go to work after their fond farewell, and Alun is happily heading to Haven. Nonetheless, I propose a toast to our Bagad, and formally ask Regin to join us. Peran, you must be his seconder." They chink bottles.

After a couple of mouthfuls of beer, Dahqin nudges Kirus. A few minutes later, all is quiet outside Third House.

July, 14th — Second House — Dahqin

Regin has knocked gently on the front door and gone into the kitchen where Briged is making lunch. I stand by the doorway as he gives her a hug.

"I want you home, Regin. The time is right, now the others are leaving, and you and Perdie have worked out a path for the children. They are welcome here whenever you want them with you. Duncn and I have had the talk about how he must not usurp you or Perdie. He promises he will learn the patience of a parent. I shall help you both all I can."

She stands back from him — sees me.

"Ah! Dahqin. You are our witness. You see me emotional again. Are you four in harmony? Don't look puzzled Regin, I mean the four of you here, now."

"Without Peran, Briged, I would still be too timid. We have left them cuddled together after our trysts."

He puts his hand out to me, and I give him the canvas slipcase.

"Dahqin has asked me to explain the context of Kaet's sketches of us. I'm leaving mine in his room. Can we go up?"

"Go. It is your room too. And shut the door between my end and this, please. I shall be using the small stairs at my end from today. I am going to see Faerachar in First House right now, and I will see both of you this evening. Duncn has invited you Regin?"

"Yes, Briged. I'm here for the rest of the day."

We're comfortable on Duncn's bed. Regin's leaning against me, or it might be the other way round. He has explained the drawing of them as teenagers, giving me a flavour of how things were. It is me and the twins

432

all over again. Now we are looking at the one he has brought. He's taken down the third of the series, that was hanging opposite the foot of the bed, and put this one in its place. They are looking at each other with eagerness, part undressed. It is sensuous with possibility.

"I had just got back from twelve weeks of Civic Service — away from him. I was two days off eighteen. I was so eager for him. We had nine days of absolute joyful frenzy, then away he went for his twelve weeks. I got withdrawn, this picture the only thing keeping me happy. Well, and Perdie. I hadn't told him what we'd got up to. Perdie is a couple of weeks younger than me. She was at school with us, and when she turned up in the training centre we carried on our conversations about wanting kids. She was two months pregnant when she arrived home, two days before she was eighteen."

He lifts the third drawing, propping it up on the chest of drawers below his. I can feel the motion of their bodies — it is alive, waking my libido.

"By the time he came home we were both mad with frustrated lust. Kaet was in here for only a few minutes. We certainly didn't stick to what we had agreed with her. A few weeks later when I told him I was to be a father he went berserk and spurned me. Kaet saved these. She gave these two back to him only a period ago. I look at this one and it makes me horny as hell, and he tells me, him too. I want to be with him so much."

He's breathing deeply, his nose by my shoulder. Our eyes meet.

"We need to head back to Kaet's."

He is away from the bed so quickly I catch up with him in the hallway of Third House. He's skittish, and I ask if he is okay.

"Dahqin, I smelled your scent on the first evening that Ardel was in Coleridge. He'd asked me to wait while he got ready and I thought it was him. He briefly held a vest to his nose, dropped his towel and got dressed in front of me. I couldn't take my eyes off him." He closes his eyes.

"Eight and a bit years of celibacy waiting for me and Duncn to find a way back together. Then on the night before you arrived, Peran crawls into my arms wearing that vest."

His eyes open and lock onto mine.

"Soon Duncn and I will be back together, in that bed. But right now ... your scent drives me crazy. I want so much to kiss you."

July, 14th — At Haven

The Blondyn is moored stern-to on the South Quay, and ready for leaving. The Harbour Master trusts them to be safe in the channel, and when they come back, she told them, they can just arrive and a berth will always be found. They are standing in the cockpit, under the canopy with the screens opened. Their small beers have been drunk in a farewell toast. Kaet puts out her arms and is embraced by the twins and Peran. As they stand back she pulls out an Earth Mother.

"This is from Briged. Peran, you are the best custodian, I think. Look after her well." She places the box in his hands.

"Thank her for us, Kaet. I'll put her safely away now. The Tents will be her real home." He grabs Regin's hand, and they disappear into the main cabin.

"And what of you, Dahqin?"

"I'll come to Douarnenez between contracts, Alun. Probably at short notice. Staying with you at the Tents. Ardel won't come very often."

"The ebb starts soon. Time for you three to go ashore. Put Peran down, Regin — we need him as ballast," Kirus calls.

There's a flurry of hugging and farewells.

"You keep them happy, Peran. Call whenever."

"You'll hear from us, don't worry. Love you, Dahqin."

The foresail is let out part-way, the ropes let go, the Blondyn moving away, turning towards the haven entrance. More sail let out, the speed picking up. Outside the sea is calm, a gentle swell, a moderate breeze. As the Blondyn goes through the entrance the mainsails are hauled out, and the boat heels slightly. Dahqin leads them onto the top of the barrier wall of the inner breakwater; the three of them waving to the three on the boat. At the fairway buoy Blondyn turns to the southwest. Dahqin lets out a big sigh. He puts his arms round Kaet and Regin.

"Ooh. It feels very, very quiet."

"Let's get back home, and the pair of you can relieve me of David's task by getting ready tonight's farewell meal. I shall put my feet up."

July, 14th — First House & Second House

Having eaten lunch together, Faerachar and Briged go up to the study. He hands her the thin ledger, lies on the daybed and puffs out breath, watching her.

"I'll await you asking questions, Briged."

She nods and starts reading. When she finishes, she closes her eyes and sets the chair into a reclined position, her feet up on the stool. Faerachar looks across at her, knows better than to say anything. He closes his eyes and eventually goes to sleep. When he starts a gentle snoring, Briged opens her eyes. She gets out her own notebook, reopens the thin ledger and starts reading from the beginning again, occasionally making notes. When she gets to the end of his list she shuts the ledger and puts her notebook back in her pocket. Then she closes her eyes and thinks long and hard about what she has seen.

Some things in his list are of no importance. Some are definitely unethical. One, maybe two, possibly criminal. All of them are related in some way to the conspiracy he and Charlie have uncovered. Some are only from the date of him reading the League files. The hardest knot is what had happened to Jarnie Paresh. It was unethical, and is likely criminal. But he cites a Law of Defence Actions. She needs to know if this law still has force. And if so, why it has. In which case it is not for her to pronounce on. That is a matter of law, not the vaguer scope of the Ethical Code. She sets the chair upright, standing noisily. Faerachar struggles awake.

"I need to go and check some things, Faerachar. I shall be back shortly."
"Mmm. Okay." He turns over, facing away from her, goes back to sleep.

In her own workroom in Second House she searches out the List of Enabled Laws he has cited. It is as he reasoned, and it is still in force. Buried away in an archaic body of laws about defence, written in the times when the Fastness was insecure after the Upheavals. It gives draconian powers to the Reever to order actions to be taken in defence of Alban. Gives him powers to order secrecy of those actions; riding roughshod over the Ethical Code, having not been brought into its ambit. This is beyond her remit.

She goes back to First House. She makes a large pot of lavender and verbena tea, adding a little honey. As she enters the study he is still asleep. Pondering her next steps she sips her tea.

She will tell him which of his actions are clearly unethical. She will tell him to pass all he has written as his Official Confession to the Clerk of the Court of Counsels. Her soundings too will be sent. The laws will then be followed. He will be assigned a Counsel to aid him in the presentation of his case.

He is a decent man with years of honourable service in the running of the Fastness, and that will be weighed in the balance. Had his actions been made for personal gain? Almost certainly not.

Only when he is in a stable condition can he face the Court of Counsels for the Official Confession. A Redemption Hearing with the joint Governing Council and Parlement will have to await the various decisions from the Court of Counsels.

Having done the Sounding ... She will hug him to her. She is his mother and still loves him. She knows he will calmly accept the findings, whatever they turn out to be, she will say.

She pours a mug of the tea for him.

"Faerachar, wake up," she says gently. "I am ready to give you the Sounding. Then it will be time for you to make ready to receive your family."

Noisily the youngsters bound through the house seeking Faerachar with shouts of "Daddy!"

Briged quickly tells Siobhagn of her findings.

"He has listened well, and appears to have taken it on the chin. But that might not last, Siobhagn. He is still teary."

They agree to meet in Second House the next day, and talk of his recovery plan, and what he might do afterwards.

"Briged, I shall try to talk him into coming to this farewell dinner for Ardel tonight. And I am going to tell him now — nothing we have agreed on already will change. I love him, as you know. At dinner I shall announce our acknowledgement."

She touches Briged's arm.

"I am also thinking — the Township could do with a rest from me. If tonight goes well and he is up to it, we three shall be living up here. We will make it happen over the next few days. The children are old enough to cope with the distance. Their friends will always be coming up and made welcome, bringing young life here. Importantly they can be with Faerachar every night. Which was the lack here I always feared. Between us three — you, me, Kaet — we will get him back to a good place."

"We shall succeed. I welcome your plan. Grandchildren up here will be a joy. I know Kaet and me together can be a bit intimidating."

"Not so much for me as you think, Briged. Talking of Kaet. Has she said anything about David to you?"

"No, Siobhagn. Why?"

"Ah! I just thought ... But I see you working it out."

July, 15th — Heading back to The Keep

Time has tripped over midnight as the launch leaves the landing. No one to wave farewell. The moon is up above the fells beyond the township, its light making the trip easy. Dahqin is happy to be afloat. He powers the boat to full speed.

"That was such a lovely evening. I shall miss all of them to varying degrees. I like Siobhagn a lot. She's a good match for the Faerachar we first met. Briged ended the evening very happy. What did you make of them all together, Grandy? Will my new-found family be good for me?"

"I think they will. They are a good group, Ardel. It's no wonder Briged is happy, with two acknowledgements to be conducted soon."

"It was a nice thought for Kaet to invite Regin. Him and Duncn are such good friends."

Dahqin's eyes roll. They sail on in silence. As they walk from the boathouse Grandy hands Dahqin an Earth Mother.

"This one is definitely yours, Dahqin. Keep her safe. I hope you weren't trying to leave her behind. Briged would never forgive you."

July, 15th — Derwent to Genève, Confederation Helvetica

Grandy, Ardel and Dahqin are seen off at the glider field below Skiddaw, by the Reever, the Castellan and Briged. They pass low over The Keep, Derwentwater and The Three Houses. Kaet, Siobhagn and Faerachar stand by the paddock, waving. The airship climbs steadily to its cruising height, setting a course towards Genève.

One of the pleasures of travelling by League airship is the space to walk around. Another the quality of the food. A third the sleeping bunks. After a pleasant lunch, taken as they pass over London, Ardel and Dahqin squish into a bunk and sleep contentedly. Grandy remains awake throughout the flight.

On arrival in Genève the two men are bright as buttons, and eager to get home. As she is about to go off with Kazzia, Grandy reminds Ardel she will see him at the usual time in the morning.

"We are due in Sion on Thursday to see Bartouche for two full days of intense debriefing. I'll discuss it with you tomorrow. Success!"

Dahqin heaves a big sigh. It was a good adventure, and it is nice to be home. But, where shall he put the Earth Mother?

Book Nine

Some Loose Ends
They sympathise, but that is what to expect

The Shadow (Marc Lafayette)

June, 29th — Douarnenez

The sea is calm when Bran anchors his boat in the shallows close in to the small sandy beach of the middle of the three blind bays on Kab y Gavr. He goes below and removes the snap cords holding the Shadow tight against the hull.

"You do exactly as I say, and you'll get to dry land. You struggle or play up and I'll dump you in deep water. I'm going to take you up on deck and get you ready to put ashore. Go with what I do, or you'll hurt yourself."

Working fast, Bran undoes the bonds around the Shadow's legs and those holding his arms bound to his torso. He massages the legs and arms while the Shadow moans at the pain of returning circulation. He is moving tape away, fixing thin rope in place. The Shadow cannot tell what he is doing, but accepts being tugged this way and that.

"I'm keeping the covers on your mouth and eyes. The last thing I'll let go is the strapping I've just put round your wrists. If you fall over I'll pull you upright. When I leave you, you'll have to work out how to take them all off. They all will come off. I'm going to put you into the water. It's not too cold. It'll come up to your chest. You'll be facing the beach. Go in the direction you're facing or you'll cut yourself on the sharp rocks. It's a short distance. The bottom's all sand. Outside the rocks the tides are very strong from now until late afternoon. You could try it. But it's straight out to the Atlantic from here."

He lifts the Shadow. Takes a couple of steps. Puts him down.

"The Guard'll find you later. There's no safe way out of here except by their boat. Have you understood all I say?"

The Shadow nods. He feels something being attached to him, then he is being winched up from the deck and swung out.

"You're lucky it's not just me involved, or you'd be out there now. Go back to the Cantons."

He catches his breath with a muffled yell as the water rises up his legs. He is twisted round, his buttocks bumping against the hull.

"You are facing the right way. There's very sharp rocks sitting both sides of this gully. Remember that. When your balls are out of the water you'll be on the beach behind them."

His feet touch the smooth bottom. There is a ripple in the water, and his chin sometimes goes under.

"Go forward a few steps, and I'll get this rope off you."

As he moves forward he feels the steep rise of the bottom — and then the rope is gone. He is alone. He hears several loud noises behind him, but concentrates on heading in a straight line. There's a surge of water pushing at him as the boat heads away. His belly comes clear of the water. Then balls. He carries on walking until his feet are barely covered, so he knows which way he is facing.

He spends many frustrating minutes freeing his hands, then his eyes, then mouth. Squinting in the bright light he gulps in huge breaths of air. As he takes the last of the tape off he finds a thin line attached round his waist. Floating in the sea a couple of metres out is a large bottle of water. He pulls it to him, and takes a deep draught.

The beach is enclosed almost completely by jagged rocks. He can only see open water directly in front of the gap through which he had walked. By the time he climbs over rocks to the small part of the cove above the high tide line there is no single boat nearby. Only a cluster of them, looking identical. Gulls are circling noisily over them. The cliffs look sheer and he is no climber. There is one spot affording some shade at the southern end of the cliffs. He heads there and lays down on a small patch of sand, making himself comfortable.

He hopes his assailant is right and the Guard will pick him up. He goes through his pockets. No persID, no Warrant, no touchpad. His wallet is otherwise intact, though wet. He can get his phone from the boarding house. Maybe get Yves to work something out. He had allowed Yves to persuade him into this by flattery and a useful sum of money. But he needs a story for the Guard. One to get him home to the Cantons without any IDs.

He watches the tide ebb away. Sees the rips and eddies in the water. Sees banks of sharp-edged rocks emerge and then be covered by the rising tide. High tide comes, the water getting uncomfortably close to his little patch of sand, and goes; the gap in the rocks slowly uncovers again. He dozes from time to time, and is asleep when the Guard cutter arrives off the cove. Its siren blast wakes him, has him jumping to his feet. They send in a boat. Back on board he's taken to the wheelhouse.

"That's a nasty cut and bruise on your head. And how did you get these abrasions at your wrists and up by your ears?"

"I got them coming in through the rocks."

"Looks clean. Salt water helps."

"Let's see your ID." The Guard officer standing by the wheel holds out his hand.

"It's in my bag. Where I went swimming. Back that way."

He points northward along the shore. He had seen the beaches when travelling on the ferry from Brest. They had seemed isolated. He hopes they are.

What had happened that he was caught in the cove?

And so his story begins.

"I was walking out along the coast towards the point, and thought it would be alright to go swimming." They listen politely, looking at the clothes he has on.

"But once out in the water, I realised the current was too strong for me to get back to the beach. So I tried to crab in to the shore, and I ended up getting into the cove. My bag might still be on that beach."

"The beaches look alright, but they aren't safe — as you've found out. You were lucky with it being a calm day and reaching that cove at the right time of the tide. Twenty minutes either way and you'd not have got

442

near because the eddies throw things away from the coast. You often go swimming with all your clothes on?"

"I was wearing a hell of a hangover too. It was supposed to be a quick dip."

The Guard cutter cruises north towards the nearest beaches.

"Tell us if you think you recognise anything."

He remembers a couple of places rather uncertainly. Eventually the cutter is loitering off the last beach before the coves.

"You think it was this one, right? About fifty metres this way from where the rocks start?" He nods. The two Guards scan the beach with binos.

"How far up the beach was your bag?"

"Quite close to the water."

"It'll have washed away then. Where have you been staying?"

"Douarnenez. In a boarding house. I know where it is but can't say the name. The rest of my stuff is there. Oh, wait..."

He pulls out his damp wallet and hands over a damp card with the name and address on. The officer takes the wallet and looks through it — hands it back.

"You should keep your ID in your wallet when you get a new one. We'll get you showered and into clean shorts and top. You need to rinse the dried salt out of what you're wearing. We'll clean the wounds too."

The two speak in Brezonheg, then the officer phones their base. There is a long conversation of which he understands only four words. Marc Lafayette, Swizzh and ID. The officer looks over at him from time to time, the other one still scanning the beach.

"We are taking you back to Douarnenez. You will be taken to our base. They will take you to the boarding house on the way."

Things get tricky at the boarding house. She tells the Guard there is nothing of his in the house.

"But my bag has to be in the house."

She goes into a rant in Brezonheg with lots of gesticulating at him. The Guards placate the woman and usher him out — back to their vehicle.

"We know her well, she's respected round here. So we believe her story. She says you sent your girlfriend to pick up your stuff. A young woman, very pleasant, came to the house, gave back the keys to your room and said you were leaving early. She said she was told not to worry about the extra couple of days' rent you'd already paid. She took her up to the room and watched her pack up your bag with your clothes and she definitely put your phone in. She did say the young woman hadn't answered any of her questions. Like you, she's an outsider, but spoke a few words of Brezonheg." They are both looking at him expectantly.

"Oh shit!" He does not manage to hide his utter surprise at this news. It is the one feeling he can display on his face with truth behind it. He simply adds more fiction to what he has already told.

The reason he was walking along the beach was because he and she had fallen out badly the night before. They had rowed over something stupid, and what with a few drinks between them had separated. In fact they'd only met one another on his first day in Brittany, after he'd left the ferry from Brest. They'd been in that place where the ferry called, where she was staying on a campsite, near one of its southern beaches. He marched off in the early hours, slept on a small beach south of there and carried on along the coast in the morning. He must have dropped the keys when he was in her tent. Her contact details are on his phone, which she's now got.

June, 29th to July, 2nd – Douarnenez, Guard Base.

Because he has no identification documents they inform him he will be held in custody until the Helvetican authorities agree he is who he says he is and issue emergency, time-limited ID documents. Once that happens, usually two days maximum, he will be released but sent directly back to the Cantons. The two days pass without news.

He has been interviewed three times and his story is perfected. He is vague about place names, because he says she knew them all and he hadn't bothered to remember any of them. He is vague about her appearance, but she was young and fit.

He can't remember the colour of her eyes or her hair colour.

"I mean, come on. Who does?"

She had a few wigs, and was always changing them. She liked pretending to be different characters, which he'd found endearing. Until the row she had been very funny.

At the end of the third day he is told the next day he will be handed over directly to officials of the Ambassadors' League, and escorted back to Genève. That is not good news for him. Can they tell him why?

They've never had a *Swizzh* in custody before. Maybe it is what usually happens. Is he comfortable and being well looked after? He says he is, but not happy to be in a cell, however comfortable. They sympathise, but that is what to expect if you go off with the first woman you run into and lose control of your dick and your ID.

July, 3rd — Douarnenez to Genève, Confederation Helvetica

He is taken by the Guard to Brest and handed over to League Runners at the railway station. By the end of the day he is in an Annex of the Council House in Genève, in the custody of the Security Section of the League.

He is of the League, one of them, and has committed serious breaches of protocol amounting to gross misconduct. Once they have ascertained exactly what he has done, he might be handed over to the Federal police, but they have the power to prosecute directly. All this is explained to him. He is arrested under League powers. They expect him to co-operate.

He is unsure what to do. If Yves and his associates are loose, then he might be in grave danger. But his questioners don't seem to have much to go on, from what they have asked so far. He clings to the story he has been given by Yves in writing. He has been carrying out a trial operation for an inspection tour Yves Penaul plans to undertake. He had got into difficulties while swimming from a beach he didn't know was unsafe. He is treated well, but remains in custody.

July, 4th & 5th — Genève, Confederation Helvetica

On the 4th, when faced with the transcripts from his touchpad and phone, and photos of his persID and Warrant Card sitting on official headed paper from the Fastness of Alban, he knows he is caught out. The transcripts undo his and Yves Penaul's defence. He is told the items will be arriving in Genève from Alban on the next day so they can listen to the actual recordings. He is assured Yves Penaul will be under arrest within a short period and will not be able to lift a finger to help him. Only co-operation will mitigate what comes next.

Marc Lafayette starts being honest, and he proves a reliable witness. With his phone and touchpad to hand it is obvious, despite all the sophistication within the League's communications systems, Yves Penaul had been tripped up by one of his own specialists when giving his instructions.

The attack on Alun Goffic happened because his instructions included the words, *Do whatever it takes to get answers as to why Grandy Emembet has suddenly gone on vacation.*

Repeated in writing was a similar form of words on his touchpad. With her and Dahqin out of reach on board the Blondyn, he had become desperate.

Bedow had been right, he intended to take the prone Alun back to the Tents and find out where she had gone. One way or another. Whatever it took.

Some Loose Ends

I'll be away for a few days

SJ Letrap (Svenjon Letrap)

July, 15th — London

It is mid-morning, and SJ is surveying the scene outside his window, watching the 'Ants'. His secretary tells him some gentlemen from the Justice Office wish to speak to him privately. SJ admits into his office two men, the first shows an emblazoned Warrant badge. They are financial policemen.

"Are you Svenjon Letrap, proprietor of the trading house registered as SJ Factors PTH?" the first policeman reads from a faxplex. The second policeman stares impassively at SJ.

"I am. What can I do for you?" His tone is neutral as he looks from one to the other.

"Svenjon Letrap, proprietor of the trading house registered as SJ Factors PTH. In the name of the citizens of the Civitas of The United Counties of England; in the name of the Confederation of Europa; under the auspices of the Rules as laid down in the Covenant of Confederation; and, on information supplied by the League of Ambassadors, I must ask you to allow us to escort you from these premises to a place properly instituted by the laws of this Civitas for the purpose of interviewing those accused of breaching the laws of this Civitas by conspiring to transgress the Rules of Confederation. You have been so accused of conspiracy to transgress.

"I must warn you that this charge is being, and anything you say from this moment on will be, recorded and will constitute part or all of your answer to these charges. Do you understand?"

SJ nods.

"The accused has nodded. You have a right to appoint a representative to plead in your case. You are informed that you may not contact this

447

person directly at this time. He will be contacted by the Justice Office, must attend you within the next six hours, and also inform your family of your whereabouts.

"Should you not allow us to escort you in a peaceful and dignified manner we have the right to detain you by other means."

He looks up from the faxplex.

"You read through this and sign it at the bottom, Sir."

He places the sheet in front of SJ and the pair watch him read through it. Shaking his head, SJ signs the document. He calls his secretary.

"I'm going out through my private entrance with these two gentlemen. I'll be away for a few days. Get hold of my brother and tell him to activate the succession plan." Then he stands up and moves around the desk.

"What now?"

The silent policeman gestures for SJ to go in front.

The other says, "After you, Sir."

The doors lock automatically behind them.

Book X

Telling Maman

Goodness, there is an opera to be written

Aoife and Robert Penaul, Ardel's parents

August, 11th, 2188 — Domaine et Cave Penaul, Villeneuve, Vaud, Confederation Helvetica

It is during the dog days that, with Dahqin, Ardel sets off to see his parents to tell his mother of her half-sibling, in a manner that will not lead to rejection. In truth, he doesn't worry about the relatives in Éire, so long as his mother will greet and adopt Briged, it shall be enough family for him. They travel by train to Montreux, then as usual, by lake steamer to Villeneuve. From the pier it is a pleasant shaded walk up into the vineyards where his parents live.

The visit goes as it normally does. Both his parents being glad to see them; openly friendly and at ease with Dahqin. It had not been a cold home to grow up in, but the affection shown him had seemed sparing, he sometimes still feels.

Pleasantries out of the way, they go to the kitchen and help get lunch ready, while drinking spritzers and talking of things they had seen and done in Alban. Lunch is taken in the dining room, with views out to the west and north across the lake, the window screens open wide, allowing a gentle breeze to moderate the heat. When they have had enough of the cheeses, *salbeimüsli* and *salateller*, they go and sit outside.

"We know about Yves being under arrest," his father says.

"He was always a bitter person, caring only for money. The person who suffered most from his nastiness was your Uncle Renaud. The patrimony was divided evenly between us three. He insisted we bought his share. At the time it was difficult financially. Especially for Renaud as the youngest.

Now I am glad we did. Let's leave him there, Ardel. Tell me how your promotion from Noviate to Ambassador changes your life. Or is it too early to tell?"

"Too early, Papa. I hope things will calm down after the Confederation has got all the trials out of the way. It seems there will never be a means to truly limit private wealth. But I have had my proposal, for visiting the Fastnesses to gather information directly, accepted. Grandy will still be my Patron while I do this work, which I'm glad about. Realistically it is a three-year programme."

"And you, Dahqin — or is it Franz? How are you living up to being a hero?"

"How did you hear of the unspoken bit of my name Robert? It's Dahqin and nothing else with my friends, never, never, never, Franz. Except to my Mam and Papa. And how did you hear of my hero status? I thought that letter was a private matter from my great-aunt. And only two people have called me Hero recently. I know who gave away my childhood fantasy — and how he's going to suffer. But so long as I never have to be a Hero again, I shall live with it very well."

"Matilde — Bartouche as she styles herself — let it out of the bag. You can't hide from us any longer. Small overlapping circles we live in. We've known her for years through the cultural bodies we patronise in Lausanne and Montreux. She dropped your name and exploits into the conversation a couple of weeks ago. We didn't know she was Ardel's maitre until he was promoted."

"Dahqin, this promotion of Ardel's means you can now travel with him as his consort. I hadn't realised he was keeping the possibility from you."

"I didn't want to put ideas in his head in case I had failed to gain my promotion, Maman."

"I shall make sure the option is kept firmly in his mind, Aoife. I'm inclined to believe his excuse for not telling me — for now."

Inclining his head slightly towards her, Dahqin grins at Ardel, who does not pick up the signal, or ignores it.

"We had such a brilliant time in Alban, Aoife. Shall I tell of the Reever and his family, Ardel?"

Ardel nods, looking relieved.

"They are such kind people. Especially his mother, Briged. They took us both, and my friends from Brittany, into their hearts. We'll be keeping in touch with them from now on, won't we, Ardel. In fact, I have a concert, maybe two, lined up for the autumn in Scotia."

"For sure we'll keep in touch. You've kept the fact of concerts there very quiet."

"I saved it for today. You've been busy and needed to concentrate on your work." Dahqin gets up. "You tell them about Briged and her family. I just need to ..." and he heads into the house.

Buying time, Ardel says, "The time in Alban has been like a tonic for him, he's been writing new songs."

"Tell us about the family he mentioned," his mother says. "Dahqin has lead you to the opening with his good linking skills."

"Well," Ardel takes a deep breath. "Dahqin is a much better storyteller than me, but I shall make a stab at it. I made a complete hash of things when I first got there. The meetings with the Reever, were not what I had expected. He is called Faerachar and has two half-siblings — Kaet and Duncn. I felt at home quite soon with Briged and those two, but with Faerachar it took me much longer. Briged is the most amazing woman I have met through my work."

"Three half-sibling children?" Aoife says. "Goodness, there is an opera to be written."

"I suppose — but that's not important." Ardel says it rather sharply.

"You mentioned them as such, so maybe it is, and are pretending it is not." Robert reasons. "Let's get past this bit. Tell us what this amazing woman and her family are like to be with."

"Warm, funny, passionate, honest, open, and very occasionally, annoying."

"You describe me so well," Dahqin quips as he comes back, making Robert laugh. He ruffles Ardel's hair.

"This isn't about you, and you know it."

"But it is perfect timing."

"They are very easy to be with most of the time. Though because of how Faerachar treated me it took time for me to trust him."

"Kaet is lovely though, isn't she, Ardel."

"Yes, and really caring. She's a very good artist, Maman. It's how she makes a living. And Duncn is a horticulturist, Papa. He has been pushing the cultivation of vines, and they have produced some very nice wines from them. They use the same grapes as you for the whites, and Dornfelder for a fine red. He's very passionate about it."

"You must get some details about the conditions, Ardel."

"I'll ask him to send me some." He changes tone. "The point I really want to get to concerns something that's been bothering me lately. Why did I never meet Grandfather, Maman?"

Aoife's face pales and she turns to Robert.

"Now is the time to tell our son about your father, Aoife."

She puts her hands up in front of her mouth, as if praying, and breathes out through them.

"I need to ask you a question, Ardel. You have swerved from talking of this woman Briged, to asking about my father. Tell me what the link is. Then perhaps we can open the can of worms that I keep."

"But a can of worms sounds bad, Maman."

"It is the right time for this, Ardel," his father says.

"If this Briged is linked to my father I will not be upset in the way you think — I am guessing wildly ... Wait, Ardel, let me finish. I shall tell you what I know. Then, if I am right, you tell me of Briged, as you know her — as she is now."

"You know something different from what I know about Briged."

"If it is the right track. You never met him, because he had no access to this family. I was sent here to finish my education, supposedly to polish my hauteur to perfection. I know I have not been as affectionate to you as you might have wanted, because of the can of worms.

"Luckily, here I met Robert. Away from the family scrutiny, and love

452

blossomed. We have tried to bring you up to be free enough to think for yourself. Parents should not overburden their children with their musts and must-nots. Having limits is necessary, or children will go somewhat wild, but crushing them under strictures is not good for them. Especially strictures coming from a pit of nastiness.

"I never allowed my father access to me after we were wed. In fact, because I was old enough, we wed without his knowledge, for I would not have sought his approval. And none of my family attended as I did not tell them. I should have told you this years ago, maybe. On one level I am glad I did not. You went to Éire to meet the siblings I know without any knowledge of him. They are the product of his iron-rod rule." She reaches across to Ardel, taking his hand.

"Ardel, he was a monster to be brought up by. My mother was cowed completely. My siblings moulded and misshapen by him. They are grouped closely in age and I am so much younger than they. From a young age I watched what happened if he was not obeyed. So I obeyed, but inside me was someone else, carefully hidden from everyone, even my mother. I hated the outer me, but kept my sanity by knowing she was but a suit of clothes to be discarded as soon as possible."

She looks at Dahqin.

"I hope this is not too horrible for you, Dahqin. But I'm glad to know you love each other and so are both my sons."

"Aoife, I need to know this story too."

Robert gets up, bends down to kiss Aoife.

"I shall make some more spritzers. I'll be back before you boys tell your story of Briged."

"Thank you, Robert. Please bring the cachou tin." She waits till he is inside the house before continuing.

"Ardel, Dahqin, I may get tearful, but I'm sure you will allow me that. I remember vividly; Ciaran, my eldest brother — when he was sixteen — told our father he had heard a story circulating in the city of a half-sister. In front of my mother, my three sisters and two other brothers, he beat him so savagely he burst an eardrum, cracked ribs and a cheek bone, covered him in bruises from his head to his feet. And the blood. No one moved except them two. I saw it from the dark of the stairwell. He said if such words were voiced again the one who uttered them would never be seen again. And it would have been so, I think. He wouldn't let my mother call an ambulance, but took Ciaran out and away to a doctor he knew — owned probably, for that's how he would have done it — bringing him back bandaged and salved. With a story to be told, in which our father did not feature. And Ciaran damaged in his living forever."

She pauses, letting out a long sigh.

"When you told me your idea of him, Ardel, on your return from Éire, you said withdrawn and private. Broken is the right word. He is broken. All his spirit went on that night. Afterwards, no humour in his life."

She has slowly sat upright in her chair as she talks. Sighing, she slumps back as Robert returns with the spritzers and the tin.

"Thank you." She takes the tin from him with both hands.

"I am nearly at the end of my story, Robert."

"My sisters he controlled with emotional violence as he did my mother. The younger brothers were never going to cross him. He chose the spouses for each one of them. And my outer self? She was his sweet darling. Who made all the right sounds. Who got her way by going to his mother and pitching a story of a desired life pleasing to the old woman, the only person he would listen to, which she fed back to him.

"At eighteen with my polished hauteur I absconded from the family, without announcing it. Though it is not how my brothers and sisters remember it. By the time it was known to him, he pretended I was doing everything he had wanted me to and that somehow he was involved in fixing me up with a good match. And I tried to shed my outer self."

She takes a sip of her spritzer.

"You only know the me I could show you, Ardel." Fumbling she opens the cachou tin. "I hope I can now be me."

She hands him the photo and the folded letter. He studies the photo closely and passes it to Dahqin, hesitating before unfolding the letter.

Aughakeel, County Longford
10th , July, 2158

My dearest, sweetest, Aoife,

I write this in readiness: it will come in its time.

You witnessed, from the shadows of the stairway, your brother Ciaran being beaten so badly by your father for speaking truth, that still he walks with a limp and looks at the world from a lopsided face.

Somewhere in this world, outside Éire, there is a half-sister only a few weeks older than Ciaran. I caressed and nurtured her till she was gone two, out here in the wilds, overlooking the Shannon Channels. Then one evening he came to take her and every trace of her. Towering over me with his threats, my sister condoning her precious son's actions. The little brown bottle with dropper-lid he placed on my kitchen table; him putting four drops into her milk. All I know is he needed her to sleep for a whole night and half a day.

He cannot harm me now, for if you are reading this I am beyond his reach for ever. No fawning priest will ever be able to absolve him for the things he has done. Nor has any such man sent me on my way. But I must confess, to someone who loves me, my fearful complicity in his plan. And there is only you I count in that number.

Maybe, through some turn of fate, you can find her. I enclose the only photo I had of her. While he went away, waiting for her to quieten, I sewed a copy into the pocket of her winter coat. Perhaps, somehow, that copy is with her.

Live well with your beloved family, my darling Aoife.
Ever loving you and your bravery,

Oona
xxx

455

Distraught, Ardel hands Dahqin the letter, and focuses on Aoife.

"Is Briged my half-sister, Ardel? Resentful of his abandonment and marked by it. But untainted by his upbringing?"

Grimacing, he nods, "Yes ... Yes, Maman."

He goes to her, hugs her as he had hugged Briged — on his knees next to her chair. She bursts into tears.

Robert places a hand on each of them.

"There ... There ... There, Aoife. There, Ardel. There ..."

"Robert. Oh, Robert, he's found her."

Robert puts his arms round her as she gets up, still crying.

"Ardel, I can only imagine what it must have been like for Aoife to have lived through that. She's been hoping to find her all this time. I really love your Maman. We have to get them to meet as soon as we can. What about the others in Éire?"

"It is up to Maman whether she goes so far. At this moment I would say not. We must walk before we run, Dahqin." Ardel says, mimicking Grandy, then smiles, drying his cheeks.

"Briged has a copy of this photo by her armchair in her small sitting room, Ardel. But this is more emotional than with Briged."

"Are you getting to be emotionally tender, Dahqin?"

"Certainly not because of you in my life. It's more I realise I had a wonderful upbringing and was allowed to go somewhat wild."

"So did I, but not wild like you."

He watches his parents hugging, rocking to a tune hummed by his father, and reaches for Dahqin.

"I just want to make sure you both realise I had a wonderful childhood. It's taken meeting Briged, and you opening your can of worms, to make me realise just how brilliant."

"The worms can be let go in the hedge, Ardel. And the tin better used." Aoife smiles as they too start to rock in the same way.

"In a moment you two can tell me more of this Briged. Do you have photos of her and her brood?"

"Yes, Maman. We'll sort some for you to look at."

Then he and Dahqin are laughing.

"We're going back to Alban." Dahqin whirls Ardel round.

"Enough! Stop now, Dahqin, or I shall ..." He holds Ardel still.

"Let's take a walk up through the vineyard," Robert announces.

By the time they reach the top of the slopes the story of their time with Briged is hardly mentioned, because the conversation spins around Aoife having gained a half-sister.

"And you really believe she shall be happy to meet me?"

"Yes, Maman. Won't she, Dahqin."

"Absolutely. We can ask Kaet when will be a good time for a visit."

"Better we ask Briged about a visit, Dahqin."

"Aoife, I'm hoping you want to go to see her, rather than the other way round. No, that's not honest of me. I want to be there when you meet her in Alban, that's the truth of what I'm saying."

"Don't try to organise this pair, Dahqin. We both would love to go with you to meet Briged and her brood."

Aoife stops at a cross path, Robert pulled to a halt, as her arm is linked through his.

"I want to talk to her today. When we get home. I want to hear her voice, to see her talk. I need to tell her I want to meet her as soon as possible. To be able to hug her to me, and feel her arms round me."

She smiles brightly.

"We both survived him and both of us have big angers to dispose of, I'm thinking. I would like it if we can dispose of them together."

A determined expression on her face, she looks at them.

"There will be tears, and I want you there with me when I see her for the first time. Who of her brood can we get to be with her on this call? Ardel, you are an Ambassador. Use your skills on my behalf. Organise it now on the walk home. Robert and I shall walk on. For once you two can do the dawdling."

"Do you want to see some photos as we are stopped, Maman?"

She nods.

"Dahqin has the best ones on his phone."

"I'll pick ten for you to see. It'll take me a moment to sort them."

He walks away from them. Ardel follows him and looks at his choices. One of Duncn stands out.

"Let me see, Dahqin ... Hmm ... I recognise that look. Right into your eyes and heart." He then whispers, "He wants you too."

"We aren't going to act on it."

"Why not?"

"Later." Dahqin flicks to a photo of Regin, he is looking to the right with a pleased expression.

"And why didn't you show these ones to me before?"

"Alun only sent the one of Duncn to me a couple of days ago. Briged knows everything that happened, by the way. He's told her. The one of Regin, came in from Kaet as we walked up here. And this one."

He flicks to the next photo, which leaves Ardel's mouth wide open.

"Stop whispering. Are the photos suitable for me to see?"

"Yes, Aoife. Ardel hadn't seen these particular ones before. Right, got them in order. They are tagged." He hands over his phone, letting her and Robert see together.

"This is how I shall look in a few years time. Oh, she is so alive. Look how her eyes sparkle, Robert." She swipes a few more.

"So this is Faerachar ... Dahqin these are very good portraits ... Kaet is beautifully vibrant."

She is looking at the picture of Duncn.

"This is the one you were whispering over, I know it. He is so beautiful ... and he seems in love with the person he is looking at."

She looks up at them both.

"Tell me. I've never asked before about anything you do. But I know I shall meet this one. Is he a threat to one of you? This is very intense." They look at one another and start laughing. She holds up her hands.

"Robert, what does that response mean?"

"I have no idea. Will one of you explain it to us?"

"Duncn is really special to both of us. He isn't a threat, Maman.

Honestly. He looked at both of us like that."

Shaking her head, she swipes again.

"Now, these three young men? Where are they from, the two with their strange names?"

"The twins, Alun and Kirus are childhood friends of mine, from Douarnenez, and Peran is their lover, from Kernow."

"They helped get Grandy to Alban. It's a really good friendship group we have gathered, Maman."

"This young man, Regin, has confidence."

"Duncn looks especially intensely at him, Aoife."

Ardel jerks his head round towards Dahqin, a deep frown gathering.

She gets to the last photo — in the background centre is the second of the line drawings. One either side, in the foreground, bare shouldered, they look at one another, awash in the colours of sunrise. Dahqin has tagged it — *Dawn. Regin and Duncn in their bedroom at Second House.*

"I see that intensity here. They look very happy."

She hands the phone back to Dahqin. Then she and Robert march off, hand in hand, down through the vines.

"Get my call organised."

As soon as they are out of earshot, Ardel sits on the grass of the cross paths.

"Here." He pats the grass next to him. Dahqin sits and leans against him. "Before we call ... Who? I want to understand what happened between you and Duncn. And then, with him and Regin."

"That photo was taken at the last lunch we all had. You and Kaet had gone out of the kitchen. I'd asked Alun if I had made the Bagad too large. He said it was possible now — because we are of an age when we are able to understand the limitations of what we think almost limitless.

"He realised Duncn was listening, and spoke to him, which made me look at him — that's the moment Alun took the shot. He told us our feelings were written on our faces for all to see. When you came back in with Kaet you focused on me so intently I thought you must have noticed.

"I approached Duncn with anger, not like you. It was that kiss. It was meant to be a theatrical shot across his bows and yours. I was scared you were falling in for him, and out with me. Anyway when you and I spoke of our love that evening, I hadn't realised what the chemistry of that kiss was doing to me. Intense is the right word, Ardel. But he loves Regin so very much. More than he does you or me."

He stands up, smiling down at Ardel.

"My desires were dampened when I heard Regin's story. That last morning you spent with Duncn, and I was at Second House, he turned up looking for Peran. He and I ended up talking in Duncn's bedroom, as he explained the relevance of the three line drawings. You must have noticed two of them. The one in this photo, was given to him by Kaet for his eighteenth birthday. It's now opposite the foot of their bed. He's back with Duncn, in Second House."

"Back with ... Oh, my goodness. How self-obsessed I've been. All the signs about Regin I wouldn't join together. I had a conversation with Kaet, wondering why Regin wasn't a draw for Duncn. She said to leave Regin be, because he's deeply in love with someone and his life is complicated. That someone is Duncn, and I suppose the complication is the children. And the look on his face that morning in his garden, telling me to have a good few days with Duncn. Embarrassing. I have to make amends."

"Stop that self-pitying thought, and accept your selfishness. The new Bagad is complete. Now I know they are together, I can fill in all the details for you — when we get home. Peran, will be so pleased. You call Kaet, thank her for the news, and discuss what Aoife wants."

"You tease me by mentioning Peran twice. I now understand better what I would not see in Derwent. I did notice the line drawings, but ... well I never saw the second person as Regin. We must congratulate them. I really am happy for them. And send me those photos."

Two large glasses of water sit on the table between their chairs when they reach the terrace.

"In about an hour, they will call us," Ardel says, taking his glass.

"We think it will be Briged with Kaet and Duncn. Faerachar might be able to make it, but that's a variable because of his breakdown."

"Thank you, Ardel. An hour." Aoife sighs.

"It seems a long time to sit shrouded in uncertain anticipation. But we have been apart for all our lives thus far. So, while we wait, take turns to tell me more about those days you spent on tour with Briged."

Harvest Moons and Mid-Summer Nights

Busy with names

October, 21st, 2188 — Second House, Harvest Moon — Dahqin

We are back in Alban — it took longer to organise than I expected. Briged has witnessed the acknowledgements of her brood of three and their consorts in this one day. I am so emotional — knowing the significance of Harvest Moon to Regin and Duncn. It's emotional all round, because the first meeting in the flesh between Aoife and Briged occurred two days back and was a total wet-face occasion. The way they are talking with each other — no one else can get a word in.

Regin moved back into Second House at the end of July.

Perdie and he worked hard to make sure Huw and Ursula really understood they weren't going to lose their Dad when he moved out. She is now with Sam, who the kids like a lot. And they like staying in Second House when Regin has them. Briged tells me she is very happy that Regin is back home; his children running free with her other grandchildren. I so admire her way of dealing with life.

Regin's chance encounter with Peran set all that in motion.

The sun is lowering beyond Nitting Haws. The moon not yet risen. Kirus is sauntering over from the front of Third House; he's left the other five chatting. I turn and walk slowly away from him, going behind Second House heading for the cowled seat amidst the camellias.

He will reach for me by the first of them. As his fingers lightly touch the nape of my neck, thrills of emotion will goose-bump down my body, while huskily he will chant ...

"Mar ham guorant va karantit, da vont in nos o he kostit."

I'll turn to see the sunset sparkle in his sea-green eyes. We haven't seen each other since July. And I'm so hungry.

January, 21st, 2189 – Third House – Kaet

In the early hours of the morning our daughter came calling. Briged says just as I did. She cried for a bit, then quietened in my arms. Before that moment I had not understood fully what love a mother has.

We chose as her name – Jenifer.

Kirus and Peran have called into Haven twice since July last year, and been fascinated by what happened to my body. Asking if they could listen to the noises and such wonderments, especially the little kicks. It so amused me and David.

When they knew I was carrying a daughter, names came from them thick and fast. David liked Gwenivar, proposed by Kirus, but it is a Breton spelling, and people are put off by names they are unsure of pronouncing. Peran assures me Jenifer is the Cornish equivalent, the f sounded as v.

I trust Peran.

June, 21st, 2189 – Third House – Kaet

I have opened all the windows and doors. The breeze is warm. Today we have an all-night gathering to prepare for – Mid-Summer Night is upon us. Tomorrow will be taken as a sleepy day. The Three Houses are busy with names, and will be for some days.

Upstairs Briged and Aoife are playing nurse-maids to Jenifer. They talk, and talk and talk, just like the first time. David has gone with Duncn, Robert and Ardel to inspect the Fastness Estates vineyards and winery.

First House holds Faerachar and Siobhagn, their children Aisling and Dùghall, and Alastair, his father. Overnight they will host Perdie, who is pregnant, and Sam, bringing with them Huw and Ursula, the children of Perdie and Regin.

In their bigger part of Second House, behind Briged's soundproofed door, Duncn and Regin will cram in the rest of the Bagad. Dahqin is on his way from Manchester where he has been performing. Peran and the Twins due anytime into Haven.

In Third House, David, I and Jenifer are joined by Aoife and Robert. And Briged does not know, but Gwyneth will soon be here.

A wild time is promised for tonight across the Three Houses. We can watch the Keswick bonfire and fireworks from the fronts of the houses and the bridge over the beck, and others right out onto the northern hills. From the rear terraces we can see those in the Derwent valley to the southwest.

Huw and his friends, Graeme and Sei-iji are really noisy outside, just as Duncn and Regin once were. I know those three, they will kip on the settees in the living room in Second House — because, though Regin is strict with them, Duncn negotiates, letting them play as he used to. Somewhere Aisling and Ursula will be allowing Dùghall to be. in their company. He has friends joining us for a while to watch the fireworks. And I have invited Mary, as she is a dear friend and straight-forward company for me. Tetchy will be in his element — he has no fear of fireworks, and loves the random food opportunities. When we greet the dawn it will be with good cheer in good company.

Duncn is happy — his work and his life with Regin both fulfilling. Faerachar is now working with Charlie to establish an ethical trading house. He is much happier away from the cares of politics, and so is Siobhagn. Briged is still impeccable as The Good Counsel of Alban.

The sight has limits, it did not prepare me for how Ardel's arrival would affect our family. I'm glad it didn't.

We must try to ensure that everyone counts for something.

The Epilogue
The Hagfish – The Keep at Derwent.

22nd, September 2189

It is the Autumn Equinox. The highest spring tide of the year is four hours off. The conjunction of Earth with Moon and Sun, has combined with steady low air pressure, and strong south-westerly winds over many days, creating an overwhelming storm surge onto the coast of Wark-in-Alban. There will be unprecedented flooding in the lower lands.

Jonat MacLachlan, the Castellan stands next to Margot Salkeld, the Reever, facing Briged and Faerachar. They are in the pump room, level with the bottom of the cistern. They watch a team of workers shut valves in the big pipes bringing sea water in on the high tides and allowing it to flush away with the natural cycle of ebbing tides. A process aided by large ejectors powered by the River Derwent.

"They'll remove the filters, they are scrap now. Those won't be going back in. After that, out will come the non-return valves and they'll reseal everything. The pipes can flow freely both ways for the next few tides. The pipes into the cistern will be filled in once the water is fresh.

It may take years, but nature will be restored."

He looks at the Reever, who nods her approval, looking serious. Then to Briged; she has a broad beam of a smile on her face, and nods too. Faerachar wears the smile of a man who has been relieved of a heavy load he had not realised he was carrying.

"Thank you, Jonat," Briged says. He is abashed at hearing her say his familiar name, and makes a deep bow of respect to her.

Faerachar comes to shake his hand.

"You are a loyal and faithful servant of this Fastness, Jonat. As Castellan you did all I ever asked of you. Rightly not without question. Disagreeing with me with wise counsel as it should be. I asked you to do things against your sound advice, and you did them because it was lawful at the time. But it was not ethical in spirit. I apologise once more for skewing your probity. I thought I was acting in the best interests of this Fastness, but I tainted that purpose by my indiscretions."

He turns to the Reever, shaking her hand. She smiles up at him.

"Thank you for asking me to witness this moment, Margot. I am glad you have taken up the burden of Reever, which I could no longer carry. You are a doughty and ethical successor. I am glad to be released, so I can do other things with my life."

The cistern will be filling to a depth not seen before. There is barely an indication this far from the sea of the surging energy of each large wave thundering onto the beaches north of Haven. Between the suction and discharge grids, set offshore, and the cistern those seventy kimetres of pipework take away the rage, leaving a slight pulsing in the water in the dark interior of the cistern.

The hagfish are going to their rightful place, out in the depths of the wild seas.

Appendices

The Masters & The Slaving

So much bloodshed for so many centuries before in a small continent.

That time it was 1914. A bullet into the heir to an imperial throne.

Rivalries and power struggles convulsed the globe.

The combination of an industrial-military oligarchy mixed into the warped ideals of nationalism

Destroyed all hopes of humane and peaceful coexistence.

Subjugated the peoples of the world under that oligarchy.

An abuse of power hidden in phrases such as 'defence of the realm'.

If a realm be not its people, what then is it?

And from the aftermath of the victors' righteous pride

It continued with nationalistic wars and horrors of the 1930s and 40s.

Then worldwide it carried into the anti-colonial wars of the 1950s and 1960s, and on into the 1970s.

There was such hope when the words glasnost and perestroika were uttered in the late 1980s.

But it was a false dawn.

Those with riches and power continued to selfishly scheme.

As governments used nationalism to manipulate the minds and hearts of their constituents;

As countries became split along ethnic lines when political unions created by imperialist ideas fell apart;

Many of those constituents demanded freedom with truth.

Demanded the right to decide for themselves.

Demanded the knowledge needed to control power.

Demanded governments be servants to their people.

Not people subjects of their governments.

As people turned to other sources for information,

As governments lost the battles of words,

They opened the gates to intimidation and violence.

Waged their wars, keeping the industrial-military coalitions in the positions gained thanks to the firing of the bullet

Killing the heir to an imperial throne.
Them and us.
The masters and the slaving.
Us hoping.
Them craving, not caring.
The haves and the have-nots,
The served and the servants.
The world in peril.
The world's children's heritage threatened,
By the power-seeking, power-glorying, power-clinging, oligarchy,
Which ruled the world's wealth as a personal fief.
Disregarding the welfare of the world's peoples for their selfish ends,
They saw the mounting environmental concerns only as a threat to their
    wealth and power.
The effects of the industrialised consumption of the world's resources on
    the environment and climate;
Downplayed by those with money to make.
For the oligarchy called into question the probity of anyone who went
    against them.
Truth — yet again — made plastic.
Denying the scientific data as questionable,
Belying the physical evidence even as the inundations and violent weather
    episodes got worse,
Belittling the hopes, dreams and futures of the children who could see
    more clearly than they,
The blighted future of humankind,
Was in humans' own hands to turn around.
Amidst the tumultuous clamour of deceitful voices from those in the
    political and religious overclasses
Was lost the voice once heard uttering glasnost and perestroika
Which warned of a world dangerous with fervour and weapons of mass
    destruction.
The most fervid, xenophobic and hate-filled zealots

Let fly with a savagery of the most awful kind.
Destroying cities and setting off weapons of mass destruction
In the swathe of neighbouring territories over which they had fought.
Killing millions.
The land made uninhabitable for an unknowable time.
The Sunderance followed.
A shocked peace rattled onto the human race
Bringing a realisation of what life could be.

Remember! Never let it be again.
Remember! Forgetfulness breeds apathy.
Remember! Consensus is better than coercion.
Remember! Probity must be our essence.
Remember! Everyone counts for something.

William Harding
Clapham Common, 1989

(Updated to include Mikhail Gorbachov's 2019 thoughts)

The Slide Into Chaos

In the early 21st century, in a way not seen for seventy-five years, the veneer of humanity was ripped apart in so many places, bringing violence against anyone who was *Other*, in a glut of killing and mayhem fuelled by irrational hatred and lies.

Old feuds between ethnic groups, now the centres of the old superpowers were entangled in internal disputes, broke out anew.

The oligarchs stood back and allowed it to happen because they made money from it, or tried to pretend they were innocent.

In the democracies, social cohesion cracked or broke down as those societies were rent by uncertainties caused by governments moving away from the international treaty-based stabilities, into an era of nationalism and protectionism framed by lies and obfuscation.

Authoritarianism and anarchy spread side by side across the world at the same time as climate change caused inundation, starvation, plague and pestilence. Parts of the world became untenable for human existence, causing massive migratory pressures. Population growth not just stagnated, but slumped, brought about by these circumstances.

As the fatalism inherent in the Abrahamic religions edged towards its illogical conclusions, the most fervent adherents let fly with a savagery of a new and awful kind. The most fervid, the most xenophobic and untameable of the religious zealots of the adherents of those faiths set off weapons of mass destruction, killing millions in the swathes of territory over which they had fought for so many decades. The land made uninhabitable for an unknowable time.

The earth shuddered. A shocked peace rattled onto the human race.

Those who are power hungry believe in control by fear.

They delude themselves that this or that makes them great.

If only as much effort could be put to peaceful co-existence.

Lily Jardine, Edinburgh, 2038

How Alban Works (*extracts*)

from a lecture given by Briged Jardine, in Victoria Hall,
Leeds, 1st May 2155

Politically and legally, the Fastness is split into two distinct parts, based
on deep-seated attachments to social and law systems, which differ in
local detail. It is a very old settled boundary. Set not only by history but
also idiom and culture. North of it is Alban proper, Scotia. South of it
are the areas that were once northern England and are now known locally
as Engeland.

At the time of the Upheavals the two parts banded together to make
what seems one Fastness. This increased their defensive strength. Across
the two parts there are fifty Regional Councils. These are the political
voice-boxes elected by the people and have wide discretion to run their
affairs in their own way. Provided always they adhere to the Ethical Code
and accept the Commonalities reached in the Governing Council and
Parlement. And they have an influence on what is debated in these bodies.

This allows regional variation to suit each population. There are
District Councils, being administrative only and serving populations of up
to roughly sixty-thousand. These are answerable to their local populations
through clearly set out service obligations to the Regional Councils. They
are supported in their work from the central administration based in
The Keep, at Derwent. The three smaller districts, Lincolnshire, Orkney,
and Na h-Eileannan Siar have much smaller populations. But have each
a Regional and a District Council.

There is a Court of Counsels, whose members ensure any proposal or
changes made meets with the Ethical Code. Any new law. Any action of
the Administration or any of its officers — including in the Law Courts
and Governing Council and Parlement.

It is a Court of Final Appeal on the rights and obligations framed
by the Ethical Code and sits in either Edinburgh or Leeds as required.
Members must have proven high moral ethical standards. The hearings

for election to it are held openly, in the highest Law Courts in both parts of the Fastness, with all Justices sitting. If we do not adhere strongly to our Ethical Code we will be wandering in a moral desert. Probity is all, should be the motto of the legal side of the Fastness.

The two parts each have a Council of Laws Peculiar. The members must be qualified in Law within the relevant part. These are partially elected bodies. They work to make into laws the outcomes from the Governing Council and Parlement. The aim is to make the laws in each part as aligned as possible. When these laws are written they are sent to the Courts of Sessions – one based in Edinburgh and one in Leeds – to be tested for practicality of application and enforcement. Then they are judged on their ethical suitability as written – again by the Court of Counsels.

At this point the proposed change to law is put back to the electors for a decision. The population will by then have all the facts about the proposed changes at their disposal. There is a period between the presentation of those facts and the vote, during which only the Factual Facility is allowed to publish and comment on the matter. We understand the power of words here, for both good and ill. And it is important the words hold their true meaning. Manipulation of important facts started the Upheavals. It must be watched for carefully in these voting periods.

Also I must mention how Education and Health and Welfare are dealt with. There are stand-alone bodies to oversee the running of these social needs. The councils do not have the right to interfere in the running of such basic requirements for making a decent society. There is close observation of the running of these bodies, by independent oversight inspectorates and well defined statements of what they have to achieve. There is a similar arrangement for ensuring there is decent housing for all at a cost that will not impoverish. Those with the wherewithal do not need recourse to this resource, for they are free to make their own provisions.

Everyone counts for something has to be more than a slogan if our society is to flourish for all. There is always a differential in human societies, but being at the bottom of society's pile should not be a cause for exclusion from a decent life, there must be equal access to the things that facilitate a good education and a decent humane experience.

We cannot hope to eliminate differentials in wealth, as people are not all savvy with life chances. But a society cannot claim to be humane, or just, or fair, or civilised — while there is abject poverty at the bottom but extreme wealth at the top.

Everyone has a desire for a decent life. And they should be treated accordingly.

Because of this members of Councils and Courts should not be paid in higher ranges as those working in Education, or Health, or Welfare. It is these professions that make for a humane and effective society. Not big egos amongst politicians, the legal professions, financiers, and administrators. And those toiling further down the ladders, to make a society tick along, likewise are crucial to everyone's well-being. All in society must be aware of their responsibilities and obligations.

Politicians most of all.

Know what is humble. Understand what is unpretentious. Do not make your career gleet with hubris and pretence, and massaged egos. Serve society with humility and purpose combined.

Note: This lecture led to the production of a book for handing to all young adults when they were conscripted into Civic Service. — *How Alban Works.*

Epiphany 2026

From the diary of Faerachar's Great-Great-Grandfather

Whenever I now see that Union Flag the rage in me feels unstoppable. I despise that flag for what it means to those who say they are prepared to defend the Union to death, all else being evil. I heard the English Prime Minister berating the Taoiseach during a televised debate only yesterday. I think the arrogance of the man has scaled new heights. There'll be no lasting solution on this island until the English ruling class stop living in their arrogant past. They colonised us and they still do their own. The checks and balances are gone. The so-called lower orders will always be servants of the ruling caste unless they are prepared for another revolution.

380 years since the start of the last.

List of characters:

❖ from *Confederation Helvetica* (*Switzerland*)

Ardel Penaul	League Ambassador
Dahqin Franz Stiwll	Ardel's consort (= *Dah-kin*)
Grandy Emembet	Ardel's patron, a Member of the League General Council
Matilde Bartouche	Grandy's patron. A Member of the Inner Table of the League
Kazzia Elizokdoa	Grandy's consort
Yves Penaul	Member of the Inner Table of the League, Ardel's uncle
Marc Lafayette	*aka* The Shadow — working for Yves Penaul

❖ from *Fastness of Alban* (*see map*)

Faerachar Strachan	The Reever of Alban (= *Fayracar*)
Briged Jardine	The Good Sounding Counsel Mother of Faerachar, Kaet and Duncn
Kaet Jardine	Faerachar's half-sister
Duncn Axelsson	Faerachar's half-brother (= *Dunc'n*)
Alastair Strachan	Faerachar's father
Siobhagn Toomey	Faerachar's consort (= *Shivawn*)
Jonat MacLachlan	The Castellan of Alban
Margot Salkeld	The Steward of Alban
David Floriot	The Communicator of Alban
Martha Jenkin	Bursar of The Keep in Derwent
Regin Peterson	Under-Bursar of The Keep in Derwent
Mary Crelin	A friend of Kaet and Duncn

❖ *Owner of a Trading House and his minions*

SJ Letrap (Sven-Jon)	Trading House owner based in London
Jarnie Paresh	SJ's Security personnel
Gabri Tabit	SJ's Security personnel
Rhys ap Griff	SJ Letrap's Factotum in Cymru

❖ from *Cantref of Wrecsam, Fastness of Cymru / Wales*

Owen ap Gaharet	Steward of the Cantref of Wrecsam
Bronwen vch Bronwen	Owen's consort
Gwyneth vch Dilys	Owen's mother

❖ from *Fastness of Brittany / Breizh*

Alun & Kirus Goffic	Twins, lifelong friends of Dahqin. Owners of the "Blondyn"
Peran Trelawn	Lover of Alun & Kirus.

❖ from *Fastness of Kernow-Devonia*

Charlie Trelawn	Trading & Shipping House owner. Based in Kernow & Hamburg Owner of the hifoil "HiTail–it"
Inez Tozer	Pilot of "HiTail–it"

❖❖

Gamboge Garcinia

So *named for its colour* — Regin's Recipe

BOLD = *ingredients*   ▶ = *cooking steps*

Amounts are approx, I don't measure, just throw in what seems right for the number of people. This is based on enough for a party of 16 - about 6 litres

Stock — vegetable — however many litres you need to make. I add it throughout as needed
I used vegetable gels at the party, so 4 in the pot, but I most often use unsalted homemade stock. Season with salt and pepper only if using unsalted stock. Cornflour is gluten-free

Coconut oil or **Rice Bran** oil — as examples of low-flavour types — or **Red Palm** oil (for its colour)
Enough to cover pan base
▶ *Heat the oil*
▶ *Then add*

Cumin seeds — 15ml or thereabouts

Cardamoms — 4 or 5 - crack the pods open, but keep the seeds in

Ginger — the size of a big thumb — chopped into fine pieces
▶ *Add the above to the hot oil and stir occasionally for no more than it takes to smell the spices*
▶ *Then add*
Sultanas or **Flame Raisins** — small handful
▶ *Stir occasionally until the sultanas plump-up, but do not let them caramelise. Add a small amount of the stock so the sultanas won't burn*
▶ *Then add*

Onion — one or two, large red - chopped into fine pieces

Turmeric — about 25ml

▶ *Stir occasionally for another few minutes until the onion starts to soften and steam. Cover to let the onion get soft without loss of liquid.*

▶ *Then add* ·

Parsnips — (8) diced (**with lemon juice**)

Carrots — (6 large) I cook carrots whole and break them up on serving

Shallots — separated into the parts, or halved if larger (at least one piece for each person, or a few more)

▶ *enough stock to cover them well. Cook for about 20 minutes.*

▶ *About half way through that time add*

Tomatoes — 6 large vine or 4 beef (peeled), or for a more intense tomato flavour, a tin of plum tomatoes

Apricots — 8 to 10 "dried" ones, soaked or soft, (*not fresh ones*) coarsely diced

Leeks — (2) sliced thinly

▶ *at end of the 20 minutes make sure tomatoes are sufficiently smashed up and add*

Broccoli — head cut into florets and each split — so they are easily picked up in a spoon

▶ *and cook for a further 4 to 6 minutes then add*

Cornflour — if needed (cornflour is gluten-free) to thicken sufficiently to your liking. All the above ingredients should be cooked through before this stage.

▶ *About 3 minutes from serving add in the*

Helda stringless beans — de-stalked and cut into 2 or 3cm lengths (they'll be squeaky when you eat them).

▶ *Dish up, and add to the bowls the*

Coriander leaves – if the eater likes it. If very fresh I use the leaves whole — otherwise chopped, stalks too.

▶ *Serve with*

Boiled spuds — smash-able, floury type, so they can be added to the stew as wanted and squashed to sop the juices, or eaten as a plain accompaniment. Alternatively rice or aquatic grass also go well.

NOTES: You can add any additional or alternative vegetables that you think will work, like white or yellow beetroots. The main thing to bear in mind is that this is a deliberately sweetish-tasting stew with a slight sour taste.

** Swash lemon juice over the prepared parsnips to stop them oxidising too much, leave for at least 10 minutes, and that goes in with them to add just a hint of sourness into the stew.**

I dice the ginger rather than grate it, so it is intense when you find it, but is not overly strong across the stew. It's my personal preference.

For omnivores I add diced chicken, or pork, or "meaty" fish to the stew — and might use a stock to suit. I do that after the parsnips and carrots are cooked but before the broccoli is added — so the meat adds about 15 minutes to cooking time. Fish about 4 minutes.

I also might add to each bowl as it is served — if with chicken or pork — thinly sliced paprika salami (as it heats, the paprika taste becomes intense, but localized), or to the fish version, brown shrimps or cold water prawns.

Gamboge **gum resin is not safe to eat** — *it is yellow and used as a paint dye or laxative. So, it is not used in any recipe.*

Garcinia is the genus of trees yielding it, along with kokum butter and mangosteens.

Author's note & acknowledgments

Work on this story was started in the early part of 1989, before it was obvious the Communist regimes in eastern Europe would fall. The first version was finished in the middle of that year, and the prehistory posited the fall of those regimes within fifteen years. I really thought it would be the case. But the Berlin Wall was down by the end of that year. While the Yugoslav catastrophe was still a few years ahead.

So I set the work aside, saying, "That's the end of that, then."

Oh! How wrong. The Masters & the Slaving was updated at the end of 2019. I heard Mikhail Gorbachev talking of an unsafe world awash with weapons of mass destruction amid the increasing madness of extreme beliefs. His utterances had started me thinking about the road travelled by humankind back in 1989, it seemed time for me to revisit the story. In these last few years we have seen how easily democracies can be dangerously unsettled. And how easily stability can be corrupted when ruthless people manipulate with disinformation and arrogance. George Orwell, for one, understood so well what many today do not.

Many of the things mentioned in the story, like mobile phones with cameras, driverless cabs powered from the road surface, and hifoil sailing boats were in development back in 1989, but mostly not available. Now all of them are here in some form or another.

The journey by the human species through a dystopian period as hellish in places as was either major war of the twentieth century, has only just begun. I'm thinking of Vietnam, Ethiopia, Iraq, Afghanistan, Syria — for example. Now, in 2022, Russia has used fictions as a pretext for an attempted annexation of an independent Ukraine — and how many others are yet to come. The government of our own country is displaying authoritarian tendencies, and complacency about international law. Add in the spreading of a virulent virus — we will not have reached the stars. The internet will probably become disjointed. No electronic system can be totally connected, and totally secure.

Society cannot move on in an equitable way as things are now headed.

Positive and equitable changes must be wrought in one way or another, or the current arrangement, even in this country, could implode.

Huge thanks to all who helped me get this book as far as the printers and beyond. Specifically the input from Gwendoline and Hermione, both of whom saved me from many a gaffe; and the many pointers from NME and you Robin. I certainly could not have done this without you all.

WH, Oulton Broad, September 2022